THE FORBIDDEN LADY

By Kerrelyn Sparks

The Forbidden Lady
Wild About You
Wanted: Undead or Alive
Sexiest Vampire Alive
Vampire Mine
Eat Prey Love
The Vampire and the Virgin
Forbidden Nights With a Vampire
Secret Life of a Vampire
All I Want for Christmas Is a Vampire
The Undead Next Door
Be Still My Vampire Heart
Vamps and the City
How to Marry a Millionaire Vampire

KERRELYN SPARKS

THE FORBIDDEN LADY

AVONIMPULSE
An Imprint of HarperCollinsPublishers

EPub Edition OCTOBER 2012 ISBN: 9780062128775
Print Edition ISBN: 9780062128782

10 9 8 7 6 5 4 3

In 2002, I dedicated this book to my husband.
Ten years later, he's still my hero.
Thank you, Don, for all the love and laughter,
and for always believing in me.

ACKNOWLEDGMENTS

I would like to thank Avon Books for bringing *For Love or Country* back to life as *The Forbidden Lady*. I'm also thrilled that the sequel will finally be published! My thanks to Erika Tsang, Chelsey Emmelhainz, and all the fabulous folks in the art, publicity and marketing departments. Another big thank you to my agent, Michelle Grajkowski of Three Seas Literary Agency.

I don't know how I would remain sane (or fake it so well!) without my critique partners: Sandy, MJ, and Vicky. A big hug and thank you to Sandy, who did a quick last-minute read-through.

My thanks to my family for always being supportive. And finally, a gigantic thank you to my readers. I love sharing my imaginary adventures with you. You guys are the best!

Dear Reader,

Welcome to *The Forbidden Lady*! Originally published in 2002 under the title *For Love or Country*, this newly revised edition is making its first appearance as an e-book! For those of you accustomed to my vampire and shifter romances, I am delighted to share something a little different with you. *The Forbidden Lady* is set in pre-Revolutionary War Boston and stars Quincy Stanton, a rugged sea captain, who is a cross between James Bond (because of his nifty spy gadgets) and Sir Percy Blakeney of *The Scarlet Pimpernel* (because he dresses like a dandy to conceal his true identity). While I was writing the book, I jokingly called it *Insatiable and Saucy*, and as you read along, you will discover exactly who is insatiable and who is saucy!

Apparently, I am incapable of writing a book without a Scotsman, so those of you who love my undead Scotsmen will be pleased to find a live one inhabiting the following pages. Some say Jamie Munro was my inspiration for Angus MacKay.

I endeavored to be as historically accurate as possible. For instance, the use of the word "receipt" for "recipe." The names of streets, wharves, and taverns are authentic. Bostonians celebrated Pope's Day on the fifth of November in the manner described. The scuffle resulting in the death of a twelve-year-old boy actually happened. And the Boston Massacre occurred on the fifth of March, 1770, in front of the Customs House, on King Street.

Like any good James Bond hero, Quincy needed a submarine, so I gave him the *Turtle*. Invented by David Bushnell in 1776, the one-man submersible is a little-known chapter in the struggle for independence. I am guilty of giving Quincy a *Turtle* in 1769. In my faulty defense, I can only claim that the existence of an earlier prototype was apparently hushed up by a top-secret government conspiracy.

For more information about upcoming books and my paranormal Love at Stake series, please visit my website at www.kerrelynsparks.com. My thanks to HarperCollins and my editor, Erika Tsang, for bringing *The Forbidden Lady* back to life, and more thanks to my agent, Michelle Grajkowski of Three Seas, for making it possible. And many, many thanks to you, my readers, who are always willing to take an imaginary journey with me. I hope you find lots of love and laughter in *The Forbidden Lady*!

Yours,
Kerrelyn Sparks

THE FORBIDDEN LADY

Friday, July 21, 1769

"What the bloody hell is happening here?" Quincy Stanton demanded as his uncle crossed the gangplank onto his schooner

Edward Stanton gave him a wry smile. "Is that any way to greet me? I haven't seen you in months."

"Sorry." Quincy glared at the soldiers in the distance. "I thought I had escaped the British, and what do I find the minute I arrive in Boston but a pack of redcoats marching up and down the wharf. Why is the British army here?"

"A good question."

Over his uncle's shoulder, Quincy spied a short man in brown carefully inching his way across the narrow gangplank. A landlubber. "Who is this?" he whispered. "An acquaintance of yours?"

"I'll introduce you later." Edward lowered his voice. "Right now, I must speak to you. Alone, in your cabin."

Quincy studied his uncle's face, noting the worry in the characteristic gray Stanton eyes. His gut reaction had been correct. Boston was in trouble. "This way." He led his uncle below deck to the captain's quarters.

Edward entered the small cabin. "How was your trip?"

"It was a disaster." Quincy shut the door with more force than necessary. He thumped two pewter tankards onto the table. "Our ship sailed as well as expected, but my father—" He grabbed a half-full jug of beer from the sideboard. "I had no idea he was such a pompous, arrogant . . . fool."

Edward winced. "I see."

Straddling a chair, Quincy pulled the cork from the jug with his teeth and expelled it onto the table. "You should have warned me."

"How could I?" Edward took a seat while Quincy filled their tankards. "You were so thrilled when my brother asked to see you after all these years. I sincerely hoped it would be the kind of reunion you wanted, that you deserved."

Quincy surged to his feet and paced about the cabin. The ugly truth was damned hard to admit, even to the uncle who had raised him. Rage he could handle, perhaps not well, but a great deal better than feeling pathetic. "When I first arrived in England, I actually believed it was the warm homecoming I had always dreamed about. My father spent a small fortune buying me elegant clothing. To please him, I shaved off my hair to wear the wigs he purchased. He showed me off like a prized stallion at the balls and soirées."

"He must be proud of you." Edward tilted his mug, taking a long drink.

"No, to him I will always be the unwanted bastard. He introduced me to everyone as his nephew, that is, *your* son."

Edward choked on his beer. "*My* son? I was only twelve years old when you were born."

Quincy swatted his coughing uncle on the back. "Obviously, ciphering is not one of my father's fortes. After a month in London, he took me to one country estate after another, and fool that I was, I thought he merely wished to show me all his property. It took me another two months to realize my father was keeping one step ahead of his creditors."

"Bloody hell! Henry is broke?"

"Aye." Quincy sat and swallowed some beer. "In one night, he gambled away ninety percent of his wealth."

Speechless, Edward stared at his nephew.

Quincy scowled at his drink. "My father was never interested in me." He downed the remaining liquid and banged his mug onto the table with a metallic clunk. He splashed more beer into the mug, spilling a portion onto the table. With the sleeve of his plain homespun shirt, he wiped the pine surface, careless of the amber streaks left on his clothing. "He wanted to see how profitable our business was."

Edward flinched. "Our business?"

"He requested I loan him our schooner, *The Forbidden Lady*, so he could recoup his losses."

"Damn." Edward gripped the edge of the table. "He would sell her to the highest bidder."

"That's what I thought, so I made a quick departure." Quincy curled his hands into tight fists. "There's more. He began legal proceedings to claim Stanton Shipping is part of his inheritance, since the money that originally financed our business came from his father."

"No!" Edward leapt to his feet. "He'll steal everything we worked so hard to accomplish. That . . . bastard."

Quincy snorted. "He considers me the bastard. And he thought I would be grateful because he deigned to acknowledge I was alive."

Edward paced about the cabin. "Damn that Henry! He inherited the title, the land. Everything was simply given to him, while we sweated for every penny. We cannot allow this."

Quincy leaned back in his chair. "He plans to send his legitimate son to Boston in a few months to learn the business."

"To take over, you mean. Damnation!" Edward bashed a fist against the palm of his other hand. "If my brother succeeds in the British courts, the courts here will yield to their decision. Our mother country never misses a chance to spank us like an ungrateful child."

"Speaking of our dear mother country, what the hell is her army doing here? Is Boston under military rule?"

With a sigh, Edward sat. "They came while you were in England."

"For what purpose?"

"To protect us from Indian attack, so they claim."

"Indians attacking Boston? And I suppose their ship patrolling the harbor needs those cannons to protect us from a fleet of canoes?"

Edward smiled wryly. "Hardly. She's a customs schooner with the sole purpose of harassing each ship that comes to port. Did they stop you?"

"Aye, and threatened to confiscate the goods I picked up

in Le Havre. After I paid off the captain, he graciously allowed me to dock at my own wharf in my own hometown." Quincy finished his beer.

"There'll be more bribes to pay to the customs officials in town. And the damn redcoats march around Boston, watching our every move."

Quincy slammed his tankard down. "This is outrageous. We're British citizens, not a pack of criminals. We must do something. Do the Sons of Liberty have a plan?"

"Aye, they do." Edward shifted in his chair, then looked Quincy in the eye. "You."

"What?"

"We know the British are here to suppress us, but we cannot make such a claim without written proof. We need someone who can socialize freely with the wealthy Loyalists in town. The redcoat officers quarter in their homes. The documents we need could be there."

Quincy waited a beat for an explanation, but then it occurred to him. "You think *I* can do it?"

Edward leaned forward on his elbows. "You're in a unique position to help the cause. You've been away ten months. What if you returned to Boston a changed man, transformed into a staunch Loyalist? You could befriend the British officers, hobnob with the other Loyalists and dazzle their wives and daughters with your incomparable charm."

Quincy looked over his shoulder to see if his uncle was referring to someone else. "Bloody hell. I'm a sea captain. Ask my men if they find me charming."

"You can do this, Quin. Just think how much information you could glean if the redcoats believed you were on their side."

Quincy tapped his fingers on the table as he considered. "Everyone knows we support the Colonial cause. Will they believe I have changed so drastically?"

"I have spread the word that you are, in truth, the son of the Earl of Dearlington. You've been away a long time, and if you act and dress the part, people will believe what they see."

"I do possess the manner of clothing that would suit the purpose, what my father bought in London. The stuff is so hideous I was tempted to throw it overboard. I only restrained myself because it is worth a bloody fortune."

"Excellent. Then you can dress appropriately. We'll stage an argument in a crowded tavern where you'll defend your Tory views and part from me in anger. Our solicitor has rented a large furnished house for you, fully staffed with servants. You need only act the role of a pompous, arrogant, totally useless English lord."

"Like my father." Quincy frowned at his clenched fists. "I'll be damned if I'll cower to the British or allow my father to steal what is mine."

"We need a decision now. The minute you leave this ship you'll have to assume your new role."

Quincy nodded. "I understand."

"We're counting on you. Will you do it?"

"Be a spy?" Quincy took a deep breath, mentally blocking the consequences of such a request. If he didn't do something, he would go mad. "Yes. I will."

"Good." Edward opened the door to reveal the short man in brown who had followed him on board. "Allow me to introduce your new employer, Mr. Johnson."

Chapter One

Tuesday, August 29, 1769

"I say, dear gel, how much do *you* cost?"

Virginia's mouth dropped open. "I—I beg your pardon?"

The bewigged, bejeweled, and bedeviling man who faced her spoke again. "You're a fetching sight and quite sweet-smelling for a wench who has traveled for weeks, imprisoned on this godforsaken ship. I say, what *is* your price?"

She opened her mouth, but nothing came out. The rolling motion of the ship caught her off guard, and she stumbled, widening her stance to keep her balance. This man thought she was for sale? Even though they were on board *The North Star*, a brigantine newly arrived in Boston Harbor with a fresh supply of indentured servants, could he actually mistake her for one of the poor wretched criminals huddled near the front of the ship?

Her first reaction of shock was quickly replaced with anger. It swelled in her chest, heated to a quick boil, and soared past her ruffled neckline to her face, scorching her cheeks 'til she fully expected steam, instead of words, to escape her mouth.

"How . . . how *dare* you!" With gloved hands, she twisted the silken cords of her drawstring purse. "Pray, be gone with you, sir."

"Ah, a saucy one." The gentleman plucked a silver snuffbox from his lavender silk coat. He kept his tall frame erect to avoid flipping his wig, which was powdered with a lavender tint to match his coat. "Tsk, tsk, dear gel, such impertinence is sure to lower your price."

Her mouth fell open again.

Seizing the opportunity, he raised his quizzing glass and examined the conveniently opened orifice. "Hmm, but you do have excellent teeth."

She huffed. "And a sharp tongue to match."

"*Mon Dieu*, a very saucy mouth, indeed." He smiled, displaying straight, white teeth.

A perfectly bright smile, Virginia thought. What a pity his mental faculties were so dim in comparison. But she refrained from responding with an insulting remark. No good could come from stooping to his level of ill manners. She stepped back, intending to leave, but hesitated when he spoke again.

"I do so like your nose. Very becoming and—" He opened his silver box, removed a pinch of snuff with his gloved fingers and sniffed.

She waited for him to finish the sentence. He was a buffoon, to be sure, but she couldn't help but wonder—did he actually like her nose? Over the years, she had endured a great deal of teasing because of the way it turned up on the end.

He snapped his snuffbox shut with a click. "Ah, yes, where was I, becoming and . . . disdainfully haughty. Yes, that's it."

Heat pulsed to her face once more. "I daresay it is not surprising for *you* to admire something *disdainfully haughty*, but regardless of your opinion, it is improper for you to address me so rudely. For that matter, it is highly improper for you to speak to me at all, for need I remind you, sir, we have not been introduced."

He dropped his snuffbox back into his pocket. "Definitely disdainful. And haughty." His mouth curled up, revealing two dimples beneath the rouge on his cheeks.

She glared at the offensive fop. Somehow, she would give him the cut he deserved.

A short man in a brown buckram coat and breeches scurried toward them. "Mr. Stanton! The criminals for sale are over there, sir, near the forecastle. You see the ones in chains?"

Raising his quizzing glass, the lavender dandy pivoted on his high heels and perused the line of shackled prisoners. He shrugged his silk-clad shoulders and glanced back at Virginia with a look of feigned horror. "Oh, dear, what a delightful little *faux pas*. I suppose you're not for sale after all?"

"No, of course not."

"I do beg your pardon." He flipped a lacy, monogrammed handkerchief out of his chest pocket and made a poor attempt to conceal the wide grin on his face.

A heavy, flowery scent emanated from his handkerchief, nearly bowling her over. He was probably one of those people who never bathed, just poured on more perfume. She covered her mouth with a gloved hand and gently coughed.

"Well, no harm done." He waved his handkerchief in the

air. "*C'est la vie* and all that. Would you care for some snuff? 'Tis my own special blend from London, don't you know. We call it *Grey Mouton.*"

"Gray sheep?"

"Why, yes. Sink me! You *parlez français?* How utterly charming for one of your class."

Narrowing her eyes, she considered strangling him with the drawstrings of her purse.

He removed the silver engraved box from his pocket and flicked it open. "A pinch, in the interest of peace?" His mouth twitched with amusement.

"No, thank you."

He lifted a pinch to his nose and sniffed. "What did I tell you, Johnson?" he asked the short man in brown buckram at his side. "These Colonials are a stubborn lot, far too eager to take offense"—he sneezed delicately into his lacy handkerchief—"and far too unappreciative of the efforts the mother country takes on their behalf." He slid his closed snuffbox back into his pocket.

Virginia planted her hands on her hips. "You speak, perhaps, of Britain's kindness in providing us with a steady stream of slaves?"

"Slaves?"

She gestured toward the raised platform of the forecastle, where Britain's latest human offering stood in front, chained at the ankles and waiting to be sold.

"Oh." He waved his scented handkerchief in dismissal. "You mean the indentured servants. They're not slaves, my dear, only criminals paying their dues to society. 'Tis the mother country's fervent hope they will be reformed by their experience in America."

"I see. Perhaps we should send the mother country a boatload of American wolves to see if they can be reformed by their experience in Britain?"

His chuckle was surprisingly deep. "*Touché.*"

The deep timbre of his voice reverberated through her skin, striking a chord that hummed from her chest down to her belly. She caught her breath and looked at him more closely. When his eyes met hers, his smile faded away. Time seemed to hold still for a moment as he held her gaze, quietly studying her.

The man in brown cleared his throat.

Virginia blinked and looked away. She breathed deeply to calm her racing heart. Once more, she became aware of the murmur of voices and the screech of sea gulls overhead. What had happened? It must be the thrill of putting the man in his place that had affected her. Strange, though, that he had happily acknowledged her small victory.

Mr. Stanton gave the man in brown a mildly irritated look, then smiled at her once more. "American wolves, you say? Really, my dear, these people's crimes are too petty to compare them to murderous beasts. Why, Johnson, here, was an indentured servant before becoming my secretary. Were you not, Johnson?"

"Aye, Mr. Stanton," the older man answered. "But I came voluntarily. Not all these people are prisoners. The group to the right doesn't wear chains. They're selling themselves out of desperation."

"There, you see." The dandy spread his gloved hands, palms up, in a gesture of conciliation. "No hard feelings. In fact, I quite trust Johnson here with all my affairs in spite of his criminal background. You know the Colonials are quite wrong in thinking we British are a cold, callous lot."

Virginia gave Mr. Johnson a small, sympathetic smile, letting him know she understood his indenture had not been due to a criminal past. Her own father, faced with starvation and British cruelty, had left his beloved Scottish Highlands as an indentured servant. Her sympathy seemed unnecessary, however, for Mr. Johnson appeared unperturbed by his employer's rudeness. No doubt, the poor man had grown accustomed to it.

She gave Mr. Stanton her stoniest of looks. "Thank you for enlightening me."

"My pleasure, dear gel. Now I must take my leave." Without further ado, he ambled toward the group of gaunt, shackled humans, his high-heeled shoes clunking on the ship's wooden deck and his short secretary tagging along behind.

Virginia scowled at his back. The British needed to go home and the sooner, the better.

"I say, old man." She heard his voice filter back as he addressed his servant. "I do wish the pretty wench was for sale. A bit too saucy, perhaps, but I do so like a challenge. *Quel dommage*, a real pity, don't you know."

A vision of herself tackling the dandy and stuffing his lavender-tinted wig down his throat brought a smile to her lips. She could do it. Sometimes she pinned down her brother when he tormented her. Of course, such behavior might be frowned upon in Boston. This was not the hilly region of North Carolina that the Munro family called home.

And the dandy might prove difficult to knock down. Watching him from the back, she realized how large he was. She grimaced at the lavender bows on his high-heeled pumps. Why would a man that tall need to wear heels? Another pair of lavender bows served as garters, tied over the tabs of his silk knee breeches. His silken hose were too sheer to hide padding, so those calves were truly that muscular. *How odd.*

He didn't mince his steps like one would expect from a fopdoodle, but covered the deck with long, powerful strides, the walk of a man confident in his strength and masculinity.

She found herself examining every inch of him, calculating the amount of hard muscle hidden beneath the silken exterior. What color was his hair under that hideous tinted wig? Probably black, like his eyebrows. His eyes had gleamed like polished pewter, pale against his tanned face.

Her breath caught in her throat. A tanned face? A fop would not spend the necessary hours toiling in the sun that resulted in a bronzed complexion.

This Mr. Stanton was a puzzle.

She shook her head, determined to forget the perplexing man. Yet, if he dressed more like the men back home—tight buckskin breeches, boots, no wig, no lace . . .

The sun bore down with increasing heat, and she pulled her hand-painted fan from her purse and flicked it open. She breathed deeply as she fanned herself. Her face tingled with a mist of salty air and the lingering scent of Mr. Stanton's handkerchief.

She watched with growing suspicion as the man in question postured in front of the women prisoners with his quizzing glass, assessing them with a practiced eye. Oh, dear, what were the horrible man's intentions? She slipped her fan back into her purse and hastened to her father's side.

Jamie Munro was speaking quietly to a fettered youth who appeared a good five years younger than her one and twenty years. "All I ask, young man, is honesty and a good day's work. In exchange, ye'll have food, clean clothes, and a clean pallet."

The spindly boy's eyes lit up, and he licked his dry, chapped lips. "Food?"

Virginia's father nodded. "Aye. Mind you, ye willna be working for me, lad, but for my widowed sister, here, in Boston. Do ye have any experience as a servant?"

The boy lowered his head and shook it. He shuffled his feet, the scrape of his chains on the deck grating at Virginia's heart.

"Papa," she whispered.

Jamie held up a hand. "Doona fash yerself, lass. I'll be taking the boy."

As the boy looked up, his wide grin cracked the dried dirt on his cheeks. "Thank you, my lord."

Jamie winced. "Mr. Munro, it is. We'll have none of that lordy talk aboot here. Welcome to America." He extended a hand, which the boy timidly accepted. "What is yer name, lad?"

"George Peeper, sir."

"Father." Virginia tugged at the sleeve of his blue serge coat. "Can we afford any more?"

Jamie Munro's eyes widened and he blinked at his daughter. "More? Just an hour ago, ye upbraided me aboot the evils of purchasing people, and now ye want more? 'Tis no' like buying ribbons for yer bonny red hair."

"I know, but this is important." She leaned toward him. "Do you see the tall man in lavender silk?"

Jamie's nose wrinkled. "Aye. Who could miss him?"

"Well, he wanted to purchase me—"

"*What?*"

She pressed the palms of her hands against her father's broad chest as he moved to confront the dandy. "'Twas a misunderstanding. Please."

His blue eyes glittering with anger, Jamie clenched his fists. "Let me punch him for you, lass."

"No, listen to me. I fear he means to buy one of those ladies for . . . immoral purposes."

Jamie frowned at her. "And what would ye be knowing of a man's immoral purposes?"

"Father, I grew up on a farm. I can make certain deductions, and I know from the way he looked at me, the man is not looking for someone to scrub his pots."

"What can I do aboot it?"

"If he decides he wants one, you could outbid him."

"He would just buy another, Ginny. I canna be buying the whole ship. I can scarcely afford this one here."

She bit her lip, considering. "You could buy one more if Aunt Mary pays for George. She can afford it much more than we."

"Nay." Jamie shook his head. "I willna have my sister paying. This is the least I can do to help Mary before we leave. Besides, I seriously doubt I could outbid the dandy even once. Look at the rich way he's dressed, though I havena a clue why a man would spend good coin to look like that."

The ship rocked suddenly, and Virginia held fast to her

father's arm. A breeze wafted past her, carrying the scent of unwashed bodies. She wrinkled her nose. She should have displayed the foresight to bring a scented handkerchief, though not as overpowering as the one sported by the lavender popinjay.

Having completed his leisurely perusal of the women, Mr. Stanton was now conversing quietly with a young boy.

"Look, Father, that boy is so young to be all alone. He cannot be more than ten."

"Aye," Jamie replied. "We can only hope a good family will be taking him in."

"How much for the boy?" Mr. Stanton demanded in a loud voice.

The captain answered, "You'll be thinking twice before taking that one. He's an expensive little wretch."

Mr. Stanton lowered his voice. "Why is that?"

"I'll be needing payment for his passage *and* his mother's. The silly tart died on the voyage, so the boy owes you fourteen years of labor."

The boy swung around and shook a fist at the captain. "Me mum was not a tart, ye bloody old bugger!"

The captain yelled back, "And he has a foul mouth, as you can see. You'll be taking the strap to him before the day is out."

Virginia squeezed her father's arm. "The boy is responsible for his mother's debt?"

"Aye." Jamie nodded. "'Tis how it works."

Mr. Stanton adjusted the lace on his sleeves. "I have a fancy to be extravagant today. Name your price."

"At least the poor boy will have a roof over his head and

food to eat." Virginia grimaced. "I only hope the dandy will not dress him in lavender silk."

Jamie Munro frowned. "Oh, dear."

"What is it, Father?"

"Ye say the man was interested in you, Ginny?"

"Aye, he seemed to like me in his own horrid way."

"Hmm. Perhaps the lad will be all right. At any rate, 'tis too late now. Let me pay for George, and we'll be on our way."

Leaning back in the seat of the closed carriage, Quincy Stanton yanked the lavender-tinted wig off his head. "The damned thing itches." He scratched his head and eyed the wig beside him. "Can wigs have lice?"

"I believe so," Mr. Johnson answered, his face expressionless as usual.

Quin scowled at the man seated across from him in the carriage. "Does anything ever disturb you?"

"Yes. Injustice."

"I see. Well, did you get the information you needed?"

Johnson patted his chest, indicating that the report from his London operative was in his coat. Someone on board *The North Star* had secretly passed it to him.

Quin waited, but the man said nothing. "Will you tell me what is happening?"

"Only what is strictly necessary for you to accomplish your mission."

Stretching his legs in front of him, Quin glowered at the high-heeled shoes that cramped his feet. "Do you think I cannot be trusted?"

"'Tis merely a precaution. You could be captured. By the way, you did an excellent job covering for me just then. No one ever notices me when you're around."

"Well, who would have known I could act like such a blooming ass? I suppose it runs in my family." Quin scratched his head again. "Damn, I was so rude to that young lady."

"You liked her."

It was not a question. Quin looked into the shrewd eyes of Mr. Johnson and didn't bother to deny it. When he had agreed to work for Johnson a month earlier, he had been surprised at the man's insight. Johnson saw right through everyone, staring at them calmly 'til they confessed the truth. No wonder the man was Boston's master of spies.

"It matters little what I think of her. She will hope never to see me again." Quin recalled the contour of her face slanted up to him, brave and indignant. She had made a clever opponent for verbal fencing, retaliating with witty ripostes. When he angered her, the smooth skin of her cheeks blushed pink. Her eyes were green, not brightly colored, but a luminous, pale green like the sun shining through a green glass bottle. There were times he had seen the sea look like that, when the sunlight would catch it just so. It was like looking into the eyes of a mermaid.

"I could find out who she is," Johnson offered quietly.

Startled from his reverie, Quin shook his head. "No need. Her father would never let me near her. Did you see the way he looked at me when I was buying the boy's papers? He thinks I was shopping for a catamite."

"Why did you buy the boy?"

"Josiah claims to be the best pickpocket in all of London."

"Hardly the best, if he was caught."

"He wasn't, but he claims the second-best pickpocket planned to turn him in out of envy. His mother brought him here, hoping to save him from prison, but her death has condemned him to fourteen years of labor." Quin hoped Josiah was still seated next to the coachman and had not tried to escape.

"And what if he steals from you?"

"I don't expect him to retire completely. He'll be my personal servant, assisting me at my social engagements. And while I am busy playing this damnable role, he will busy himself, locating documents and so forth. Servants can go about unnoticed, and a child, even more so."

"Not a bad plan. You've been very helpful, though I wish you wouldn't tell people I was a criminal."

Quin grinned, wondering if he would, at last, shake this man's cool demeanor. "'Tis my revenge for allowing you to ruin my life."

Johnson nodded. "I figured as much. But your life is hardly ruined."

"You think not? Boston is my home, and now, all my former friends and acquaintances think I'm the biggest jackass ever to come to town." They thought he was betraying them and the Colonial cause. *She* thought he was a foppish, arrogant numbskull. Her father thought he was a pederast. And if she knew the truth, that he was a bastard, it would be even worse. He could just imagine her adorable little nose turned up in disgust.

Quin sighed and rested his head against the seat as he rocked with the motion of the carriage weaving through the congested streets. The sea breeze had loosened her dark auburn hair from its bun, allowing a few stray curls to drift along the nape of her graceful neck. She had the perfect hair color for a mermaid.

"If you can take your mind off that young lady for a moment, I need to explain a few things."

Quin straightened with an annoyed glare at his director. "How do you do it? Do you have a pact with the devil?"

Johnson shrugged, neither insulted nor surprised. "We have made a few adjustments to your carriage. If you'll sit beside me for a moment, I will demonstrate."

Quin moved to the front seat of the coach and watched as Johnson lifted the cushioned lid of the backseat.

"As you can see, there's a hidden compartment underneath," Johnson explained. "'Tis stocked with three muskets, a powder horn, a sack of musket balls, and a few knives." He removed a walking stick and small cloth bag, then dropped the seat back into place. "This is a new snuffbox for you, designed by Revere." He opened the cloth bag and handed a round silver object to Quin.

"I already have a snuffbox."

"Not like this. Open it."

Quin clicked it open. "'Tis rather large, don't you think?"

"Notice how the top lid has a mirror inside. While you pretend to take snuff, you can watch whatever happens behind you. And this—" Johnson grasped the snuffbox and demonstrated a small switch that made part of the box slide out from a hinge. "This is a magnifying glass with a special edging of phosphorescence that will make it glow in the dark. This way, you can examine papers in a darkened room without having to light a candle which could obviously alert someone of your presence." He slid the round glass back into place, and it deftly disappeared into the design of the box.

Quin practiced operating the switch that popped out the magnifying glass. "This is very clever. Thank you."

"Now, take a look at this walking stick. A simple twist of the silver knob and *voilà*." A razor-sharp knife sprang out of the tip, transforming the ebony stick into a bayonet.

Quin cocked a brow. "Tory pigs on a skewer. My favorite dish."

Johnson gave him a bland look. "You forget, Stanton. As far as most of Boston is concerned, *you* are a Tory. You may need this stick to protect yourself from some overzealous patriots."

"You have a point, no pun intended." Quin frowned, recalling an incident when a group of patriots had tarred and feathered a Tory merchant for refusing to sign the nonimportation pact. He twisted the silver knob, and the knife receded into the walking stick.

Johnson continued, "We're also experimenting with small explosives that can be thrown after they're lit, but we're experiencing a delay in their manufacture. The man who was working on them blew his hand off."

With a gulp, Quin sneaked a sidelong glance at his employer. "How inconsiderate of him."

"Yes. Now, let's move to the backseat while I demonstrate the latest addition."

Quin grabbed his wig from the backseat and tossed it onto the front one. Once they were seated, Johnson reached up to pull on a looped silken cord hanging from the ceiling.

Immediately, a trapdoor over the front seat swooshed open. A heavy iron bar fell out and slammed onto the cushions and the wig with a muffled thud and a puff of lavender flour.

Quin winced. "Ouch. That would really hurt."

Johnson nodded. "Aye, guaranteed to knock a fellow traveler unconscious. Just in case you find yourself in poor company. Now, help me put it back. 'Tis rather heavy."

After helping him, Quin pressed on the trapdoor 'til he heard a distinct click. He eased back, wary of being caught underneath in case the heavy rod decided to drop unexpectedly. He lifted his flattened wig. "Perhaps it killed the lice."

"There's one more item in the experimental stage. A submersible vessel, operated by one man. I believe you are just the man to help us with it."

"Why? Did the others lose their hands?"

Johnson sighed. "Pray, don't be ridiculous, Stanton. There is no danger to your hands, only a slight chance of drowning. You do swim well, don't you?"

CHAPTER TWO

Monday, September 18, 1769

"You call her the *Turtle*?" Quincy studied the egg-shaped submersible that bobbed like a cork in the Charles River. "She's rather small."

"Yes, only seven feet in depth, and the ballast tanks occupy the bottom portion." Johnson looked Quin over. "'Twill be a tight fit."

Quin winced. *Damned tight.* "How do I move her about?"

"There are two propellers attached to hand-cranks inside the vessel. The propeller on top controls your descent. The one on the side beneath the surface of the water will control your horizontal movements. The rudder is operated by foot."

"I see." Quin removed his sky-blue velvet coat and laid it on the grassy riverbank. "Assuming I can move her about, how will I know where I am?"

"The vessel is equipped with a depth gauge and a compass, surrounded with fox-fire phosphorescence," Johnson explained. "'Tis dark inside, of course."

"Of course." *Cramped and dark.* With a silent curse, Quin dropped his tricorne and wig onto the ground. "What are those openings on top?"

"Vents to supply the *Turtle* with air. In theory, once you submerge, the vents will close."

"In *theory?*"

"It hasn't been tested. Until now."

"Splendid." Quin unwrapped his lacy silk cravat and tossed it onto his coat. "How does she submerge?"

"There are two ballast tanks, fore and aft. You'll open valves on the bottom to allow water into the tanks—"

"And then, you sink. That makes sense." Quin rolled up his sleeves. "Do I dare hope there is a way to ascend?"

Johnson gave him a slightly annoyed look. "Of course. You will eject the water with two brass pumps, operated by foot. Unfortunately, they haven't been tested in this particular situation."

Quin frowned at his employer. "Is there anything else I should know?"

"Yes, once you submerge and the air vents close, your supply of air will be limited."

"How long will I have?"

Johnson shrugged. "We're not quite sure. It hasn't been—"

"Tested," Quin interrupted him. "I understand. Next you'll ask me to test some milk to see if it has turned?"

"Don't be ridiculous, Stanton. I need you in good health."

"If you don't kill me first." Quin strode onto the small pier. Two men in a rowboat waited for him.

"Good luck," Johnson called.

Quin nodded and stepped into the rowboat. He must have

been crazed to agree to this. The two men rowing the boat certainly looked at him like he'd lost his mind. He glanced back at his employer. Johnson had gathered his discarded clothes and was taking them to the coach.

The rowboat pulled up alongside the *Turtle*. Constructed of oak planks, she was reinforced with iron bands and covered with pitch. The rowers unhooked the ropes that had kept the submersible tethered a distance from the pier.

Quin scrambled on top and lowered himself through the open hatch. A wooden beam extended across the middle of the *Turtle* with a leather seat centered on it. Straddling the beam, he sat.

He studied the interior, memorizing the location of each instrument so he could find them in the dark.

He looked up. Damn, the hatch would close less than an inch above his head. Given the size and number of devices to work, the *Turtle* was better suited for an octopus than a man. He reached for the hatch and hesitated.

The sky above was blue with only a few wisps of clouds. He swallowed hard. *So 'twill be dark. You knew that.* The metal scraped as he slid the hatch into place. His eyes adjusted to the dim light that filtered through the air vents. He turned the side propeller's crank, moving the vessel away from shore.

"No wonder they call her a turtle. She has to be damn slow. God help me, I'm talking to myself." He cranked for what seemed a long time. In spite of the air vents, it seemed stuffy inside.

He checked the compass. "We're headed in the right direction. Let's try to submerge." He opened the valves.

The water came in, gurgling and sloshing as it filled the

tanks beneath his feet. He could feel the vessel sinking. The vents overhead shut, enveloping him in darkness. He should be grateful the vents didn't leak, but the blackness surrounding him felt oppressive. The phosphorescence around the compass and depth gauge glowed an eerie green. He reminded himself this was merely a machine, and he was in control.

Still, he fought an odd sensation of panic as he sank into a world uninhabited by men. He gripped the cold metal of the hand crank by his head and rotated it to control his descent. The air about him grew thick, pressing down on him like a cold blanket. Was it his imagination or was it difficult to breathe? How long would his supply of air last?

The walls felt like they were closing in. *Ridiculous.* He couldn't even see the walls. *Concentrate.* He checked the depth gauge. The *Turtle* had proven her ability to sink. He closed the valves to the ballast tanks, then went back to working the cranks.

Suddenly, the *Turtle* tilted backward. Quin slid down the beam and knocked his head against the back wall.

"Damn!" He pulled himself forward and read the depth gauge. The vessel was still sinking. He held his breath and listened. Yes, the stern tank was still taking on water. This explained his lopsided position.

He twisted the handle again to shut the valve. No luck. The depth gauge showed increasing descent. He opened the second valve to fill the forward tank. The *Turtle* regained her upright position, but continued to sink. The air grew thicker. A pain throbbed in his ears.

Finally, the *Turtle* stopped. He assumed the tanks were full. A thick silence surrounded him in the darkness, interrupted only by the sound of his breathing. Would he know if he was out of air before it was too late? *Damn.* Would he be able to ascend? He closed the valves. If they were both working this time, he could eject the water and rise to the surface. He worked the pumps with his feet.

With a sudden lurch, the *Turtle* rolled onto her back.

He slammed against the back wall. "Damn it to hell!" The valve on the stern tank hadn't closed.

Water dripped onto his face. With his hands, he examined the air vents by his head. In the *Turtle*'s tilted position, they were starting to leak. Eventually, the whole vessel would fill.

He couldn't reach whatever was wrong from the inside, the inside of a dark, watery tomb. What were his choices— drowning or suffocation? No, he could abandon ship. It was the only way. He took a deep breath and reached for the hatch.

It wouldn't budge. He fought a surge of panic. *Remain calm. Reserve your air.* There was no choice on this. He would have to purposely flood the *Turtle* in order to open the hatch.

He skimmed his fingers along the interior 'til he located the first set of vents. He shoved the flaps open and water poured in. Damn, it was cold. He found the second air vent and pushed it open. More cold water gushed in. His heart thumping, he forced himself to wait patiently as the water level crept higher and higher up his legs.

It was taking time. Would he run out of air to breathe before he could escape? And if he couldn't move the hatch, he would drown. Johnson's prophetic words echoed in his throbbing ears. *There is no danger to your hands, only a slight chance of drowning.*

The water soaked his breeches where he sat, straddling the beam. He shuddered as the water level reached his waist. His chest. When the water lapped at his chin, he took a deep breath of air and tried the hatch.

It opened.

He hauled himself through the opening, against the current rushing in, and swam for the surface 'til he broke through. The sky welcomed him with fresh and glorious air. He gulped it down. The sun glinted off the sparkling water. *Thank you, God.* He was alive.

The rowboat floated by the pier. The men stared at him, surprised by his sudden appearance.

"Bring the ropes back," Quin shouted. "I'll dive down and tie them off."

"What happened?" Johnson yelled from the shore.

"She rolled over to play dead."

Quin dove four times to the *Turtle* to attach the ropes. These were harnessed to oxen on the shore, and slowly, the beasts dragged the vessel out of the river.

Resting on the riverbank in his sodden clothes, Quin watched the men cart the *Turtle* off to a nearby barn. The rays of the sun were suddenly blocked, and he turned to see Johnson standing beside him. "You were right. There *is* a slight chance of drowning."

"We'll have the problem fixed before you try again. For now, I suggest you change. You'll find some dry clothes and a towel in the hidden compartment of your coach."

Quin hefted himself onto his feet. So Johnson had known he might have to swim for it. That damned *Turtle.*

He trudged toward the carriage, his feet squishing in his

wet shoes. "Be sure to fix the problem before we move the *Turtle* to her new home. I wouldn't want to swim from the bottom of Boston Harbor."

He had changed into dry breeches and a cambric shirt when Johnson hopped into the coach and rapped Quin's walking stick on the ceiling. The coach jolted to a start.

Quin fell back against the seat, his foot stuck in the air with a silk stocking halfway on. "Why the hurry, Johnson? I haven't finished dressing." He tugged the hose past his knee and tied the garter.

"Redcoats are nearby. We need to return to Boston."

"Fine." He slid on his other stocking. "You do realize these rivers will freeze over in a few months?"

"Of course. The storm that blew through on the eighth put us behind schedule, but we'll have the *Turtle* ready and hidden in the harbor before winter sets in."

Quin shrugged on his brocade waistcoat. If he had to abandon ship again, the water would be very chilly.

"Her name is Virginia Munro."

Quin paused with his hands on one of the many buttons of his waistcoat. He glanced at his employer who was staring out the carriage window with a blank face. "Excuse me?"

"Her name is Virginia Munro, daughter of James Munro, a farmer from North Carolina." Johnson shifted his gaze to Quin. "Do you wish to know more?"

As Quin fastened the buttons of his waistcoat, he considered feigning ignorance, but he knew exactly to whom Johnson was referring. How many times in the past three weeks had he found himself staring out a window, picturing a pair of bottle-green eyes and a turned-up nose? He met Johnson's watchful eyes and knew it was useless to pretend. "I told you there was no need."

"But you didn't mean it."

Sighing, Quin wrapped his cravat around his neck. "Her father will not let me near her."

"Her father left, headed south. I assume he has gone home."

Quin paused in the process of tying the cravat. "She stayed in Boston?"

"Yes. She and her sister are staying with their aunt, Mary Dover, the widow of Charles Dover."

"The merchant?"

"Yes. I believe he did business with Stanton Shipping in the past."

"Aye, my uncle did a great deal of business with the man, though I could never understand why." Quin thrust his arms into the sky-blue velvet coat. "Dover was a snide and grouchy old bastard. And a Loyalist."

"Your description is accurate."

"The aunt is a Loyalist, also?"

"It would appear that way."

Quin recalled the young woman's words aboard *The North Star*. She had given every indication of sympathizing with the Colonials. Even her name was patriotic. *Virginia*.

"The aunt is in mourning, but I hear she's accepting invitations to Loyalist social functions."

"I see." Quin stuffed the ends of his cravat into the top of his waistcoat, where the top three buttons remained undone. His heart was beating fast, but he attempted to appear nonchalant. "They might attend the same parties as I."

"Most probably. I felt I should warn you beforehand and remind you of your priorities." Johnson eyed him as if he were an errant child. "You're to look for information, not a pretty face. What we need is written proof that the British army came here not to protect us as they claim, but to suppress us."

"I understand, sir." Quin pulled on an uncomfortable pair of shoes. If he saw her again, he would still be trapped in his role. How could he possibly impress her when he behaved like a pompous ass?

Johnson glanced out the window. "We're approaching the Neck."

Quin leaned out his window for a better examination of the narrow strip of land that led into Boston. "Damn. Redcoats, ahead."

"We'll have to stop." Johnson rapped the cane on the ceiling. "Find out what's happening."

"Yes, sir." Quin reached for the door handle as the coach slowed to a stop.

"Your wig, Stanton."

"Oh, right." Quin plopped the wig onto his head with a grin at his employer. "You know, as my servant, you should open the door."

Johnson raised his eyebrows. "Very well." He exited and waited by the open door.

Quin stepped out of the coach and into his role. "I say, a lovely day for a ride in the country, is it not?" Presenting a lazy smile, he quickly assessed the situation.

A dozen British soldiers blocked the road leading into Boston. A man in plain homespun clothing, his wrists and ankles tied, sat beside the road.

Quin glanced over his shoulder at Johnson. "Don't just stand there, old man. Make yourself useful." He flicked his fingers at him. "Go . . . do something. Write a letter."

Johnson bowed his head. "Yes, sir, Mr. Stanton." He climbed back into the carriage.

The leading officer came forward, his scarlet woolen coat richly embellished with gold epaulettes and buttons. A crescent-shaped silver gorget hung around his neck, matching the silver-mounted pistols that jutted from his belt.

The officer bowed. "I apologize for the inconvenience, sir. We're stopping all traffic in and out of Boston. Caught this one here, trying to desert." He motioned to the man in restraints. "Some local people were helping him, had him hidden in their cart."

Quin widened his eyes as he removed his snuffbox. "Sink me! 'Tis a crime to leave Boston?"

The officer's face hardened with an irritated expression. "He's a British soldier who tried to desert."

"Oh, my! Now, why would a man do that? The uniforms are so dashing, don't you know. I absolutely adore the bright colors. And those drums you play—so exhilarating. *Mon Dieu!* My heart goes pitter-pat."

"You don't say."

"Would you care for some snuff? 'Tis a special blend we call *Grey Mouton*. Captain . . . ?"

"Captain Breakwell, and no, thank you." The officer gazed over Quin's shoulder with a frosty look.

Quin took a pinch and sneezed into his powerfully perfumed handkerchief. The mixture of musk oil, licorice, and ambergris was a foul concoction Josiah had proudly discovered and poured onto his master's handkerchiefs.

Quin blinked to keep his eyes from watering. "I say, I was thinking of having a suit of clothing made for me in the military style. I hear the ladies positively swoon over a man in uniform. Have you found that to be true, Captain?"

Breakwell clenched his jaw. "You are free to enter Boston, sir. There's no need to detain you further."

"Oh, how kind of you." Quin waved his handkerchief in the air, dispersing noxious fumes under the captain's pinched face. "I say, what will you do with that man over there?" He eyed the captured man's homespun clothing and shuddered. "*Quelle horreur*! It should be a crime to dress like that. I would suggest you put the man's tailor in the pillory."

"His crime is desertion. Fifty lashes."

"*Mon Dieu*! And you say the local peasants were helping him?"

"Aye, the Americans are happy to help a British soldier desert."

"Hmm. Then, might I suggest, Captain, that instead of whipping the young man before his regiment, that you punish him where the townsfolk will see it, also? That might discourage the locals from assisting more soldiers in the future."

Captain Breakwell considered this. "I believe I will. It could prove an effective deterrent."

"Always happy to help. Good day, Captain." Quincy retreated to the coach and glanced at Johnson through the window. "Well, hurry it up, old man, and open the door. You cannot see my hands are full?" He lifted his hands in a helpless gesture, displaying a snuffbox in one and a handkerchief in the other.

Johnson stepped out and waited for Quin to climb in. He reentered, closing the door behind him.

"You enjoy that, don't you, Stanton?" Johnson sat across from him and rapped the cane on the ceiling.

As they rolled past the soldiers, Quin looked out the window at the man who would soon receive fifty lashes. "I should have helped that man escape instead of acting like a fool."

"You were outnumbered. And you would have given away your true identity. But that was a good move, suggesting they lash the man in public."

Quin yanked the wig off his head. "I'm sure the man would not agree."

"No, but it will greatly anger the people of Boston, particularly when the British give more than the scriptural thirty-nine lashes."

They continued their drive along the Neck, and Quin noted the gallows. An iron gibbet hung there, swaying gently, the decaying body of an executed criminal encased inside. He looked away, stunned for an instant by the risk he was taking as a spy. "With the British army quartered here, 'tis like a powder keg waiting to explode. It could blow up in our faces."

Johnson shrugged. "Let it blow. 'Tis for a good cause."

"'T is for a good cause," Mary Dover told her nieces in the parlor of her Boston home.

"Aye, but it sounds dangerous." Virginia frowned as she sat on the ochre-yellow settee.

Caroline Munro paced silently across the thick imported rug. "But 'tis so exciting! Ginny, we must help Aunt Mary." She whirled in front of the fireplace to assume a dramatic pose. "'Tis our patriotic duty."

Virginia flinched as her younger sister's skirts narrowly missed the flames. After a deep breath to calm herself, her voice revealed only the slightest tremor. "Please don't stand so close to the fire."

With an impatient huff, Caroline sat across from her in a Windsor chair.

Aunt Mary deposited a tray of refreshments onto the round mahogany table. "I'm afraid you misunderstand me. I only mean to explain my own actions. I'm not expecting you to assist me."

"Well, why not?" Caroline asked. "I thought we stayed in Boston to help you."

"Father agreed we should keep Aunt Mary company during her period of mourning," Virginia explained. "He certainly did not give us permission to spy."

"You're right." Mary passed a linen napkin and silver plate of sugared biscuits to Virginia. "Your father would never forgive me if I put you two in danger."

Caroline leaned back in her chair, pouting. "Why can I not help? I'm just as much a rebel as you are."

Mary sighed. "I know, but this is something *I* must do."

Virginia selected a biscuit and passed the plate to her sister. "Does this have something to do with your late husband?"

"I suppose." Mary handed Caroline a napkin. "He was a difficult man to live with. He wouldn't allow me to voice any opinions of my own. I was told I must learn to speak properly, meaning not like a Scot, so I wouldn't cause him embarrassment." She shook her head as she returned the plate of biscuits to the round table. "I could never be myself."

Virginia exchanged a glance with her fifteen-year-old sister. Father had told them about Mary's abusive Tory husband. Now, at last, Aunt Mary was free. Free and determined to strike a blow against the Tories by spying on them.

"How exactly do you plan to go about this?" Virginia asked.

"'Tis quite simple." Mary filled the china teacups with her latest attempt at patriotic pine-needle tea, instead of the overly taxed tea imported from England. "Since my late husband was a Loyalist, I was forced to socialize with the other Loyalists of Boston. I receive invitations to all their parties. Even though I'm in mourning, I have the perfect excuse for attending because I have two lovely young nieces I wish to show off."

Caroline clapped her hands together, grinning widely. "Oh, I love parties."

With a smile, Mary delivered full cups of tea to her nieces. "First, we shall go to the best seamstress in town and spend a small fortune."

"Oh, no." Virginia set her cup on the small table beside her. "We cannot allow you to spend money on us."

"Why not?" Caroline asked, then blushed under her sister's pointed stare. "No, you really should not," she protested weakly and set down her cup of tea.

"Nonsense!" Mary pivoted to face them. "The money is mine now and I intend to enjoy it. We shall go to all the parties, and since many of the British officers will be there, I hope to overhear something important."

"I see." Virginia nodded, relieved her aunt was not planning a more aggressive approach to espionage. "I suppose that would be safe enough."

Caroline snorted. "Don't be so cautious, Ginny. To be a good spy, one must be absolutely fearless, bold, and daring. And that is exactly how I shall be."

Virginia glared at her sister. "If you're overly bold, you'll be caught, and they'll be hanging you by your daring neck. The more cautious spy will live to spy again."

Caroline rolled her eyes. "This is not the time to be afraid."

She thinks I'm a coward. Virginia winced inwardly. For years, she had avoided the memory of what she had done. Or rather, what she had not done, out of cowardice. She'd allowed her fear of fire to continue, never once attempting to conquer it. Instead, she had lived with a secret sense of shame.

How could she ever atone for the past? For the loss of life? She twisted her napkin in her hand as she considered. Could she somehow watch over her aunt to keep her safe? Perhaps the best way to keep her aunt from taking risks would be to take the risks herself. After all, she was a patriot, too. And even though the prospect of spying was frightening, it would afford her the opportunity to prove she could be brave. *And not a coward.* Just like her aunt, this was something she needed to do for herself.

She took a deep breath. "Very well, Aunt Mary. I shall assist you."

"Yes!" Caroline leapt to her feet. "We'll send the British packing."

"Caroline." Frowning, Mary set her napkin and half-eaten biscuit on her plate. "We must be careful. And realistic."

"I agree." Virginia smoothed out her napkin, mentally smoothing her frayed nerves. "We'll think this through, step by step. Now, if we overhear something important, how do we relay the information to the proper channels?" She bit off a piece of sugared biscuit.

"I know exactly the person we should tell," Mary said. "He did business with my husband. And everyone knows he supports the Colonial cause. Edward Stanton."

"Sta—?" Virginia choked on her biscuit. To ease her coughing, she grabbed her cup and gulped some tea. The resinous taste of pine needles burned a trail of bitterness down her throat.

"Are you all right, Ginny?" Mary asked.

"*Stanton?*" Virginia returned her cup to its saucer with unsteady hands. "You cannot be serious."

"I am. Edward Stanton is a highly respected man." Mary blushed slightly. "I have always found him quite . . . reasonable."

Virginia wiped her watering eyes with her napkin. "If you think lavender silk reasonable for a man. I cannot believe that fop is a patriot."

"Fop? Oh, I see. You mean Edward's nephew, Quincy." Mary pursed her lips in disapproval. "A sad story, that is."

Caroline leaned forward. "Why? What happened?"

"Quincy Stanton went to see his father in England and returned a dandified Loyalist," Mary explained. "Poor Edward is not even speaking to him now."

"I'm not surprised." Virginia grimaced. "The man is downright insulting."

Mary's eyes widened. "Did Quincy offend you in some way?"

Caroline grinned. "What did he do?"

Virginia paused as warmth swept up to her cheeks. "Nothing. 'Twas a mere trifle."

"A trifle insulting?" Mary asked.

Caroline squirmed in her chair. "Come on, Ginny. Tell us."

"Very well. He wanted to . . . purchase me."

Caroline gasped. "He thought you were a doxie?"

"No, of course not." Virginia's cheeks blazed with heat. "He thought I was a . . . a criminal."

Caroline collapsed against the back of her chair, giggling.

Virginia crushed her napkin in a tight fist.

Mary covered her mouth, attempting to hide her grin. "Why would he think that?"

"'Twas the day Father and I found George. Quincy Stanton tried to buy me as a servant."

"So how much was he willing to pay?" Caroline gave her a sly grin. "And what sort of services did he have in mind?"

Virginia grabbed a sugared biscuit from the table and threw it at her sister, thumping her on the head.

"Ladies, please." Aunt Mary cleared her throat. "If we're to be successful in our mission, we must blend in with the most elite of Boston society. This sort of behavior will not do."

"Yes, Aunt Mary." Caroline picked up the biscuit from her lap, where it had fallen, and eliminated the assault weapon by eating it.

"Dear Lord." Virginia caught her breath with a startling thought. "Since Quincy Stanton is a Tory, he might attend the same parties we do."

Her sister stifled a giggle.

"I'm sure he will." Mary smiled. "I've heard every Tory hostess in town wants the charming Quincy Dearling Stanton at her party."

"Quincy *Dearling*?" Virginia wrinkled her nose as if a skunk had marched into the parlor and promptly died.

"'Tis a family name," Mary explained. "His father is the Earl of Dearlington. 'Tis not an endearment."

"I should say not." Virginia shuddered. She recalled the moment his gray eyes had locked with hers and the intense, searching look he had given her. If they met again, would he remember her? "I only hope I will not see the horrid Quincy Stanton again."

CHAPTER THREE

Saturday, October 7, 1769

"**O**h, no. 'Tis the horrid Quincy Stanton." Virginia turned her back to the elegantly dressed man as he made an entrance at the Higgenbottoms' ball. "Aunt Mary, I cannot remain here."

"It would be rude to leave this early. Come." Mary led her to the far side of the huge parlor. "There are so many people here, I doubt he will notice you."

Virginia opened her fan with trembling fingers. "I shall be forced to hide behind a fan for the entire evening." She peeked over the top of her fan, observing the man in sky-blue velvet with silver buttons as he made a leg to the hostess. Beside him stood the young boy purchased on *The North Star*, well groomed and also dressed in blue velvet. The boy's appearance closely matched that of his employer, from his white powdered wig to the polished silver buckles on his shoes.

Without a glance, Quincy Stanton tossed his silver-tipped ebony cane to the side. The boy nabbed it in midair.

Quincy removed his lace-edged tricorne and dropped it to the side without a look. The boy caught it, also. During the entire scenario, Quincy conversed with the hefty Mrs. Higgenbottom with apparent charm, for she responded with booming laughter.

"He certainly has that boy well trained," Mary observed.

Virginia snorted behind her fan. "I wonder how many hours they practiced that ridiculous little scene."

Across the room, a young lady in rose brocade let out a delighted squeal. "Quincy Stanton!" She skipped toward him, blond curls bouncing, with both hands extended. "How marvelous of you to come. And fie on you for arriving late. I was quite terrified I would languish to death from boredom."

Virginia could not make out his low comment from across the room, but the young lady responded with a high-pitched giggle, rapped Quincy on the shoulder with her fan, and announced to everyone with her strident voice, "Oh, Quincy Dearling, you are insatiable!"

A rainbow of silk-gowned, beauty-marked ladies joined in with a musical score of trilling laughter.

Virginia shut her fan with a snap. "I think I am going to be ill."

"Pay him no heed, Ginny. We're here for more important matters."

Virginia checked on her sister, who, with her emerald green eyes and flaming red curls, was collecting her own group of admirers. "I wish we had not included Caroline in our plans. She's only fifteen and thinks this is nothing more than an amusing game."

Mary whispered behind her fan, "I made it very clear to

her that she must not introduce the subject of politics. So, if she finds out anything, it will be quite by accident."

Virginia nodded, relieved. She suspected the older, higher-ranking officers would make the best targets, but Caroline had surrounded herself with a group of the youngest soldiers in the room. "I doubt she will learn anything useful from those boys, though it appears she *has* learned how to flirt."

"It wouldn't hurt you to try a little flirting yourself. You look absolutely beautiful in that pale green. I wouldn't be surprised if you found yourself surrounded by suitors."

Virginia winced as a sudden thought struck her. Had Father agreed to let her stay in Boston in hopes she would attract a suitor? "Aunt Mary, I didn't come to Boston to look for a husband. I wanted the chance to finally meet you. Father always told us about you, about how much he missed you since your husband had forbidden you to see your family."

"That's all over now, thank the Lord. Still, it wouldn't hurt for you to mingle a little."

Virginia fiddled with the button on her glove. "Did Father tell you about the rumor at home that I'm unfit for marriage?"

"Posh! Utter nonsense."

Virginia sighed. "I suppose it doesn't matter. There's no one at home I'm interested in." Even so, it had stung.

Mary patted her arm. "Perhaps you will meet someone here."

"I doubt it." Virginia scanned the crowd before her. The men were either British officers or exquisitely dressed Tories. "All these men hold political views opposite of my own. They might suit our purposes for information gathering, but I couldn't possibly find a husband here." She caught her breath. The speech of nearby people melted into incomprehensible mush.

Quincy Stanton, head and shoulders above his female admirers, was looking straight at her.

"Oh, no." She flipped open her fan to cover the blush that warmed her cheeks.

He was watching her, no, staring at her. His smile was gone, the remaining expression serious and alert.

She ceased fluttering her fan as the flutters concentrated in her stomach. Stunned, she found herself staring back at him.

He bowed his head slightly, his eyes darkening. A chill slipped up her back as if the man had somehow managed to touch her from across the room.

When a woman's fan struck him on the shoulder, he instantly resumed his smiling display of charm and elegance for the pleasure of his admirers.

Lowering her fan, Virginia resumed breathing.

"Ginny!"

She jumped, startled by the sudden appearance of Caroline beside her.

"Ginny, you must meet my new friends."

"They're not our friends, Caroline."

"Oh, fiddlesticks. You're being far too grumpy, hovering over here with all the old women. Oh, begging your pardon, Aunt Mary."

With a smile and a shake of her head, Mary took a seat. "Never mind, my dear. I'm glad you're enjoying yourself."

"Oh." Caroline leaned closer, her eyes sparkling with excitement. "The man who wanted to buy you is here. Quincy Stanton, himself."

Virginia shrugged. "I noticed."

Caroline perched on a chair next to her aunt. "Did you hear what he said? It made the ladies squeal, especially Miss Higgenbottom. She's the one who called him 'Quincy Dearling.'" Caroline grinned at her sister.

"How quaint." Virginia slid the looped handle of her fan over her gloved hand so the fan would dangle from her wrist.

Caroline continued, "When Miss Higgenbottom said she would languish to death from boredom, he confessed to causing many women a *little* death, but never from boredom. I asked one of my friends to explain, and he said he would be honored to demonstrate. Then all the men laughed—"

"*My stars!*" Aunt Mary sprang to her feet. "That is enough of that kind of talk, young lady. You will not speak of such matters again. Do you understand?"

Caroline's eyes opened wide. "But I don't know what it means, Aunt Mary. Do you, Ginny?"

Mystified, Virginia shook her head.

Mary sat down with a huff. "I will explain the matter at home in private, but for now, there will be no discussion of little . . . *deaths* with anyone. Understood?"

Caroline agreed, then dragged Virginia over to meet her friends as the strains of a contredanse filled the room.

Virginia accepted her first offer to dance and lined up with the other dancers. To her dismay, she spotted Quincy Stanton further down the men's line. As the dance progressed, a lady partnered each man in turn, so in a few moments she would have no choice but to dance with him.

When her partner gulped, looking at her with the frantic eyes of a hunted animal, she realized she had been scowling at the poor man and forced herself to smile. He returned her smile with a nervous twitch of his lips, and the dance began.

The dreaded moment soon arrived.

She curtsied to Quincy Stanton. He made a leg to her. She approached, keeping her eyes focused on his lacy cravat. She didn't need to see his face to know he was examining her with those gray eyes. She could feel it. It made her heart quicken, her skin tingle.

They turned, standing side by side, though the wide skirts currently in fashion kept a man at a distance. She lifted her hand. It was instantly enveloped in his larger, gloved hand. She was tempted to snatch her hand away, but as if he had read her mind, he tightened his fist.

She avoided looking at him, pretending not to notice the firm grip on her hand that defied proper dance etiquette. She glided through the steps as fluidly as possible. Whatever the man might think of her, he would at least think she was graceful.

The dance required that he release her and pass behind her. He whispered, "We have not been introduced."

She remained silent, determined to ignore the sensation of his breath stirring the tiny hairs on the back of her neck. If he expected her to announce her name, he was sadly mistaken.

The dance separated them as they each circled around another person. Her heart pounded in her ears so she could scarcely hear the music.

He neared her once again. "You're still angry with me?"

So, he remembered his attempt to buy her. Her cheeks flooded with warmth. Of course, he did. When he had stared across the room at her, his recognition had been startlingly clear.

She waited until their time together was about to end, then spoke, "To sustain anger over a period of time, I would have to be acquainted with you. Since we have not been introduced, I remain indifferent." She turned to her new partner and curtsied with shaking knees.

She danced in a daze, moving mechanically through the next two partners. Then she slanted a glance down the row of men to see if he conversed with his current partner.

He was dancing with Caroline. She was biting her bottom lip, her eyes glittering like emeralds. It was a look Virginia knew well. Her sister was trying hard not to giggle. And Quincy Stanton—he remained silent, his expression bored and aloof, apparently immune to her sister's dazzling good looks.

When Virginia returned to her original partner, she curtsied, glancing sidelong to see whom Mr. Stanton had asked to dance. Of course. 'Twas the pretty Miss Higgenbottom, who was smiling at him, displaying dimples in her rosy cheeks.

Virginia declined any more invitations to dance. Enough time had been wasted. It was time to go to work.

She spotted a lone officer and casually approached. The portly major stood bleary-eyed at a table stocked with wine bottles. His red coat was stained; his white waistcoat strained at the numerous buttons, threatening to pop them off. He poured his glass with an unsteady hand, downed the entire contents, then noticed her presence.

He adjusted his frizzled wig, which was slipping to the side. "Good evening, my dear. Would you care to join me in a scientific pursuit?"

"You're a man of science, Major?" She wondered if his wig had been groomed by the winner of a cockfight.

"Indeed, I am." He selected another wine bottle and refilled his glass. "I'm conducting research into the quality of European wines, a comparative test, don't you know. Which is better—the French, the Rhenish, or perhaps, this sweet little Madeira I have here?" He guzzled it down and smacked his lips. "Hmm. It is hard to say. I'll have to try this one again."

Virginia eyed his flushed cheeks and the red nose accenting his round face. "I can see you are an expert."

He downed a second Madeira and readjusted his tilted wig. "This one is excellent. It will require further study. Perhaps you will assist me?" He filled two glasses and offered one to her. His bloodshot eyes lit up when he noticed her low neckline. "Such a delight to find a delicate rose such as yourself, blooming in this backward wilderness."

"Why, thank you. Will you be in Boston for long? I would enjoy the opportunity to see you again."

The officer stumbled closer to her, still focused on her breasts. She eased back, fearful he would drool down her décolletage.

He emptied the contents of his glass down his throat and licked his full lips. "I would love to see you again, mistress, but I'll be very busy for the next few months."

"Oh?" Uncomfortable with the man's leering, she gulped down some wine. He seemed to be holding a conversation with her bosom.

"At the end of the month, my men will be leaving Castle Island in the harbor and moving to a new location in town."

Her heart quickened. This could be important. "Indeed? I do hope you will like your new quarters."

"Oh, I suppose they'll do. 'Tis the old warehouse where they once stored barrels of pickled meat. We'll be close to the customs house in case there's any trouble." He narrowed his bloodshot eyes as if his continued ogling required a great deal of concentration. "And we do expect there'll be trouble."

"Trouble?"

"Aye, the damned rebels won't like what's in store for them." He rubbed his ample stomach and belched, dispersing a strong smell of alcohol in the air.

She blinked as her eyes watered.

He swayed toward her, offering her a grimy handkerchief. "Dear gel, no need to cry. I—" His pupils rolled back in his eye sockets, and he crumpled onto the floor at her feet. His frizzled wig tumbled off, revealing a shiny, bald head.

"Oh, dear." She grabbed his wineglass and set it on the table. Fortunately it was empty and unbroken. She peered down at the unconscious major. Perhaps she could roll him under the table like a fat sausage, and no one would notice.

"Shame on you, *mademoiselle*. Did you frighten the poor officer into a faint?"

She would know this voice anywhere.

Quincy Dearling Stanton.

She pivoted to see Mr. Stanton and his grinning female entourage fanned out before her. He raised his quizzing glass to examine the inert officer.

Virginia glanced down. The major's coat had fallen open, revealing his enormous, round belly squeezed into the white waistcoat. His bald head glistened in the candlelight while the frizzled wig lay beside him like a porcupine on alert.

Mr. Stanton lowered his quizzing glass, his mouth quirking with amusement. "Your husband, I presume?"

His ladies twittered with laughter.

Virginia focused a stony glare on him. "You need not interfere, sir. We have not been introduced."

His eyes gleamed like the silver buttons on his coat. "Now where have I heard that before? *Mon Dieu*, by the looks of his wig, I would say our dear major has been flying kites with Benjamin Franklin."

She bit her lip when an urge to laugh caught her by surprise. The major's wig did look like it had been struck by lightning. "Could you help the major to a settee where he would be more comfortable?"

"*Moi?* Dear gel, this colonial self-reliance may be admired in the backwoods of North Carolina, but here, we have servants."

Her mouth fell open. How did he know where she was from? She inhaled a quivering breath, uncertain if she was frightened or excited. She dared a quick look at his face, then turned away.

He was watching her again with that serious, searching expression.

A servant grabbed hold of the unconscious major by the

arms and dragged him across the floor like a lumpy sack of potatoes.

"Allow me to assist." A sandy-haired redcoat captain grasped the major's ankles, and with the servant's help, he heaved the officer onto a blue brocade settee. The major's legs sprawled awkwardly, and one hand slid off his round belly to dangle on the wooden floor.

"Bravo!" Quincy Stanton sauntered over to the table stocked with wine. "You have beached the great white whale."

His ladies giggled. The major responded with a tremendous snore.

"And there she blows!" Quincy poured a glass of wine and raised it in salute. "To our first brave soldier, fallen in the line of duty."

His toast was greeted with cheers from the men and peals of laughter from his ladies.

The young captain plucked the major's wig off the floor, holding it at an arm's distance between his forefinger and thumb as if it were some kind of vermin. After plopping the wig askew on the major's head, he approached Virginia.

"I apologize for the major's inattentiveness." He bowed. "I am Captain Breakwell. May I be of further assistance?"

"No, but I thank you. You have been most helpful, unlike some gentlemen." She glanced at Quincy Stanton crossing the room with a woman on each arm. "I have no idea why the poor major fainted like that. 'Twas most unexpected."

"I fear he tends to overindulge. I assure you, a sober man would never leave a woman of your charms unattended."

She smiled. "Thank you." What a shame, the enemy had such nice manners.

"Would you care to dance?"

"Yes, thank you, Captain." She felt at ease during the dance to "Rickett's Ride" since Quincy Stanton was not participating. She searched the room for her aunt, eager to tell her the information she had learned from the drunken major. Caroline was dancing, as usual, but Aunt Mary was not in the room. Neither was Quincy Stanton, though Miss Higgenbottom and his other admirers were dancing. Perhaps the two missing persons had retired to the adjoining parlor to partake of the buffet.

She executed the final curtsy to the dance. "Will you excuse me, Captain, while I visit the buffet? I'm absolutely famished."

"Allow me to accompany you." He led her into the other parlor. "May I crave your name, mistress?"

"Oh, of course." She gave him a fleeting smile as she introduced herself. "I'm visiting my aunt who lives here in Boston." She scanned the room for her aunt in vain.

"May I fetch a plate for you?"

"Yes, thank you, Captain." She pretended to be admiring an elaborate bombé chest, topped with an Oriental vase. Where was Aunt Mary? She needed to pass on her information before Captain Breakwell returned with her food.

A set of glass-paned doors led to the garden outside. Perhaps Aunt Mary had stepped out for some fresh air. She glanced at the captain. He stood stiffly erect in line, the back of his scarlet uniform turned toward her, his gold epaulettes gleaming in the candlelight of flickering wall sconces.

She approached the French doors, intending to slip out, when she noticed through the glass a strange iridescent glow in the garden. As her eyes adjusted, she spotted two people—a tall man and a much shorter, slighter figure, perhaps a boy. The man bent over the glowing object, apparently studying something. He straightened, passed something back to the boy, and the glow abruptly disappeared, casting them in darkness. Virginia blinked, unable for a moment to discern their movements.

The man was coming toward the house.

She spun around and took a seat, tucked back into a poorly lit corner.

Captain Breakwell had advanced to the buffet table, where he stood filling two plates. He must be planning to eat with her.

The French door inched open without a sound.

She held her breath. A man's gloved hand rested on the door handle, the sleeve above it made of sky-blue velvet.

Quincy Stanton.

He eased into the room. She looked away quickly, pretending not to notice, but her eyes disobeyed her better judgment and she peeked back.

His smile was gone, his brow knit with concentration. He surveyed the room, in particular the line at the buffet, and his mouth thinned with disapproval. He tugged at the lace at his wrists as his gaze dropped to the floor. Virginia leaned forward, tilting her head to see his expression.

He looked sad. *How strange.* The man who was the life of the party was not enjoying the party.

As if he felt her watchful eyes, he suddenly turned his head in her direction. She looked away, straightening in her chair as the warmth of a blush spread across her cheeks. Her fingers curled around her closed fan in a tight grip. *You're being ridiculous to pretend like this.* He must know that she'd been staring at him.

She took a deep breath and looked at him.

He had advanced toward her a few steps. He glanced around, then continued 'til he was in front of her. And there he stood, frowning at his high-heeled shoes.

She waited for him to speak. *Amazing.* The charming Quincy Stanton was hesitating, apparently unsure of himself.

She peered down at the oversized silver buckles adorning his black leather pumps and back up to his face. "Are they uncomfortable?"

His eyes met hers. "Excuse me?"

"Your shoes."

He paused, then nodded. "Aye, they are. You . . . pardon me, but you're looking very lovely tonight."

She raised her eyebrows. "*Moi?* This is not the backwoods of North Carolina. Shouldn't you have a servant deliver your compliments? You wouldn't want to strain yourself."

His eyes responded first. They shone with a warmth that communicated a keen appreciation of her boldness. His mouth followed, the corners turning up with a slow smile 'til a hint of his dimples showed. "Some things are better in person."

She flipped open her fan in what she hoped was a nonchalant gesture. Her heart was racing, her cheeks burning. Blast this man, she was reacting like one of his brainless admirers.

He lowered his voice to scarce more than a whisper. "I owe you an apology."

"Only one?"

His eyes twinkled as he smiled. "At least half a dozen."

Her heart took a leap. "At least."

"I do apologize. May I introduce myself?"

"Excuse me." Captain Breakwell stepped around Mr. Stanton, cutting him off.

Virginia caught a glimpse of Quincy Stanton's hostile glare, directed at the officer's back.

Then, the transformation occurred. It was so abrupt, so affected, how could others fail to notice?

Quincy Stanton leaned on one leg in an elegant pose and smiled sweetly as he plucked a round, silver snuffbox from his pocket. "I say, is it not the dashing young Captain Breakwell? How delightful to see you again." He helped himself to a dainty morsel of snuff. "Tell me, have you trounced any more deserters lately?"

The captain peered back at Mr. Stanton, frowning. "No, I have not."

"Now, now, good captain, no need to be modest." Mr. Stanton flipped a heavily scented handkerchief from his coat and dabbed at his nose. "This clever young lady would be quite impressed with your exploits—capturing runaway soldiers and giving them a good lashing. I say, do you apply the whip, yourself?"

"No, I do not. If you will excuse me?"

"Of course." Quincy Stanton stepped back. "Though I wonder, do the men you have whipped excuse you? Are they happy to be back in the service of their king?"

The captain pivoted toward Mr. Stanton, his knuckles white as he gripped the two plates in his hands.

Quincy Stanton stared back, his eyes as hard and cold as

slate. "So sorry, I have forgotten my manners." He lifted his snuffbox. "Would you care for some *Grey Mouton?*"

"No." Captain Breakwell gritted his teeth. "We would like to enjoy our meal in peace."

"Ah, a redcoat who wants peace. Of course." Quincy Stanton slipped his snuffbox back into his pocket. "The uniform works wonders with the ladies, does it not? I simply must have a red coat made for me. And so clever of you to wear that silver gorget around your neck. The way it sparkles in the sun, a rebel marksman will know exactly where to aim."

One glance at the captain's enraged expression and Virginia sprang to her feet, determined to put a stop to this before her plate of food ended up in Quincy Stanton's face. "Come, Captain. Let us return to the other room."

She led Captain Breakwell toward the door. Why was Quincy Stanton provoking a British officer? They were both loyal to the crown. It made no sense, unless he objected to the captain's attentions to her, personally. But that made no sense either when he had so many women fawning over him.

A crowd of people around the door slowed their progress, and they waited their turn. Nothing about Quincy Stanton made sense. A tall man who wore high-heeled shoes he disliked, who stole outside to the garden to do mysterious things, who insulted the same people who shared his political views.

Captain Breakwell took a deep breath and visibly relaxed his shoulders. "I'm sorry you had to endure that man's company. I fail to understand how so many can find him charming."

Virginia peered over her shoulder just as Quincy Stanton slipped through a door leading to parts of the house not being used for the night's festivities. Where was he going now? And for what purpose?

She narrowed her eyes. "I fail to understand him at all." But not for long. She knew exactly where to direct her investigative talents next.

She would solve the puzzle of Quincy Stanton.

CHAPTER FOUR

Sunday, October 8, 1769

Edward glanced up from his desk. "Did anyone see you?"

"No. I waited 'til the servants would be asleep." Quincy ambled into the study of his uncle's north-side home. "I grew up in this house. I can find my way in the dark."

Edward stacked his papers to the side. "How are you?"

Quincy shuffled about the room. Along one wall stood the shelves of ledgers that documented the history of Stanton Shipping. "My ship left this morning." *Without me.*

"It made no sense to leave *The Forbidden Lady* idle, so I promoted your first mate to captain. They're off to the Caribbean, trading fresh timber for sugar and molasses. You know the route."

"Aye." Quin could hardly blame his uncle for using his ship. He was painfully aware that he no longer earned his living and poor Edward was paying the bills. He roamed about the study, glancing at book titles—some he had enjoyed, others he had endured to please his uncle.

"Is something amiss?" Edward asked.

Quin shrugged. "It goes well enough, I suppose."

"You seem restless."

"I don't usually stay in town this long."

"Ah." Edward scraped back his chair and wandered to the sideboard to pour some sherry in a glass. "You miss the sea."

Quin paused in midstride. His uncle was right. He always felt at peace at sea. He reveled in the endless horizon, even slept on deck sometimes under the never-ending canopy of stars. He loved the vastness of it all, so much the opposite of the prison-like interior of the dreaded *Turtle*.

Edward sipped his sherry. "Johnson told me you're doing fine work."

"You asked him about me?"

"Of course. I always do, at the Sons of Liberty meetings. I worry about you. You're like a son to me."

Quin felt his cheeks redden and strode to the sideboard for a drink. "Like a son, am I?" He splashed some sherry into a glass and gave his uncle a wry grin. "I remember when you threatened to throw me overboard to feed the sharks."

Edward smiled. "You were not responding well to authority at the time."

"And you also threatened to sell me once."

"You refused to go to school, so I explained the importance of a good education. But you're a man to be proud of now."

Quincy took a quick gulp. His family in England would not agree. "Any news from my father?"

"Aye. Your brother should be here any day now."

"My half brother."

Edward sighed. "Your half brother. I believe his name is Clarence. I was wondering, Quin. When he comes, will he be suspicious of your newfound loyalty to the crown?"

"No, I don't believe so. I barely met him. When I arrived, he was leaving for Paris, taking a tour of Europe which he couldn't afford, of course."

Edward shook his head and returned to his desk.

Quin continued, "I kept my political views to myself and tried so damned hard to fit in, I don't think they ever considered the possibility I could be an American patriot. After all, they're so convinced their ways are superior, who in their right mind would not wish to emulate them?"

"I see." Edward lounged back in his chair. "So their snobbery works to our advantage."

Quin resumed his aimless wandering about the room, a half-filled glass in his hand. "I don't see how my father can prove the money that financed Stanton Shipping is his. My grandfather gave it to you. I saw it." He stopped in front of the hearth and gazed into the flames. His memories of twenty-one years ago were hazy, overshadowed with fear, anger, and confusion.

His grandfather had arrived shortly after his sixth birthday and whisked him away to a busy port. There, he had been informed he was going to the New World with an uncle he had never met. His grandfather handed a bulging sack of money to Edward and left without a word or glance at his illegitimate grandson.

Quin looked at his uncle, who sat quietly at the desk. Edward shifted in his chair and stuck a finger inside his neckcloth to loosen it.

Quin swallowed more sherry as an uneasy feeling settled in his gut. "My grandfather gave you the money to start our business, right?"

Edward leaned an elbow on his desk and rubbed his forehead. "He gave me the money to do whatever I saw fit to do. There were certain . . . stipulations."

"Such as?" When his uncle remained quiet, Quin turned toward the fireplace and placed his glass on the mantelpiece as if it might shatter into tiny pieces. "Tell me."

"I was to make certain you never stepped foot in England again."

Quin closed his eyes. "You agreed."

"I needed the money."

Quin opened his eyes and glared at his uncle. "I thought I was like a son to you."

"You are." Edward rose to his feet. "It was a long time ago. I had never met you before that day. Hell, I didn't even know you existed. You were a well-kept secret."

Quin balled his fists. *Secret.* Damn, he had forgotten. *You wanted to forget.* A memory of a small, dark room flitted through his mind. "What do you know of me? Do you know who my mother was?"

"I was told that Henry seduced an innocent, impoverished young lady of gentle birth. She had no father or brothers alive to force Henry to marry her. I don't know her name, but she actually believed she *was* Henry's wife."

"How is that?"

"According to my father, Henry was so determined to have her, he used the fake vicar ruse and staged a false wedding. He never intended to stay with your mother. He was courting an heiress at the time and was not about to give up all that money. Your grandfather allowed your mother to keep you in the country at his expense, as long as she remained silent about Henry's dishonorable behavior."

The flames of the fire blurred before Quin's eyes. His father had victimized his mother worse than him. At least he had had the chance to start over in the New World. "I can barely remember her."

"She died when you were four. My father paid some poor relations to take you, but they neglected you."

Quin placed his hands on the mantel and leaned toward the warmth of the fire. They were the ones—paid by his grandfather to keep the little bastard a secret. The ones who had locked him in the cellar whenever a visitor came by. And if the visitor stayed the night, the bastard was left in the small dark room, alone.

Edward continued, "By the time I met you, you were a wild, unkempt hellion."

"You must have needed the money badly."

Edward winced. "I did. I know what it is like to be rejected, Quin. I was the third son, entirely useless to my father. When I told him of my ideas on ship design, he made it clear he would not give me a farthing. I was eighteen, unwanted by my family, about to embark on a voyage to a strange new world. When he showed up that day, I would have adopted a hideous monster for that money."

Quin snorted. "You did."

"No. You were an angry six-year-old child." Edward stepped toward him. "I understood your anger. I felt it, too."

Quin turned away and paced across the room. "Where does that leave us now?"

"I'm afraid Henry may have tricked us."

Quin stopped. "How?"

"If Henry knows I accepted the money on the condition that you never return to England, he may have invited you there to make it seem like I broke the agreement."

"Then the money would revert to him?"

Edward nodded. "Aye. I should have told you, but I didn't think Henry knew. He must have found the paper I signed. It was so long ago, and my father is long dead. You were so happy when Henry asked you to come—"

"I know." Quin lowered himself into his favorite chair by the fire and breathed out a long sigh.

"I'm sorry. I should have explained it to you years ago, but I wanted to spare you."

Quin closed his eyes and leaned his head back. "'Tis all right, Edward. I always knew, deep inside, they didn't want me." He heard his uncle's footsteps leading to the sideboard and the splash of sherry filling a glass. Was it always to be this way? Would he live his entire life as the unwanted bastard? "Have you ever told anyone in Boston that I'm a bastard?"

"No, of course not."

"Do you think a woman would find my illegitimacy offensive?"

Edward's footsteps approached him. "Are we talking about any woman in particular?"

Quin shrugged, keeping his eyes shut as he pictured a pair of mermaid eyes.

"I suppose it would depend on the woman. If she's a decent sort, she shouldn't mind. How does she feel about you?"

Quin opened his eyes. "She hates me."

His uncle grimaced. "Off to a rocky start."

Quin nodded. "'Tis this damned role I'm trapped in. If I don't continue to play the obnoxious dandy in public, it could look suspicious." For a moment at the Higgenbottoms' ball, he had risked lowering his mask to talk to Virginia Munro. It had gone well 'til that damned redcoat captain had interfered.

"That is a tricky situation. You mustn't endanger yourself."

"I don't plan to." Quin took a deep breath. The solution was clear. He needed to be alone with her. And soon.

Edward Stanton dodged a fresh pile of horse manure in the street and quickened his steps. Monday morning, and already he was swamped with work.

The British required massive amounts of paperwork to prove whatever he transported was legal with all duties paid. And their customs schooner, *The Sentinel*, patrolled the harbor daily. Her crew grew more outrageous in their demands, helping themselves to whatever they liked. Edward had no time for a social call, but this one, this one was special.

Mary Dover had sent a note to his home, asking him to come. Mary Dover, the inspiration for the name of Stanton Shipping's most prized vessel, *The Forbidden Lady*.

Her house was on the corner, two stories high, built of brick in the Georgian style. He bounded up the steps to the colonnaded entrance and knocked.

A young girl with fiery red hair showed him to the parlor. He checked his appearance in the gilded mirror over the fireplace and cleared his throat so his voice wouldn't sound like a croak.

The door behind him opened, and he spun around to make a bow. "Mrs. Dover, I trust I find you well?"

"Yes, of course." She bobbed a small curtsy. "It is good of you to come, Mr. Stanton, and so quickly."

He cleared his throat, fearing he appeared too eager.

She whisked by him with a swish of wide skirts and a scent of lavender. "Please have a seat. Our pine-needle tea will arrive shortly."

He sat on the ochre-yellow settee. "Pine-needle tea?"

"Yes." She smiled as she sat across from him in the Windsor chair. "You see, everyone believes I'm a Loyalist, but in truth, my feelings are quite the opposite."

He stared at her, speechless. Her husband had certainly been a Loyalist. Two years ago, in 1767, he had refused to sign the nonimportation pact after the British had laid a tax on a few items, including tea. The Sons of Liberty had wanted to sack Charles Dover's home. Edward had dissuaded them for Mary's sake. He cleared his throat again.

"Have you been ill with the morbid throat, Mr. Stanton?"

"No. You're not a Loyalist, Mrs. Dover?"

As she shook her head, the movement of her curls launched more lavender scent into the air. His heart swelled in his chest.

The young redheaded girl entered carrying a silver tea tray, which she placed on the round mahogany table. Mary rose to her feet and introduced the girl as her niece, Caroline.

The young girl curtsied and left as Mary poured tea into a pair of china cups.

He cleared his throat.

She passed him a cup of steaming pine-needle tea. "Perhaps this will help?"

"Yes, thank you." With the cup raised to his lips, the strange, resinous aroma assailed his nostrils. "I believe I'll let it cool a bit."

He placed the cup and saucer on the small table beside him. "Is there a matter in which I can assist you, madam?"

"Yes, there is. You see, I was looking for a man." A pink blush colored her cheeks as she returned to her chair. "That is, a man I could trust, one with political views similar to my own and, I must say, I thought of you, Mr. Stanton."

He shifted forward to rest his elbows on his knees. "Dear lady, please call me Edward."

"As you wish. You see, Edward, you're the most suitable man I could think of, under the circumstances."

His elbow slipped and he nearly plummeted onto his face. Was he dreaming? Was she proposing to him? "Dear God, yes, Mary. I am delighted."

She blinked. "You are? But I have yet to inform you of this private matter I wish to discuss."

"Oh, but I understand completely."

Her face paled as she leaned back in the Windsor chair. "My stars! How could you know? I thought I was very discreet."

"You have been, Mary. In my wildest dreams, I dared not hope this could be true."

Her brow puckered. "I'm not sure I understand."

"You wish to . . . form an alliance with me, do you not?"

"I suppose you could call it that."

He nodded his head. "I believe we understand each other very well."

"Well, perhaps." Frowning, she helped herself to a sip of tea. "Then, you will not be surprised when I say I have information that may prove important to the Colonial cause, and knowing you to be a fine patriot, I trust you'll know how to deliver the information to the proper channels."

"Excuse me?"

"Saturday night at the Higgenbottoms' ball, we overheard some important news."

He frowned. "You went to the Higgenbottoms' ball?"

"Yes. Now, about this infor—"

"But they're Tories. They entertain the British officers."

"Yes, I know. How else could we hear something important?"

"*What?*" A horrifying suspicion snaked into his thoughts. "You *wanted* to acquire information?"

She gestured toward his neglected cup. "Have some tea, Edward. It may help to calm you. 'Twas quite by accident that we learned of this, I assure you."

He stared at her, uncertain what to believe, while he waited for his heart to regain a steady rhythm.

"We plan to attend more functions in the future, so I would appreciate it if you could stop by from time to time, just in case we accidentally hear anything else."

He leapt to his feet. "Dammit, woman, you're behaving like a spy!"

Returning from the market, Virginia stepped into the kitchen, followed by George, who hefted his full baskets onto the long trestle table.

The cook, Mrs. Robertson, unloaded the first basket. "Help yerself to the scones. They're fresh from the oven."

George stuffed a scone in his mouth and dropped three more onto a wooden trencher.

"We're making apple pies." Caroline smiled with triumph as she finished paring an apple with one long, unbroken spiral. "Don't they smell wonderful?"

"Yes." Virginia sat across from her sister and picked up a knife and an apple. "Where is Aunt Mary? I thought she wanted to teach us her receipt for apple cider."

Caroline sliced her apple into a waiting piecrust. "She's in the parlor with a man."

Virginia winced as her knife slipped. "A man came to see Aunt Mary?"

Caroline's emerald eyes twinkled. "A very handsome man, and she insisted on being alone with him."

The apple popped from Virginia's grasp and bounced across the table onto the piecrust Mrs. Robertson was rolling out.

"Sorry." Virginia grabbed the apple and set it on the table in front of her. The poor thing looked like it had been pared with a crochet hook. She poised her knife over the apple, ready to slice. "Who is this man?"

George wiped his mouth on his sleeve. "'Tis Mr. Stanton."

"What?" Virginia pressed her knife down with a jerk. The apple skittered across the table, dropped onto the wooden floor and rolled away. She jumped to her feet to follow its trail.

"Good Lord, lass." Mrs. Robertson frowned at her.

Virginia groaned inwardly. A five-year-old would be more capable. She gave her sister a warning look. *Don't tell them, please.* But if she continued to do this poorly, it would be all too evident. She had avoided kitchen chores all her life because of her fear of the fire in the kitchen hearth.

Caroline grinned at her. "Mr. Stanton? You mean the man who wanted to—"

"You needn't say it, Caroline." Virginia poured water over her runaway apple to wash it off. "How do you know 'tis Mr. Stanton, George?"

"Mrs. Dover sent me to his house this morning to ask him to come here."

"Oh, it must be Edward Stanton." Saturday night, at the Higgenbottoms' ball, Virginia had relayed her information to her aunt. Mary's disappearance had been nothing more than a trip to the necessary room. Now, Aunt Mary must be passing on the information. "Has anyone served them refreshments?"

"I took in a tray of pine-needle tea." Caroline titled her head, considering. "I wonder if he's still alive."

George snickered.

Mrs. Robertson snorted. "Ye doona have work to do, young man?"

"Aye, Mrs. Robertson." George trudged out the back door.

"I'll take them some scones and jam." Virginia wiped her hands on a linen towel and readied a tray.

She knocked softly on the parlor door but doubted they heard her. The voices on the other side reverberated with tension. A man's voice suddenly shouted.

She flung open the door. Aunt Mary and a gentleman faced each other in front of the fireplace.

He *was* Edward Stanton, without a doubt. The family resemblance was undeniable. Startled, the man glanced her way and blinked.

Virginia placed the tray on the round table, next to the tray of tea. "I've brought scones, freshly baked." She took the plate of scones to Edward Stanton as he seated himself.

"Thank you." He grabbed a scone, which he dropped on the saucer next to a full cup of tea. "You are . . . ?"

"Virginia Munro, sir, from North Carolina." She bobbed a curtsy.

"You look much like Mary did . . . a few years ago."

Aunt Mary smiled wryly as she sat. "More than a few years ago. Ginny and Caroline are the nieces I was telling you about."

"I see." His expression turned grim once again. "And how would their parents feel if they knew these girls risked their necks spying?"

Virginia glanced quickly at her aunt.

Mary responded with a helpless shrug.

Virginia felt the plate in her hands being lifted. She looked down to see Edward Stanton adjusting the plate. In her surprise, she had tilted it and two scones had slipped off and landed in his lap.

"Oh, excuse me." Virginia returned the plate to the table.

Edward tossed the two scones onto the small table beside him and surged to his feet. "I will not tolerate this. This is exactly the sort of trouble that happens when there is no male guidance in the home."

Virginia paused with a scone halfway to her mouth. "I beg your pardon?"

He paced about the room, his steps silent on the thick rug. "I insist you cease this activity at once."

Mary stood and touched his sleeve as he paced by. "Edward, please. I need to do this."

"Why? Why must you risk yourself? Dear woman, it is not your fault that your husband was a cruel, selfish bastard and did damage to our cause. You do not have to make amends for him."

Mary sat down abruptly, clasping her hands together.

"I'm sorry." Edward rubbed his furrowed brow. "I should not speak ill of the dead, but I . . . I care too much for the living."

"I have to do this for myself, for my own peace of mind."

He went down on his knees in front of Mary and covered her clasped hands with his own. "Stop doing it, please, for *my* peace of mind."

Virginia's mouth dropped open. The handsome man was on his knees, his passion unveiled in his eyes. A twinge of longing lodged in her chest.

She turned away, suddenly averse to witnessing a tender scene that would probably never happen to her. Why couldn't the nephew be more like his uncle? Why did he possess such a pompous, wretched character?

Or *did* he? For a brief moment Saturday night, he had seemed sincere and . . . vulnerable.

Mary spoke softly, "Edward, pray, do not be vexed. You're the only one who knows. No one else will ever suspect. If you truly care for our safety, promise me you will tell no one."

"I could never cause you harm, madam."

Virginia peered over her shoulder. Edward was still kneeling and holding her aunt's hand.

Mary asked, "Will you promise to tell no one?"

He heaved himself to his feet. "Aye, I will."

Aunt Mary rose, also. "Thank you. I knew I could trust you."

He shook his head and trudged toward the door. "I have failed you if I cannot turn you from this folly."

Mary followed him, smiling. "Come now, Edward, don't be so dramatic."

Virginia heard their voices grow fainter as they approached the front door. With a forlorn sigh, she collapsed on the settee and helped herself to one of Edward's uneaten scones.

Mary returned. "There, it is all taken care of. Our secret is safe with Mr. Stanton." She reached for her cup of tea.

"Of course, we can trust him. The man is in love with you."

Aunt Mary's cup slipped from her fingers and landed with a clatter on the saucer.

"May I sit with you during the performance, Miss Munro?" Captain Breakwell asked.

"Of course." Virginia forced herself to smile.

A small orchestra of five warmed up their instruments for the performance Monday evening. She and Aunt Mary had come alone to the concert, hosted by the Ashford family. Caroline had stayed home, declaring that a night without dancing would be a complete and utter bore.

"I believe the composer we're to hear is British." The captain sat beside her. "Have you ever been to England?"

"No, but I do wander about the harbor and imagine what it would be like to travel to faraway, exotic lands."

"It is hardly exotic, but you should consider visiting Dorset. I stand to inherit a sizeable estate there."

"Oh, how nice." Perhaps she should tell him she was not impressed. "I have no plans at the present to go anywhere."

He leaned toward her. "I fear Boston is not the safest place to be at the moment. As much as I enjoy your company, I would prefer to see you safely elsewhere."

She was tempted to tell him the tense atmosphere in Boston would disappear if he and the army would simply go away. To her relief, the concert began.

Most of Tory society was in attendance, along with a number of British officers—some in scarlet uniforms like Captain Breakwell, some in the black uniforms of the cavalry or the red and blue of the Royal Marines. Several of the highest-ranking officers quartered here in the Ashfords' home in grand style. Virginia hoped to acquire more information, but it would be difficult with a redcoat captain dogging her every step.

Her attention drifted to the tall man seated in the row in front of her. Quincy Stanton wore the lavender silk again with the lavender-tinted wig. To one side of him sat the young Miss Higgenbottom and on the other, the slender, silver-wigged Mrs. Ashford, tonight's hostess.

Virginia watched, aghast, as Mrs. Ashford burrowed a gloved hand under Quincy Stanton's coat. The woman was old enough to be his grandmother. What was she doing to him?

He calmly removed the lady's hand from his coat and kissed her gloved fingers. She winked with a grin that threatened to crack the paint on her face. He patted her hand and held it through the rest of the performance.

Virginia noted he wore gloves again. Did he wear them purposely to conceal hands that were as tanned as his face?

He lounged back in his chair. The silk of his coat stretched across his broad shoulders, shoulders that must have experienced some sort of physical labor in the past. Curiously, her fingers itched to touch him, to slide across the taut silk in search of hidden padding.

Applause interrupted her thoughts as the concert ended. She asked Captain Breakwell to fetch refreshments so he would be occupied. She then surveyed the room, hunting for the most likely target for information gathering. A glimpse of a lavender-dressed man exiting the parlor caught her eye. Quincy Stanton on his way to a rendezvous with the elderly Mrs. Ashford? He should be ashamed.

She continued her perusal of the room, aware of the anger building inside her. *Blast that Quincy Stanton.* It was becoming difficult to concentrate. Why should she care if he met women in secret? She spotted Miss Higgenbottom flirting with a cavalry officer and the grasping Mrs. Ashford besieging an embarrassed young lieutenant. So, where was Quincy Stanton?

She ambled out of the parlor and into the empty hallway. Was he in the room across the hall? No light appeared at the bottom of the shut door. She pressed her ear against the door to listen, crushing her ringlets against the wooden surface.

She heard voices—low, whispering voices. Then, the sound of muffled footsteps drew near. She stepped back from the door, alarmed to see the latch slowly moving.

She dashed into the parlor and stood next to the entrance, her heart beating fast. Faint steps sounded in the hallway. She caught her breath, leaning against the wall for support.

Slowly, the footsteps faded away. When she peeked around the doorjamb, she spied Quincy Stanton ascending the last few steps of the staircase.

She darted into the room across the hall and noted that the drapes at one window stirred with a light breeze. Whoever had been talking to Quincy Stanton had exited through the open window.

Another breeze of autumn air fluttered the curtains. She shivered. If she wanted to know what Quincy Stanton was doing, she would have to follow him up the stairs.

Her cautious nature rebelled as she ascended the first step. The second step creaked. She glanced about to make sure she was alone. *Be brave. You're here to discover secrets.* She lifted her midnight-blue skirts and dashed up the narrow stairway.

Investigating the hallway to the right, she tiptoed down the corridor, silent in her satin slippers. Though she stopped to listen at each doorway, she heard no sound. She reached the end of the hall, where a half-full moon glowed through the casement window, casting shadows of intersecting lines onto the wooden hallway floor.

A door slowly opened.

Quincy Stanton emerged. Without a sound, he closed the door and slid something from his hand into his coat.

Virginia froze—trapped between a dead end and Quincy Stanton. If she were lucky and remained perfectly still, he would turn toward the stairs and not notice her presence.

"Good evening, mademoiselle." He bowed slightly.

So much for luck.

CHAPTER FIVE

Virginia's mind raced to furnish her with a likely excuse. She curtsied. "Pardon me, I was searching for the . . . convenience room, and I appear to have lost my way."

"Indeed." Quincy Stanton sauntered toward her, removing a round silver snuffbox, unlike the one he had used on *The North Star*. "Are you here alone?"

"I . . . my aunt is downstairs. She'll be expecting me." Virginia watched curiously as he held the open snuffbox at eye level and moved it from side to side, peering at it.

He shut the box without removing a pinch and pocketed it. His brow furrowed as he studied her from head to foot. "I know why you lurk about these halls. You plan to meet your young captain up here."

"Of course not. What impertinence." She moved to go around him.

He blocked her path. "My deepest apologies if I offend."

"If you weren't so offensive, you wouldn't spend so much of your time apologizing."

"You are correct." He inclined his head, though the glimmer in his eyes made her wonder if he found the situation amusing. "May I introduce myself, at last? Quincy Stanton, at your service."

She extended her gloved hand. "Miss Munro."

His gloves were off.

It was just as she suspected. The stark white of her glove emphasized his deep tan.

He lifted her hand to his lips. Her gaze flickered to his bronzed face and discerning gray eyes and she knew, without a doubt, this man was not the simpering dandy that he pretended to be. Nor was he hesitating or unsure, now that he was alone with her.

"I am delighted, Miss Munro." His deep voice seemed to rumble right through her bones. He continued to hold her gaze and her hand.

With a quick breath, she pulled away her hand. In spite of her gloves, she felt a curious sensation prickle the skin up her arms. His mouth quirked up slightly as if he knew.

It nettled her, his ability to unnerve her. A sudden notion urged her to turn the tables on him, to make him just as uncomfortable.

She eased toward him 'til she was only inches away. Her heart pounded wildly; her voice was whisper soft. "I won't lie to you, Mr. Stanton. I saw you go up the stairs. And I followed you."

She placed her hands on his shoulders, the lavender silk cool and smooth against the slightest pressure. *Definitely no padding.* Her fingers pulsed with each hammering beat of her heart as she raked her fingertips down his chest. With one hand, she could feel the round, hard outline of his snuffbox and with the other, the rapid staccato of his own heart as it drummed in his broad chest.

She *did* have an effect on him. Her fingers spread out, searching for whatever he had secreted inside his coat.

His hands covered hers, halting her quest. "You're playing a dangerous game, *chérie*."

"And what game are you playing that has you stealing into bedchambers in the dark?"

"An assignation with a lady who apparently has changed her mind." He rested his right hand lightly on her shoulder and crooked his thumb inside her neckline, wedged between the midnight-blue silk and her skin. "But since a younger, sweeter morsel has come along . . ." He slid his thumb down, watching its descent as it followed the curve of her breast. "He put in his thumb and pulled out a . . . plum?"

Virginia jumped back, pressing her hand across her chest. Her agitated breathing caused her breasts to rise and fall rapidly against her palm. "I must ask you to keep your hands to yourself, sir." She should have known not to flirt with a man like this, a man who radiated so much raw masculinity in spite of his silk trappings.

He shrugged. "You touched me first." His eyes gleamed like quicksilver as he stepped toward her. "My dear *mademoiselle*, you would be amazed what a . . . well-placed thumb can do."

"And you would be amazed what a well-placed knee can do."

His chuckle was deep. "You are determined to prove yourself less than proper this evening. I'm quite intrigued."

"You're not what you seem, either, Mr. Stanton."

He tilted his head as he considered her carefully. "And how, may I ask, have you reached that conclusion?"

"You pretend to be a lazy fop, yet you have the tanned complexion and muscles of a man who has known true labor."

His dark eyebrows lifted. "Have you been studying me? I am flattered."

She felt her face redden with a rush of heat. "I'm merely an observant person."

"You're very clever, Miss Munro, but other equally observant people may have noticed your disappearance. I suggest you return at once to the parlor. To be seen with me will only harm your reputation. I'm rumored to be . . . insatiable."

"I'm not sure what you are, Mr. Stanton." Virginia whisked by him and down the hall. She heard his soft voice behind her.

"Likewise, *chérie*."

Quincy glared at his glass of Madeira, his fourth one this afternoon, and set it down on his drop-leaf desk. If he kept up this pace, he would be unfit to work tonight. He rubbed his forehead. He had been doing so well. No one knew of his secret profession. Until last night, when a beautiful, clever girl with mermaid eyes had seen right through him.

You're not what you seem.

At first, he had been delighted by whatever accident of fate had caused him finally to be alone with her. But had it been an accident or, as she claimed, a deliberate design? Damn, she had tempted him like a siren at sea, the way she had touched him.

What was the purpose of her saucy behavior? Did the prim and proper Miss Munro enjoy torturing men in private? His grip tightened around his glass, threatening to crush the crystal in his hand. Did she flirt that shamelessly with that damned captain who followed her around like a sick puppy?

He gulped down more Madeira. Captain Breakwell had the luxury of oozing out charm with every well-rehearsed compliment.

I'm not sure what you are, Mr. Stanton.

He was an ass. Every time he was near her.

He sighed and finished his drink just as Mr. Johnson sauntered into his study.

"Do you have anything for me, Stanton?" The short man, dressed as usual in plain brown buckram, sat in the corner chair next to the secretaire.

"Aye, I do." Quin retrieved a paper from a small drawer and handed it to his employer.

Johnson scanned the contents of the military report, which named the new quarters a British regiment was moving to in a few weeks. "Where did you acquire this?"

"I found it last night in Colonel Farley's bedchamber. He's quartering with the Ashfords."

Johnson nodded. "And servicing his hostess, I hear."

Quin rose from his chair, frowning. "I'm not surprised." The rapacious old woman had tried to fondle him in public. He had been forced to hold the lady's hand all through the concert to keep her fingers from roving about. He stopped at the walnut sideboard and poured two glasses of Madeira.

Johnson folded up the paper and pocketed it. "I hear the British are preparing for some kind of trouble. This is old news."

"It was new to me."

"Someone found out last Saturday."

"Who?" Quin handed him a glass.

"I don't know where the information came from. That's why I'm here—to see if you know."

Quin lounged back in his chair. "I don't follow you, Johnson. If I had known before, I would have reported it. How did you find out about it?"

"I was at the Bunch of Grapes Tavern last night, meeting with the Sons of Liberty, when your uncle asked for a word with me in private. He gave me the report but refused to name his source. Said the information was gathered at the Higgenbottoms' ball."

Quin set down his glass. "I was at the Higgenbottoms' ball."

"Exactly."

"'Twas not me."

Johnson leaned forward. "Then who was it? Think about it. Who was there, acting a little peculiar, disappearing for minutes at a time, being nosy?"

Nosy? An instant vision of a pretty face with an adorable, turned-up nose flitted through his mind. *No, impossible.* But a redcoat officer had fainted at her feet, and last night, she had wandered alone upstairs and traced the outline of a paper in his coat with her fingertips. "Bloody hell."

"So you know. Who is he?"

"I . . . I cannot say for sure."

Johnson's eyes narrowed. "I will not have amateurs snooping about, Stanton. My professionals will be tripping over some well-meaning fool in the dark. He must be either stopped or brought into the organization. Understood?"

Quin nodded his head slowly as his hands balled into tight fists. "Don't worry. This . . . amateur will definitely stop." *I'll wring her pretty little neck . . . if the British don't do it first.*

"Very well. I'll leave you to take care of it." Johnson set down his glass, still full, and moved silently to the door. He paused. "'Tis a woman, is it not?" He peered over his shoulder, his eyes honing in on Quin with their usual, startling perception.

"Dammit, Johnson. There's a job for you on Judgment Day, giving counsel to the Lord. No one could hide anything from you."

He almost smiled. There was a definite twitch at his mouth. "It simply makes sense. You and your uncle are reluctant to divulge the name. Only a woman could inspire such protectiveness."

Quincy doubted if a woman could inspire anything in Johnson. From what he could tell, the man never ate, never drank, never laughed or smiled, and never slept. "I'll take care of the matter. You have my word."

That night, Quincy sneaked into his uncle's north-side home and entered the study to find his uncle still at his desk. "You're working too hard."

Edward glanced up. "Quin, did anyone see you?"

"No. I miss living here. I cannot continue with this charade for long, Uncle. 'Tis too expensive for you and too irritating for me. I miss my old life."

"Johnson is happy with your work."

"How can you tell? The man never smiles." Quin sat in his

favorite chair. "He tells me you had a conversation with him last night at the Bunch of Grapes Tavern."

"And he sent you here to find out the name of my source." Edward pushed back his chair and stood. "I knew he wouldn't leave it alone. So, he has my own flesh and blood spying on me?"

"I'm not spying on you. I already know who your source is."

His uncle paled. "Did you tell Johnson?"

"No."

Edward let out a deep breath. "Good. Would you like some whiskey? I need a drink." He poured himself a dram and immediately downed it. "So, who do you think he is?"

"Nice try, but this is a woman we're talking about."

"Damn." Edward refilled his glass and offered one to Quin. "And you didn't tell Johnson?"

"No, but he surmised we're protecting a lady."

Edward paced the length of the room, shaking his head. "You must never tell. I cannot bear for any harm to come to her. She's too important, too special to me."

Quin shifted in his chair to keep an eye on Edward, aware of a growing, gnawing sensation in his gut. She was special to his uncle? "Will you tell me her name, so I can be certain we're talking about the same person?"

"No, I promised her I would tell no one, that I would never cause her any harm. I will be true to her."

Quin's stomach lurched. "You could write her name down, then burn the paper."

Edward looked askance at him. "'Twould be the same betrayal of confidence. I'll not do it. Not to her."

"You . . . you care for her that much, then?"

Edward halted in front of the hearth and gazed into the fire with a faraway look. "You cannot imagine the depth of my affection for her."

Quin gulped down his whiskey so fast his eyes watered.

"She has the most beautiful shade of hair—a soft, dark red you want to lay your face in, and eyes—she has eyes like . . ."

"Like a mermaid." Quin banged his glass down on the table beside him. Damn it to hell! His uncle was infatuated with the same woman as he. Infatuated? Was he? *Dear Lord, no.*

"A mermaid? 'Tis a bit whimsical, but—Quin, are you all right? You look a little green."

"I . . . yes. You don't believe she's a bit . . . young for you?"

Edward shrugged. "The difference is not great. I believe we're perfectly suited. God knows I've waited long enough for this. But I am distressed by this dangerous game she's playing. I tried to dissuade her, but she'll not listen."

"Aye, she has a mind of her own, a very clever one, too."

"Exactly. I even begged her on bended knee to no avail."

Quin surged to his feet. "You knelt in front of Virginia Munro?"

"Who? Oh, you mean the niece? I suppose you could call her an accomplice."

"Accomplice, my ass! She's the bloody ringleader behind the whole operation."

"No, you're wrong. My Mary is the leader."

Quin paced toward his uncle. "'Tis Virginia, I tell you. I know." He stopped with a jerk. "Wait. Who are you talking about?"

"Mary, Mary Dover. Damn! If this was a trick to make me confess her name, so help me . . ."

"No, Uncle." Quin took a deep breath. "I believe the trick was on me. You're not in love with Virginia, then?"

"Egad, no. She's hardly more than a child."

"Believe me, she's not a child." That nicely rounded breast he had skimmed with his thumb was definitely larger than a plum and looked every bit as sweet and succulent. Quin closed his eyes, remembering the soft, smooth texture of her skin, the light scent of lavender in her auburn ringlets.

Realization slowly seeped into his lust-filled brain. His uncle was not competing with him for the same woman. He blew out a breath of air and smiled. "We're a couple of besotted fools. For a while I thought your heart was set on Virginia."

"No, I—oh, you have your eye on Mary's niece, have you?"

I've had more than an eye on her. Quin sat down with a groan. This was the last thing he needed right now. He was immersed in a spying operation. His business was in jeopardy, threatened by his own father. He had no time for a dalliance.

Edward chuckled as he threw another log onto the fire. "Mary and Virginia are alike in appearance. It would seem, Quin, that you and I have similar tastes."

"I suppose."

"I've been in love with Mary Dover for years. I plan to marry her as soon as possible."

"Marry? Are you crazed? She's a widow. You could just—"

Edward whirled around. "I *will* marry her. She's a respectable lady." He gave Quin a pointed look. "And, by the way, so is her niece."

Quin gulped. "I'll have another drink."

As he made his way home, Quin pondered over this latest twist in his life as a spy. How was he to stop Virginia Munro from spying? If he simply told her what he knew, she would wonder why a Loyalist refrained from turning in a traitor to the crown.

Perhaps he could say he disliked the thought of a woman being executed. That might ring false, since executions were considered great social events with all the trappings of a fair. People came from a radius of fifty miles to enjoy the entertainment, and everyone knew a female execution drew the biggest crowd.

You could tell her the truth—that you're a spy yourself. Damn, as clever as she was, she might already suspect. She'd seen him upstairs at the Ashfords' home. He wasn't sure how much she'd seen at the Higgenbottoms. If other people thought he was sneaking about to conduct illicit affairs, he could live with it, but he hated for Virginia Munro to believe it. Her opinion of him was already low enough.

He was tempted to confide in her. If she were truly spying for the Colonial cause, he could let her know that he secretly agreed with her patriotic feelings. He might have a chance to court her then. But if he was wrong and she was a Tory, it would be his execution advertised in the broadsides.

No, he couldn't confide in her. Out of the question.

A faint glow filtered through the grimy casement windows of a seedy tavern, dimly lighting the road before him. The path he should take with Virginia Munro was just as obscure. How could he possibly deal with her without exposing himself?

Sounds of drunken laughter and naughty songs sifted through the walls of riven siding. He recognized the words from the ballad, "Our Polly Is a Sad Slut." A pink-and-black spotted pig rooted through the overripe garbage piled in the street, the smell bad enough to make him wish he had one of his pungent handkerchiefs with him. He hurried past the tavern.

You could tell her how you feel about her. Splendid notion. Tell the proper Miss Munro that the local bastard was lusting after her. That would impress her. Besides, she didn't need his attentions. She had a redcoat captain panting after her panniers. A captain who would inherit a large estate in England. A captain who was obviously not a bastard.

He swatted an empty bottle in the street with his walking stick. It rolled away in the dirt 'til it stuck fast in a pile of pig manure, shocking the flies into scattering away in search of another pile. They wouldn't have to go far.

He had to give her credit; she made a damned good spy. His accomplishment that night had been pathetic. Josiah had sneaked into the Higgenbottoms' study and stolen what he thought was an important document. When Quin had examined it in the garden, he'd discovered it was a receipt for hasty pudding and battalia pie.

After that fiasco, he'd sent Josiah to grammar school to improve the boy's lamentable reading skills. In protest, Josiah decided to be the class clown and spent the last two days standing on a stool with a dunce cap on his head and a sign around his neck that said *Idle-Boy.*

Actually, Quin thought, he shouldn't be surprised if the lovely Virginia Munro made a better spy. All he had was a few fancy spy contraptions. She had creamy skin, silky auburn curls, and pale green eyes. The British army didn't stand a chance.

Neither did he.

"And what have we here? A real fancy one, eh?"

Quin glanced up to see three rough-looking sailors blocking the street. *Damn.* He should have been paying more attention. "Stand aside. I don't want any trouble."

"Oh, do ye hear that?" sneered a sailor with a thin, white scar jagging through an eyebrow and down his cheek. "His Majesty's royal ass kisser don't want no trouble."

"Aye," agreed one with an oversized, battered tricorne. "We wouldn't want to frighten a delicate gent like you. Maybe ye be willing to pay for no trouble?"

The third sailor laughed nervously and wiped his nose with a filthy sleeve.

Quin eyed them carefully for signs of weapons. "I'll find an alternate route. Good day, gentlemen." He turned to leave, listening for a whisper of movement.

They didn't bother to be quiet.

Quin wheeled around, swinging his cane hard into the stomach of the first assailant. The man doubled forward onto his knees, groaning and clutching his midsection.

The man with the scar pulled out a foot-long knife. His eyes danced with anticipation as he crouched into an attacking stance. The third man hung back, still laughing like a fool.

Quin twisted the knob on his cane. The knife snapped out, sharp and lethal. "I suggest you keep back, scar-face, unless you'd like a matching set. I have a much longer reach."

The sailor halted. "Here now, what's a fancy fop like you doing with a weapon like that?"

Quincy backed away. "I would love to stay and chat, but I'm late for my dance lessons." When he spotted a side street, he sprinted down it. He heard their voices rising in anger as they rallied their courage for the chase.

"Mister, over here!" A voice called out from a doorway. "Come in."

Quincy slowed his pace, wary of this sudden invitation.

The voice belonged to a boy, about twelve. "Don't worry, you'll be safe here."

Quincy stepped inside, and the boy quickly shut and barred the door.

"You can stay here awhile, Mister. They'll give up soon enough."

"Who are you?" Quin peered around the darkened storeroom. "What is this place?"

"A print shop. I'm the apprentice."

"Why did you help me?"

The boy moved toward an open doorway. "They had you outnumbered. Come to the front room. I have a candle lit there."

Quin followed the dim outline of the youth. "Is your master a Tory, that you would help me?"

The boy laughed. "The master's a businessman. He'll print anything, Tory or Whig, as long as they pay up front."

After a wait, Quin slipped out the front, thanking his young rescuer, and made his way home.

What a rotten night, he thought, heading for his study. He might as well drink himself to sleep. He didn't want to think about his former friends who considered him a traitor. He definitely didn't want to analyze his feelings for a certain saucy young lady. Even so, he had a disturbing feeling that mere lust would not inspire this strong a desire to protect.

He opened the study door.

In front of his drop-leaf desk, reading *The Gentlemen's Magazine*, sat a younger, stockier reflection of himself. Dressed in claret velvet, the man lounged in Quin's chair with his legs propped up, his silver-buckled shoes stacked on the wooden seat of a nearby chair. He glanced up at Quin, his eyes the familiar gray that all Stanton males possessed. He lowered his magazine onto the secretaire, a cold imitation of a smile pasted on his pale, flaccid face.

"I intended to stay with my uncle, but when I passed by his house—well, shall we say, I can see why you no longer live there. At least, your residence comes close to respectability. Your stay in England must have had a positive effect on you. Hope you don't mind, dear brother, I've made myself at home."

Quin smiled back. Indeed, better to keep the enemy close at hand. "Welcome to America, Clarence."

CHAPTER SIX

Wednesday, October 11, 1769

The next morning, Quin ambled out the back door to the detached kitchen in search of a strong cup of coffee. The cook, Mrs. Millstead, was kneading bread dough while her son and Josiah ate a breakfast of sausages and eggs.

The scrape of spoons on pewter plates reverberated painfully through his head. "Josiah, hurry it up. You'll be late for school."

The youngster took a quick gulp of weak ale. "I was thinking, Mr. Stanton, that I'd be more help to you if I stayed close at hand."

"You'll help yourself to an education first. Off you go."

"But—"

"Go!" Quin rubbed his forehead. He should know better than to yell after all the drinking he had done the day before. He winced as the door slammed, signaling Josiah's protest of his cruel fate.

Mrs. Millstead punched the dough with a meaty fist.

"'Tis a queer way to treat an indentured servant, sending him to school."

Quin sighed and sat at the kitchen table. He missed his ship and the crew that never questioned his orders. "Make me some coffee, please, Mrs. Millstead."

She continued to complain as she prepared his coffee. "Don't see why that little orphan should get an education and not me own boy, Samuel."

Quin examined Samuel, who held a plump, greasy sausage in his equally plump, greasy hand, calmly chewing on one end while his dull eyes focused on the wall in front of him. "How old are you, Samuel?"

The boy chewed slowly while he frowned over the difficulty of the question. "I dunno, about fifteen."

"Why don't you apprentice yourself to learn a trade? 'Tis not too late."

Samuel shrugged. "I tried working at a chandler's shop. He made me work too hard."

Quin closed his eyes and massaged his aching head. The boy thought cutting candlewicks was hard work? "Has my brother wakened yet?"

"No, his lordship gave me instructions last night," the cook said. "Gave me a complete menu of what he expected for breakfast. Said he always slept 'til noon and don't want nobody bothering him before then."

"He's not a lord, Mrs. Millstead. Not unless my father has died."

"Well, he was very precise about that, he was. Insists that we all call him 'his lordship.'" Mrs. Millstead's eyes shone with a malicious gleam. "Said he was the heir and not you."

"I see." Quin rose wearily to his feet. So, his younger brother was wasting no time informing everyone that he was a bastard. "I'll have my coffee and breakfast in the study, Mrs. Millstead, and you can remember that 'tis I, and not his lordship, who is paying your wages."

Quin wandered into his study. He sat at his drop-leaf desk, dipped a quill into a crystal inkwell and began a letter.

> Dear Edward,
>   Clarence arrived last night and is staying with me. Notify our solicitor. There must be a legal way to outmaneuver him.
>   Meanwhile, I'll keep him occupied with a hectic social life. If he goes to parties all night and sleeps most the day, he'll not have time to cause trouble.
>   Regards, Q

Quin folded the letter and secured it with sealing wax. When Samuel stumbled in with his breakfast tray, he jumped to his feet to relieve the boy of the burden, fearing the clumsy Samuel would spill his coffee.

Quin set his tray on the walnut table as the man in brown entered the room. "Good morning, Johnson. Would you care for some breakfast?"

"No, thank you."

Quin noticed Samuel hovering at the doorway. "Samuel, the shoes I wore last night need to be cleaned and polished."

"Yes, sir." The boy shut the door after him.

Quin poured himself a cup of coffee and sat, waiting for Johnson to join him.

His employer remained at the door, cracked it open for a peek, then closed it. As he approached Quin, he withdrew a small cloth pouch from an inner pocket of his coat.

"The latest from Revere." Johnson removed a pair of silver shoe buckles from the pouch and laid them on the table next to the breakfast tray. "They each hold a small amount of gunpowder. I suggest you wear them always."

Quin took a sip of coffee. "Very well."

Johnson placed a silver ring on the table and returned the empty pouch to his pocket.

Quin cocked an eyebrow. "I'm touched. Does this mean we're betrothed?"

With a faint twitch at his mouth, Johnson pulled back a chair to take a seat. "This is no laughing matter, Stanton. I hear your British brother has arrived and is staying here. While it may confirm everyone's belief that you're loyal to the crown, it makes your situation more dangerous. Watch your back. Trust no one, not even this enterprising female you're determined to protect."

"I know how dangerous it is, Johnson."

"Good. The ring is a precaution in case you're captured. The British fear that a jury of Colonials would not convict, so they would send you to England to stand trial. Not only would the British condemn you in a minute, they would execute you as a traitor, and that is a great deal nastier than a simple hanging."

"I know." Quin's appetite withered away at the thought of near-fatal strangulation, followed by disembowelment and decapitation. He picked up the ring to examine it. "What's inside? Poison?"

"Yes. 'Tis not painless, but it is quick. I would recommend it if the time comes. You can at least cheat them out of deciding your fate."

Quin turned the ring around in his hands while a vision of a female with bottle-green eyes sailed through his mind. There was too much unknown sea to explore with a mermaid hidden in the elusive depths. He would not give it up. He slipped the ring on a finger of his left hand. "I'll wear the deuced thing, but I'll not be caught."

"Good. I'll be on my way then." Johnson rose to his feet. "You have another practice session with the *Turtle* tomorrow. 'Tis almost time to move her to the harbor."

"Fine." Quin groaned inwardly. After six practice sessions, he still hated the sensation of being closed up in the dark little submersible.

"In case your brother asks, how will you explain your absence from the house tomorrow?"

"I could be visiting friends in Cambridge."

"A mistress would sound better," Johnson observed. "He'd be more inclined to respect your privacy then."

"Very well." Quin fetched the letter he had written from the desk. "Can you see that this reaches my uncle?"

"Of course. And remember, Stanton, put a stop to a certain young lady's attempts at espionage."

Friday, October 20, 1769

An excellent night for spying, Virginia thought, eager to try her hand once more. It had been two weeks since her last, successful attempt. She surveyed the gaily lit parlors of the Oldhams' luxurious home. The doors between the two large parlors had been opened wide and the gilded baroque furnishings pushed up against the flocked wallpaper to allow room for dancing.

At the entrance to the parlor, she stood with her aunt and sister. They curtsied and exchanged pleasantries with the host and hostess. She had made one adjustment to her green silk gown, adding a sheer scarf around her neck, tucked into the bodice to conceal the low décolletage. When Caroline had questioned her sudden attack of modesty, she had mumbled an excuse about the old major at the Higgenbottoms' ball drooling on her.

The truth was the major and his drool were far from her thoughts. Ever since that night at the Ashfords, she had not been able to dress or undress without recalling the touch of Quincy Stanton's bare thumb gliding down the curve of her breast.

Her pulse speeded ahead of her thoughts, quickening at the mere possibility of seeing him again. She squelched the anticipation. She would remain calm.

And she would discover exactly what he was doing.

He was easy to spot. With the help of his high heels, he stood considerably taller than the other men. His green silk coat and breeches nearly matched the color of her own gown. She watched his back as he sauntered across the adjoining parlor, accompanied by a shorter, stockier dandy in plum velvet.

"Good evening, Miss Munro." Captain Breakwell made a leg to her. "'Tis my greatest pleasure to see you." He offered his arm to escort her across the room.

"Good evening, Captain." What was she to do with this redcoat? He seriously interfered with her plans. It was too early to send him for refreshments. And the last time she had done that at the concert, he had questioned her disappearance. "Could I ask a small favor of you?"

"Of course, and I would be honored if you would call me William."

"As you wish. You see, my sister loves to dance, and I was wondering if you could partner her for the first set?"

Though he looked taken aback, the captain rallied with a small smile. "But do you not wish to dance also, Miss Munro?"

"Perhaps later. I fear I'm quite fatigued today. I helped my aunt in the garden, you see . . ."

"Of course." He guided her to a chair. "Please rest yourself, my dear."

Virginia forced herself to smile as he hovered over her like she might break. This was not working. Perhaps she should suddenly take ill. With a sigh of relief, she heard the musicians warming up.

William sat beside her. "May I address you by your given name?"

"Yes, 'tis Virginia." She leaned slightly to the side in order to see into the adjoining parlor. What was Quincy Stanton doing? And who was that shorter man in plum velvet at his side? She jumped in her seat, startled when the captain suddenly clasped her hand in his.

"I remember your name, Virginia, from when you first introduced yourself. I have called you that in my mind ever since."

She blinked dumbly at him, wondering why she was not

more affected. Didn't young ladies dream of receiving attention like this? He was very handsome with his sandy blond hair and clear blue eyes. Shouldn't her heart pound?

Perhaps, having convinced herself of the unlikelihood of her ever marrying, she was now immune to such feelings. But her heart *did* race when she encountered Quincy Stanton. She had told herself it was her natural curiosity that excited her in his presence, the enticing lure of solving the mystery that surrounded him and his puzzling behavior.

She frowned. But what if it was something more?

The captain patted her hand. "I beg your pardon, Virginia. I see by your countenance I am too forward and have shocked your delicate nature."

She bit her lip to keep from grinning. Her delicate nature? She once took revenge on her brother by stuffing a frog down his breeches. And the captain thought he was bold for using her name and holding her hand? He should take lessons from Mr. Stanton.

The now-familiar memory swept over her—Quincy Stanton inserting his thumb into her neckline and sliding it down. She responded in her usual manner. Her cheeks heated up, and she grew short of breath. *Be honest with yourself. You feel more than curiosity for him.*

"Forgive me." William released her hand. "I can see I have rushed you."

"Excuse me?" She cast the captain a confused look. She truly should pay more attention to the poor man. He tried so hard.

An unexpected shriek distracted her. She glanced up to locate the source.

Quincy Stanton leaned against the door frame between the two parlors, studying her, apparently unfazed by the feminine sound of horror that had erupted from the room behind him.

Virginia's eyes met his. The searching look he gave her seemed to reach down into her soul. She gripped her hands together as her heart expanded in her chest.

The source of the shriek, Miss Higgenbottom, stormed out of the adjoining parlor, her normally white skin flushed pink from her neckline to her hairline. She halted beside Mr. Stanton, her blue eyes flashing and blond curls trembling as she shook with anger. "How dare you deceive me, Quincy!"

Everyone in the two parlors hushed. All eyes turned to witness the evening's entertainment.

Quincy Stanton retained his casual pose and calmly removed his snuffbox. "Come now, Miss Higgenbottom. I behave like a bastard. Surely, it should come as no surprise that I am one."

A collective gasp surged across the two rooms, followed by a wave of hushed whispers.

Miss Higgenbottom clenched her closed fan in tight fists. "You said you were the eldest son of the Earl of Dearlington."

"I am, but if you're interested in the title, I suggest you focus your efforts on my brother." He shrugged one shoulder in an uncaring gesture. "C'est la vie, chérie."

The fan snapped in Miss Higgenbottom's hands, and she stumbled back. Her mother bustled over, and with a contemptuous glare directed at Quincy, she escorted her daughter from the room.

"Well, well," William Breakwell whispered to Virginia.

"The truth about the ill-mannered Stanton has finally come to light."

Virginia pondered the satisfied look on the captain's face. "You don't like him."

"He has no place in polite society."

"He cannot help the way he was born." She glanced at Quincy Stanton. His face was stiff, implacable, and cold, as he slipped his unused snuffbox back into his pocket.

Excited whispers hummed around the room as the well-dressed elite of Boston discussed Quincy Stanton's illegitimacy in his presence. A slow churning sensation started in the pit of Virginia's stomach and crept up her chest. It burned her throat with a foul taste of hypocrisy. She knew, in that moment, he was in pain.

And she felt rage.

She turned toward the captain and kept her voice calm. "Would you excuse me for a moment? I would like to see if Miss Higgenbottom is all right."

William nodded his head with an approving smile. "You have a kind heart, Virginia."

Kindness was not what she had in mind. She strode toward the parlor entrance. The hall was empty, the door across from her slightly ajar.

She peeked inside, steeling herself for a confrontation. Miss Higgenbottom sat on a settee, sobbing into a handkerchief, while her mother paced back and forth like a British officer inspecting his troops.

"Hush those tears this instant, Priscilla." The mother major shook a chubby finger at her. "Do you want Clarence to think ill of you?"

Priscilla lowered her handkerchief and sniffed. "'Tis not fair. Clarence is not as handsome as Quincy. He's short and boring, and in few years he'll probably be fat."

Mrs. Higgenbottom loomed over her daughter. Overly plump herself and dressed in oversized panniers and skirts of scarlet silk, she was as wide as the settee where Priscilla sat. Her white-powdered wig added another foot to her intimidating height. "You listen to me, Prissy. If you want to be a countess, you will behave like Clarence is the most handsome man in the world. Understand me?"

Priscilla's bottom lip trembled. "Yes, Mama."

Virginia's anger dissipated as quickly as it had emerged. She knocked gently on the door. "May I be of some assistance?"

Mrs. Higgenbottom whirled around with a huge swish of red silk skirts, like an enormous tomato and just as poisonous, although Virginia had serious doubts that tomatoes were actually poisonous. The woman's eyes, heavily lined with lampblack, narrowed on her. "And you are?"

"Virginia Munro." She stepped into the room. "I'm visiting my aunt, Mary Dover."

"I see." Mrs. Higgenbottom inspected her from head to toe. "Are you married?"

Virginia blinked at the woman's bluntness, but realization soon followed. Mrs. Higgenbottom looked upon her as competition for her daughter. "I doubt I shall ever marry."

"Umph," Mrs. Higgenbottom snorted. "This young generation, so foolish to think you should do as you please. If you could keep my daughter company while I fetch some water to clean her face, I would appreciate it." She barreled past Virginia and out the door, closing it firmly behind her.

Virginia perched on the settee next to Priscilla Higgenbottom. "Are you all right?"

The young lady shook her head, her blond ringlets swaying with the movement. "I'm mortified. I shall never be able to show my face in public again."

"Surely, 'tis not that bad."

Priscilla dabbed at her eyes with the handkerchief. "The sad truth is I actually like Quincy."

"Then why did you humiliate him like that?"

"I didn't mean to. His brother, Clarence, was spreading the news. Everyone would have known soon enough."

"Clarence is the man in plum velvet?"

Priscilla nodded her head.

"And Clarence told everyone his brother is illegitimate? That was cruel of him."

"No more cruel than I." Priscilla sighed. "Poor Quincy. My heart breaks for him."

Virginia felt a strange unease in her stomach. "You truly care for him?"

"I know some say he's ill-mannered and arrogant, but he was always kind to me. He made me laugh." Priscilla twisted the handkerchief in her hands. "Now, I must forget about him and concentrate on Clarence."

"For goodness sake, why?"

"My mother is determined I should live in England and have a title. She says the Colonials are about to destroy our lives."

"Oh." Virginia bit her lip. In her patriotic fervor, she had not considered how dismal the future might seem to a Loyalist.

"Mother has prepared me all of my life so I would be able

to catch the man of her choosing. When I was fifteen months old, she put me in stays, and I've worn them night and day since."

"You sleep in your stays?"

Priscilla nodded. "Aye, I cannot support myself without them now. I was dressed like a lady since the moment I could walk, so I was never allowed to play. I had to wear long gloves and a mask over my face to keep my skin white and pure."

Virginia's sympathy turned to horror. In comparison to this girl's life, her childhood in North Carolina had been free and unconfined. Her parents had always given her love without question. Even her terrible fear of fire was indulged with gentle patience.

She excelled in sewing, embroidery, and all sorts of handwork. Her knowledge of gardening was extensive. She could read, write, cipher, dance, and speak French, but she could not perform any tasks that required a fire.

A woman in the hills of North Carolina was expected to know how to cook, make soap, and do the laundry without assistance. Servants were extremely rare. News of her inadequacies had somehow leaked out, causing the rumor that she was unfit for marriage.

Virginia sighed. "Surely your parents would not force you to marry against your will?"

"They know what is best for me." Priscilla took a deep breath. "I must devote my attention to Clarence now."

Virginia couldn't help but wonder—if the well-trained and beautiful Priscilla had continued to pursue Quincy Stanton, would she have succeeded?

"Where did you go?" Aunt Mary whispered to Virginia.

"I was talking to Priscilla Higgenbottom." It seemed strange, but Virginia had made a new friend tonight, a Loyalist friend. Of course, most of what she felt for the girl was sympathy, but poor Priscilla needed a friend.

"Oh." Mary sounded disappointed. "I thought perhaps you had discovered something useful."

"Aunt Mary, what will happen to the Loyalists if—never mind." She watched Priscilla dancing to "Sukey Bids Me" with Captain Breakwell. After encouraging her new friend to rejoin the party, she had asked William to dance with her.

"Are you having second thoughts about what we're doing?" Mary asked.

"No, but it is more complicated than I thought it would be."

Mary closed her fan with a sigh. "Aye, lass, it always is."

Virginia scanned the parlors. Her sister was dancing as usual. She spotted the man who must be Quincy Stanton's younger brother. Priscilla was right. He was shorter and a bit too stocky. Though still handsome, his pale, soft features did not compare well to the tanned, chiseled countenance of his older brother. "Did Quincy Stanton leave?"

"No," Mary answered. "He was dancing a moment ago as if nothing had happened. The ladies seem more fond of him than ever. Nothing like a bit of notoriety to pique the interest."

"I don't see him."

"Perhaps he stepped out for some air. It is stuffy in here."

Virginia remembered the night of the Higgenbottoms'

ball. She had spied him in the garden with a curious, glowing object. "I believe I need some air, myself. Excuse me, Aunt Mary."

She wandered to the glass-paned doors that opened onto the side of the Oldhams' house. One last look about her reassured her that everyone was occupied with dancing, drinking, and gossiping.

She eased onto the colonnaded porch and stood perfectly still while her eyes adjusted to the dim light. A cool October breeze caressed her shoulders and neck. It was a clear night, for a multitude of stars shone overhead. If she looked hard enough, she would spot the comet that everyone was talking about—when they weren't discussing Quincy Stanton's accident of birth.

Where was he?

She descended two brick steps into the garden. The scent of roses drifted toward her, along with the smell of rosemary and lavender. The light of the moon picked out the thick, lumpy outline of an intricate knot garden. She was alone.

She closed her eyes and listened, shuttering out the muffled sounds of dance music and laughter. The low murmur of voices emanated from the garden behind the house.

Quietly, she crept to the back, the ground hard and cold beneath the thin soles of her dancing shoes. A thick row of tall bushes grew close to the side of the house and rounded the corner to the back. She positioned herself at the corner, concealed by the hedge, and gently pulled back a leafy section at eye level.

There he was.

His back was to her. The moonlight gleamed off his powdered wig. He pivoted to the side, holding a paper in one hand, the glowing object in the other, a few inches above the paper. He murmured something as he pocketed the paper. With a faint snick of a sound, the glow disappeared.

Virginia blinked. What was that strange object? She had never seen anything that could glow in the dark, other than a few fireflies.

Quincy Stanton moved slightly, revealing his smaller companion. She recognized the boy from *The North Star*, just before he turned on his heels and sprinted away toward the far side of the house. Whatever secretive business these two were conducting, it had come to an end.

Quincy Stanton swiveled in her direction. She pulled back and dashed toward the colonnaded porch. Halfway there, she skidded to a stop.

Captain Breakwell and Priscilla were exiting the house onto the portico.

"I wonder where she could be?" William's voice carried through the cool, crisp air.

Virginia backed up. How could she explain this to a British officer? But where could she go? She jumped when a leafy branch scraped her back.

The hedge.

It was tall enough to conceal her.

She slipped around the first bush and into the narrow space between it and the house. With her back flattened against the brick wall, she scooted sideways.

The gritty surface of the brick tugged at her silk gown. She winced. Hopefully, her dress could be repaired. She reached out, running the palm of her right hand along the grainy texture 'til she felt the sharp edge of the corner. She rounded the corner and continued for a short distance before stopping. Completely concealed between the back wall of the house and a seven-foot hedge, she took a deep breath to calm her frayed nerves.

All she had to do was wait, then return to the party. She could claim to have spent her time in the back garden.

A whispered curse sounded on the other side of the hedge. She froze, her back pressed against the cold, rough brick.

Quincy Stanton.

He must have spotted William and Priscilla standing on the porch. What would he do?

Just to the left of her, the hedge suddenly parted as two tanned hands reached through and shoved the leaves apart. Quincy Stanton squeezed through. He dropped his hands, and the branches snapped back together.

Virginia grimaced, closing her eyes. How could she explain her presence here?

It was an unlikely place to look for a chamber pot.

CHAPTER SEVEN

Virginia opened her eyes and peeked to the side. Quincy Stanton had recovered quickly from any surprise he may have experienced. He leaned against the brick wall, positioned as close to her as her wide skirts would allow. There was just enough light to see the sides of his mouth curl up and the dimples appear in his cheeks.

"I can explain," she whispered.

He placed his forefinger in front of his lips in a warning to remain quiet.

She frowned in spite of the reprieve that allowed her a few more minutes to manufacture an excuse. The sound of voices drew closer.

"I don't see her," William Breakwell said from the other side of the hedge. "Do you?"

"No," Priscilla answered. "Perhaps she's still inside."

"Her aunt told me she went out for some fresh air." William sighed. "This is very disturbing."

Not as disturbing as Quincy Stanton's behavior. Virginia

watched him as he tilted toward her and closely inspected the scarf that covered her bosom.

"I'm sure she's perfectly safe," Priscilla said.

Virginia glared menacingly at Quincy Stanton. He appeared not to notice, although the dimples in his cheeks deepened. *Why did the rascal have to be so handsome?*

"You know," Priscilla continued, "it is odd, but Quincy disappears every now and then, too."

"Nothing odd about that," William replied. "The cad has most likely cornered a poor, unfortunate female in the dark to take advantage of her."

Virginia gave Quincy Stanton a questioning look to see if he was offended. His white teeth became visible as he grinned.

"Perhaps we should look for Virginia inside," Priscilla suggested. "I do hope she's all right."

Quincy Stanton leaned in close, his breath warm against her brow.

"I worry about all gentlewomen, such as yourself," William said. "I fear dangerous times are ahead."

Virginia shoved Quincy back. He placed his forefinger in front of his smile, reminding her to remain silent.

"My parents agree with you, Captain." Priscilla's voice faded as the two wandered back to the side entrance of the house.

Virginia heard the click of the door shutting. She was alone with Quincy Stanton.

She took a deep breath. "Well, that's enough fresh air for me. I believe I'll be going now." She moved to the right.

He reached across her, planting a hand against the brick

wall to stop her. He eased himself in front of her, sandwiched between her and the hedge. "Why are you hiding here?"

She avoided looking him in the eye. "Why are you?"

"I asked you first."

"I hardly know you. Why should I talk to you?" She scooted to the left.

He blocked her movement with his other hand, pinning her in. "Fine, then I'll do the talking. You cause British officers to faint, you wander about upstairs in homes where they quarter, and you hide from them behind a hedge. 'Tis an odd way for a Loyalist to behave, is it not?"

He knows. Her breath caught in her throat, rendering her speechless, unable to defend herself. A horrifying vision crept through her mind of him dragging her back into the house and flinging her at the feet of the British officers as he accused her of treason. *Admit nothing that can be used against you.* "I . . . I'm trying to avoid one officer in particular, for personal reasons."

"Captain Breakwell? As much as I would love for that to be true, I doubt your sincerity. The man's too good a catch for a woman to pass up."

"I don't think he's such a good catch." She glared at him. "And I'm not interested in catching anyone." She ducked under his arm and scooted away.

"Wait." He grabbed her arm, pulling her to a stop.

"Let me go." *Please, Lord, don't let him turn me in.*

"What do you mean you don't want to catch anyone?"

Blinking, she stared at his face. His furrowed brow and narrowed eyes told her he was serious about the question. "I . . . I don't see that it is any of your business."

He leaned against the brick wall, frowning. He seemed unsure of himself again.

"Will you release me, please?"

He shook his head. "We have to discuss your . . . behavior."

"There's nothing wrong with my behavior."

"You always hide behind hedges?"

"Aye." She gave him a pointed look. " 'Tis very popular tonight."

"I believe you were spying on me."

He *did* know. Her heart raced. "That's—that's utter nonsense."

"Then why are you hiding?"

Give him an excuse and escape. "I told you. I was hiding from Captain Breakwell."

"Tell the man to leave you alone. I'll do it for you, if you like."

"I'll take care of the matter, myself. Now, if you will excuse me?" She lunged to the right, pulling away from him.

He released her and followed her along the hedge. "Miss Munro, we have to talk about this. What you're doing is far too dangerous."

"Oh, aye, a hedge can be a very treacherous thing. I'm a wee frightened for it looks so big and fierce."

"Saucy as ever."

She shot him a look of disdain just before she reached the center of the back wall, where another brick porch jutted out from the house and the row of shrubbery came to an end. The porch was knee-high, so she lifted her skirts to step up.

He grabbed her around the waist to help her up. She squirmed to get away from him. Twisting to the side, she lost her balance when her wide skirt stuck in the branches of the hedge.

"Oh!" She grappled at the hedge to steady herself, but the branches merely gave way. She fell back against Quincy Stanton.

His chest didn't budge. His arms swept around her for support. "I see what you mean. The vicious hedge has attacked you."

"Let go of me!"

"No, you'll fall and tear your skirt. 'Tis caught in the clutches of a treacherous hedge."

"This is not amusing, Mr. Stanton."

"I'm not laughing." He rubbed his chin against her temple. "I see two possibilities, *chérie*. I free your skirt from where the hedge has snagged it or . . ."

"Or?"

"I remove your gown."

"Ah!" She tried to wiggle away, but he held her tight while he chuckled. She elbowed him in the ribs. "You said you weren't laughing."

"Careful, sweetheart, or you'll rip the skirt clean off. Of course, you could tell everyone I did it while I was ravishing you."

"Get me out of here!"

"The problem is with the panniers. They stick out too far."

She gritted her teeth. "I know that. They'll collapse if you press on them."

"Mmm, I thought you'd never ask." His hand slid along her hip, groping in the dark in search of the branches that held her hostage.

She closed her eyes, agonizingly aware of his arm wrapped around her waist, his other hand exploring her skirts, his sturdy chest against her back. It expanded each time he inhaled. It vibrated when his deep voice rumbled through him. She trembled as she felt his breath against her ear.

"Are you cold?" he whispered.

"No." *Get ahold of yourself. He's a dandy, an oaf in high heels, not a strong, handsome man with his hand in your skirts.* "Why aren't you wearing lavender?"

"I've developed a fondness for green." He rubbed his nose in the ringlets about her ear. "But I like the scent of lavender. There, I have it." He pushed her onto the porch, free from the hedge.

She dashed down the steps into the garden and shook out her skirts, examining them for damage in the moonlight.

"You will stop spying immediately." Quincy Stanton stood at the top of the dark porch, a large, looming shadow threatening to swoop down upon her.

She froze. "I don't know what you're talking about."

He descended the steps, coming into the moonlight as he positioned himself in front of her. "If you know what is good for you, you'll figure it out."

She swallowed hard. Was he threatening her? "What do you want from me?"

"I shall call on you tomorrow and explain."

"I've done nothing wrong! You will leave me alone." She turned on her heel and marched toward the side of the house.

"Virginia."

She halted and peered over her shoulder. "You know my name? And how do you know where I'm from?"

His eyes appeared black as night as he strode toward her. "Who could forget such a name? I consider it a challenge."

She shuddered in the cool air as she faced him. "A challenge? How is that?"

He stopped in front of her and spoke, his voice soft and distinct. "To render your name obsolete."

Her mouth dropped open as comprehension sank in.

"I know what you've been doing, Virginia, and you will cease the spying forthwith."

She laughed, but the cadence sounded brittle and false to her ears. "Of all the ridiculous things to say. I do believe you've been drinking too much rum punch."

"Is that your technique? You select an officer who's too much in his cups, gaze at him with your beautiful green eyes, and the poor sot tells you everything?"

"I've had enough of your nonsense." She whirled around.

He touched the back of her neck, curled his fingers around her scarf and gave it a tug. The ends of the scarf popped out of her neckline and she spun around, grabbing at it.

He yanked it off completely. His gaze dropped to her breasts and shifted back to her face. "What a shame, *chérie*. You are . . . exposed."

She covered herself with a trembling hand, aware of the double entendre in his warning. Was this it? Did he intend to turn her in now? "What will you do?"

"Keep it close to my heart." He tucked the scarf inside his coat.

She bit her lip. He was a Tory who accused her of spying, yet he planned to keep it a secret? Why? Did he want something in exchange? "Give me my scarf." She reached for his coat.

He stepped back. "I prefer you this way."

Her agitated breathing nearly caused her breasts to pop out of the tight bodice. His eyes glimmered in the moonlight as he looked her over. So that was what he wanted, blast him. The spurt of anger that shot through her came as a welcome relief. It gave her strength whereas her fear had made her feel weak.

She lifted her chin, glaring at him. "I will not play the tart to you, sir."

His gaze quickly met hers. "I would not ask you to."

"Oh, I believe it is quite clear what you have in mind."

"I cannot deny I'm inclined toward certain . . . thoughts." He grinned, his white teeth flashing in the dark. "They do say I'm insatiable."

"You're insufferable!"

"You're in error. I have another kind of bargain in mind."

Did he intend to blackmail her? Red-hot rage burst inside her, burning her eyes with unshed tears.

She lunged forward and snatched the wig from his head. "There! I have something of yours. Two can play this game, Mr. Stanton. I know you sneak around in the dark, meeting that young boy, looking at papers with some sort of glowing object. You won't say a word about me. You won't dare. I can expose you, too."

"Damn." He grimaced. "Virginia, I would never harm you in any way. You must believe me."

She crushed his wig in her fists. "You . . . you're just saying that so I'll stay quiet about you and return your wig."

"No! I only want you to stop. I don't want you in danger. And you can have the damned wig."

"Well, you cannot have my scarf."

He shrugged. "As you wish." He stepped toward her.

She noted his hair was short and black, his appearance younger without the wig. She stepped back. "I dare not trust you."

He removed the scarf from his coat. "I will not harm you." He looped the silken material around her neck and pulled her gently toward him.

She shivered as cool silk pressed against the back of her neck, so much softer than the noose that would strangle her if he turned her in.

"You can trust me, Virginia. I'll see you tomorrow. All will be well."

Dear Lord, she wanted to believe him. She wanted to believe he was honest and trustworthy.

His dimples appeared as his fingers hovered over her neckline. "Shall I . . . tuck this back in for you?"

She ripped the scarf from his hands and jumped back. In response to his grin, she hurled his wig into the garden. Then, she wheeled around and fled to the side porch. As she entered the Oldhams' parlor, she knew her escape from Quincy Stanton would not last long.

The man was not a dandy, and certainly not a lazy numbskull. He was a hunter, in pursuit of his prey.

And she was it.

Quincy wandered about the garden, allowing the time to pass, so no one would know he had been alone with Virginia.

Thanks to a hedge, he had managed to hold her in his arms tonight. He smiled at the memory of finding her behind the shrubbery. The woman was full of surprises.

And suspicion. She didn't trust him, that much was clear. Somehow, without exposing himself, he needed to convince her that his intentions were honorable.

He snorted. Honorable? Why would she ever believe that? Especially now, when everyone knew he was a bastard.

As he neared the portico on the side of the house, a sudden shrieking noise erupted from within. He bounded up the steps and entered the parlor. The music cut off abruptly as the guests crowded into the hall. He looked about but couldn't spot Virginia and her family.

He peered over the heads of the murmuring crowd. Mrs. Ashford was escorting a hysterical Mrs. Oldham down the stairs.

"'Tis gone, my brooch is gone," Mrs. Oldham cried.

Mr. Oldham dashed halfway up the stairs to his wife. "What has happened, my dear?"

"The diamond brooch you gave me last week," Mrs. Oldham whimpered. "I wanted to show it to my friends, but when I went to my room, 'twas not there!" She collapsed on the steps in tears.

Her wails were soon drowned out by the excited speculations of the guests.

Clarence shouldered through the crowd and stopped beside Quincy. "A robbery, eh? This sort of thing happens often in London. Probably one of the servants."

Several redcoat officers offered to investigate. Quincy watched the soldiers as they ascended the stairs. *Damn.* It would be impossible for him to sneak about the house. His work for the night was over.

He located a footman. "My hat and walking stick, please."

"Mine, too," echoed Clarence.

Quincy eyed his brother. "You're coming with me?"

"Of course. I say, old boy, how about a visit to Madame Minuette's House of Earthly Pleasures? I hear it is the best in town."

"I'm going home."

"What? The night is still young."

Quincy collected his hat and cane and made his way through the crowd to the front door. Josiah sat on the front steps, waiting for him.

"Josiah, find the coachman. I'm ready to leave." Quincy put on his hat.

Clarence followed him onto the porch. "How about we stop at a tavern for a few drinks?"

Quin clamped down on his growing anger. "I'm surprised you want to be seen with me, Clarence. After all, you made sure everyone would know I'm beneath you."

Clarence shrugged. "I have no problem with you being a bastard, old boy."

"That's very big of you."

Clarence waved a hand in dismissal. "I didn't realize my little snippet of information would cause such a stir. I naturally assumed that you'd been honest about yourself all these years and everyone already knew. Didn't mean to embarrass you, old boy."

Quin noted the amused glint in his brother's eyes. He was certain Clarence had enjoyed his humiliation. Still, his brother undoubtedly had a deeper purpose for spreading the news. He wanted Stanton Shipping.

All of Boston knew that Quincy was part owner and stood to inherit the entire business eventually. But now, no one would question if Clarence inherited it instead. Not when he was the legitimate one.

"I say, what happened to your wig, Quincy?"

"I lost it in the garden."

Clarence chuckled. "So that's where you disappeared to. A frolic in the grass, eh? No wonder you're not in the mood for Madame Minuette's. You've already rogered a wench tonight. Who was she?"

Quin curled his hands into fists. "A gentleman never tells."

Clarence snorted. "Have you never heard of using a bedchamber upstairs? 'Tis much more pleasant than a tumble underneath a hedge."

"I've developed a sudden fondness for hedges."

The coach pulled to a stop in front of them. Josiah sat on the bench next to the coachman. Quincy descended the brick steps and grasped the door handle.

"Oh, I know who she was." Clarence joined him with a grin. "That pretty redhead. What the deuce is her name? She came in from the garden looking like used goods."

Quin seized Clarence by the cravat and slammed him against the coach. His brother's eyes widened.

Quin twisted the cravat in his hand. "You may impugn my name to the delight of your vicious little mind, but say one word about the lady and you'll regret it."

"Threatening me, are you?" Clarence's voice rasped. "I would expect as much from a bastard."

Quincy heard voices behind him on the porch as more guests left the party. He released his brother. "I will be civil to you in public. Do not expect more."

Clarence glared at him. "I *do* expect more. I expect to have it all."

Quin wrenched open the carriage and climbed inside.

Clarence settled on the seat across from him.

Quin thumped his walking stick on the ceiling, then laid the cane across his lap as the coach lurched forward. He took a deep breath to control his anger. If only he could deny his brother shelter.

For over a week now, he'd entertained the enemy. Living with Clarence was increasingly hard to bear. Quin flexed his hands, tightening his grip on the cane. He would have to continue enduring his brother. He was more believable as a Loyalist fop with Clarence in his house and accompanying him to parties.

Clarence adjusted his cravat and cleared his throat. "You should know better than to threaten me, old boy. Don't you realize you'll be working for me someday?"

Quincy snorted. "You'll never have Stanton Shipping. Why don't you try another means of fattening your wallet? Marry an heiress. Priscilla Higgenbottom would do."

"She's not worth as much as a fleet of ships. Besides, Father has his heart set on Stanton Shipping. I won't disappoint him." Clarence leaned back against the cushions and whispered, "I dare not disappoint him."

A sense of unease settled in Quincy's gut. His brother sounded fearful, even desperate. Until now, Quin had assumed a favorable court decision would put an end to the family squabble. But now, he wondered—how far was Clarence prepared to go in order to achieve his goal?

Saturday, October 21, 1769

"Promise me, Caroline, that whatever happens to me, you and Aunt Mary will stay out of it." Virginia held fast to a bedpost while her sister tightened the laces on the back of her dress.

Caroline yawned noisily. "Whatever are you rambling on about? And why did you wake me up? Aunt Mary said we could sleep late on mornings after a party."

"I have to be prepared, in case . . ." Virginia's words drifted off without admitting the possibility of doom. Would Quincy Stanton turn her in as a traitor? He said he wished her no harm, but how could she trust such a man? A man who stuck thumbs in her neckline and tore scarves off her neck? "Quincy Stanton said he would come see me today."

Caroline marched around to face Virginia. "And you're wearing this plain, homespun dress? Have you lost your senses?"

"No. I simply have no wish to impress the man."

Her sister plopped down on the bed. "You mean because of that silly notion of yours that you'll never marry?"

Virginia rested her forehead against the carved bedpost. "This has nothing to do with marriage."

"Are you sure? I've seen how he looks at you. The man is wealthy, Ginny. He'll have servants. You won't need to do any chores that—"

"Lace me up. Please."

Caroline crossed her arms with a mutinous lift of her chin.

Virginia's confession came out in a whisper. "He accused me of spying."

"Good Lord!" Caroline fell back onto the bed, her face as white as the lace-edged pillowcase. "Oh, no. This is terrible."

"I know." Virginia leaned on the bedpost, wrapping her arms around it. "If the worst happens, I want you and Aunt Mary to act like you know nothing about it."

"We will not."

Virginia pushed away from the bedpost. "You must!" She sat on the bed beside her sister. "There's no point in all three of us hanging for treason. I will certainly take no comfort in your company at that time, I assure you."

"How does he know? We've only just begun."

"He caught me spying on him, twice."

Caroline popped up to a sitting position. "Why would you spy on Quincy Stanton? He doesn't know anything. 'Tis the officers who would know—"

"I know, but he was behaving strangely and—he's not what he seems."

Caroline shrugged. "So he has a few secrets, or did. Everyone knows he's a bastard now."

"I don't see why that should matter, or why everyone takes such delight in talking about it. I'm sure there are thousands of . . . illegitimate people in the world."

Caroline gave her a quizzical look. "Are you defending the man?"

A blush heated Virginia's cheeks.

"And you were spying on him?"

"He was behaving oddly."

Caroline gave her a pointed look. "He's not the only one." She rose to her feet and threw on a robe over her white woolen nightclothes. "I'll fetch Aunt Mary. She'll know what to do."

Virginia collapsed on the bed as her sister dashed from the room. What a mess she had made of Aunt Mary's plan. Perhaps she should leave town immediately, go home to North Carolina and be a spinster for the rest of her life. She closed her eyes, trying to imagine the green hills of home, the forests of tall trees, the wild rhododendrons in bloom— but the vision in her mind's eye took the form of Quincy Stanton.

Aunt Mary and Caroline burst into the room.

"Close the door, Caroline." Mary sat on the bed. "Now, do I understand this correctly? Quincy Stanton accused you of spying and plans to come here today?"

"Yes." Virginia sat up. "He says he means me no harm, but I'm not sure I can trust him."

"I see. Caroline, tell George to go to Edward Stanton's house and tell him I must speak to him immediately on an urgent matter."

Caroline nodded and left to complete the task.

"There." Aunt Mary rose to her feet. "If you cannot talk sense into Quincy Stanton, then his uncle will. Now we must prepare you for his visit. That dress will not do, Ginny. How about the midnight-blue silk?"

"No!"

"Why not? You look lovely in it."

With a moan, Virginia fell back on the bed. "I cannot

wear that one." The midnight-blue with the low neckline, the one that he had stuck a thumb in.

"Well, you cannot wear the pale green silk. It has not been repaired yet."

Virginia covered her face, moaning again. After her struggle with the hedge the night before, she had rejoined the party in such a bedraggled state that Aunt Mary had insisted they leave.

"Caroline's right." Mary perched on the bed beside her. "Your behavior has been odd. You never explained how a walk in the garden could tear your skirt or remove your scarf."

Virginia lowered her hands. "I wasn't alone."

"Quincy?"

She nodded, her cheek rubbing against the quilted counterpane. "I went outside to spy on him."

"Hmm." Mary pursed her lips. "I believe there is a simple way out of this."

Virginia sat up. "How?"

"There's no proof you were spying on British officers and committing treason. Quincy Stanton can only say you were spying on him, an American. There's no need for you to deny something that innocent. 'Tis no crime to be infatuated with a man."

"What?"

"When he comes, you can simply explain the situation. I'm sure he'll be very flattered. Any man would—"

"*What?*" Virginia leapt to her feet. "Tell Quincy Stanton I'm infatuated with him? Are you crazed?"

"No, Ginny. I'm trying to save your neck."

"I'd rather hang!"

Aunt Mary rose with a shake of her head and proceeded to the clothespress. "If you don't tell him, I'll tell him myself."

"'Tis not true!"

Ignoring her, Mary pulled out a lavender-and-white-striped cotton gown with white lace at the neck and sleeves. "This will do."

"Oh, no, not that one."

Aunt Mary turned to her with an exasperated look. "What is wrong with this one?"

"'Tis lavender."

"So?"

Virginia sighed. How could one man make all her clothes seem unwearable? "All right. I'll wear it." She slipped out of her homespun dress and stepped into a lacy white petticoat her aunt passed to her.

Caroline returned, and soon she and Aunt Mary had Virginia looking her best. Mary bustled out of the room, in a hurry to ensure Mrs. Robertson had something ready to serve the guest when he arrived.

"Well?" Caroline drew a daffodil-yellow cotton gown over her head. "Did you and Aunt Mary decide what to do?"

Virginia took hold of the laces on the back of her sister's gown. "Yes, but I don't believe I can do it."

Caroline peered over her shoulder with a grin. "Why not? Are you supposed to seduce the man?"

Virginia gave the laces a hard tug before tying them off. "'Tis not amusing, Caroline."

"I was right? No wonder Aunt Mary told me to make sure you two had privacy."

Virginia groaned.

A knock sounded at the door and Aunt Mary peeked in. "Your first guest has arrived."

Caroline giggled.

"My *first* guest?" Virginia asked.

"Aye, Captain Breakwell is in the parlor."

Virginia poured two cups of tea, real tea that Aunt Mary kept stored in a small locked chest in the kitchen. It was necessary to behave like the Loyalists that they pretended to be in front of the captain. She handed William a cup and sat across from him.

"I know it is forward of me to come without an invitation, but I was concerned about you after your hasty departure last night." He sipped his tea.

"I'm quite all right, I assure you. 'Twas silly of me to tear my gown in the garden. I do so love roses, but I forget about the thorns." Virginia heard a muffled giggle from the other side of the door. Caroline, no doubt. Her sister was eavesdropping.

William cleared his throat. "I fear you and your family missed the great event of the evening. After you left, Mrs. Oldham collapsed into a fit of hysterics, screaming that she'd been robbed."

"Oh, my! How dreadful."

"Yes." He drank more tea. "It appears that someone stole into her bedchamber and helped himself to her diamond brooch."

"While the party was in progress?"

"Mm." He took another sip. "Mr. Oldham checked the

servants and their quarters, but 'twas not one of them."

Virginia frowned. Was one of Boston's elite a thief?

William set down the cup and saucer. "I'm concerned for you and your aunt. With this burglar about, you're not safe here without a man."

"We have George."

"Who is he?"

"A servant."

Captain Breakwell stood, tall and resplendent in his scarlet uniform, a brace of silver-mounted pistols jutting from his white belt. "I wish to offer my services to protect you."

"I . . . I'm certain we're not in danger, but I appreciate your concern."

"The atmosphere in this town is growing more dangerous by the day."

She forced herself to smile. "Come now, Captain. What danger could possibly happen to someone like me?" She jumped when her sister flung open the door.

Caroline bit her lip to keep from giggling. "Excuse me, Ginny. Your next guest has arrived."

CHAPTER EIGHT

Quincy Stanton strode into the parlor, dressed in his clothes of lavender silk, and stopped short when he spotted Captain Breakwell.

Virginia curtsied. *Blast him. He would choose to wear lavender today.* "I believe you two gentlemen have met."

Captain Breakwell acknowledged the other with a slight nod of the head.

"Sink me!" Quincy leaned on his ebony walking stick. "You didn't tell me you were inviting more than one, Virginia. I thought I would have you all to myself."

William inched toward her. "You invited him here?"

"Of course, she did." Quincy propped his walking stick against the settee and began to remove his gloves. "I wouldn't be so rude as to come uninvited."

The captain's face turned pink. "I asked Virginia the question."

"I was expecting him, William." She moved toward the hall. "But it was very kind of you to stop by."

Captain Breakwell passed by Quincy Stanton, giving him

a suspicious look, and accompanied her to the front door. "Are you certain you want to be alone with that man?"

She opened the door. "There's no need for you to worry. Thank you for coming by."

With one foot outside, William hesitated. "I didn't realize the two of you were well acquainted."

"Ginny and I have become very close recently." Quincy glowered at the captain from the parlor door.

Virginia winced.

"I see." William strode down the steps, his face red.

She closed the door and glared at Quincy Stanton. "How dare you!"

He pivoted around and marched into the parlor.

Virginia spotted her sister lurking in the shadows under the staircase. "Caroline, go to the kitchen. So help me, if I catch you by the door, I shall cut off your hair while you sleep."

"All right, don't fuss at me." Caroline grinned. "Are you going to fuss at Mr. Stanton?"

"Go!" Virginia took a deep breath to steady her nerves, entered the parlor and closed the door firmly behind her.

Quincy Stanton was pacing back and forth. As usual, she thought his long-legged stride seemed incongruous with the lavender-tinted wig and high-heeled shoes.

"William," he muttered. "You call the man by his given name? What was he doing here? I thought you wanted rid of him."

"He stopped by unexpectedly. I don't believe it is any of your business. You certainly didn't have to be rude to him or infer that there is something more to our relationship than—"

She stopped talking when he pulled a small bundle from his coat and flung it onto the table. "What is that?"

He scowled at her. "A gift."

Her mouth fell open. "You brought me a gift?"

"Aye, is it so strange?"

She approached the round mahogany table, where the package lay next to the tea tray. "Why did you bring me a gift?"

" 'Tis not a keg of powder set to blow up in your face. 'Tis a simple gift." He turned away with a frown. "You wouldn't question it if it came from that damned captain."

He was jealous, the realization finally dawned. Quincy Stanton was bringing her presents and jealous of other men giving her attention. Her heart skipped a beat as she unwrapped the bundle. Perhaps his jealousy meant he cared for her and she could actually trust him.

She pulled out a delicate black silk shawl, painted with colored flowers and edged with imported black lace. " 'Tis . . . so beautiful. I've never seen such a beautiful shawl." She slipped it around her shoulders, admiring the way it draped so gracefully, the way the vibrant colors splashed across it with abandon.

"Then you like it?"

She glanced his way, spotting once again the hint of vulnerability that touched her heart. "I've never received such a lovely present. Thank you, Mr. Stanton."

His cheeks actually reddened. "I would prefer you call me Quin. After all, we battled the treacherous hedge together and emerged victorious."

"Very well." She decided to go straight to the heart of

the matter. "About your accusation—I don't believe you can accuse me of anything other than . . . misplaced curiosity. Do you intend to turn me in?"

"No, but I intend to make you stop this dangerous game you're playing."

She shrugged. "I'm not playing a game."

"Fine, deny it to your dying breath, just before the rope tightens around your pretty neck."

"Are you threatening me?" She paced toward him. "Is that your aim—to gain my confidence with the lure of lovely presents 'til I confess something that would give you the power to destroy me?" She whipped the shawl off and held it out to him. "You have wasted your time and money."

His jaw tensed. "You made your point. I'll not expect you to make a dangerous confession to someone of dubious character, such as myself." He strode toward the fireplace. "Keep the damned shawl. 'Tis a gift."

She felt a twinge of regret, knowing she had hurt him. She wrapped the shawl around her shoulders. "Thank you."

He stood with his back to her as he watched the fire burning in the hearth. "The facts remain the same. I caught you twice where you shouldn't be. For your own safety, you must stop sneaking about."

She sat in the Windsor chair. "What about the way you sneak about?"

He turned, his gaze meeting hers. "We will not discuss it."

"That hardly seems fair. You wish to interfere in my life, dictate what I can or cannot do, yet you will not answer my questions?"

He stepped toward her. "Virginia, you must trust me. I know what is best."

"Why should I trust you when you will not trust me?"

He balled a fist and hit it lightly on his thigh. "Damn." He paced across the room, frowning at the floor, then glanced up. "Would it help if I said espionage is too dangerous for a woman?"

She wrinkled her nose and gave him a doubtful look.

He smiled. "I know, you're very brave." He wandered to the window and stood there, looking out.

Dumfounded, she stared at his back. *He thinks I'm brave.* Her eyes misted with tears. For as long as she could remember, she had thought herself a coward. *He thinks I'm brave.* She blinked back the moisture from her eyes. But he would think her a coward if he knew the truth.

He spoke, his back still turned to her. "I know 'tis difficult for you to believe I have your best interests in mind, especially when I've been so rude to you in the past. I can only say, I have the utmost respect for you and wish you no harm. Indeed, I could not bear for any harm to befall you."

Her heart filled with longing. He sounded so sweet, so sincere. God help her but she could easily fall for him. She realized now, the physical attraction had always been there. Why else did she spend so much time studying his broad shoulders and long muscular legs, or respond as she did to his deep voice? His eyes, his dimples, everything about him appealed to her. It had only been his outrageous behavior and clothing that had set her off.

Now, he seemed kind, caring, and dependable. If this

were his true nature, she could readily trust him.

But no, she couldn't. He still acted like a pompous dandy in public. How could she trust someone who purposely deceived the people around him?

And what if she were deceiving herself? Her heart yearned to believe him, to trust him. She was so desperate to satisfy this aching need, she might fool herself into thinking he matched her vision of the ideal man.

If only she knew the truth.

He turned around to face her. "I'd like to ask for your help, if you don't mind. Josiah has behaved so poorly, the schoolmaster will no longer accept him. I can tell you're well educated, and I thought—"

"Wait." Virginia interrupted, flustered by the unexpected turn of the conversation. "Who is Josiah?"

"The boy I bought on *The North Star*."

"Oh." She smiled slowly. "The day we met."

He shifted uncomfortably. "Yes. As I was saying—"

"Why did you send Josiah to school?"

He shrugged. "For an education. The boy can hardly read."

"He's a servant. Why should you care?"

"No one else does. Someone has to."

She examined the man before her. He was full of surprises today. All the time he had been behaving like a pompous oaf in public, he'd been secretly caring for an orphan boy for the simple reason that someone needed to. But why dupe people into thinking he was a lazy, arrogant fop? "Can you tell me why you pretend to be a dandy?"

He frowned. "No."

"Why not?"

"I will not discuss it."

She rose to her feet. "How can you come in here, asking me to trust you, when you refuse to tell me anything about yourself?"

"Virginia, it is very simple. I know you were spying, but you have my word I will not report you. I only want you to stop."

"And I'm supposed to believe that and trust you?"

"Yes. You can trust me with your life."

"With my *life?*" She marched up to him. "I don't even know who you are. You act like a nonsensical fop when you're around other people, but with me, you act sincere and—I don't know what to believe. Who *is* the real Quincy Stanton, the one with the wig or the one without?" She reached up and yanked the lavender-tinted wig off his head.

His eyes darkened to a stormy gray. "Dammit, Virginia, I'm a man of my word."

"Hah! Would an honest man deliberately deceive people into thinking he was something other than his true self?"

He gritted his teeth. "I have my reasons."

"Which are?"

"Which are none of your business!"

With a cry of frustration, she threw his wig to the side. It landed in the fireplace.

"Oh, my God! Oh, no!" She ran toward the fire, halting in front of it as panic seized her in its grip.

"Leave it be. It doesn't matter."

"No, no! Oh, God, I didn't mean to." She covered her mouth and shook her head.

"Virginia." He touched her shoulder. "It doesn't matter. You can burn all my wigs. I don't care."

She pulled away from him, captivated by the fire. She watched the flames race up the hairs of the wig. The powdered strands curled and turned black 'til the wig bore a grotesque resemblance to a human head.

Her hair had been gray. She had come to help when Caroline was born. They had called her Auntie, for she had been her mother's aunt. Mother was in bed resting when Auntie asked the six-year-old Virginia to help her cook dinner.

Virginia glanced at the side of the hearth, and for an instant saw her young self in a homespun dress, her hair braided into neat pigtails. She was turning the spit. The roasting meat smelled delicious. The fat dripped into the fire, hissing with little sizzling sounds.

She took a deep breath. The smell of burning hair assaulted her nostrils. *"No!"* She backed away.

"Virginia, what's wrong?" Quin followed her.

With a whimpering sound, she covered her face to keep from seeing the horror.

But the memory hunted her down without mercy. Determined to torture her again, it played itself out in her mind's eye. She saw Auntie raking the coals to the side, her skirt brushing too close to the hearth, the flames leaping up her clothes 'til she was engulfed in fire. And Auntie had screamed and screamed.

"Ginny." Hands grabbed her shoulders.

Virginia screamed, jumping away.

"Ginny!" Quin grabbed her again. "What's wrong?"

She gasped for air. The smell of burnt hair filled her

senses. Nausea swept over her. She covered her mouth, broke loose from him and bolted from the room.

Quin stared at the door, listening to her footsteps fading away down the hall.

"Damn." He leaned over and picked up the shawl from the floor. It had slipped off her shoulders without her noticing. He glanced back at the fireplace. The flames had entirely devoured his wig—and *terrified* Virginia.

He wandered into the empty hall and stood there pondering his next move. He couldn't leave with her distraught like this. It was partly his fault. She had thrown the wig out of frustration because he refused to confide in her. But he had to remain silent about his participation in Johnson's spy ring. The information would be dangerous for her to know. And dangerous for himself.

He opened the door at the end of the hall and found himself in the kitchen, surrounded by scowling faces. Virginia's aunt and sister, an older, square-shaped woman, and the boy that James Munro had purchased on *The North Star* glowered at him, the accusations clear in their expressions.

"What did you do to her?" the younger sister demanded.

"Nothing. I—I gave her a shawl." He lifted up the shawl to prove his words. "Where is she?"

"She came through here, crying, and ran outside to the garden," the aunt explained. "I was about to go to her."

"Are you going to turn her in?" the sister asked.

"No. I would never hurt her."

The square-shaped woman snorted. "Ye made her weep."

"My wig fell in the fire. I told her it didn't matter, but she was so distraught, I don't think she heard me."

The aunt approached him. "Here, let me take the shawl. 'Tis lovely, and you're crushing it. She's in the garden, if you wish to see her."

Quin passed her the shawl and stepped outside. The autumn air felt cool and crisp. The sun shone brightly in a clear blue sky.

He ambled down the path through the kitchen garden. On each side the vegetable rows hid beneath a thick layer of hay, protected from the threat of an early frost. Two rows of beans stretched between poles connected with lines of twine. A tool shed and privy stood in the distance against the wooden fence.

The back half of the garden contained a small orchard of a half dozen fruit trees, the branches almost completely bare of leaves. He spotted her, propped against a cherry tree with her back to him.

"Virginia?"

She sniffled. "Please, go."

He hesitated, wondering if he should. This was an uncharted sea for him, comforting a crying female. But he couldn't turn his back on her. He advanced toward her. "Are you all right?"

She shook her head.

He winced. *Dumb question.* "Do you need a handkerchief?" He held his out to her.

She looked askance at it. "Does it stink?"

"No. I wouldn't bring a foul one to your house."

She turned, leaning her back against the tree, and accepted the handkerchief. Her tear-filled eyes and damp cheeks tore at his heart. He didn't know what to say, only felt a powerful need to take her in his arms. He clenched his fists, fighting the urge.

She wiped her eyes. "I'm sorry. It must have looked strange, the way I behaved."

"I'm only sorry to see you so distraught."

She sighed and turned away. "Now you know the truth about me."

"That you're afraid of fire?"

She pushed away from the cherry tree and strode toward the neighboring apple tree. "'Tis more than that. I'm a coward. I let her die."

"Who?"

"My great-aunt. She came to help when Caroline was born. I was helping her cook supper, when she . . . caught on fire."

"She burned to death?"

Virginia nodded. "I just stood there. I was so horrified."

"Of course you were. How old were you?"

"Six." She twisted the handkerchief around her fingers. "I was so afraid, I didn't run for help."

"You were a young child. You shouldn't blame yourself."

She crushed his handkerchief in her fist. "You don't understand. I did *nothing*. There were fire buckets on the hearth. I didn't even throw water on her."

He walked toward her. "Don't blame yourself. It was an accident."

Her voice broke as the tears began to flow. "But she screamed and screamed! She needed my help, and I was too afraid."

He reached for her and wrapped his arms around her shoulders. "'Twas not your fault." He searched his mind for comforting words. "Couldn't other people hear her screaming? Didn't they come to save her?"

Her head nodded against his chest.

"Don't you see? They tried to save her. 'Twas not your fault."

She sniffed and rubbed her cheek against his coat. "That's what Father said."

"He was right."

"It was so long ago. I should be over it by now, but it still haunts me."

"I know." He brushed back her hair from her brow. "There are some things we carry with us forever." Like being an unwanted bastard. Or the memory of a small, dark room in a cellar.

She squeezed handfuls of his coat in her fists. "I didn't want you to think I'm a coward."

"I don't."

She glanced up at him. "You don't?"

"No." The sight of her red-rimmed eyes struck at his heart. "Ginny, don't cry." He touched her damp cheek. Her lips were parted slightly, perfectly shaped pink lips. How would the curves, the fullness of them feel, how would they taste? He leaned down.

"Oh, no, I've ruined your coat." Releasing him, she stepped back.

"What?" *Damn.* He had come so close to kissing her.

"Your pretty silk coat is wrinkled and wet. I'm so sorry. And I destroyed your wig, too."

"Actually, you've destroyed two of them. But don't worry, I still have more."

"Two? How did I . . . ?"

He smiled. "The one you threw last night in the garden, it landed in the Oldhams' ornamental fish pond."

"Oh, no!"

He shrugged. "I truly don't care."

"That's not so. You love your fine clothes."

"Why do you think that?"

"You always dress so well, and it must cost you a fortune."

"I don't care about the clothes. Look." He paced toward the fence and removed one of his high-heeled shoes. "I hate these blasted things." He hurled the shoe over the fence.

"Ouch!" A shout returned from the other side of the fence. "What the hell is this?"

Quin stared at the fence, his mouth dropped open. "Sorry!" he shouted. "I didn't know anyone was there." He gave Virginia an apologetic look. "Oops."

She slowly smiled. "There's been a boy on the corner there for a week now, selling roasted chestnuts."

"Oh." With one shoe on, Quin stepped toward her with a lopsided gait.

Her smile widened.

He returned her smile, relieved to see her happy again. He removed his other shoe and left it behind as he drew closer to her. She was still smiling at him. He wouldn't have to lean over so much to kiss her now.

"Virginia." He touched her shoulder.

"You shouldn't walk home without shoes."

Was that a dismissal? Perhaps she had been through

enough today. He withdrew his hand and wandered toward the path. When he glanced at the house, he spotted four faces glued to the window. "We're being watched."

She rested against the apple tree. "They cannot see back here amongst the trees. The bean rows block the view."

Was that an invitation? He looked at her. She watched him steadily, then raised her hand to brush away the moisture on her cheek. Within seconds, he was in front of her, pulling her into his arms.

She gasped. "Quin?" She dropped his handkerchief and pressed her hands against his chest.

"Ginny, I want to kiss you." He cradled her face in his hands. Her eyes widened with a look of alarm. He would have to start slow. He bent down and touched his lips against hers. A light kiss.

He pulled back to gauge her reaction. She was gazing at his mouth, the look of alarm transformed to one of wonder. He slipped his hands to the back of her head and kissed her again, a little longer.

This time when he checked her reaction, her eyes were closed, her lips parted. She looked so sweet, so trusting, he kissed the tip of her nose. Her eyelids flickered open. With a shy smile, she eased closer to him, sliding her hands up to his shoulders.

He grinned, wrapped his arms around her, and pulled her close 'til her breasts pressed against him. "Yes." He planted soft kisses across her cheeks. The taste of salt lingered upon her skin, making him thirsty for more.

He kissed her mouth again, much more thoroughly. He wanted inside, but restrained himself for fear of frightening her. Instead, he concentrated on the shape and fullness of her lips. They tasted of sweetened tea. He raked his fingers into her hair. The ringlets curled around his fingers, tickling soft. The scent of lavender filled his head.

Her lips began to move with his. *Yes.* She was feeling it, too, this desire that ran hot through his veins. He pulled her tighter. Her hands stole up to his neck. Her breasts moved against his chest with each excited breath. Within seconds, the pleasure became torture. He groaned, realizing his appetite far exceeded what he could realistically expect.

He wanted her. Now.

He released her and stepped back. Her lips were pink with a just-ravished look that made him want to beg for more pain.

Gritting his teeth, he attempted to mentally halt the erection in process. "I . . . I have to go. I'll call on you again soon."

He loped down the path, spotted a gate in the fence, and made his escape. Pausing on the side of the street, he breathed deeply to clear the lust from his mind. She was a lady, a proper lady. He had to control himself.

"Sir?" the boy on the corner yelled. "Do you want your shoe?"

Quin peered down at his feet in sheer hose. "Aye, I suppose." He padded over to the boy selling roasted chestnuts. "Sorry I hit you. May I buy some of these?"

"Aye, sir." The boy grinned, handing him a cloth bag and pocketing the coin.

"Quin?" He heard Virginia's voice from the other side of the fence. A fraction of her face appeared between two riven boards. "Don't you need this?" She tossed his other shoe over.

He pulled both shoes on and with his added height peered over the fence. "Are you all right, Ginny?"

She smiled shyly, her cheeks coloring. "Yes, I am."

"I forgot to ask. Do you mind helping me with Josiah?"

"No, of course not. Should I pay for the wigs I destroyed?"

"No, of course not. Here." He passed the bag of roasted chestnuts over the fence. "I'll see you soon."

Quin strode home without his wig, without his walking stick and gloves, without feeling the pinch of his high-heeled shoes. Never had he wanted a woman before like he wanted Virginia Munro. When it came to his green-eyed mermaid, what the Boston elite said was definitely true.

He was insatiable.

CHAPTER NINE

Virginia returned to the apple tree with the bag of roasted chestnuts. On the ground lay Quincy Stanton's handkerchief. She must have dropped it just before he kissed her.

She picked it up. His initials were embroidered in a corner. With a smile, she smoothed her thumb over the raised letters. She lifted the handkerchief to her nose. It didn't possess the foul fragrance he had used before, the scent of a dissolute dandy. It smelled clean and masculine. It smelled like Quin.

Leaning back against the tree, she gazed through the twisted branches to the blue sky overhead. Only a few colored leaves remained on the tree, fluttering in the breeze. It had finally happened. Her first real kiss. Oh, there had been friendly and flirtatious pecks in the past, but nothing like this. Nothing that had left her breathless and unable to think. Nothing that had awakened a need to have more.

She inhaled a deep breath and let it out slowly. She needed to keep her wits about her. How much did she really know about Quincy Stanton? She knew he was handsome, intelligent, and charming, but he masqueraded as a vain, pompous fool. Did she dare involve herself with a man capable of such duplicity?

'Twas not your fault. He had been so kind and sympathetic. He knew everything about her now, yet still found her attractive.

You shouldn't blame yourself. Perhaps he was right. She was twenty-one years old. The memory of Auntie's death, as horrible as it was, should be put to rest and not allowed to control her anymore. Quincy thought she was brave. If she were truly brave, she would face her fear and deal with it.

She pushed away from the tree and strode toward the house.

"Are you all right, dear?" her aunt asked as she entered the kitchen.

"I'm very well." Virginia sat at the kitchen table, placing the bag on the surface. "Quincy bought us some roasted chestnuts."

"Why did he run away?" Caroline sat across from her.

"Excuse me?"

"We were watching from the window," Caroline explained, "and all of a sudden, Quincy Stanton ran down the path and out the gate."

Virginia felt the warmth of a blush across her cheeks. She had sensed the tension in Quin, the desire, the control he had exercised. It had engulfed her to the point she had been unable to think. "Aunt Mary, I have a confession to make."

Her aunt gasped. "What did you do with him?"

Caroline clapped her hands together. "I knew it. You seduced him."

"No." Virginia glared at her sister. "This has nothing to do with Quincy." She shifted her gaze to Aunt Mary. " 'Tis about me. Since the age of six I've been so terrified of fire, I've allowed this fear to dictate how I live my life." She steeled herself for her aunt's reaction, but Aunt Mary simply nodded her head.

Virginia glanced at her sister. "You told her?"

Caroline turned bright red and shook her head.

"Your father told me before he left." Aunt Mary sat next to Caroline. "He was explaining about that ridiculous rumor that you're unfit for marriage."

"I am unfit," Virginia said. "I don't know how to build a fire, how to make soap, or do the laundry. I cannot cook at all. 'Tis ridiculous for a woman my age to be so ignorant."

Caroline shrugged. "Just marry a wealthy man like Quincy Stanton."

Virginia frowned at her sister. "Neither one of us will have much of a dowry. Wealthy people tend to marry other wealthy people. Besides, marriage will not cure my fear of fire. I need to do that myself."

"How do you propose to go about it?" Mary asked.

"She could learn to cook." Mrs. Robertson stirred the pot of stew over the fire. "I'll be happy to teach the lass."

Mary nodded. "Aye, that would be a step in the right direction."

Virginia examined the large kitchen hearth and swallowed hard. "All right, I will. And when I go back home, those nasty people will have to find someone else to humiliate with their vicious gossip."

Caroline covered her face and burst into tears. "I'm so

sorry. I wanted to tell you, Ginny. I was afraid you would hate me."

Virginia blinked. "What are you talking about?"

"It was all my fault," Caroline wailed. "The rumor at home. I told one of my friends. We were telling each other secrets, and I told her you couldn't cook, that you were afraid of fire. I didn't think she would tell anyone, but she did. It was all my fault, and now, everybody will hate me." She lowered her face into her hands, sobbing.

Virginia skirted the table to sit next to Caroline.

Aunt Mary scooted down the bench and hugged the crying girl. "Hush now, lass. Nobody hates you."

Virginia hugged her sister from the other side. "Come now, there's been enough tears for one day."

Caroline sniffed. "I'm afraid that, because of me, you'll never want to go home. And Mama and Papa will hate me."

Virginia handed her Quincy's handkerchief. "Nonsense. No one could hate you. Besides, I'm not afraid of what a few people in North Carolina think of me. You know there's no one there I want to marry."

Caroline smiled tremulously with bleary eyes. "Not even Hans Schroeder?"

Virginia laughed. She and her sister had teased each other in the past, saying that the chubby widower Hans would come courting one of them, looking for a wife to take care of his five chubby children.

"As far as I'm concerned, you two can stay with me forever," Aunt Mary said. "I would be terribly lonesome without you."

George barged into the kitchen. "We have another guest. I showed him into the parlor."

"Who?" Virginia asked.

"Edward Stanton. Remember? I went to his house this morning and left him a message."

"Oh, my." Aunt Mary popped up from the bench and smoothed out her skirts. "Do I look all right?"

Virginia stood and adjusted the lace cap perched on her aunt's auburn curls. "You look lovely."

"Oh, my." Mary dashed from the room.

Virginia exchanged a look with her sister. "I have a feeling Aunt Mary won't be lonesome much longer."

Caroline grinned, her unsinkable spirit bubbling back to the surface. "Perhaps there'll be a double wedding?"

Virginia scoffed. "In a hurry to be rid of me?" She glanced at George, who stood by the door. "What is that you're holding, George?"

"A walking stick. It was in the parlor."

"Oh, may I see it?" Virginia skimmed her palm along the smooth ebony surface. "This belongs to Quincy." She fingered the silver knob on the end. "The knob feels a trifle loose. Perhaps we can fix it." She gave it a twist and jumped when a sharp blade sprang out the other end. "Good Lord!"

They stared at the transformed walking stick.

"Godsookers," George whispered.

Josiah arrived Monday morning, brown hair wet and neatly tied back, clothes clean, shoes polished, hornbook in hand, and a surly expression on his freshly scrubbed face.

"Good morning, Josiah." Virginia gave him a friendly smile. "Won't you come in?"

He glowered at his clipped nails. "The master made me come. I don't need no education."

"You don't need *an* education," Virginia corrected him.

"Right!" He flashed a grin at her and bolted down the front steps.

"Josiah, come back here!"

He was rounding the corner with no indication of returning.

"That little scoundrel." Virginia darted down the hall into the kitchen. "George, run out the side gate and catch the boy. He's running away!"

She dashed after George as he sprinted to the side gate. At the street, she paused to catch her breath. Josiah was ahead a few feet with the older George quickly gaining on him.

The boy selling chestnuts stuck out a foot. Josiah tripped and splattered into a puddle of water and filth.

George yanked him up and hauled him back to the garden. "I caught him, Miss Virginia!"

She inspected Josiah, now covered with foul-smelling muck, the hornbook in his hands filthy. "Were you this much trouble in school?"

The boy grinned. "Oh, aye."

"You're too filthy to let in the house."

"Then I can go home?"

"No." Virginia smiled. "You can have a bath here in the garden."

With George standing guard, she succeeded in washing Josiah in a tub of cold water while the boy complained loud enough for the entire south side of Boston to hear. George was left with the task of cleaning Josiah's clothes and hornbook as she marched the boy into the parlor and sat him down at the table. Wrapped in a linen towel, he scowled at her.

She removed the vase containing flowers Quin had sent the day before and placed it on the mantelpiece in front of the gilded mirror.

"Do you know the alphabet?" She fetched paper, inkwell, and sharpened quill from the secretaire against the wall and set the items on the table in front of Josiah.

"Aye, I ain't no muddlehead. Ye're giving me real paper? And ink? Ye're not afraid I'll make a mess in yer fancy room?"

"If you do, you'll clean it up." She sat across from him.

He chewed his lip, apparently judging the situation.

"I'm waiting."

Frowning, he went to work and finished quickly. "There." He passed the paper to her. "I can write real fast when I've got a good chair."

She examined his work. "What do you mean?"

"That scurvy old schoolmaster, he made me sit on the unipod for a week."

"Unipod?"

"Aye, a stool with one leg. 'Tis a punishment for bad boys like me." He lifted his chin with pride.

"You're not bad, Josiah, and I've never heard of anything so ridiculous in my life. What kind of schoolmaster is he?"

Josiah beamed. "That's what Mr. Stanton said. He fussed at the old man, said he didn't know how to handle the clever ones like me."

"Well, perhaps, but I don't believe you made it very easy for your teacher."

The boy squirmed in his chair. "I don't need no education." He glanced at her with a hopeful look.

She smiled. "I try not to make the same mistake twice. And you do need an education. You can do very well in America if you're willing to learn and work hard."

"Ye sound like me master. He said if I gets an education, he'll cut me time in half. Seven years instead of fourteen."

"That's very generous of him."

Josiah grimaced. "Seems like forever to me."

"How old are you?"

"Nine."

"I see." Virginia studied the boy before her. Seven years would seem like forever to a nine-year-old. The boy needed more immediate rewards for his efforts.

"I could make a living for meself, I could. I don't need no big people taking care of me."

"What would you do?"

He sat up straight in his chair, puffing out his scrawny chest. "I'd be the best damn pickpocket in the New World!"

She kept her face expressionless, aware the boy was trying to shock her. "That's not a profession with a promising future. Now let's see how good you are at ciphering."

The rest of the lesson proceeded well enough. Josiah was correct; he was not a muddlehead. She rewarded him with a big piece of apple pie. Without mentioning she had discovered the hidden blade inside, she gave him the walking stick to return to Quincy. Then she sent him home in his damp but clean clothes.

Friday, October 27, 1769

Virginia fanned herself, seated next to her aunt and sister in Concert Hall. The air was warm and stuffy with so many Bostonians crammed into the building, eager to hear the band of the 64th Regiment play. Virginia sighed. The inhabitants of Boston lacked consistency. They hated the British army's presence in their town, but loved their music. Of course, the fact that the concert was free might account for the heavy turnout.

Her eyes scanned the crowd, searching for one Bostonian in particular. Josiah had come by that morning for a quick lesson and had confided that his master would attend this evening. She needed to discuss the boy's lessons with Quin, but she knew that was a convenient excuse.

The truth was she longed to see him. She ached to see him with a hunger that worried her, for the overwhelming nature of it defied clear thought.

Every night she went to sleep with the memory of his mouth against her own and his arms around her. For a week she had dreamed of him, and where was he? Was he so occupied with business that he didn't come visit her?

Her heart leapt in her chest when she spotted him entering with his younger brother. Quin's gray silk coat and breeches fit him to perfection. Buttons of engraved silver lined his waistcoat of black-and-silver brocade. With his gray wig and gray eyes, he epitomized wealth and elegance.

Her initial excitement dwindled into uncertainty. He claimed not to care for rich clothes, yet he looked like he had spent half the day dressing. His frilly flock of peahens gathered around him, fawning over his fabulous plumage. His natural charm eased out with flowing speech and a dimpled smile, and his ladies responded with twitters of laughter. So intent was he on entertaining them, he never noticed her presence.

A slow throb of pain crept from the middle of her forehead to lodge in her temple, and she pressed her fingers against the side of her brow. With his wealth and handsome looks, Quincy Stanton was one of Boston's most eligible bachelors. The group of females surrounding him attested to that fact. So, why would he be interested in her? Did his duplicity extend to his treatment of her, so that he not only pretended to be a dandy, he also pretended to be attracted to her? Was that why he kissed her, then never came back?

"Virginia, how marvelous to see you."

She gave Captain Breakwell a halfhearted smile. "How do you do?"

"Is this seat not taken?" He helped himself to the seat she had saved for Quincy.

She glanced sadly at Quin and his brother where they held court. Another sad face, that of Priscilla Higgenbottom, peered back.

"Oh, look, there's Priscilla." Virginia raised her hand in greeting.

Mrs. Higgenbottom loomed over her daughter, whispering, and Priscilla turned her attention to Clarence Stanton.

"Poor Priscilla." Virginia resumed fanning herself. "Her mother insists she flirt with Clarence Stanton."

William frowned. "Does Miss Higgenbottom not care for the man?"

"No, she doesn't, but her mother is determined that she marry a man who will take her to England."

"Oh." William shifted uneasily in his chair. "I was wondering how you would feel about living in England."

Virginia swallowed hard. Was this man that serious about her? Dropping her fan in her lap, she rubbed her temple where the throb was quickening its pace. "I . . . I've never given the notion any thought."

"Please do."

The music started with a great pounding of drums that reverberated through her head. When the music finally ended, the pounding in her head continued with a life of its own. In the midst of the applause, she spotted Quincy Stanton headed for the door.

She rose from her chair. "I need to step outside for a moment."

"Allow me to escort you." William jumped to his feet. "You shouldn't be alone."

Outside, she spied Quin rounding the corner of Concert Hall, but she didn't dare follow him with William shadowing her. If her suspicions were correct, Quin was involved in some sort of activity that must remain a secret from the British authorities.

"Perhaps we should go to the side of the Hall," William said. "'Tis a bit muddy here in front."

"Oh, no, this is fine." She patted William's arm, determined to keep him away from Quin. "Is that not the major who fainted at the Higgenbottoms' ball?" She motioned to the portly man crossing the street with a group of British officers.

William introduced her to them. She curtsied to each

one, exchanging pleasantries to keep them distracted so Quin would have time to do whatever he was doing in secret.

The major weaved toward her, ogling her low neckline with his bloodshot eyes. "I remember you. I never forget a br—I mean, a face."

She stepped back, opening her fan to cover her bosom. "I remember you, too." A sharp twinge shot through her temple. Her headache was worsening.

The major lurched toward her, his frizzled wig listing to the side. "I've been looking for you, my gel. Been alone for much too long, don't you know."

"I'm not surprised." She retreated, peering over her shoulder. She was on the edge of a low spot in the road where horses and carriages had churned up a slippery quagmire of mud and manure.

When the major lurched toward her again, she simply stepped to the side and watched the major sprawl into the filth.

"Oh, dear. William?" She looked helplessly at the captain.

He paused in the middle of his conversation with another captain and offered a hand to the major to help him up. The major was almost erect, when his feet skidded in the mud, knocking into William's boots and causing him to lose his balance. William yelped, reached out for the other captain, and all three men toppled with a tremendous splash, splattering mud and filth all over Virginia's face and green silk dress.

"Aagh!" She wiped her face. "This is horrid! And I repaired my gown just yesterday."

"Virginia, I'm so sorry." William scrambled to his feet, his scarlet uniform coated with foul-smelling mud.

The people exiting Concert Hall stopped to point and

snicker. She turned her back to them, but discovered another audience enjoying the show on the far side of the street.

"I've never been so embarrassed." And she had done this to protect Quin and his secret activities.

William held her shoulders lightly with his soiled hands. "Let me take you home."

"**W**hat news of my ship?" Quin questioned his uncle. He had arranged to meet Edward briefly after the concert.

"*The Forbidden Lady* was returning when *The Sentinel* confiscated half our goods," Edward said. "That damned customs schooner has gone too far."

Quin ground his teeth. While he was occupied spying and entertaining his obnoxious brother, his business was suffering. "What excuse do the British have for doing this? We've done nothing illegal."

"They don't bother with excuses. They do whatever the hell they like. Last week, they came ashore and cut down half of Pitman's orchard, just for firewood."

"Aye, I heard about that. Have you lodged a complaint with the customs office to get our goods back?"

Edward nodded. "Aye, for all the good it will do. We cannot afford to take many more losses like this one."

Quin lowered his voice. "Johnson and I are cooking up a little surprise for *The Sentinel*. In the meantime, proceed with business as usual."

"What are you up to, Quin?"

"I don't have time to go into it now. Any other news?"

"No, other than my meeting with Mary Dover a few days ago. She asked me to convince you to spare her niece from a hanging."

Quin smiled. "I could never hurt her. Besides, it is all settled. Virginia has her hands full teaching a rascally boy named Josiah. I can assure you the female spy ring has come to an end."

"Thank God. I was worried about them."

Quin nodded, also relieved that Virginia would be behaving herself from now on. "I have to go. We'll talk again soon."

Quin strode to the front of Concert Hall and stopped short. He blinked, hoping his eyes were in error. She was not behaving herself.

Virginia stood with Captain Breakwell by a patch of muck in the road, the two of them splattered with mud, while two more filthy officers heaved themselves to their feet. Why the hell did that damned captain have his hands on her?

Quin clenched his fists, ready to plant one of them in Breakwell's face. "What a touching sight."

Virginia looked his way and paled. She jumped back from the captain, but her foot slipped in the mud. The captain grabbed her and pulled her against him.

Quin charged toward them. "Get your hands off of her!"

Breakwell glared back.

"Please!" Virginia turned to face Quin.

A scream came from behind them, piercing the air.

Mrs. Higgenbottom barreled out of Concert Hall, screeching at the top of her well-sized lungs and knocking people out of the way as she made a wide lane through them.

"I've been robbed! My ruby ring. It was on my finger." She held up a gloved hand. "It was there, and now, it is gone!"

Priscilla ran up to the muddy soldiers. "It must have happened when someone was kissing her hand. She's so distraught. Can you help us, Captain Breakwell?"

The captain released Virginia. "Aye, of course. Will you be all right, Virginia?"

"Yes, I will."

Breakwell and Priscilla rushed off.

"I thought he'd never leave." Quin nabbed Virginia by the elbow to lead her off. To his surprise, she jerked her arm away from him.

"I'm going home with my aunt and sister. Good day."

Quin stared at her as she marched away. She was mad at him? "We need to talk, Virginia."

She didn't answer.

He stalked after her. "We have an understanding."

"Oh?" She pivoted, putting her hands on her hips. "Which understanding was that, pray tell? The one last Saturday when you promised to see me again soon?"

"I meant that. I intended to see you tomorrow."

"Oh, and where have you been the past week? With your tailor?"

"Dammit, I was busy." He could hardly explain they had transported the submersible to the harbor and run practice tests. And why was Ginny acting like a shrew? "I sent you flowers."

"I don't want flowers. I want—" Her eyes brimmed with tears. "There's my aunt. I must go."

He pulled her into his arms. "What do you want?"

A tear rolled down her grimy cheek. "I wanted to see you."

"Ginny." He brushed away the tear. "I wanted to see you, too. I couldn't."

"Why not?"

"I cannot say."

She shoved him away. "You'll soil your pretty clothes."

He snatched her back. "I don't give a damn about the clothes."

"*Oh là là.*" The younger sister grinned. "'Tis rather warm for an October night."

"That's enough, Caroline," Mary Dover said. "We should give them a little privacy."

The two ladies wandered off a short distance, Caroline's remark drifting back. "Better not give them too much privacy."

Quin released her and spoke softly, aware now of the people around them, watching. "Is this your latest technique? Do the British spill their secrets when you wallow in the mud with them?"

"Don't you dare fuss at me, Quincy Stanton. You're the one with secrets, and this was all your fault."

He snorted.

"I mean it. I saw you go to the side of Concert Hall for one of your mysterious meetings and—"

"Wait." He held up a hand to interrupt her. "I told you to stop spying on me."

"You should be glad I did. I stopped those officers from coming around the side and seeing you."

"I don't need your help, Virginia."

She glowered at him. "I humiliated myself in public to keep you safe, and not only are you not grateful, you refuse tell me what you're doing. I don't even know why you have a hidden knife in your walking stick."

She wiped her eyes as the tears spilled over. "You still dress like a dandy and flirt with every woman in sight. You fuss if any man gives me attention, but there's always a pack of women all over you. I don't see why I should do anything you ask." She dashed away to her aunt and sister.

He watched them walking away. She had discovered the knife in his walking stick? Thank God she had not impaled her foot with it.

"I say, Quincy, shall we go to a tavern?" Clarence sauntered up. "You know, you really should start a decent men's club here."

"There are clubs. I belong to a few." Quin watched Virginia disappear around a corner.

"Yes, I know, the Freemasons and that captains' club you belong to."

"The Marine Society."

"Mmm, dreadfully boring." Clarence opened his silver snuffbox engraved with the Dearlington crest. "I meant a club for drinking and gambling. I say, having a bit of lady trouble, old boy?"

"'Tis none of your business."

Clarence helped himself to a sniff, then sneezed into a lacy handkerchief. "Perhaps she found out about that other woman of yours in Cambridge."

Quin gritted his teeth. He'd used the imaginary mistress

to excuse his absence most of the week. "Have you been talking about me again?"

"*Moi*? Why should I find it odd that you keep two women? 'Tis a family custom, old boy." Clarence gave him a wry smile. "Like father, like son, don't you know."

CHAPTER TEN

Monday, October 30, 1769

Josiah arrived in the morning, a basket of oranges in hand, and his freshly scrubbed face scrunched into a menacing glare.

He stalked into the parlor and dropped the basket on the table with a thud. "These be for you. The master said ye not be wanting no flowers. He be in a foul mood for days, growling at everybody."

"Oh, dear." Virginia kept her face serious, even though she felt like smiling.

Josiah raised his skinny arms in exasperation. "What did ye do to him, Miss Munro?"

"Nothing." She shoved the basket of oranges to the side and placed paper, quill, and inkwell in front of the boy.

Josiah collapsed in his chair. "That's what he said. I asked him what ye'd done. He said nuthin'." He pulled a letter out of his pocket. "This here be for you."

"Oh." Her heartbeat quickened as she turned the note

from Quin over in her hands. "While I read this, why don't you try writing a letter? 'Twould be good practice for you."

"I ain't got nobody to write to."

Breaking the seal on the letter, she strolled over to the window for more light. "You can write to me."

"Well, ain't that a blockheaded thing to do? Ye're right here in the room. I could just talk to you."

"Sometimes, you can say things in a letter that you would hesitate to say in person. Try it."

"Oh, all right." Josiah proceeded to write, sticking out his tongue to the side of his mouth as he concentrated.

She quickly read Quin's letter.

> *Dear Ginny,*
>
> *My deepest apologies. I assure you that my reluctance to confide in you is not grounded in a lack of trust, but rather in my fear for your safety. I look forward to the day when I can share my thoughts with you. As for now, I ask for your patience.*
>
> *Q*

She folded the note carefully, savoring the moment. He *must* care for her if he feared for her. She wandered over to the basket of oranges and held one up to her nose. The cool, pebbly peel smelled sweet and tangy. He must have paid dearly for these.

Josiah was still laboring away when she sat across from him to write a letter to Quin. She started twice, changed her mind, and tore the papers in two. Her final letter was impersonal and to the point. She stated that Josiah's lessons were progressing well, but he needed a series of immediate, small rewards and an interesting book to read.

"Here." Josiah shoved his finished letter across the table. "Can I have a piece of pie now?"

"No pie today, but I can give you a piece of Queen's Cake."

The boy chewed his lip, frowning. "Did ye make it yerself, Miss Munro?"

"I . . . helped." Her cheeks felt warm as she rose to her feet and left the room. Her first attempts at baking had not been entirely successful. She returned with a piece of cake and settled on the settee to read Josiah's letter while he ate.

> Dear Miss Munro,
>
> Ye look real purty today. Me Master thinks yer purty. I think ye should be nice to him cuz he likes you so much. I want him to be happy cuz he is nice to me, not like that scurvy retch Samule. I hate Samule. He hits me when no one is looking. He eats like a Pig. He locked me up in the privy so I would be late and the Master be mad at me. He is mad cuz the Master likes me best. He gives me fancy clothes and takes me to fancy Parties and sends me to you for schooling. I like working for Mister Stanton. He is nice to me. Please be nice to him, Miss Munro.
>
> Josiah

"Who is this Samuel?" Virginia asked.

"He's Mrs. Millstead's son." Josiah shoveled in another big bite of cake and talked with his mouth full. "She's the cook. She likes Clarence, cuz he be an earl. She calls me master a bastard when he's not around."

"That's terrible. Mr. Stanton should dismiss her."

Josiah shrugged. "He hopes he won't be living there much longer. He don't like the big house and all the servants."

"And he doesn't like the fancy clothes?"

Josiah shook his head. "He likes to be captain of his own ship and sail the seas, killing pirates and sea monsters!"

"Indeed? Is that what he said?"

"Well, not exactly, but he does have his own ship, and he said I could sail with him." Josiah pulled out a crumpled sheet of newspaper from his pocket. "He asked me to buy this on the way home, but I bought it on the way here. I'd rather read this than that *Tommy Thumb's Little Story-Book*. That thing is for babies."

Virginia smiled and patted the space beside her on the settee. "An excellent idea. Is there anything interesting in the paper?"

"Aye." He snuggled up close to her. "There's a story here about the Boston Burglar. That's what they're calling the man what's stealing jewelry from the ladies."

"Do they have any idea who he is?"

"No, the bugger must be good."

Mrs. Higgenbottom's ruby ring had brought him a tidy sum. Satisfied, the man pocketed the money and stepped out of the dimly lit establishment into a narrow street close to the waterfront. These stupid Colonials never suspected him. By the time he returned to England, he would be a wealthy man.

Josiah returned the next day with news. The British customs schooner had seized a merchant's sloop. Josiah had delivered Quincy's letter of protest to the customs house before going to his lessons.

"Why did the British take the man's ship?" Virginia asked.

"They say he was smuggling." Josiah took his usual seat at the mahogany table. "Me master says they're greedy leeches plaguing the hard-working man."

"Indeed." She pondered this latest indication that Quincy was not the Loyalist he went to great expense to portray.

"Me master said he'll fix them good."

"What do you mean?" She sat across from the boy.

He squirmed in his chair, chewing his lip. "I dunno. He didn't tell me."

"You know some of the things he does because you help him. I saw you with him in the gardens behind the Oldhams' house. He had a strange object in his hand that glowed in the dark."

Josiah scowled at the table. "I ain't supposed to tell nobody, not even you."

She tapped her fingers on the table. "Did Mr. Stanton say that?"

"Aye." The boy peered up at her. "Ye ain't mad at me?"

"No. Let's start with ciphering. I wrote some problems for you." She passed him a sheet of paper. He hunched over the problems, sticking his tongue out the side of his mouth.

Rising to her feet, Virginia picked up the cloth she was using to dust the furniture and knickknacks in the parlor. Quin trusted Josiah, a nine-year-old, but not her. She wiped the mantelpiece and the Oriental vase centered in front of the gilded mirror. The wilted flowers from Quincy needed to be thrown out.

He warned Josiah not to tell her anything. Over the past week, she had given a great deal of thought to Quincy's mysterious behavior. If he so easily suspected her of spying, then he could be engaged in the same activity. It would explain his secretive behavior and animosity toward the redcoats. It could also explain his possession of a walking stick with a hidden blade and an object that glowed in the dark. Yes, the more she thought about it, the more convinced she became.

Quincy Stanton must be a spy.

A knock at the front door interrupted her thoughts. A youth at the door handed her a package.

"What is this?" she asked.

"I work at the bookseller's shop on Hanover Street," the boy explained. "Mr. Stanton ordered these yesterday. Said to deliver them here. Good day, miss." He scampered down the steps and around the corner.

Virginia reminded the curious Josiah to complete his work as she opened the package on the round table. She smiled at Quin's choices: Swift's *Gulliver's Travels* and Defoe's *Robinson Crusoe*. Josiah would not have to endure a stuffy discourse on man's role in the universe or the origin of mathematics. The last book was a surprise. She opened it up to find a note, written by Quin.

> *This one is for you, dear Ginny. Enjoy.*
>
> *Q*

Quin had given her a book titled *Love in Excess* by a woman author, Eliza Haywood. Virginia grinned. This must be the sort of book the reverend back home preached against—the sort of book that destroyed a God-fearing woman, corrupted her moral standards, making her prey to wicked passions, and causing her to neglect her housekeeping chores. After the preacher's ferocious sermon denouncing the evil books penned by women scribblers, the women of the community had searched desperately for a copy, but none were to be found.

Now, she had one.

She couldn't wait to read it.

"Me master made ye happy, Miss Munro?" Josiah peered up at her with wide blue eyes.

"Yes, he did, and I believe you'll like your books, too."

"Can I start one now? I finished me ciphering."

"Good. Let's sit on the settee together, and I'll help you."

Long after Josiah had left, she remained in the parlor, reading the book Quin had given her. She thought ruefully that the reverend might have a point. She had no interest in doing any chores today. With a shrug, she smiled and continued reading.

Sometime in the afternoon, Aunt Mary burst into the parlor with a wide grin and flushed cheeks. "I have wonderful news!"

"What is it?"

"I've just returned from seeing my manager of Dover Mercantile. Our latest venture with Stanton Shipping was very successful. Edward Stanton, himself, dropped by with the good news. He has deposited the note in my bank."

"That's wonderful! I'm so proud of you."

Mary shrugged. "My manager does all the work. I only stop by every week to take a peek at the books. I think we should celebrate. How about new gowns for each of us?"

Virginia winced. "'Tis far too expensive. You've spent enough on us."

"I insist. Besides, that poor green gown of yours has taken a beating lately. We'll find Caroline and be on our way."

Friday, November 3, 1769

After completing his schoolwork, Josiah settled on the settee next to Virginia to read another chapter from *Robinson Crusoe*. She smiled as she heard his young voice stumble over a word. Although he would never admit it, Josiah was very eager to please. His reading had improved to the point that he rarely needed her help.

She reached down to a basket on the floor to retrieve her knitting. Since the boy walked to her house Monday through Friday, she intended to keep him warm in the increasingly cold temperatures with a new hat and mittens. The blue yarn she had selected reminded her of his eyes.

She gave him a glance when he stopped reading.

His brow puckered with a frown. "I thought ye wanted to listen to me read."

"I am listening." She continued to knit.

"No, ye're not. Ye're using those clickety sticks."

"I'm knitting *and* listening, Josiah. I've been knitting since I was four years old. I could do it in my sleep. Go on."

His frown deepened, but he turned back to his book. He started reading in sporadic bursts, occasionally glaring at her hands.

She lowered her handwork to her lap. "I'm sorry if it disturbs you. I was not raised to be idle."

"It don't bother me none." He started reading again. After a few sentences he stopped, his eyes focused on the book in his lap.

She had leaned closer to see if he was stuck on a difficult word, when a large tear fell onto the page. He slammed the book shut and dropped it on the floor.

She stuffed her knitting in the basket. "Josiah, what's wrong?"

Wiping his face, he turned away from her. "Nuthin'. Ain't nuthin'."

She touched his shoulder. "It is something. Can you not tell me?"

He swung around and dove into her lap, wrapping his skinny arms around her waist. His tears spilled out, sobs shaking his bony shoulders, his cries filled with raw pain.

She held on to him. "Josiah? Dear boy, what is troubling you?"

His words came out, smothered and broken against her skirt. "Me mum . . . I miss me mum . . . I wish I had me mother back."

"Oh, dear Lord, of course you do." It occurred to her now that she had never heard him speak of his mother before. "'Tis only natural to grieve for her, lad. You must miss her sorely."

"She told me not to cry for her. She said I had to be brave. I tried . . . I truly tried."

"Oh, Josiah." Virginia brushed back his hair that had tumbled loose from its tie. "You are brave. I've never known a boy as fierce as you."

"Really?" Turning his tear-streaked face toward her, he wiped his cheeks. "Ye'll not tell me master I cried like a baby?"

"A few tears are nothing to be ashamed of."

He sniffed. "Me mum used to knit at night by the fire. I always fell to sleep with that sound in me ears."

"I see."

"After me father left, she did laundry and sewing and knitting for people, so we would have money. But 'twas not enough. I was always hungry. So, I took to stealing. Me mum didn't like it none."

"I'm sure she was worried about your safety."

"She thought I would have a better life here. She was always giving me part of her food on the ship, cuz I'm always so bloody hungry, but she . . . she took sick and. . . ." Covering his face with his hands, he sobbed again. "I shouldn't have taken her food."

Blinking back tears, Virginia lifted him and hugged him tight. "'Tis not your fault, Josiah. They never give enough food." She rocked him like a baby 'til his shoulders stopped trembling and his whimpers faded away.

His voice sounded old and weary. "I wish me master were me father."

"Quincy?"

"Aye, he would never leave us like me real father. I told him me father didn't want me and he said he understood." Josiah yawned and closed his red, swollen eyes. "His father don't want him neither."

"His father rejected him?" Virginia glanced down at the boy in her arms. His body sagged against her, limp and worn out.

Carefully she settled him on the ochre-yellow settee, but he never woke, so exhausted he was. She brushed back his soft brown hair and let him sleep.

Quincy read the latest news from his uncle.

> Dear Quin,
>   Clarence has hired a solicitor. They requested a court date in order to present their case. Our solicitor will arrange to have this proceeding postponed 'til we can come up with a solution.
>   Edward

Quin sighed and held the letter to a candle flame. So, Clarence had finally made his first move. It probably meant that the court in England had ruled on the case there. And if Clarence was proceeding, the ruling must have been favorable to him and his father. *Damn*. The court here would simply follow suit.

No wonder Clarence had been in such a jolly mood lately. It didn't bother him at all to steal from his own brother.

Quin dropped the blackening letter onto a silver tray and watched it smolder to a pile of ashes. Clarence wasn't concerned about hurting a brother. In fact, he probably felt justified in saving the family business from a bastard.

Scraping back his chair from the drop-leaf desk, Quin

stood, then ambled to the walnut sideboard to fill a glass with Madeira. He paced back and forth, sipping the sweet wine, considering yet another problem. When he had arrived home, Mrs. Millstead had complained in her usual whining voice that her son Samuel had done his and Josiah's chores for Josiah had never returned from his schooling.

Quin knew he should rush to Virginia's house to see what had happened, but he hesitated. The taste of her lips, the feel of her body against him, the sensations tormented him every night. He couldn't deal with this infatuation right now. Besides, she was still angry with him. Just as well. She deserved better than a bastard. A bastard who might soon be penniless.

A sound at the door drew his attention. Josiah peeked in, blue eyes wide with guilt.

A wave of relief swept over him. The boy had not run away. With effort, he kept his expression stern. "Where have you been, Josiah? You were due back hours ago."

Josiah glanced to the side as a voice whispered to him. He whispered back to the person standing outside Quin's study.

Quin set his glass down and advanced toward the door. "Who are you hiding back there?"

"Whom." A feminine voice corrected him.

Josiah grinned.

"Virginia?" Quin opened the door wide.

There she was—a woolen cape of dark green wrapped about her. The hood had fallen back, and strands of auburn hair curled around her face. The brisk weather outdoors had left her cheeks bright pink. She was dressed in plain wool, and he had never seen her so lovely.

"Virginia, come in."

"I shouldn't stay. I walked Josiah home so I could explain his tardiness."

Quin glanced down at the boy. "Why are you late?"

Josiah scratched his head and shifted from one foot to another. "I . . . I fell asleep."

"Asleep? When you had chores to do?"

"Please allow me to explain," Virginia said.

Quin frowned. "Very well. Josiah, go have your supper."

"Yes, Mr. Stanton." Josiah turned away, then tugged on Virginia's cape. "Ye won't tell him I . . . ye know."

She patted his shoulder. "Everything will be fine."

Josiah scampered off to the kitchen.

When Quin looked at Virginia she was studying him with her mermaid eyes. He clenched his fists to keep from pulling her into his arms.

She cleared her throat. "I allowed Josiah to sleep this afternoon because he was exhausted."

"Exhausted? I haven't overworked him."

"No, he was . . . emotionally drained. He experienced . . . an episode."

"What are you saying?"

She sighed. "He doesn't want you to know, but he collapsed into tears, grieving for his mother."

"Oh, I see." Quin leaned against the doorjamb. A vague memory of a lullaby and soft arms flickered in his mind. He couldn't remember what his mother had looked like, but he remembered the pain of losing her. "I wondered when he would finally break."

"Break? You were expecting this?"

"Aye. I never saw Josiah grieve for her. 'Twas not natural."

Virginia's eyes glistened with tears. "His mother told him not to cry. He was still trying to mind her."

"Damn." Quin wandered into his study and downed the last of the Madeira from his glass. "I didn't mean to involve you to this extent. I'm sorry you were put through this." Poor Ginny. He had only meant to keep her occupied with Josiah so she would give up spying. He shouldn't have used the boy so shamelessly to further his own plans.

"'Twas natural he would turn to me. He would be mortified to cry in front of you, Quin. He thinks very highly of you."

Quin set his glass down on the sideboard, planning to refill it. "Not highly enough, obviously."

"I disagree. He wishes you were his father."

Quin spun around, stunned. How had that happened? He spent most of his time fussing at the boy.

Virginia smiled as if amused. "I should be going now before it grows dark. Good evening."

"Wait." He grabbed his coat from the back of a chair and stuffed his arms into the sleeves. "I'll walk you back."

"'Tis not necessary."

He offered his arm. "I want to be with you, Ginny."

Chapter Eleven

"Lob, buy lob!" The lobsterman pushed his red-and-blue wheelbarrow down Union Street, selling his wares.

Virginia smiled at Quin as they strolled arm in arm. "Thank you for the book. I enjoyed it very much."

"You're welcome."

She breathed in the crisply cool air, surveyed the pink-and-gold clouds painted by the setting sun, and felt a surge of pure happiness. She stole another sidelong glance at her escort.

Quin was not dressed in his usual finery. His plain but well-cut blue woolen coat and breeches emphasized his tall, muscular frame. Dark whiskers shaded his jaw. She wondered if it would feel prickly against her fingertips. His short hair, without a wig, reminded her of the time he had kissed her in the orchard. She had slipped her arms around his neck and burrowed her fingers into his hair.

"Would you like a flip?"

She jolted into the present. "A what?"

"'Tis a popular drink—a beer mixed with a little sugar,

molasses, dried pumpkin, and rum. Before they serve it, they plunge a hot chunk of iron in it."

She grimaced. "Why? Is it not bad enough as it is?"

"It gives it a burned and bitter taste." After a glance at her expression, he chuckled. "All right. Perhaps you would like a hot chocolate."

"Oh, I do like chocolate. My father treated us to one before he left. I believe it was this place on the right."

"Then you shall have another." Quin led her into the coffeehouse and to a table in a quiet corner. He sat across from her as a young waitress approached.

"Lord, ain't you two a handsome pair." The waitress grinned at them.

Quin glanced at her. "Good evening."

"Me name's Sukey. What can I fetch for you?"

"A coffee for me and—"

"And for yer wife?"

He hesitated as his gaze flitted to Virginia. He cleared his throat and shifted in the chair.

Virginia came to his rescue. "We're not married."

"Oh, I see how it is." Sukey nodded her head knowingly. With a hand on the table, she bent over Virginia. "Fallen for a married man, have ye? Poor lass, there's nuthin' but heartache in store for the likes of you."

"He's not married. I mean"—Virginia glanced at Quin—"I don't believe he is."

His dimpled smile confirmed her belief.

"What?" Planting her fists on her hips, Sukey pivoted her short, square frame toward her male customer. "A handsome man like you, not married? What are ye waiting for?"

"A coffee. And a hot chocolate for my . . . friend."

"Hmm, well, suit yerself, but I'm telling you, if ye don't snatch her up quick, someone else will." Sukey wheeled around in a huff and marched off to the kitchens.

Quin frowned at Sukey's departing figure.

An awkward silence ensued while Virginia scoured her mind for a pleasant topic. "Oh, I have good news. Aunt Mary made a great deal of money on her last venture. We have all ordered new gowns. Mine is a golden color. Aunt Mary assures me the color suits me, but I . . ." She drifted off as she noticed the incredulous look on his face. "Is something amiss?"

"What ship did she have her merchandise on?"

"One of your uncle's ships, I believe. *The Forbidden Lady?*"

"That's my ship."

"Oh, I didn't realize—"

"British customs seized half the goods when she came in. We took a loss."

Virginia's mouth dropped open. "I don't understand. Edward Stanton told my aunt the good news himself. He gave her the money from the profits."

Quin shook his head. "There were no profits. He must have given her his own money."

"But why?" Virginia observed Quin's eyes fill with heat and desire, similar to the way Edward Stanton viewed her aunt. "Oh, dear." She studied her clasped hands on the table.

Quin reached over and took her hands in his. "Edward has been in love with your aunt for years."

"We cannot possibly keep the money."

"It must be what my uncle wants. I would do the same." He squeezed her hands gently.

She looked at him and became lost in his gray eyes that darkened to twilight. She felt the pressure of his fingers against her own, his steady pulse against her skin. Slowly, her pulse matched the rhythm of his as if their life's blood sought to become one. The world around her grew dim, and she wanted it to last forever.

She started when a coffee and hot chocolate were banged down on the table between their outstretched arms.

"Just friends, are you? Looking at each other like a pair of cats eyeing the cream. Ye're not fooling me none." Sukey gave them each a saucy look. "We've got rooms upstairs we rent out for the likes of you."

Virginia grasped her mug, her cheeks as hot as the mug of chocolate.

Quin cleared his throat. "That will not be necessary."

"In a hurry, are you? I could talk to me boss, see if I can get ye in for fifteen minutes—"

"That's enough!" Quin glared at the waitress. "Leave us be."

"Humph!" Sukey spun around and marched off, mumbling to herself. "Try to help people and see what it gets you."

"Damn." Quin reached for his mug. "I thought this was a normal coffeehouse."

Virginia sipped her drink. It slid down, hot, rich, and comforting to her frayed nerves. "The chocolate is good."

"I apologize for her behavior, Ginny."

"At least you're apologizing for someone else this time."

His dimples deepened as he smiled. "And not myself?"

She smiled and enjoyed another sip of chocolate. "I'm sorry about your ship."

"I was at the customs house today, trying to get our goods back. Still, it could be worse. They confiscated Derby's sloop, and now they're taking him to the admiralty court."

"What will happen there?"

"They'll probably sell the ship and her cargo. The governor will get a third of the proceeds, the customs official another third, and our mother country the last third. 'Tis not in their interest to be fair about it."

Virginia grimaced. "It sounds like robbery to me."

"Aye, it is, but unlike the Boston Burglar, 'tis legal." He took a long drink of coffee. "The mother country sees us as slaves, laboring for the sole purpose of feeding her greed."

"You don't sound like a Tory, Quin." She hoped he would confide in her just a little.

"Neither do you."

"I'm not. What are you?"

He finished his coffee, giving himself time to consider a response. "I am what you see."

She frowned at her almost empty mug. What a ridiculous answer. Then again, he was not dressed as a fop today. Perhaps he was telling her something.

His mouth quirked with a playful smile. "Of course, if you would like to seduce me to the Colonial cause, I would be a willing victim. Shall I call Sukey over?"

"No, I'm a patriot, not a martyr."

Chuckling, he tossed a few coins on the table. "Shall we go?"

He escorted her to the south side of Boston in the fading twilight.

As they turned onto Milk Street, she surveyed the stars

as they became visible in the darkening sky. "Do you know the stars well?"

"Aye. You can see them better at sea. And if the sea is calm, it can reflect their light so that you feel completely surrounded by them."

"That sounds beautiful."

"Aye, it is, though you don't make good time. Do you see the bright one there?" He pointed over her shoulder. "That's the North Star."

"Oh, like the name of the ship where we met."

"Aye, it has always guided me true." He smiled at her. "It led me to you."

Blushing, she mounted the steps to the front door. "Would you like to join us for supper?"

He appeared surprised by the offer. "I would enjoy that, but I've already made arrangements to eat with Clarence."

She wondered why he spent so much time with the man who had announced his illegitimacy to all of Boston. "Do you get along well with your brother?"

"'Tis better to keep the enemy under close watch."

"You call your brother an enemy? Is that because of the rumor he spread about you?"

"'Tis no rumor. I am a bastard."

She winced at his sharp tone.

Frowning, he studied his shoes. "I should go. Thank you for your help with Josiah."

"You're welcome." *No wonder he refuses to confide in me.* Trust had to be difficult for a man when he was rejected by his father and his brother was his enemy. "Will you be at the Ashfords' ball next week?"

"Aye. 'Tis a ball for Tories."

"Or those of us pretending to be Tories."

He placed a foot on the bottom step, leaned forward, and took her hand. "No more spying, Ginny, please."

"I'll try to restrain myself."

"I'll hold you to that." He pressed his mouth to her hand and strode away.

She closed the front door and rested against it, deep in thought. Quincy Stanton had been a puzzle from the day he had tried to purchase her, but she felt she was beginning to understand him. He was a mixture of pride and doubt, of strength and pain. He needed love, but was afraid to trust in it. He was a challenge, but definitely a worthy one. And she was falling in love with him.

Monday, November 6, 1769

"I feel it would be best for me to quarter here in your home," Captain Breakwell announced.

Virginia gulped. She had been surprised when the captain arrived uninvited at her door close to midnight, but this latest statement astounded her. "I cannot believe we're in that much danger."

"Did you go out this evening?"

"No, Aunt Mary said we should stay inside because of the celebration."

"Aye, Pope's Day, they call it." William sat across from her on the settee. "I have been there, and I can tell you 'tis nothing more than two unruly mobs trying to kill each other."

"Surely, 'tis not that bad—"

"Your aunt can tell you I'm not exaggerating. A few years ago, the mobs killed a young boy. Ran him down with a cart or some such nonsense. These Colonials are barbaric! You should not live here amongst these savages."

As shocked as she was by the death of the boy, Virginia felt increasingly vexed by the captain's opinion of her countrymen. "I would not call them savages, William."

"Do you know what they did? First, the groups from the north and south sides of town swarmed each other, trying to get each other's effigy of the Pope. Then, they dragged the effigies to the gallows at the Neck to burn them."

She shrugged. "'Tis a simple demonstration against Catholicism."

"There were thousands of them, as wild as animals. At least they were fighting each other, but if they gang up against us—I'm telling you, Virginia, if they turn against the mother country, this will not be a fit place for a dog to live."

She rose to her feet. "This is a fine country, and there are many well-educated, intelligent Colonials."

"I doubt their intelligence when they purposely incite these mobs to violence."

"They have legitimate complaints. No one should have to live under tyranny."

William rose to his feet. "Tyranny? Surely it is better to live safely under one tyrant who is three thousand miles away than to live under the threat of three thousand tyrants here. These people cannot possibly manage to rule themselves."

"I will take my chances here." She took a deep breath and sat down. "I am sorry, William. We simply do not agree."

"I had not realized you had such feelings for this country." He sighed and wandered about the room. "I can hardly blame you. 'Tis the only country you know." He stopped to stare out the window. "My father plans to marry me off to an heiress back in England. I had hoped to thwart his plans."

"You do not wish to marry the heiress?"

"No. We're not suited, but my father thinks we need the money."

"I certainly don't have much in the way of a dowry, but there are other young ladies in Boston who do."

He shrugged, still gazing out the window. "I have other plans for acquiring the money I need. Still, I would like to return already married so my father cannot force me to his will."

"I have no doubt you can be successful. I've been told you are a good catch."

He peered back at her. "But you do not believe it?"

"I do, truly. 'Tis merely that I am . . ."

"In love with someone else?"

She studied her hands in her lap as heat invaded her cheeks. Was she that obvious? No, she couldn't be. Quin didn't seem to know. But would he recognize love if it grabbed him by the nose and shook him?

"I hope he knows how fortunate he is." With a curt nod of his head, Captain Breakwell paced toward the front door. "Good evening, Miss Munro."

Saturday, November 11, 1769

"I'm so envious of you, Ginny." Caroline sighed dramatically as they rode in a carriage. "You have two suitors vying for your hand. Perhaps, if you're lucky, they'll fight a duel for you."

Virginia winced. "I certainly hope not. Besides, I wouldn't say I have two suitors."

"Of course you do. Now if I were you, I'd take Quincy Stanton. He's absolutely perfect."

Virginia couldn't help but wonder by what criteria her sister judged perfection. "Why do you think so?"

"He sends presents. The oranges were nice and the book was wonderful. And the chocolate he sent us this week—well, any man who gives you books and chocolate must be perfect."

Aunt Mary laughed. "I believe you are correct."

Virginia's heart beat faster as they approached the Ashford home. Perfect or not, Quincy Stanton would be there. This was the house where she had followed him upstairs and he had slipped his thumb into her neckline. Something even more exciting could happen tonight.

She smoothed out her skirts, hoping the ride in the rented carriage would not cause wrinkles in her new gown. A white-and-gold brocade panel across the front of the bodice narrowed as it reached her waist. Her full overskirt of gold silk was slit up the front to reveal an underskirt of matching brocade. As much as she loved this golden gown, she felt a twinge of guilt about it. She had not told her aunt that their new clothing had been purchased out of Edward Stanton's own pocket.

"Now, about your other suitor," Caroline continued. "I

know Captain Breakwell would ask for your hand if you gave him the slightest encouragement. Of course, I don't really want you to marry him, because he would take you to England and 'tis too far away. But it would be exciting to hear him propose."

Virginia narrowed her eyes on her younger sister. "Exciting for you, no doubt. You were listening at the door again, weren't you?"

Caroline blushed. "Well, I wouldn't need to if anything exciting ever happened to me. 'Tis not fair. You have two men who want you. Even Aunt Mary has a suitor."

"I do?" Mary chuckled. "Now that's news to me."

"You would have to be blind not to see it, Aunt Mary. Edward Stanton looks at you like you're a goddess. And all that money he gave you—ow!" Caroline glared at her sister. "You kicked me!"

Virginia scowled back. She had told her sister to refuse any more gifts from their aunt since the money came directly from Edward Stanton. She had also warned Caroline not to tell Aunt Mary the truth.

"Edward paid me the money earned by Dover Mercantile on the last voyage," Aunt Mary explained.

"Oh, absolutely, of course, you're right." Caroline nodded her head, red curls bouncing. "That's exactly what happened. Right, Ginny?"

Virginia noted her aunt's suspicious expression.

"Is there something I should know?" Mary asked.

Simultaneously, Virginia answered "no" as her sister answered "yes."

Mary frowned at her nieces. "I want the truth."

The carriage slowed to a stop in front of the Ashford home.

Virginia caught her breath as the dance ended.

Quincy escorted her to a chair. "Shall I fetch you some punch?"

"Yes, thank you." She admired his retreating figure, dressed in elegant gray silk.

"Ginny!" Caroline startled her, then perched on the chair beside her. "Everyone is talking about you and Quincy Stanton. They say he's besotted, that you've blinded him to the charms of other women."

Virginia smiled, recalling the moment when Quin had arrived at the ball with Josiah. He had exchanged words with the hostess while tossing his tricorne and walking stick to the young boy. When he spotted her seated by Aunt Mary, he headed directly for her. His usual flock of peahens swooped down upon him, surrounding him. He smiled, nodded his head, and slipped right by them, continuing on to Virginia. Then he asked her to dance three times in a row.

From what Caroline reported, Boston society had received his message. Everyone knew Quincy Stanton had chosen her.

Caroline leaned close to whisper. "You're in love with him, aren't you? You should see yourself, Ginny. Your skin is rosy and glowing, and with that golden gown of yours, I vow you're as radiant as the sun. And in gray, he gleams like the moon. You're perfect for each other."

Virginia blinked and stared at Caroline. So often, her exasperating sister blurted out things she shouldn't say, but she always spoke from the heart. "I think that's the loveliest thing you've ever said to me."

" 'Tis the truth. I'm so happy for you. You don't know how much I've prayed that my foolish words back home would not ruin your chance for happiness."

Virginia squeezed her sister's hand. Caroline, in her youthfulness, seemed to think all was simple and rosy, but the future was far from settled. She watched Quin approaching with two glasses of rum punch. He had not declared any intention of marrying her, nor had he claimed any special affection for her. True, he'd kissed her under the apple tree very sweetly at first, then with undeniable passion, but he had probably kissed many women before. He still kept his secrets from her, refusing to discuss himself.

Quincy handed her a glass and turned to her sister. "Would you care for some punch?"

"Not for me, but I'll take it to Aunt Mary, if you don't mind." Caroline accepted the glass and strolled across the room to where Aunt Mary sat in a daze.

Quin took the seat vacated by Caroline. "Is your aunt all right?"

"I fear she's suffering from shock." Virginia sipped her punch. "She now knows her recent earnings were a gift from your uncle."

"She didn't take it well?"

"No. She insists she must pay him back, but she hasn't the funds now. I wish there was something I could do."

Quin shrugged his broad shoulders. "Edward wouldn't take her money. He's in love with her, wants to marry her."

Virginia drank more punch. How easily Quin spoke of

other people wanting love and marriage. Would he be able to admit it so freely of himself? She glanced up to see his younger brother, dressed in claret velvet, approaching them.

"I say, old boy, are you going to introduce me to this lovely lady or keep her all to yourself?"

Quin rose to his feet. "Virginia Munro, my brother, Clarence."

"Charmed." Clarence raised her hand to his lips. "The other men in the room are too cowardly to ask you to dance, fearing the wrath of Quincy, but I shall do so." He cast an amused glance at his brother. "What say you, old boy, can I dance with the most beautiful woman in the room without fearing your glove slapping me in the face?"

Quincy's smile did not reach his eyes. "Of course you may dance, but one wrong move and 'twill not be my glove but my fist you will feel."

Clarence chuckled. "Come, my dear. Let us show my oafish brother how the steps look when properly executed."

She passed her half-empty glass of punch to Quin and allowed Clarence to lead her to the floor for the next dance. Odd, she thought, that Quin would agree to this when he didn't seem to trust his brother. She peered over her shoulder and spotted Quin slipping out the parlor door. *Of course! Blast the man.* He wanted her occupied while he sneaked about on his secret errands.

The music started to "Balance a Straw." She curtsied to Clarence. The entire time the man made a leg to her, his eyes inspected her bosom. Normally, such ogling would have embarrassed her, but she could only feel vexation with Quin. He had purposely left her with his leering brother so he could wander about the house doing his mysterious deeds.

She moved through the steps, wondering where he could be. The last time they had been in this house, he had gone across the hall to the study and then upstairs. It occurred to her that the open window in the study had been where Josiah had exited.

Her anger doubled. It was bad enough for Quin to risk his own neck, but to involve an innocent young boy? The courts would suffer no qualms at sentencing a boy to hang. How could Quincy use Josiah like this? She would certainly let him know how she felt. If she could find him.

When the dance ended, she excused herself, presumably to find the necessary room. She crossed the hall into the study and closed the door behind her. A quick survey of the dimly lit room yielded nothing. Quin must have gone upstairs. She listened at the door, planning a quick exit and dash up the stairs. The sound of footsteps reached her ears as someone else crept up the stairs.

She hesitated, wondering what to do. The light of the moon shone through the windows, illuminating the desk and the stack of papers on top. Papers, so easily within her reach. She had agreed to stop spying, but what harm could come from a quick peek? No one would know.

She scurried over to the desk and rummaged through the papers. Most were simple letters or bills, but one caught her eye. Written by the chief customs official, it was addressed to Colonel Farley, who quartered in the Ashford home. It supplied the names of merchants and ship owners, all described as major Colonial sympathizers, along with a list of their ships which the customs official clearly stated he planned to seize.

Virginia skimmed down the list and found Edward Stanton's name. Quincy needed to see this. For that matter, all of Boston needed to see this. The British were singling out the more rebellious of the Colonials for financial ruin. She folded up the paper and jammed it down the bodice of her gown.

She peeked out the door. The coast was clear. She sauntered into the parlor, displaying a calm demeanor to mask the pounding excitement that coursed through her veins. Quincy was not there. She sat down beside her aunt.

"Where have you been?" Mary whispered. "You shouldn't wander off with Quincy Stanton. 'Tis not proper to be alone with him."

"I wasn't with him. Aunt Mary, I have discovered the most incredible information. I have it tucked inside my gown."

"Oh, my! This is wonderful."

"You must show it to Edward Stanton tomorrow."

"Oh, no! This is dreadful. I canna see the man."

"Aunt Mary, you must. It involves him."

Her face paled. "Is he in danger?"

"Not physically, but it is bad."

Mary pressed her hand against her chest. "Puir Edward."

Virginia realized her aunt's speech had reverted to a Scottish brogue. "You do care for him, don't you?"

Mary closed her eyes, not answering.

Scanning the room, Virginia spotted Quincy slipping into the parlor. He ambled to the refreshment table. Another dance began, this one to "Money in Both Pockets." She won-

dered what Quin had hidden in *his* pockets. Clarence sauntered into the parlor, breaking into the line at the refreshment
table to stand beside his brother. Caroline was dancing with
a young lieutenant; Captain Breakwell partnered Priscilla
Higgenbottom.

The elderly Mrs. Ashford burst into the parlor with a
high-pitched screech. The music ground to a stop as she continued to scream. "Thieves! Robbers! My emerald ring was
missing from my hand. I went to see if it was in my bedchamber and discovered my emerald necklace was gone!"

Captain Breakwell and the lieutenant who had partnered
Caroline darted out the room and up the stairs to search for
the burglar. Women squealed and checked their jewels. Men
examined their pockets and rings.

Over the noise, Clarence Stanton's voice boomed out.
"Calm yourselves! We can unmask this hideous Boston Burglar tonight."

A hush fell over the room as the crowd listened to Clarence.

"I suggest we all submit ourselves to a search. Colonel
Farley can search the men. Mrs. Ashford and Mrs. Higgenbottom can search the women in another room."

Mrs. Ashford gasped. "You believe a woman could be the
burglar?"

Clarence smiled. "My dear Mrs. Ashford, I have known
women to be capable of most anything."

Mrs. Higgenbottom planted her hands on her wide hips.
"His lordship is correct. We will catch the fiend tonight. If all
the women will step into the study, we will commence with
the search." She barreled out of the room, like a cannon rolling to the front line.

"Oh, God." Virginia pressed a trembling hand against the bodice of her gown. "Oh, no."

"Ginny," Aunt Mary whispered. "Is that paper on you?"

"Yes." Virginia gripped her aunt's hand. She gasped for air, finding it difficult to breathe. If they found the paper on her, they would know she was a spy. "What shall I do?"

Tears filled Mary's eyes. "Give it to me."

Ginny released her aunt's hand, jumping back in her seat. "No!"

Suddenly, Quincy Stanton appeared before her, his eyes flashing like a storm cloud, his granite jaw clenched. "We're getting out of here now."

He hauled her to her feet and dragged her past the others and out the front door. With a viselike grip on her arm, he towed her along to his carriage.

Virginia had never seen him so angry. As stunned and frightened as she was, she went along with him for the consequences of staying behind seemed worse.

He yanked open the carriage door and tossed her inside like a sack of cornmeal. She sprawled on the backseat with a flurry of skirts as a perverse thought sneaked into her shocked and confused mind. Was he fleeing the scene not to protect her, but himself? If they searched him, would they find the jewels? It would explain his secretive behavior. And he was always present when the thefts occurred.

Quincy Stanton could be the Boston Burglar.

CHAPTER TWELVE

"We're getting out of here now." Quin escorted Virginia out the door.

One look at the panic-stricken terror on her face and he had known she was in trouble. What could she have done? She had promised not to spy, and he knew she couldn't steal. Unless, the thought sizzled through him, she was stealing to help her indebted aunt. Anger boiled inside him, threatening to explode.

He helped her into the coach and yelled to the driver to return to his house with all haste. He leapt in and slammed the door behind him. Ginny's wide skirts covered most of the backseat as she struggled to sit up properly. He sat across from her, frowning with the realization he might have been a little too forceful. As the coach lurched forward, he braced himself by grabbing the edge of the open window frame.

The sudden forward movement of the carriage sent her careening backward again with a bewildered exclamation. Flailing her arms about, she reached for the looped silken cord that hung from the ceiling.

"*No!*" He lunged for her.

She toppled onto her back, pulling the cord as she fell.

The trap door swooshed open to release the iron bar.

"Umph." He landed on top of her just seconds before the heavy iron rod smacked the cushions of the front seat.

She slapped at his shoulders. "What are you doing? You knocked me down!"

"You nearly knocked me out." He seized her wrists. "Calm down, Ginny. You're safe, now."

"Safe? You jumped on me. You attacked me!"

"No, I . . ." He realized he was on top of her, his face only an inch from the rounded curves of the exposed portion of her breasts.

"Get off of me." With each frantic breath she took, her breasts rose toward him, tempting him.

He released her wrists. "Dear Lord."

She shoved at his shoulders. "Go back to your seat."

"I cannot." He grazed her soft, pliant skin with the tip of his nose. She was warm and smelled of lavender and sweet woman.

"Go back to your seat!"

He breathed deeply, reveling in her scent. "I cannot. The rod fell out."

"The *what?*"

"The rod. It fell out."

"Why do you have a rod?"

Grinning, he nuzzled his face against her breasts.

"Stop that." She pushed at his head. "Go back to your seat this instant."

"There's no room. The rod takes up the entire seat."

"I don't care how big your rod is. Get off of me!"

He buried his face in her breasts to stifle his laughter.

"Why are you snickering on me?" She shoved at his head. "Get your face off of me."

He lifted his face when he felt his wig coming off.

"Oh, blast!" She scowled at the wig in her hand and threw it behind her.

He raised himself onto his elbows. "Ginny, you threw my wig out the window."

"What?" She twisted around to look at the open windows of the carriage. "Oh, no! We should go back for it." She struggled to sit up.

"Forget about it." Chuckling, he leaned down and knocked heads with her as she was coming up.

"Ow!" She fell back on the cushions.

He winced. "Sorry. I didn't mean to run into you. Are you all right?"

"Yes. I'm sorry about your wig."

"Where did I hit you?"

"My chin."

He stroked his fingers along the line of her jaw. "Sweet Ginny. Can you open your mouth?"

"Yes, of course. I'm talking, aren't I?"

He closed in, sliding his hands behind her head. "Open your mouth."

"I said I was all right. What are you doing?"

He planted his mouth on hers. She made a startled noise and tensed beneath him.

He eased the pressure of his kiss, persuading her with gentler, nibbling kisses.

With a moan she responded. She wrapped her arms around him and scrunched her lips tightly against him. He pulled back, awed by her innocent eagerness.

"Quin?"

"Open for me." He pressed his lips against hers and felt them mold against his, soft and giving. She made a small noise of surprise when he slipped his tongue inside.

Her mouth tasted of rum punch; her tongue grew bolder as she adjusted to his exploration. He took his time, relishing her willingness. He moved down her neck, his lips on one side, his fingertips on the other. Her skin was velvet to touch and smelled of lavender soap.

He traced the delicate curve of her collarbone and proceeded to her breasts. She moaned, running her fingers into his hair. Her heart pounded beneath his mouth. He brushed his lips over her skin, the rise and fall of her breasts like the foamy white waves of the sea, the sea calling him home.

He slipped his fingers into the neckline of her dress, hoping to disclose more sweet flesh. His fingers brushed against something loose inside her bodice. It crackled against the pressure of his fingers.

Paper.

"What is this?" He pulled the folded paper from her bodice.

"What?" Her voice sounded drowsy.

He tossed the paper to the side and jammed his fingers back inside her bodice. "What else are you hiding?"

"Nothing." Now alert, she yanked his hand out of her dress.

"Do you have the jewels?" Sitting up, he ran his hand up her legs.

"What are you doing?" She kicked her legs at him and squirmed to a sitting position.

"I saw your face when they were planning to search for the missing jewelry. You were terrified."

She stared at him, stunned, then huffed with indignation. "You believe I'm a common thief? How . . . how could you?"

"I don't believe you would do it for yourself, but you are concerned about your aunt's financial situation, and you were present when the theft took place."

"I cannot believe this! You would kiss a woman you believe to be a criminal?"

He took a deep breath and shoved a hand through his hair. "You're right. I don't know how I . . . I panicked. I'm sorry."

"You should be." She crossed her arms across her chest. "I have never been so insulted. Are you aware the same logic works against you, Quincy Stanton? You sneak about people's houses. You refuse to explain your activities. You're always present when the thefts take place."

He blinked, dumbfounded. "You're saying I'm the Boston Burglar?"

She shrugged. "What am I to think when you won't confide in me?"

He clenched his teeth. Was her opinion of him that low? "If the same logic applies to me, then so does the same insult. You kissed me, you laid down on the cushions beneath me, thinking I'm a criminal."

"I couldn't think at all. Besides, you pushed me."

"Oh. So like a bastard I forced you?"

Her mouth fell open. She covered her mouth to stifle a groan.

The carriage stopped.

He glared out the window at his rented house. He had been so frantic, he had not thought clearly. He should take Ginny to her house. And then he would have to return to the Ashfords' for Josiah.

"Oh, no." He sat back. Josiah, the best pickpocket in all of London.

"What?" Ginny asked.

"We must go back immediately. I forgot Josiah." He leaned out the window and yelled to the coachman to return to the Ashfords'.

The carriage moved with a jolt.

"I believe you're a spy."

Astonished by her sudden accusation, he could only stare at her a moment. "Ginny, don't ask me—"

"I'm not asking, for I would not have you lie to me. But 'tis what I believe, and I think it is unconscionable of you to involve Josiah. The courts would hang him right alongside you."

"And you would not object to me hanging?"

She huddled back in the corner, frowning at him. "Of course I would."

He breathed out a sigh of relief. "You have my word. Josiah will not be placed in danger again. I should never have taken him to these parties. The temptation was too much for him."

"Temptation?"

"Aye. Josiah could be the burglar."

"Nonsense! He's only a boy."

"A boy thief, the best pickpocket in London." He moved to the front seat and lifted the iron rod.

"Do you need help getting it up?"

Grinning, he stashed the bar overhead. "I'm sure I can manage when the time comes." With a click he closed the trapdoor. *When the time comes.* He felt sure it would. "If you don't mind, Ginny, I would prefer to share your seat. I hate sitting under this thing."

"Why do you have such an odd contraption?"

He settled in the seat beside her. "'Tis for protection, in case I find myself in poor company. The silken cord from the ceiling releases it."

"Oh, so that's why you pounced on me."

"Originally, yes. Once there, I remained for the sheer pleasure."

She studied her hands folded in her lap. "You didn't force me."

He smiled, remembering her sweet eagerness. "No, but I went too far." He picked up the paper from the floor. "Is this what caused your terror of being searched?"

"Yes."

He unfolded it. "I thought you agreed to stop spying."

"I know, but this was too important to pass up. You'll understand once you read it."

He removed his snuffbox, flicked open the magnifying glass outlined with phosphorescence, and held it over the paper.

She gasped. "That's what I was seeing in the garden. It truly does glow in the dark. How does it work?"

He forgot to answer her as he scanned the contents of the paper twice. "This is invaluable. This is incredible." He gazed out the window, unseeing. This was proof the British were using their power to suppress, not protect.

"May I see your snuffbox?"

Without thinking he passed it to her. "Where did you find this?" He folded the paper. It was exactly what Johnson had been hoping for, and Ginny had found it. Not him.

"In the study. I found it by accident. I was looking for you."

He had been upstairs, rummaging through Colonel Farley's bedchamber. "Can you move to the front seat for a moment?"

"Hmm?" She studied her hand under the magnifying glass.

"Ginny, raise your arse for a moment." He lifted her up, ignoring her huff of indignation, deposited her on the front seat, and slipped the paper into the compartment beneath the back one.

"There." He sat back down and reached for her, pulling her onto his lap. "Now if they want to search us, they'll find nothing." He took the snuffbox from her hand and closed it.

"That is the most amazing machine."

He slipped it into his pocket. "You're the amazing one, Ginny, but please, no more spying."

She rested against him, nestling her head against his shoulder. "Do you worry about me?"

"Aye."

"You're wrong about Josiah being the thief."

"I hope so."

Hidden in the shadows, he saw the carriage roll to a stop in front of the Ashford home. Quincy Stanton jumped out, followed by Miss Munro. The pair scurried to the front door.

Interesting. *The saucy Miss Munro likes a quick frolic in a carriage.* He would remember that for the future. Even so, it might not be the sole reason they ran away. Did Quincy have a reason to avoid being searched? A closer watch was warranted from now on. Meanwhile, he had to stash the jewelry somewhere and return to the party to be searched.

He approached the carriage, careful to remain unseen. With open windows, it was a simple matter to reach inside. He stuffed the ring and necklace between the cushion and side wall of the carriage. He would retrieve the goods later.

As he withdrew his hand, an idea struck him. *Of course!* He was a genius. He would plant one of his stolen items amongst Quincy Stanton's possessions, then alert the authorities. Everyone would believe the bastard was the Boston Burglar.

Quincy would hang. He'd be rid of the bastard once and for all.

And Virginia Munro would be his.

Wednesday, November 15, 1769

"This here be the paper for today." Josiah handed the sheet of newspaper to Virginia, then settled down at the table to write his assignment for the day—what he would do if stranded on an island like Robinson Crusoe.

Virginia scanned the paper, which for three days in a row had printed the information she had stolen from the Ashfords' study. A surge of pride shot through her. She, a woman, had successfully aided the Colonial cause.

All of Boston was in an uproar, demanding the immediate withdrawal of British troops. The paper reported a number of brawls between apprentices and British soldiers. She could only hope the British would leave before serious injury occurred.

Aunt Mary had been greatly relieved that Quincy had taken care of the matter and informed his uncle. She refused to see Edward Stanton until she had the money to pay him back.

Virginia's thoughts turned to Quincy as they so often did these days, flooding her with warmth and excitement. Quin's arms around her, his fingers caressing her, his lips moving on her. She took a deep breath and fanned herself with the paper. She had accused him of spying, but he had avoided speaking of it. If only he would learn to trust her.

"Finished," Josiah announced. "Can we read me book now?"

"Yes, but first, I have something for you. Your reading has so greatly improved, I believe you deserve this small reward." She reached through the slit in her skirt and removed a small package from the sewing pocket tied around her waist underneath the skirt.

Josiah ripped off the ribbon and homespun cloth to discover his present. "A sack?" He wrinkled his nose.

"A sack of marbles. Look inside."

He upended the sack, shaking a few marbles into his outstretched hand. His eyes lit up. "I ain't never had nuthin' like this before."

She winced as she rose to her feet. "That was three negatives in one sentence."

He grinned. "Then I'm improving?"

"Hah! You rascal, you know better than that." Her laughter stopped abruptly when he flung his arms around her waist for a tight hug. She closed her eyes and hugged him back. He had not disappointed her. When she and Quincy had returned to the ball, he had already been searched and declared innocent.

Josiah admired the marbles in his hand. "Thank you, Miss Munro."

"'Twas Mr. Stanton who picked them out for you."

"Oh, I just remembered. Me master said if ye wanted to see something exciting, ye should come to the rally on the north side next Wednesday night."

"A rally? For what?"

"The rebels are gathering at Hancock's Wharf, giving out free rum. I'll be going."

She frowned at her young student. "Not to drink rum, I hope."

Wednesday, November 22, 1769

The crowd roared, incited to a feverish pitch, as the speaker rained insults on the mother country from the makeshift stage.

He shook his fist in the air. "What kind of mother, I ask you, does not nurture her young, but drains them dry to feed her own lust for power?"

"A venomous bloodsucker, that's what!" The slovenly man next to Virginia bellowed so loud, her ears hummed.

She turned to her sister beside her. "Let's go home. 'Tis too loud."

Caroline yelled back, "I cannot hear you. 'Tis too loud!"

Virginia huffed with annoyance, her breath vaporizing in front of her face. It was a very chilly night, only made bearable by the warmth of the boisterous crowd and the torches held by numerous men.

The man on stage stopped shouting to confer with his cronies. The grubby man beside Virginia took a big swig from one of the many bottles of rum being passed about.

"Here, lass." He rubbed the mouth of the bottle on his filthy coat, and handed her the bottle with a loud belch. "Have a drink. 'Twill warm ye up."

"Thank you." Virginia passed the bottle on. Caroline lifted the bottle to her mouth.

"Don't you dare!" Virginia ripped the bottle from her sister's hands.

"I'll take it," George Peeper said.

"You will not. You're supposed to be protecting us, not getting drunk."

"Here now, lass." A young man behind her tapped her shoulder. "Don't hog the rum."

"You're welcome to it." Virginia passed the bottle back.

"Now that's a sweet lass." The young man thanked her with a pinch on her backside.

She jumped. "Aagh! I've had enough." She shouldered her way through the drunken crowd.

Breaking free from the mob, she strode past Revere's silver shop to the water's edge. Hancock's Wharf jutted far out into the harbor, a number of sloops docked along its length.

Larger ships lay anchored in the distance. A breeze of chilled, salty air blew across the dark waters to sting her cheeks. She wrapped her green woolen cape more tightly about her and raised the hood to cover her head. It warmed her ears, but did little to lessen the noise of the crowd.

She wondered if everyone in attendance was truly patriotic or merely interested in the free rum. Grudgingly, she admitted that Captain Breakwell might have a point. Inciting a crowd of this size with treasonous words and free liquor did not show a great deal of responsibility. Had the Colonial leaders reached the point they no longer wanted a peaceful solution but were purposely pushing for war?

She groaned inwardly. War would cause her father and brother to risk their lives in battle. And what of Quincy?

"Is that you, Miss Munro?"

She spun around. "Josiah, you startled me. Are you here alone?"

He nodded, his head covered with the blue cap she had knitted for him. "Me master said he would be here later."

"Oh." She gazed out over the dark waters. "I suppose I can wait awhile. What is that there?" She pointed to a black shape moving on the water.

"'Tis a small boat, full of people." Josiah squinted. "They're rowing toward the wharf."

"There's two more, I believe." She gestured to another pair of boats headed for Hancock's Wharf. "They're coming from that ship out there."

"Oh, I know that one. See the big flag? 'Tis the customs schooner, *The Sentinel*. Me master curses it every time we see it."

"They're all leaving the ship. Oh, no, you don't think they mean to cause trouble at the rally, do you?" She watched the first boat reach the wharf. As the men disembarked, the ropes tying their wrists became visible. Two men, dressed as native Indians and armed with muskets, ordered them to sit.

"Miss Munro, the savages have taken them prisoner!"

She shook her head. "They're not savages. They're white men dressed in war paint."

The second boat unloaded at the wharf.

She hunched her shoulders under her green cloak as a shiver crept up her spine. "I want you to go home now, Josiah."

He shook his head. "I ain't missin' this."

The last boat of hostages tied off at the wharf. The men disembarked and sat on the wharf's wooden planking.

One of the false Indians ran to the stage and leapt on top to make his announcement. "Good friends, let us welcome our guests from *The Sentinel*!"

The crowd cheered when they noticed the hostages on the wharf. They shook their fists at the British, shouting curses that became more and more innovative.

"Now, good people," the war-painted man yelled. "Be kind to our guests. They have come to witness the night's entertainment. Cast your eyes to the harbor, and you shall see a most glorious sight!"

The eager crowd pressed forward to the water's edge. Fearing they would push her and Josiah into the freezing water, Virginia headed north, towing the young boy along.

Boom! An explosion split the air, knocking her back a few feet. A flash of light blinded her.

She heard Josiah's excited voice. "They blew it up!"

Holding up a hand to shield her eyes, she blinked as the scene before her came into focus. The crowd hooted and leapt like savages in a victory dance. *The Sentinel* was ablaze, fire racing up the masts and ropes.

She froze, stunned by the sheer size of the fire and the brilliance of the flames—flames that mesmerized her 'til her eyes watered, flames that threatened to leap across space with fiery tendrils to singe her hair and sear her flesh.

When she gasped for air, she choked on the taste of smoke. Her stomach lurched. She covered her mouth and nose. The fire crackled with a snapping sound that made her cringe.

"Damn!" Josiah laughed. "That looks wondrous fine!"

She stumbled along the waterfront, headed north.

Josiah tagged along behind. "Don't go now, Miss Munro."

The crack of gunshots rang out, followed by the pounding boots of a British regiment advancing up Fish Street, their muskets still smoking from the warning shots they had fired.

The crowd panicked, screaming and shoving, some dropping to the ground, some dashing away.

"Halt!" a British officer shouted. "You're under arrest for the destruction of His Majesty's property!"

A second explosion ravaged *The Sentinel* as flames discovered a stash of gunpowder. Debris rained down, inciting more panic. The inferno raged, lighting the tumultuous scene on the wharf.

Virginia recognized the British officer as Colonel Farley. She backed away, pulling her hood close about her face.

The redcoats fought their way through the frenzied mob to Hancock's Wharf, determined to reach the men dressed as savages. The more dedicated rebels in the crowd pushed the soldiers back to allow the false Indians time to escape.

"Back into the sea with you, ye Lobsterbacks!" They shoved redcoats off the wharf and cheered when the men splashed into the icy water.

"Caroline! George!" Virginia tried to spot them in the crowd, but the scene was too chaotic, the noise too deafening for them to hear her screams.

She grabbed Josiah and charged further north. Perhaps, if she waited a safe distance from the struggle, she would be able to see her sister and George leaving.

Suddenly, in the harbor not far from them, a large round object popped to the water's surface. A door on top opened, and a man's head appeared.

Amazed, Virginia and Josiah stopped to look.

"What is that?" Josiah asked.

From his position on Hancock's Wharf, Colonel Farley pointed to the odd vessel in the water. "Stop that man!"

Soldiers lined up beside the colonel and leveled their muskets at the man emerging from the hatch. He dove into the water and disappeared under the dark waves.

Virginia gasped. "They mean to kill him."

"He's headed for Scarlet's Wharf!" Josiah sprinted onto the next wharf, north of Hancock's.

She raced after him. "The redcoats will follow us!"

"I'll slow 'em down." Josiah toppled over barrels to roll them down the wharf.

She spotted the man's head coming into view as he hauled himself up a rope ladder. He heaved himself onto the pier, then straightened to his full height. A large man, dressed entirely in black, he presented a mysterious, dripping, dark silhouette against the backdrop of the burning ship.

As she ran toward the man, she noted the violent shakes of his body. She whipped off her cloak and threw it over his shoulders. "You must hurry. The redcoats are coming."

"G-Ginny?"

She froze in shock. "*Quin?*"

CHAPTER THIRTEEN

"Dammit, Ginny, get out of here n-n-now!" Quin gritted his teeth as another violent shudder coursed through him.

"No, I won't leave you."

He noted the soldiers advancing toward Scarlet's Wharf. *Damn.* If they caught Ginny helping him, she might hang alongside him. But what choice did he have but to take her with him? "Josiah!" he called the boy over.

"Master? Is that you?" Josiah grinned. "That was a fine show."

"Can you sneak off the wharf unnoticed? G-go to my uncle. Tell him I'll be on my sh-ship, waiting for him. He'll understand."

"Aye, sir." Josiah slipped away, blending into the darkness.

"Come with me." Quin grabbed Virginia by the arm and charged to the end of the wharf.

She ran to keep up with him. Her voice sounded frightened and near panic. "Where are you going? 'Tis a dead end."

"Tr-tr-trust me." His icy, wet clothes glued themselves

to his body as if a cold-blooded snake had coiled around his vitals, squeezing the air out of him. His feet squished painfully in sodden shoes. Lightheaded and dizzy, he forced his stiffening limbs to obey his command to run.

He halted in front of *The Forbidden Lady*, the last ship tied off at the wharf. The gangplank had been removed to keep unwanted visitors from boarding.

He clenched his teeth to keep them from chattering. "Stay here." He heard her gasp when he made a running leap off the pier.

As he cleared the dark abyss between ship and dock, his frozen feet slammed against the gunwale of the ship. Red-hot pain exploded in his feet and surged up his legs. He landed on deck with a clumsy splat like a net full of fish.

"Bloody hell!" He hobbled to the gangplank and set it into place. "Come on."

She stepped carefully across.

"Hurry." He snatched her off as soon as she was within reach.

"Aah! Your hands are like ice."

"Head for the s-stairs." He dropped the gangplank into the water. If the redcoats wanted to board, they would have to jump for it.

"This way." He led her to the stairs leading below deck. As she descended, he glanced back to see if he had left a watery trail. Yes, his wet footprints were discernible. It would take too long to dry them all. He spotted a fire bucket nearby and splashed water over the deck. Not the best solution, but all he could manage in a hurry.

He joined Virginia below deck. To avoid leaving another trail straight to his cabin, he whisked off her cloak and dragged it behind them.

The bright fire from *The Sentinel* cast a golden glow through the wide windows of the captain's cabin. Virginia paced about examining his living quarters. He shut the door, flung her cloak onto the pinewood table, and yanked open the trunk at the foot of his bed.

"Damn." He dropped the lid. All his clothes were gone, replaced by those of his first mate, who had captained the schooner on her last voyage.

"What's wrong?" she asked.

"The clothes won't fit." He yanked his soggy black shirt off and threw it on her cloak.

Her eyes widened at the sight of him undressing. "Oh." She turned and looked out the window. "What if the redcoats come aboard?"

"Don't worry. I have a p-plan." He dragged the wide trunk away from the bed, revealing a pair of ropes attached to the bottom corners of the trunk which led into two holes in the floor. He curled his fingers around a metal ring and pulled. A narrow trapdoor, situated between the two ropes, opened to a compartment hidden under the bed.

Leaning against the bedpost, he removed his black, sodden shoes and stockings. The stinging pain still throbbed through his feet.

She was staring out the window at the burning ship. "Why did they blow it up? 'Twill cause so much trouble."

He tossed his shoes and stockings into the hidden compartment along with his wet shirt. "Actually, they didn't. Their job was to m-make sure everyone was off before it blew."

"Well, someone blew it up. Who—" She pivoted around to look him in the eye. "Oh, no, you didn't."

"I—" He heard noises overhead, the thumping sounds of bodies landing on deck. "Quick! Pull the blankets off the bed and drop them in the hole."

"What hole?" She ran to the bed and gathered up the blankets.

With her woolen cloak, he dried any visible wet spots.

She dropped the blankets down the hole. "What is this place?"

"A French bottom." He tossed in the cloak and slid into the narrow opening.

"Are you a smuggler?"

"No, but I'm prepared for the p-possibility." His chest now level with the floor, he turned to face her. "Right now, I'm just a spy." He reached his arms up to her.

She stared at him. "I was right."

He winced as he heard more soldiers landing on deck. "Ginny, come on. Trust me."

She bent down and he lowered her into the smuggler's hole. She clutched at his shoulders to steady herself. He held her close, enjoying the glorious warmth of her body as he reached around where part of her skirts had remained behind. He stuffed her skirt into the hole. "There. You're all in, now. Can you sit down?"

"Yes." She sank to her knees in front of him, her hands trailing down his bare chest to keep her balance.

He swallowed hard. It was a good thing he still wore his breeches. He shut the trapdoor, immersing them in total darkness.

On his knees, he groped along the ceiling for the knotted ends of the ropes. He grasped them and pulled. The trunk, attached to the ropes, scraped along the floor as it moved back into position at the foot of the bed. He tied the ropes together so the soldiers would be unable to budge the trunk. They would assume the trunk was bolted to the floor like most things in the cabin. The door to their secret place would remain hidden beneath the immovable trunk. They would be trapped inside until Edward came.

By the sound of her breathing, he could tell Ginny was close by and frightened. "We'll be safe. The m-men from *The Sentinel* never figured it out. The redcoats won't either. Of course, we'll have to r-remain completely silent."

"I understand. Here, you'll need this blanket."

He wrapped the blanket around his shoulders and shoved his pile of wet clothes out of the way. With numb and clumsy fingers, he unbuttoned his drenched, icy breeches and peeled them off. Damn, but it was a dark, little hole they were in, as small as the submersible he hated. A person couldn't even stand up in this place. He tugged his linen underdrawers off and flung them aside. At least it was too dark for Ginny to see his nudity. Not that he cared, but she probably would.

Shivering with his bare arse on the cold wooden planks, he adjusted his blanket so he would be sitting on it. God, he hated small places. He caught his breath. Why had he never made the connection? Most probably because he had always refused to dwell on bad memories. This secret hole and the damned submersible were too much like the small, dark room in the cellar where he had been stashed away as a child. He had dreaded being alone in the dark, not that he was afraid of the dark, but afraid of being unwanted. At least this time he wasn't alone. Ginny was breathing softly beside him.

The door to the cabin squeaked as it opened overhead. The heavy footsteps of booted feet reverberated across the floor.

The soldiers wandered about, their voices too muffled to comprehend. He heard the loud slam of cupboard drawers and the sound of pewter tankards banging on the table. The damned redcoats were helping themselves to his rum.

He huddled in the blanket, racked with shudders as the chilly, damp air in the secret compartment tormented him. One thin blanket was not enough. He felt another blanket being placed around his shoulders and knew Ginny was giving him her own. He shook his head in vain. She couldn't see his refusal in the dark, but he didn't want her to be cold either. He opened his mouth to whisper. His teeth chattered.

A redcoat opened the trunk above them.

He clenched his teeth together to stop the chattering. In the dark hole, it seemed incredibly loud.

Ginny's arms wrapped around him and she pressed her warmth against him. He released his blanket and clung to her, jamming his mouth against her brow to stop his chattering teeth.

When she tilted up her face, he found her mouth with his own. She gave her warmth to him so sweetly, so selflessly, he drank it in, reveling in the taste of her. He reclined on his discarded blanket and pulled her body on top of him like a sun-warmed quilt.

He rubbed his hands up and down her back 'til the numbness in his fingers subsided. He nestled his cold nose into the snug crook of her neck, inhaling her scent. She laid her heated palms against his ears and breathed against his brow. The light-headedness dissipated; the stiffness from his joints melted away into warm, soupy comfort.

"Yes," he whispered, then remembered the redcoats overhead. He listened, but heard no sound.

"Are they gone?" Her voice was faint against his ear.

"They could still be on board. We'll have to stay here until Edward comes."

"All right." She moved to shift her weight off of him.

"No, don't go." He pulled her back. "I . . . I'm still cold."

She settled on top of him, inching down his body 'til she could lay her head on his chest. "Is that better?"

He groaned as he felt her legs entwining with his.

"Am I too heavy?"

"God, no."

"What was that strange vessel you were in?"

"A submersible, for traveling underwater. I used her to attach a keg of gunpowder to the ship."

"Oh." She sighed, her breath puffing against his bare chest. "I'm relieved you're not a Tory, and I'm grateful that you've been honest with me about the spying, but blowing up a British ship—this is too much. What am I going to do with you?"

"I don't know." He located the laces at the back of her woolen gown and slowly pulled.

"Quin?"

He stopped. "Yes?"

"My aunt will be worried sick about me."

"Josiah will get through to my uncle. Edward will tell your aunt what has happened."

"How long do you think we'll stay here?"

"Perhaps the entire night." He tugged and felt the bow unravel.

"Oh, dear. Then perhaps we should discuss the situation. You are, no doubt, as tense about this predicament as I am."

"Tense, yes." He gently loosened the laces. What the hell was he doing? She could be left with child, a bastard one. She deserved better than that. And the child did, too. He had no choice but to marry her. But damn, she deserved a better man for her husband. If only he could persuade her, woo her with kisses, then make love to her. All night long.

She turned her head to rest her other cheek on his chest. "This is the sort of situation that could potentially expand into a much larger, unwieldy type of circumstance. Do you not agree?"

"Aye, it is expanding by the moment."

"I want you to know, Quincy, that I will not hold you responsible for being trapped in here with me. No one need know other than your uncle and my aunt."

"I *am* responsible."

"There's no need for you to be so noble about this."

He crooked his finger in her laces and pulled. Noble, his ass. He was definitely a bastard.

"Are you warm now?" She wiggled up his body to touch his brow. "Goodness, you're hot. I hope you're not feverish."

He grimaced as her upward movement rubbed against his erection. "Perhaps you should get off now."

"Oh, of course. You no longer need me."

He snorted.

She shifted her torso to his left and slid onto the wooden

planks beside him. Her leg, moving across his hips, bumped against his stiff erection.

He groaned.

"I'm sorry. I'm trying to move aside, but there's some sort of impediment here." She jiggled her leg against it.

He reached down to stop her movement. "Careful with that."

"What is it—part of your spy equipment?"

"Oh, aye. I use it to explore hidden passageways."

"Indeed? Does it glow in the dark?"

"Bloody hell, I hope not." He reached down to lift her knee and push her leg to the side.

"Then how do you see where you're going?"

He groaned.

"Oh, dear, you don't sound well. Perhaps, if you can move, we should find a doctor."

He surged onto his elbow and leaned over her, pressing her against the wooden floor.

"Oh, you can move. That's a good sign."

"Forgive me."

"This is not your fault, Quin. I told you I will not hold you responsi—"

His mouth found hers with startling accuracy in the dark.

"If you've come for the money, Edward Stanton, you have wasted your time. I do not have it."

Baffled, Edward stared at Mary Dover. "What money?"

"The money I owe you. Don't pretend ignorance with me."

"How? Never mind. May I come in?" He slipped past her into the hall, a cloth sack in his arms.

With a frown, she closed the front door. "'Tis extremely late to come visiting, but if you're concerned about the money, I assure you, I will pay you back."

"I don't want your money, Mary."

"Well, I don't want yers! How dare ye lie to me."

He winced. His plan to help her had gone awry. Somehow she knew the truth. "I meant no harm. I knew you would need it."

She paced about the hall. "But now I'm in debt to you. I canna bear this. 'Tis the same nightmare all over again!"

"You make too much of this, Mary."

"Too much? You have no idea, Edward Stanton. My father gave me in marriage to settle a debt. Against my will. I canna, I willna endure this again!"

Edward gaped, dumbfounded by her confession. "Your father used you to settle a debt?"

Mary flushed a bright red and stammered, "I . . . I shouldna have told you. Please, doona repeat it."

"I would never. Mary, I'm so sorry."

Her bottom lip trembled, and she bit it. "I will pay you back somehow. Now, if ye'll kindly leave, we have enough problems to deal with tonight. My niece went to the rally and hasna returned. George is out looking for her—"

"I know where she is. She and Quin are hiding on his schooner."

"What? Why?"

"The redcoats were after them."

"My stars!" She paled and covered her mouth.

"Josiah told me about it. I'm sure they're perfectly safe, but I wanted to relieve your concerns as soon as possible. I'm going there now to check on the situation."

"I see. What do you have there, some food for them?" She gestured to the sack in his arms.

"No, dry clothes for Quin. Josiah said he swam to safety in the harbor. He'll be needing these if he's not already frozen."

"Good heavens." Mary grabbed her cloak from the peg on the wall. "I'm coming with you."

When he first kissed her, Virginia feared he was merely trying to put a stop to her nervous babbling. She had been experiencing a confused jumble of emotion, from the chilling possibility of being caught by the redcoats to the heated excitement at being trapped in a dark hole with the man she loved. A man who wore no clothes.

At first, she shivered when he pressed her down onto the cold wooden planks, but his heat soon seeped into her. His mouth moved over hers, demanding and hungry. No, he wasn't hushing her up.

He wanted her.

She tried to think, but too many sensations bombarded her. His tongue invaded her mouth, his hands explored, his bare legs rubbed against hers. And something hard and thick strained against her.

She jerked away from his kiss with a gasp.

"Ginny, please."

"I . . ." How could she say she had just now realized what the impediment was? She moaned with embarrassment. He must think her a fool. She was so nervous, so naïve. Her only experience in seeing a male prepared to mate had been with animals in daylight.

He laid his head on her chest. "I cannot bear it."

She ran her fingers through his thick hair, wanting to comfort him but afraid where it might lead.

He exhaled, and his warm breath tingled her skin. "There's no help for it. We will have to marry."

Her hands halted their caress. "Marry?"

"Aye. I have too much respect for you to misuse you, and I will not bring a bastard into the world."

She frowned into the darkness. So much for the proposal of her dreams—misuse and bastardy were so romantic. Was respect all he felt for her? No, obviously, he also experienced a goodly amount of lust. And a small amount of trust. He was beginning to confide in her. He had admitted to being a spy.

He raised his head from her bosom, and she knew he was waiting for an answer. She slipped her hands down his neck and across the smooth, bare skin of his shoulders. To be honest, she felt a goodly amount of lust, herself, and she loved him with all her heart.

She loved him enough not to entrap him. "Quin, if you're feeling honor-bound by tonight's events, 'tis not necessary."

His grip on her shoulders tightened. "It *is* necessary. I want to marry. I want you in my bed."

"Is that the only reason?"

"Seems like a damned good one to me. Ginny, there are many good reasons we should marry. I . . . I need you."

Her heart melted. That was, she suspected, as close as he could get to a confession of love at the moment. Without the benefit of growing up with loving parents, he had difficulty recognizing what he was feeling. In time, with the help of a loving wife, he would tell her what she wanted to hear. But for now, she had to be honest with him.

"Quin, because of my fear, I never learned how to do the chores that require a fire. I'm only now learning how to cook." She felt his shoulders shrug underneath her hands.

"Eating is highly overrated. I've lived for days at a time on hardtack and grog."

"But at home, they say I'm unfit for marriage."

"They're idiots. Will you marry me?"

She laughed, relishing his easy dismissal of her secret failing. "Yes. Yes, I will."

"Good." He tugged her bodice down to her waist.

She gasped. When had he untied her laces? "What are you doing?"

He untied her chemise and cupped her bare breast with his hand. "Celebrating."

CHAPTER FOURTEEN

Edward helped Mary cross the makeshift gangplank onto the schooner he had secretly named for her. He wished he could divulge that secret, but the forbidden lady had become the angry, indebted lady, still impossible to pursue. Damn her father for using her that way.

Carrying a lantern to light their path, he escorted her along the deck. The cold night air smelled of burnt ashes and tar. In the distance, the charred remains of *The Sentinel* floated on the water like a blackened skeleton. Good riddance.

"What if there are redcoats still aboard?" Mary tucked the sack of dry clothing under her arm.

"I have every right to be here." He led her down the stairs. "The ship belongs to Stanton Shipping."

"How will you explain my presence?"

"Easy. You're my guest for the evening. We've come to be alone."

She narrowed her green eyes on him to let him know she was insulted. He turned away so she wouldn't see his smile.

He set the lantern on the table in Quin's cabin, noting the three pewter tankards and empty bottle of rum. "The redcoats were here."

"Aye, they searched the place." She dropped the sack of clothing onto a wooden chair. "But where are Quincy and Ginny?"

"Under here." Edward grasped the trunk and gave it a yank. It moved slightly, then stuck fast.

He hunched down on the floor. "Quin, do you hear me?" There was a pause while he waited for a response.

Nothing.

He swallowed hard, not wanting to consider the possibility that the two had been captured. He yelled louder, "Quin, if you're there, answer me!"

"Dammit, Edward, come back in the morning!"

Relief swept through him and he grinned. Quincy was all right. More than all right.

Mary stomped her foot on the wooden floor. "We will not go. Now you come out of there this instant and release my niece."

"Aunt Mary?" A female voice sifted through the floor.

"Ginny?" Mary fell to her knees on the floor. "Are you all right, dear?"

"Yes. Uh, perhaps you *should* return in the morning."

Edward snorted with laughter.

Mary swatted his shoulder. "This is not amusing. God knows what he's doing to my innocent niece."

Edward leaned close to her. "I could show you."

She huffed. "'Twas merely an expression. I know quite well what he's up to, and you should be ashamed of yourself for not teaching him better morals." She raised her voice. "Ginny, you come out at once!"

"I've untied the ropes," Quincy yelled. "You should be able to move the trunk now."

Edward scooted the trunk away from the bed.

Mary rose to her feet. "Edward Stanton, are you a smuggler?"

"Not yet." He hooked his fingers around the metal ring to lift the trapdoor. "But I'm glad these two had a place to hide." With the door open, he spotted his naked nephew behind Virginia Munro, tying the laces of her gown. "Mary, hand me that sack of clothing we brought."

She passed it to him with a suspicious glance at the smuggler's hole. "'Tis black as pitch in there."

Virginia stood up, her shoulders now level with the floor. She brushed her disheveled hair back from her face. "Good evening."

Edward handed her the sack, carefully keeping his face blank. "I believe my nephew can use these."

Virginia passed the sack to Quin, her cheeks bright pink.

Quin's voice drifted up from the hole. "I'll give her a boost. Then you can pull her out, all right?"

"Yes." Edward grasped Virginia under the arms and with Quin's help, he lifted her out.

Mary escorted her to the table. "You poor dear, trapped in that awful hole. Let me pour you a drink." She bustled to the cupboard for clean glasses and a bottle of wine while Virginia rested in a wooden chair.

"I'll have a drink." Edward wandered over to the table. "Is

it true, what Josiah says, that Quin is responsible for blowing up *The Sentinel*?"

Virginia nodded. "Yes, he attached the gunpowder using a submersible."

"My stars." Mary poured herself a drink and collapsed in a chair.

Smiling, Edward poured wine into the remaining glasses.

"I could use one of those." Quin tossed blankets and a pile of damp clothing out of the hole. Dressed in blue woolen breeches and an unbuttoned white shirt, he heaved himself out of the hole. He padded to the table in his bare feet and grabbed a glass.

Edward patted him on the back. "You struck quite a blow for the cause. I'm relieved you two are all right."

Mary snorted and crossed her arms. "That remains to be seen. Did he force you, Ginny?"

"No, of course not."

"I'm not blind, young lady. Your laces are not properly tied. Your father will never forgive me if you're ravished while in my care."

"I was not ravished," Virginia whispered. "I didn't even experience one of those little deaths you told me about."

Quin sputtered his wine. "Bloody hell! I'll do better next time."

Mary jumped to her feet. "There will not be a next time."

"There will." Quin slammed his glass onto the table. "Ginny has agreed to marry me."

Mary gasped and collapsed back into her chair.

Allowing his elation free reign, Edward laughed as he

shook his nephew's hand. "Congratulations, Quin! I'm very proud of you."

"Proud?" Mary asked. "He blew up a ship and ravished my niece, all in one night."

Virginia frowned. "He didn't ravish me."

Edward finished his glass of wine. "I say we clean up here and return to Mary's house. Quin, you may need an alibi for this evening. You'll say you were visiting Virginia at her home and proposed to her there."

Quin nodded. "Agreed."

In the wee hours of the morning, Quin crept into his house, exhausted and hoping to sleep through the rest of the day. Overall, the night had been a success. *The Sentinel* was gone, and Virginia had agreed to marry him.

"A late night, old boy?" Clarence sauntered from the study, a glass of brandy in his hand.

"Aye." Quin passed by him to the stairs.

"'Twas an exciting night. Quite a show those Colonial hoodlums put on. After the explosion, I went to the harbor to see the rumpus for myself, but I didn't see you there."

Quin paused with a foot on the first step. "I was at Mary Dover's house."

"Indeed? What a pity. I would have thought you'd enjoy watching *The Sentinel* burn."

"I was occupied with another matter. You may congratulate me. Virginia Munro has agreed to marry me."

Clarence pasted a cold smile on his face. "How fortunate."

"Yes. Now, if you'll excuse me, I'm off to bed." Quin started up the stairs.

"Very well, since you have no interest in what happened at the harbor. Though you might wonder why Colonel Farley thought it necessary to search *your* ship."

Quin stopped and peered over his shoulder. Clarence stood at the base of the stairs, his gray eyes gleaming with challenge. He lifted the glass of brandy slowly to his mouth.

Quin turned to face him. "Why would they search my ship?"

"Why, indeed?"

"I have no idea." Quin continued up the stairs.

"Such a lack of curiosity. 'Tis not like you, old boy."

"I'm tired."

"Of course. The proposal must have been exhausting. It certainly was timely. A shame you didn't dress better for the occasion."

"Good night, Clarence." Quin reached the top of the stairs.

"Sleep well, old boy. I'm sure the two painted rebels the British captured will not be sleeping tonight."

Quin gripped the balustrade, hesitating only an instant in his stride. *Damn it to hell.* The two men were probably his friends.

He glanced down at Clarence with a bland look. "I hope they hang."

Shortly before noon, Quin woke and remembered. Ginny would soon be his wife. And two of his friends would not be at the wedding. He jumped out of bed to pull on his clothes. There had to be something he and Johnson could do.

He strode to the kitchen in search of coffee. Mrs. Millstead poured him a mug, setting it down with a clunk on the table. She returned without a word to the large pot of boiling water where she was washing clothes. Quin decided she must be protesting his interference with her duties.

Josiah and Samuel sat at the table, polishing silver. Josiah grinned at him, squirming on the bench.

Quin picked up his mug. "Josiah, I need to speak to you in my study."

"That's not fair. I'll be left with all the work," Samuel whined. "Me mum said if we finished, we could go see the rebels' submersible."

Quin paused at the door. "Submersible?"

"Aye." Josiah jumped to his feet. "The British pulled it out of the water this morning. 'Tis at the town dock by Fanueil Hall."

"Indeed? Perhaps I'll go with you boys and take a look. But first, I need some food. Josiah, bring me a tray to the study."

Quin sat at his drop-leaf desk, sipping coffee. So, the British had the *Turtle* in their possession. They could take the vessel apart, but there would be nothing to connect him to it. Only a few men knew he was the pilot.

Ginny and Josiah knew.

The boy came in with a tray of bread, cheese, and cold ham and set it on the walnut table. "'Tis cold, Master. Mrs. Millstead fixes a nicer tray for yer fancy brother."

"It doesn't matter. Have a seat and help yourself if you're hungry." Quin crossed the study and peered out the door before closing it.

He sat at the table next to the boy. "You did very well last night."

Josiah grinned. "Not as good as you. That was splendid, the way ye blew up—"

"Josiah, I didn't do anything. In fact, I wasn't at the harbor. I was at Miss Munro's house with her. Do you understand?"

"Oh. Aye, I do."

"Now, even though you've done excellent work, I will no longer require your services in the evening. You'll remain home from now on."

Josiah bit his lip. "What did I do wrong?"

"Nothing. I have simply realized I can no longer endanger you." The boy looked so miserable Quin tried to cheer him up. "I have good news. Miss Munro and I will be married."

Josiah's eyes opened wide. "Oh, Master, that is fine news! Then she'll be living here with me?"

Quin sat back in his chair. "No, you rascal. You're too young for her. She'll be living with me."

The boy laughed and threw his arms around Quin's neck.

Surprised, Quin patted the boy on the back. "Josiah, you must never tell anyone what you saw last night. Not only would they arrest me, but they could possibly arrest Miss Munro for aiding in my escape."

"I won't never do that, Master. I couldn't stand to lose you or Miss Munro."

Quin felt a strange twinge in his chest. He had purchased the boy to help him spy, without any qualms that he was risking Josiah's life. Now he only wanted to protect the boy. He had an odd feeling he had experienced this before. A young boy who no one wanted and a man who cared for him.

He swallowed hard when he realized what had happened. He had become Uncle Edward, and Josiah was himself.

He surged to his feet and paced to his desk. He grasped his mug and gulped down some coffee. "Fine. Then you know nothing of the submersible, and you never saw Miss Munro or me at the harbor. We were at her house, making wedding plans late into the night."

Josiah frowned at his shoes.

"What's wrong?"

The boy grimaced. "I didn't say nuthin' about the submersible, but last night when I came in so late, Mrs. Millstead fussed at me and I said I was at the harbor with you."

Saturday, December 16, 1769

The banns had been read thrice; the day had arrived. Virginia rode to her wedding in a rented coach, accompanied by her sister and aunt. George, dressed in the late Charles Dover's best clothes, sat next to the driver.

Virginia smoothed out the skirts of her golden silk gown, mentally reviewing her list of preparations. Right now, Bostonians would be cramming into the Old North Church—Aunt Mary's Loyalist friends and Edward Stanton's rebellious friends and business associates. A group of musicians would be arriving at Concert Hall for the party while servants from two taverns and a bakery delivered food. Aunt Mary had worried over the cost of renting Concert Hall, but every other place was currently occupied with troops. Edward Stanton insisted on paying as a wedding gift.

"Now I feel even more indebted to that man. How will I ever pay him back?" Aunt Mary adjusted the hood of her blue woolen cloak as a gust of cold air blew through the coach.

Virginia pressed her hand to her chest, suddenly finding it difficult to breathe in spite of the crisp air that pinched her cheeks. It had snowed last night, but thank goodness, the gray skies had cleared by morning. The sun now shone bright on her wedding day. Certainly that was a good sign.

Mary fiddled with the tasseled cords that fastened her cloak under her chin. "And he will be at the wedding and festivities to follow. I canna bear this."

"Please." Virginia could feel her heart racing beneath her hand. "You're not the one getting married today. I don't know if *I* can bear this." With all the preparations, the last three weeks had flown by so fast she had not realized the frightening truth.

Today, she attached herself to a man for the rest of her life.

Aunt Mary clutched her gloved hands together. "I knew it. This is happening too fast. You should have waited for Twelfth Night."

Virginia winced. "'Tis a wee late to postpone it now. And Quincy was very adamant about doing it today."

"Don't worry, Ginny." Caroline squeezed her hand. "Everything will be fine."

"I wish Mother and Father were here. Dear Lord, they won't even know. With all the rush, I forgot to write a letter."

Caroline smiled. "I took care of it for you. I sent off a letter two weeks ago."

Virginia let out a sigh of relief. "Oh, thank you."

"Papa will be so surprised. I told him you were marrying the man who wanted to buy you."

"Good Lord!" Virginia gasped, pressing her hand to her chest. "I cannot breathe."

The carriage stopped in front of the church. A crowd of people gathered around the open doors, indicating the church was already packed full.

Quincy Stanton emerged from the church and weaved through the crowd. He wore the gray silk with silver buttons, a lavish abundance of lace at his neck and sleeves. Obviously, she had not destroyed all his wigs, for he wore another one, curled and powdered snowy white with a gray silk bow around the ponytail.

Virginia groaned. "I cannot do this. He's prettier than me."

Aunt Mary reached over and patted her hands. "Ginny, he's a good man. Remember, it is important right now for him to be seen as a Tory. But you know who he truly is."

As Virginia accepted Quin's arm and descended from the carriage, she could only pray that she did know who he truly was.

CHAPTER FIFTEEN

She refused to dance with him. Hell, she wouldn't even talk to him. Frowning, Edward poured more wine into his glass. The more money he spent, the more vexed she became. Perhaps Mary would like him more when he became a pauper.

He shouldered his way across Concert Hall, greeting people as he went. The wedding had gone well, even with a nervous bride and groom. Lively music filled the hall. The guests ate, danced, and laughed at bawdy jokes. It seemed that patriots and Loyalists could forget their differences when the wine was free.

He stopped to talk to his solicitor, Obadiah Winkle. "Is everything set?"

"Aye, the papers are ready. I have them here." The solicitor tucked a brown leather envelope under his arm.

"Quincy doesn't know about the plan yet. I'll send him over so you can explain it."

Obadiah Winkle squinted through his spectacles. "What if he doesn't want to do it?"

"He has no choice. None of us do." Edward downed the

last of the wine in his glass. "When you're done, tell him to go to the Green Dragon Tavern."

"Why?"

"Don't worry, Winkle. 'Tis not business, but pleasure." As Edward passed by the dancers on his way to the newly wedded couple, he motioned to four of his friends to join him.

He set his empty glass on the table where the bride and groom were enjoying a meal. "Quin, you need to talk to our solicitor. He's over there by the first window."

Quin frowned. "Surely it can wait."

" 'Tis extremely urgent. Don't worry. I'll take good care of your bride while you're gone."

"Very well." Quin pushed back his chair and stood. He gave his wife an apologetic look. "I'll be back soon."

She nodded.

Edward watched his nephew disappear into the crowd. His four friends arrived, lining up in front of the table where the bride sat alone. "Virginia, may I introduce my friends from the Sons of Liberty. We have come to liberate you."

She blinked. "Excuse me?"

"You'll come with us. We're kidnapping you." Edward noted her apprehension and sought to reassure her. " 'Tis but a jest, my dear. No harm will come to you."

She frowned, eyeing the four men who had surrounded her. "Aunt Mary," she called. "What is happening here?"

Mary hastened to her side, ignoring Edward's presence. "What is wrong, dear?"

Virginia glanced at Edward with a look that questioned his sanity. "Quin's uncle wants to kidnap me."

Mary snorted. "Indeed? You would think the man was too old for such a childish prank."

Edward placed his palms on the table and leaned toward them. "I'm young enough for you, Mary."

"Humph." Mary gave him a look of disdain. "You should be ashamed of yourself. Frightening this poor girl on her wedding day."

He smiled slowly. "Are you speaking to me now?"

Mary narrowed her eyes at him.

"What's happening?" Caroline Munro approached, examining the men curiously.

Virginia shook her head. "I have no idea."

Edward straightened. "It is a custom in Boston for friends of the groom to kidnap the bride and take her to another location. The groom then comes to rescue his bride."

Caroline clapped her hands, grinning. "How marvelous! Can I be kidnapped, too?"

Edward bowed to her. "Of course, my dear. We aim to please."

Mary crossed her arms. "This is ridiculous. I cannot allow you and your ruffians to abscond with these young women without a chaperone. I will have to accompany you."

Edward grinned. "I am delighted, Mary. Shall we go? Our carriage awaits."

Virginia rose to her feet. "Will Quin know where we are?"

"Aye." Edward noticed the young servant that lived at Mary's house hovering nearby. He was the same height as Virginia. "You there, what is your name?"

"George Peeper, sir."

"You're coming with us."

Outside Concert Hall, Edward helped the ladies into Quin's carriage, while the boy servant climbed up next to the driver. "To the Green Dragon," he called to the driver.

He settled in the front seat next to Mary, giving her a smile which she ignored. His friends, the four Sons of Liberty, rode their horses alongside the coach as they proceeded to the tavern.

Caroline beamed. "I've never been kidnapped before."

Mary rolled her eyes. "I certainly hope not."

"What's this?" Caroline reached for the silken cord hanging from the ceiling.

Virginia gasped and shoved her sister's hand away. "Don't touch that! It releases an iron bar over the front seat."

Edward studied the trapdoor over his head.

"What manner of carriage is this?" Mary asked.

"Quin's been using it." Edward turned to Mary, eager to maneuver the conversation away from Quin's secret activities. "What do you know of this George who lives with you?"

"He's a fine boy. My brother selected him."

"He only stole food to help his family," Caroline added.

Edward frowned. "He's a thief?"

Mary shook her head. "He was desperate. His family was evicted from their home when a fancy lord decided sheep were more profitable. They moved to London and when his parents took ill, George tried to care for them. Obviously, he didn't make a very good thief."

"What happened to his family?" Edward asked.

Mary shrugged. "We don't know. He suspects his parents have died, but he has a younger sister he worries about."

Edward nodded. "If you'll give me the names and descriptions of his family members, I'll have my factor in London search for them."

Mary shifted on the seat to face him. "You would do that?"

"I may be a kidnapper, but I'm not an evil man." Edward saw the hope lighting her beautiful green eyes. "Mary, the chances are not good that we'll find any of them alive. I would hate to disappoint you."

They stopped in front of the Green Dragon, and Edward helped the ladies out of the carriage. As George jumped down from the driver's seat, Edward patted him on the back.

"George, I have an unusual request."

Quin strode through the streets, accompanied by three old friends who teased him for losing his wife an hour after the wedding.

"You're the lucky one, Quin." One of his friends grinned. "I wish I could lose my wife."

"How could you?" another one asked. "She's as big as a barn."

"Here now," the third man joined in. "That's not true. She's no bigger than a horse."

The offended one knocked the other two's tricornes off their heads.

Quin shook his head and quickened his pace. He was not in the mood for frivolity, not after his conversation with Obadiah Winkle. He had known that Edward and Winkle intended to foil Clarence's plan to take over Stanton Shipping, but the solution was much more drastic than he had imagined. He was in a shocked state of mind when he had discovered his wife was missing.

Perhaps Edward thought he needed some silliness to take his mind off the grave situation.

"Actually"—one of the friends veered closer to him and lowered his voice—"we wanted a chance to see you alone."

Quin glanced at him. A few months ago, the man had accused him of being a traitor. "Do you plan to give me a beating?"

"No." His friend smiled. "But I was tempted to before."

The second companion positioned himself to Quin's left. "We heard you're still working for the cause."

Quin shook his head. "I'm afraid you're mistaken. I'm a King's man."

The third friend spoke behind him, "We heard you're the one responsible for the . . . incident in the harbor."

Quin skidded to a stop. *Damn.* Someone was talking who shouldn't. His friends reached out to steady him.

"The road's a bit icy, don't you think?" Quin resumed walking.

The man on his right said, "Your secret is safe with us, but we thought you should know there are rumors floating about."

The one to the left added, "We want you to know if you ever need any help, we'll be there."

Quin stopped again and regarded his old friends. A part of him felt relieved they no longer considered him a traitor. Another part warned him of imminent danger. Too many people knew about him.

He thanked his friends silently with a quick smile and a nod of his head. "And now, old friends, I have to find my wife."

They grinned and fell into step beside him.

Quin spotted his carriage, parked in front of the Green Dragon Tavern. If Edward was following custom, he would persuade Ginny to exchange clothes with her sister or aunt. Then, everyone would enjoy a big laugh when he rescued the wrong woman.

He slammed open the door of the Green Dragon. "Edward, my blockheaded uncle, what have you done with my wife?"

Snickers and stifled laughter greeted Quin as he stalked into the tavern followed by his three friends. He spotted his uncle seated with his back to him.

Edward rose from the long trestle table and gestured to the figure in gold silk next to him. "She's perfectly fine, as you can see."

Quin advanced slowly. A dark veil covered his alleged wife's head. *A trick, to be sure.* He scanned the establishment. Ginny's aunt and sister sat at the trestle table facing him, so she could not have exchanged places with either of them.

He halted behind the figure in gold. "Ginny?"

"My hero, you saved me!" A strange, falsetto voice answered.

The occupants of the room erupted in laughter.

Quin ripped off the veil and lurched back. "Bloody hell!"

George Peeper flushed red as he rose to his feet, dressed in Virginia's golden gown. "Sorry, sir. They made me do it."

Quin gritted his teeth as laughter and bawdy jests filled the room. His friends shook his hand, congratulating him on his lovely young bride. He surveyed the room. Where was she?

In the corner sat a slight figure in breeches and a loosely

fitted coat, an oversized tricorne pulled low over the brow, a giant pewter tankard raised to conceal the face. He ambled over and caught a glimpse of bottle-green eyes watching him.

When he yanked the tricorne off, auburn curls tumbled out. "Good day, madam wife."

Hours later, as the sun was setting, Virginia settled into the carriage for the ride to her new home. She fastened her green woolen cloak under her chin. The party still raged inside Concert Hall, showing no sign of winding down. The last of the revelers would not wear out 'til the wee hours of the morning.

After exchanging clothes with George, she had accompanied her husband back to the hall for an afternoon of dancing and feasting. Worn out and grateful the day was over, she lounged against the cushions of the carriage. As Quincy climbed in beside her, her heartbeat quickened. The day was not over yet.

He smiled and took her gloved hand, turning it over to undo the button at the wrist. "Finally, we shall have peace."

A tremendous, jarring clatter sounded behind them as the coach sprang forward. People alongside the road added to the clanging noise with their whistling and shouted jests.

"Damn. What has happened now?" Quin shouted to the driver to stop. He opened the door and jumped out.

Virginia heard him curse again and peered out the window. "What is it?"

"Come and see." He helped her dismount, then climbed in the carriage and lifted the backseat.

Behind the carriage, she spied half a dozen ropes attached

to the rear axle. On the other ends of the ropes dangled an assortment of old dented pewter tankards, an oversized corset, and a banged up chamber pot.

Quin hopped out of the carriage, knife in hand, prepared to cut the ropes. As he bent over, his wig plummeted into the chamber pot.

The crowd roared in response.

With a resigned sigh, Quin bowed to the audience. He proceeded to saw through the ropes, one by one, while the crowd cheered him on.

Virginia returned to the carriage door. If they could just survive the wedding, the rest of their lives would seem easy.

"May I kiss the bride?" a voice spoke behind her.

She pivoted around. "Oh, Clarence, how are you?" She extended her gloved hand to her new brother-in-law. "Did you enjoy the party?"

"Indeed." He took her hand, lifting it to his lips. "But I shall enjoy living in the same house as you even more." He slipped a finger into the unbuttoned opening of her glove and stroked her skin.

She jerked her hand away. Was he perverse or merely drunk? "Good evening." She retreated to the rear of the carriage, where Quin was located. "Can we go now?"

"Aye." Quin flung the last severed rope to the side.

"Congratulations, old boy, on your lovely bride."

She winced as she heard Clarence's smooth, aristocratic voice close behind her.

Quin straightened, tilting his head to keep his brother in view. "Thank you."

Clarence stepped around Virginia, assessing her with his

leering eyes. "I say, I wonder if your bride will still want you when you lose all that money. Or did you not tell her, old boy, that you'll soon be penniless?"

She noticed Quin's fingers flex around the handle of the knife. He had once told her his brother was an enemy, but she'd always seen them behave cordially to each other. Until now.

Quin spoke softly, "She didn't marry me for my money."

"No?" Clarence smiled. "We'll know soon enough, won't we? Enjoy your wife while you can, dear brother. The court date is set for the end of this month."

"I'll be there." Quin passed by him, eyeing him coldly.

Virginia shivered and followed Quin to the side of the carriage. What was going on between him and his brother?

"Leaving so soon?" Clarence ambled into view, his smile looking more like a sneer. "Perhaps you'll give me the name of your mistress in Cambridge, now that you no longer need her services?"

Virginia gasped.

With a chuckle, Clarence sauntered back into Concert Hall.

No, it couldn't be true. She gave Quincy a questioning look.

With a soft curse, he hurled the knife into the carriage.

She hesitated at the carriage door, spotting the knife embedded in the opposite door. The blade glinted in the setting sun. She glanced at her new husband. How well did she really know him?

His eyes had chilled to the icy color of sleet. "Shall we go home?"

Chapter Sixteen

"This is our bedchamber." Quin thrust open the door.

Virginia swallowed hard and stepped inside. The large canopy bed immediately caught her eye, for it dominated the room. She searched for something else to focus on. Two small tables flanked the bed, topped with silver candlesticks. Two plain wooden chairs rested in front of a hearth of glowing coals.

She fumbled with her gloves. "How nice. I've never had a fireplace in my . . . bedchamber before."

He shoved open another door. "This is the dressing room." Entering, he gestured to a clothespress. "I had this put in for you. Your trunk arrived this morning."

She laid her gloves on the top shelf of her clothespress. Examining the small room, she noted her trunk on the floor next to an empty bathing tub and a second door. "Where does that door lead to?"

"Another bedchamber. No one is using it." He pulled off his gloves and dropped them in a drawer.

His clothespress stood across from her own, and above it,

on a shelf, she noticed five wooden heads lined up in a row—four without wigs. "You have only one wig left."

"Aye. I had the tub put in here, so you would have privacy. Josiah will bring you hot water later. He's the only servant here tonight. I gave the others the night off."

"I see."

He paced to the fireplace. She hovered at the dressing-room door and watched him toss a handful of twigs onto the hot coals. His back to her, he spoke softly. "I need to talk to you."

She frowned as she approached. Tension radiated from him. He had remained in a brooding silence on the ride home, refusing to explain his brother's behavior. Did he remain silent because Clarence was correct? Had Quincy frequented a mistress at the same time he had courted her? "I need to talk to you, too. About what your brother said."

"The court proceedings? I'll explain."

"No, the . . . mistress."

He swiveled to face her. "You believed that?"

She could see the pain in his eyes. "I don't want to believe it."

"Then don't." With a curse he hunkered in front of the hearth and jabbed at the small fire with a stick. "I lied to my brother, told him I had a mistress so he wouldn't question all the afternoons I was gone, practicing with the submersible."

"Oh."

He straightened and looked at her. "You believe me?"

"Yes." She attempted a smile. "I suppose your brother is hoping to cause trouble, though I cannot imagine why."

Quin planted his fists on the mantel and glowered at the

fire. "My father in England gambled away a fortune. In hopes of regaining his wealth, he sent Clarence here to steal Stanton Shipping."

"Your father would take away your livelihood? But you're his son."

Quin shoved away from the mantel. "I don't count, Ginny. I'm a bastard."

"That's ridiculous. I won't have you talking that way."

" 'Tis the truth." He sat in one of the plain wooden chairs and removed some papers from his coat.

She took a seat, facing him. "What will you do?"

He unfolded the papers. " 'Tis already done. When Clarence arrives at court to take over the business, he'll be in for a surprise. Stanton Shipping no longer exists."

"Oh, no! You sold it? Oh, Quincy, it was everything to you and your uncle."

"No, it is not truly lost. We sold it to you."

Her mouth dropped open. "I . . . I didn't buy anything. I haven't the money."

He handed her the first paper. "This is a betrothal contract where I agreed to pay you a bride price."

She scanned the document, noting the huge amount of money cited. "I didn't agree to this."

He handed her two more papers. "The second page is the contract where Edward and I sold you all our shares of Stanton Shipping for the agreed price. The last page changes the name to Munro Shipping and names you as sole owner."

She stared at the papers. Without her knowledge, she had already received a fortune and spent it. "I don't understand. You helped me buy your business with your own money?" She shoved the papers back to him. "It sounds like a silly game."

" 'Tis entirely legal. The business belongs to you."

"I cannot believe this."

He folded the papers and pocketed them. "It was the only way to save the business. We had no choice. We were desperate."

She clenched her hands together, shifting her gaze to the hearth. Close to the fire, a glowing red twig smoldered to a white skeleton. *We had no choice.* She ought to feel relief that Quin had saved his business. She ought to feel relief.

She felt used.

The twig crumbled into a pile of ash. Quin had pushed for the wedding as quickly as possible. Was it because his day in court was coming soon? He admitted he was desperate. Desperate enough to marry. What were the words he had whispered in the smuggler's hole? *There are many good reasons we should marry.*

And this was one.

He had known all along. He needed a wife to save his business.

She swallowed hard. "I didn't realize our marriage would be so . . . convenient."

He rose to his feet and added a log to the fire. "I know this has come as a shock to you, but it needn't worry you."

"Doesn't it worry *you*? What if I sell the business?"

He propped an elbow on the mantel. "You cannot. As a married woman, you cannot sign a contract."

"Oh." What few rights she had possessed had disappeared with marriage. And now she was saddled with a shipping company. A glimmer of hope flickered in her heart. Quin had given her his life's work. "Then you trust me to run the business for you?"

"As your husband I have the right to run your business and spend the profits as I see fit."

"Oh." The glimmer faded away.

He passed by her to take a look out the window. She blinked as hot tears stung her eyes. She was nothing but a decoy, a name to hide behind. For all practical purposes, Quin still owned his business—for she, as his wife, was his property.

She felt strangely numb, sitting by the hearth. And cold, in spite of the warmth from the fire. Shouldn't she be raging against the fates, against tyranny, against a God that gave man dominion over all creatures including herself?

She glanced at the man she had married—the spy who was so adept at portraying himself falsely. Was his desire for her a pretense?

No, she wouldn't believe it. She couldn't.

He was a man who risked his life rebelling against a world designed to use him and a family that rejected him. Were his dreams, his needs so different from hers? Didn't he want freedom and respect? Didn't he want to be loved?

He returned to the fire and plucked out a burning twig which he used to light one of the silver candlesticks. He tossed the twig back into the fire and strode to the dressing room, taking the candlestick with him. "I have to go now."

Her heart lurched in her chest. "You're leaving?"

"I'll be back as soon as possible."

She wandered to the open dressing room door and peeked inside. His gray silk coat lay on a nearby chair. He unbuttoned his black-and-silver brocade waistcoat while kicking off his silver-buckled shoes. The candlelight gleamed off the numerous silver buttons and cast a large, flickering shadow of Quincy against the far wall.

"Where are you going?"

He tossed the waistcoat onto the chair and proceeded to unbutton his lacy cambric shirt. "The night *The Sentinel* burned, the British captured two of my friends." He yanked the shirt over his head and threw it onto the chair. "We intend to rescue them."

She stumbled back against the door, her weight pushing it shut. "You mean to steal them out of jail?"

"No." He pulled on a long, plain shirt of homespun. "The British are transporting them tonight to a frigate due to set sail in the morning. So the deed must be done tonight."

Her heart pounded wildly, and she pressed her hand to her chest. "You plan to attack the British when they move the prisoners?"

"Nothing that drastic." He exchanged his gray silk breeches for a pair of brown woolen ones. "The officers of the British frigate were at the party drinking like fish, and I sent several more casks to the ship in honor of our wedding. By now everyone on board should be in a drunken stupor."

He pulled on plain woolen hose and a pair of old battered shoes. "A companion and I will impersonate two sailors aboard the frigate. When the British arrive with the prisoners, we'll be there to take them. Then we'll take them to another sloop. By morning the two men will be in Rhode Island."

"What if the British recognize you?"

He pulled an old, battered tricorne low on his brow. "Then, I suppose, you'll be a very wealthy widow."

She grimaced. "That is not amusing, Quincy. Why must you do this tonight?"

"The men will die if I don't. Don't worry. I have the perfect alibi. No one would ever believe I could leave you on my wedding night."

She swallowed hard. She found it hard to believe herself. "How long have you known about this?"

"A few weeks. I'll tell Josiah to bring the hot water. You look tired."

She'd be alone in the house with Josiah. What if Clarence returned? The memory of how he had looked at her and stroked her skin sent a quiver of alarm up her spine. "Quin?"

He shrugged on a thick woolen coat. "Yes?"

She hesitated, reluctant to make matters worse between the two brothers. Perhaps Clarence had simply had too much to drink. And she couldn't insist that Quin stay with her, not if it would cost the lives of two men. "Do . . . do you know where your brother will be this evening?"

"Edward is keeping him entertained 'til the wee hours of the morning. I couldn't afford to let Clarence see me leaving the house for this mission."

Virginia exhaled with relief. Now if only her newly wedded husband could survive the night. "Be careful. Please."

"I will." He gave her a fleeting smile. "Don't worry." He strode out the door, his face grim with determination.

He was gone.

She picked up his discarded shirt and slumped in the chair, lifting the soft cambric to her cheek. It was still warm from his body. She buried her nose in it and breathed in his scent. *Please, Lord, don't let him be captured.* Too much, it was all too much.

When Josiah came in, hauling buckets of hot water, she was still in the chair, feeling dazed and numb.

Quin hunched his shoulders against the freezing wind as he hurried home in the dark. He rounded a corner and met an onslaught of snowflakes in the face. Gritting his teeth and holding on to his hat, he strode against the buffeting wind to the back gate of his home.

With a wind like this, the sloop transporting his friends would make excellent time. The plan to rescue them had worked without a hitch. The British had asked no questions, eager to hand over the prisoners and return to their warm barracks. Now a warm bed waited for him. A bed with Ginny.

He opened the gate to the garden. Caught by the wind, the gate banged against the fence. The loud noise echoed down the street. He winced and looked about. The street was empty.

He stepped into the garden, pulling the gate shut behind him. Only Ginny and Josiah should be in the house, for the party was still raging at Concert Hall with all the servants in attendance. Everyone would naturally assume he was in bed enjoying his new wife, not sneaking onto British frigates to abscond with their prisoners.

He passed by the kitchen, his shoes crunching on the frozen ground. A glimpse of movement caught his eye—a shadow moving along the brick wall.

"Who goes there?" He heard no response, only the wind whistling through the trees, swirling snowflakes in the air.

The shadows of buildings and trees wavered as a cloud passed in front of the full moon. He swiveled full circle but saw no one. A gust of sleet-filled air swept the hat from his head, stinging his cheeks. No one would stand about in this miserable weather. It had been nothing more than clouds drifting across the moon. He retrieved his hat and sprinted to the back door.

Ginny would be waiting for him in bed.

He bolted up the stairs, three steps at a time, and raced down the hall. He halted by the bedchamber door to catch his breath. She might be sleeping. He shouldn't barge in and startle her. Better to sneak in and wake her with a kiss.

He slipped inside and closed the door without a sound. The glowing coals in the hearth provided the only light in the room. He crept over to the bed.

It was empty.

He scanned the room. Where was she?

He flung open the door to the dressing room. "Ginny?"

The room was dark. He swallowed hard. Did someone steal her away? He dashed into the bedchamber to light a candle. Bringing the light into the dressing room, he noted the tub still full of water and her trunk, open and empty. She had neatly deposited her clothes on the shelves of the clothes-press.

"Quin, is that you?"

"Ginny, are you all right?" He frowned as he realized her voice was coming from the bedchamber on the other side of the dressing room.

He opened the door and spotted her in bed, the covers pulled up to her shoulders. "What are you doing in here? This room is icy cold."

"Are you all right? Did you rescue your friends?"

"Aye. Why are you here, Ginny?"

"I . . . I was thinking."

"Well, come out of there before you freeze. Come sit by the fire. I'll put on another log." He set the candlestick down in the dressing room and returned to the hearth. As he built up the fire, he puzzled over her odd behavior.

All through the wedding festivities, he had endured teasing from other men. *Women make no sense. Logic doesn't apply to them. Don't try to understand them. You'll end up a broken man, crazed and worthless.*

He had dismissed their warnings, considering it all nonsense. Now he wondered.

Back in the dressing room, he spotted her hovering in the doorway to the adjoining bedchamber. Thick woolen stockings covered her feet, and a white woolen shift reached from her neck to her ankles. She clutched a crocheted shawl around her shoulders. The ruffles of a white mobcap framed her flushed cheeks. Her hair, braided on each side, lent her the appearance of an innocent child.

Of course. She was an innocent. He would need to be more understanding and patient.

He smiled. "Come in." As she inched forward, he reached behind her and shut the door. "Ginny, I would prefer you share a bedchamber with me."

Her knuckles whitened as she gripped her shawl tighter.

He flicked his fingers in the tub of water. "A little cold, but 'twill do." He pulled off his coat and started on his shirt buttons. "Are you hungry? Do you need anything?" He yanked off his shirt and sat in the chair to remove his shoes and stockings.

"No, I'm fine."

He stood to unbutton his breeches. "'Tis snowing outside." He dropped his breeches to the floor.

"Excuse me." She whisked by him into the bedchamber.

He grinned as his underdrawers hit the floor. *Who said you couldn't understand women?* She was merely shy. He stepped into the tub and sat in the cool water. His Virginia was experiencing a normal virginal fear. He reached for the soap, remembering how he had once boasted about rendering her name obsolete.

He lathered up quickly. He would start with gentle kisses and flattery, then draw the sweet passion out of her 'til she was as eager as he. He was definitely eager, in spite of the cool water he sat in. Hopefully, the process wouldn't take too long. He dunked under the water to rinse off.

He stepped out of the tub and reached for a towel. As he dried off he heard her voice from the bedchamber.

"I think, under the circumstances, we should maintain separate rooms."

He halted. "What?"

"Under the circumstances, I think—"

"I heard you." He wrapped the towel around his hips and marched into the bedchamber. "What circumstances are those?"

"The wedding was obviously a decoy in order to provide you with an alibi for the rescue mission and to provide a way for you to maintain control of Stanton shipping."

"*What?*"

"I said—"

"*Wait.* You think I endured that hell today for an alibi?"

She stiffened. "'Tis likely to be the only wedding I will ever have. I'm sorry it was hell for you."

"I didn't mean . . . damn, what is this about an alibi?"

"You used the word, yourself. You said no one would believe you could leave a wedding night. I cannot object to being used if it saved the men's lives for I'm greatly relieved they're safe, but I do think you should have been forthright about it from the beginning."

"The devil take it. What are you talking about?"

She twisted the ends of the shawl around her fists. "I think it is obvious. The timing of the wedding was orchestrated to coincide with the rescue mission. Since the wedding was a ruse to cover your actions tonight, there's no reason to consummate the marriage."

"*What?*"

"As a fellow rebel, I entirely agree with your objectives. Your plan tonight was brilliant. I am pleased to do my part to aid the cause."

He snorted. "Is this some sort of jest? Did my uncle put you up to this?"

Her eyes flashed with anger. "Believe me, this is no jest. I find nothing amusing about entering into a marriage of convenience without foreknowledge. I may not have many rights in this world, but I do believe I have the right to the truth. You should have been honest with me—"

"Dammit, I was honest. I explained everything."

"Yes! *After* the wedding. You should have told me *before*

the ceremony that you were using me to solve your business problem."

"Bloody hell!" He ripped off the towel and flung it aside. *"Does this look like a business problem?"*

Her eyes widened. Her mouth dropped open. She shifted her focus to the ceiling. "I . . . I realize you may be experiencing a small amount of"—her gaze flickered down to his erection and quickly away—"that is, a huge amount of lust, but it is only temporary. Once your problems with your father are over, you may feel the need to annul the marriage—"

"*Enough!*" She wanted to leave him? *Never.* He stalked toward her. "You listen to me, Virginia."

He plucked off her mobcap and tossed it across the room. "There will be no separate rooms."

He yanked the shawl off her shoulders. "There will be no talk of convenience."

He seized the drawstring at her neck and jerked it loose. "There will be no annulment."

"And mark my words." He grasped the opening of her shift in his fists. "The marriage *will* be consummated."

He ripped her shift down the middle.

She jumped back, grabbing at her clothes. "How dare you!"

"I'm just getting started." He snatched her up and deposited her on the bed.

CHAPTER SEVENTEEN

Virginia rolled to the far side of the bed and landed on her feet, facing her husband. "So help me, Quin, you will not take me in anger."

He clenched his fists, breathing heavily. "You will not leave me."

She pulled the halves of her shift together to cover her breasts. "I do not intend to. I'm prepared to remain in the marriage and honor my vows."

"Indeed? Then get in bed."

She stepped back. "No. Not like this. I've endured enough humiliation today."

His face paled. "You're ashamed of me? I realize you could have done much better than a bastard for a husband, but I will be good to you."

Her anger seeped away when confronted by this unexpected vulnerability. "This has nothing to do with an accident of birth. The fact is I was used."

He frowned. "I haven't misused you. I . . . I'm sorry about your shift. I'll buy you another."

"This is not about a shift."

He looked about the room as if searching for answers. "Why are you vexed, Ginny?"

She realized he truly didn't know. "I object to the contracts you made. You're using me to save your business."

He sat on the edge of the bed, frowning. "'Twas not my idea. I never saw the damned contracts 'til today, when you sneaked off with my uncle."

A rebirth of hope simmered in her breast. "Are you serious? You didn't know before the wedding?"

He shook his head. "No. But what difference does it make? Whether the business is in your name or mine or my uncle's, Edward and I will still run it the same way."

"It makes a difference to me."

"I thought you would be happy the business is safe. Surely, you would not have us penniless."

"No." His reasoning made sense from a practical standpoint, but she'd wanted a marriage based on something more than cool logic. Foolishly, she'd hoped for love and desire. Perhaps even a bit of passion.

She perched on the other edge of the bed, holding her shift together. He had ripped it down to her belly. "Did you purposely plan the wedding to coincide with the transportation of your friends?"

"Aye. Does that disturb you?"

She peered over her shoulder, uneasily aware of his nudity. His bronzed arms and torso contrasted with the paler skin of his hips and legs. "I . . . I don't know. I'm grateful the men are all right, but . . ."

"Ginny, I asked you to marry me in the smuggler's hole of

my ship. That was before I knew anyone was captured. The wedding would have happened whether I needed an alibi or not. I wasn't going to let you go."

The woolen shift blurred before her tear-filled eyes. Apparently, she had fallen prey to misplaced fears, but how was she to know how he truly felt about her? He never spoke of love.

Standing, he pulled back the quilted counterpane. "I believe you were disappointed that night for not experiencing a little death. We could take care of that now."

She lurched to her feet, her heart racing as she examined the man she had married. His broad chest expanded with each breath; the black mat of chest hair narrowed to a line, crossing his narrow waist, ending in the thick patch around his swollen manhood.

He slid between the sheets, pulling the counterpane up to his hips. "I haven't used you, Ginny. At least, not yet, but I would surely love to." He patted the bed beside him as his mouth quirked with amusement. "Do you think you could, how did you put it, do your part to aid the cause?"

She scoffed, blinking back hot tears. "And what is the cause? Pleasing my master?"

"I intend to please you. And the cause is becoming husband and wife."

She swallowed hard and perched on the edge of the bed. There had been a few occasions on the farm when she'd seen the mating ritual of animals. It had seemed necessary and natural, as routine as the yearly coming of spring. So she had not expected this amount of trepidation. It was more than a shedding of clothes, a baring of one's breast. She felt as if her very soul would be exposed for his taking. The level of intimacy astounded her.

"Are you afraid of me?"

She took a deep breath and looked him in the eye. "I'm in love with you."

He stared at her, stunned.

She turned away, sniffing as the tears threatened to fall. What had she expected? A dramatic declaration of everlasting love? She squeezed her fingers around the torn edges of her shift, waiting for a response. Any response.

"I . . . I don't deserve you."

She felt the bed shift as he moved behind her. She closed her eyes. He was coming for her.

His breath tickled the back of her neck. "I'll be a good husband."

A good husband would say he loves me. She took a deep breath and opened her eyes. Someday he would tell her. Someday.

He touched the top of her head. Slowly, he traced the line where she had parted her hair. Then he trailed his fingers down her braided pigtails to her shoulders. He kissed a path from the back of her neck to her ear, then whispered, "Lie down with me."

She glanced back at him. His eyes glimmered with heated desire. That much she had expected, but there was more than lust in his eyes. A need, a fear of losing her that tugged at her heart. He hadn't lied in the smuggler's hole. He did need her. She suspected he even loved her. He just didn't realize it yet. But that was something she could help him with.

She turned to him and touched his face. "I'm all yours."

With a grin, he pulled her down on the bed.

A spurt of panic swept through her, and she clutched her shift together. *Calm yourself.* She had enjoyed his kisses in the smuggler's hole. Surely she could enjoy this, too.

"You're frowning." He kissed her brow, then trailed kisses to the tip of her nose. When he placed his mouth on hers, he moved so slowly, so leisurely, that she felt the tension in her body melting away.

Her grip on the shift loosened. There was no need to hold it together. His body pressed against her would keep it from falling open.

It was all right to touch him, too. He wouldn't mind. His shoulders were warm and smooth, the muscles in his arms taut as he kept his weight from crushing her. She buried her fingers in his hair, still damp from his bath.

He deepened the kiss and invaded her mouth with his tongue. His desire seemed to pour into her with liquid heat, sliding down her throat and past her belly to her most intimate flesh. Good Lord, she felt hot and . . . tingly. She pressed her thighs together, but that made her even more sensitive.

He moved his hand down her woolen shift to her breast. With his thumb, he made a wide circle around the nipple. He circled closer and closer on the woolen fabric. Gasping, she pulled away from the kiss in need of air.

It was all right. She was still dressed.

His thumb brushed across her nipple. She shuddered.

It was not all right. Her shift was in the way. "Take it off."

He peeled the material back. "Yes." He took her nipple in his mouth.

She gasped, then gripped his head as he suckled and tugged at her. With each flick of his tongue, she squirmed. It was too wickedly wonderful. Leaning forward, she covered his hair with kisses. It felt damp against her cheek and smelled familiar. He had used her soap in the tub.

He sat up abruptly and tossed back the sheets. Cool air wafted over her moistened breast, causing her to shiver.

"I'll buy you a new one." He grabbed the torn sections of her shift and ripped.

"Wait! I'll take it off." She sat up and pulled her arms out of the sleeves. "It can be repaired."

Grasping the shift, he tugged it past her hips to her knees. He paused, looking her over.

She saw where his eyes were focused and squeezed her thighs together. Heat pulsed to her face. "Must you look?"

A slow smile caused his dimples to appear. "Aye." He touched her, his fingers furrowing into the curls. "You're beautiful."

Her legs disobeyed her, opening slightly. "Quincy?"

"'Tis all right." His fingers slipped between her legs.

She jolted, shocked at the feel of him exploring her, circling and pressing. He found a superbly sensitive spot and tickled it gently. It was ungodly. No, it was heavenly.

He leaned over to kiss her breasts.

She kicked the shift completely off. "I cannot . . ." She opened her legs wider. "Is it wrong for me to want more?"

"No, sweetheart. Enjoy it." He rubbed her harder. And faster.

Her hands clutched at the sheets. "Oh, God." Her toes curled at the slick sound of moisture.

He inserted a finger inside her, teasing her opening, widening it. She felt more moisture seeping from her core. And a delicious coiling of passion, growing hotter and increasingly more intense.

"Quin." She grabbed ahold of him. His fingers quickened to a desperate pace, and she raced with him. Her legs tensed, raising her hips, as the sensations grew stronger, more overpowering.

She was rushing toward something, but she wasn't sure what. Her body jerked when a rhythmic pounding seized her. Wave after wave coursed through her.

"Dear Lord." She gasped for breath. "What did you do to me?"

He grinned. "'Twas a little death, though I would say not so little in your case." He gave her a quick kiss and rose to his knees.

"'Tis an odd name for it. I never felt so alive."

He moved between her legs. "Raise your legs a bit."

She gulped, eyeing the enormous size of him. "Are you sure you want to do that now?"

"Aye." He lifted her knees.

"I don't think we should."

"Of course, we should."

She scooted back. "The fact is, Quincy, I . . . I'm quite certain I do not possess an opening of that magnitude anywhere on my body. Well, my mouth, perhaps, but that would be too strange to lend credence to."

Chuckling, he pressed himself against her. "Don't make me laugh now. I'm barely in control as it is."

She eased away. "But it will not fit."

"It will." He inched closer and positioned himself against her.

She wiggled away. "I know you don't care to admit it, but it cannot fit."

"Will you hold still? Think of doing your part to aid the cause."

"Hah!" She struggled to sit up.

He reached under her and raised her hips, causing her to fall back onto the bed.

"Umph." Her head hit the pillow, and she stared at the white canopy overhead. Dear Lord, he meant to go through with it.

He rose to his knees, dragging her close to him and lifting her hips level with him. She squirmed, but he tightened his grip on her hips.

He positioned her against him. "This may hurt." He plunged in and pulled her to him.

She screamed as much from shock as pain. It felt awful, like a red-hot iron.

Embedded inside, he slowly lowered her hips. "God, it feels good."

"I don't think so."

"Oh, Ginny, you're beautiful."

She frowned, suspecting he was not referring to her face.

He propped himself on his elbows, leaning over her. "I'm sorry I hurt you."

"Can you get off of me now? You've proven your point."

"Aye. My point has been . . . well taken." He glanced down at where their bodies joined and smiled. "But I am not done." Slowly, he eased out and back in.

She closed her eyes. It was such an odd sensation. He was moving inside her. She could feel the length of him filling her completely, then withdrawing, gliding up and down the passage, creating a friction that was slowly becoming quite enjoyable. The burning sensation melted into heated pleasure.

This was not bad, not bad at all. She wrapped her arms and legs around him, her feet still encased in woolen stockings. In fact, it was quite . . . exciting. She felt the pleasure building, the tension coiling tighter and tighter. She had an idea now what they were rushing toward, so she held on to him, enjoying the wondrous sensations he was causing.

He quickened his pace, breathing heavily in her ear 'til he raised his head with a groan. He thrust into her deeply, repeatedly. She gasped when she felt herself reacting, shattering and pulsing around him. He collapsed beside her with a moan that sounded both tired and satisfied.

She closed her eyes, enjoying every little throb that coursed through her. They were one now, husband and wife. She turned to him and touched the dark whiskers on his cheek.

His eyes opened, and he smiled. "Sweet Ginny. My sweet Ginny." He closed his eyes, falling asleep with the smile on his face.

Her heart swelled as she watched him sleep. She had said she was all his, but now he was all hers. She smoothed back his thick black hair. "Quincy Dearling, I love you so."

Thursday, December 28, 1769

Quincy sat in the courtroom next to his uncle and solicitor, keeping his face carefully blank as he watched the proceedings.

"Your Honor, may I present the decision from the court in London?" Clarence handed the paper to the judge. "It clearly states that the capital used to finance Stanton Shipping belonged to my father, the Earl of Dearlington."

"I see." Judge Jeffries adjusted his spectacles as he studied the document from London.

Clarence pivoted, facing Quincy. "Furthermore, the court in London has decided that Stanton Shipping belongs to my father."

Quincy balled his fists under the table. His father had gone through with it, seeking to rob the bastard son of everything he owned. He stared coldly at his brother, who had taken center stage in this farce.

Clarence's eyes gleamed with anticipated victory. He had insisted his solicitor remain at their table and allow him the pleasure of the presentation.

Judge Jeffries removed his spectacles and laid the papers on his desk. "In light of the decision of the British court, I must yield to their authority and rule in favor of the plaintiff. Stanton Shipping now belongs to Henry Stanton."

Quincy felt his uncle flinch. Poor Edward. Now that the business was in Virginia's name, Edward was simply listed as an employee.

With a triumphant grin, Clarence whipped another paper off his table and turned to the judge. "If it may please the court, in this document the Earl of Dearlington gives his son the right to assume immediate control of Stanton Shipping."

The judge frowned. "And which son would that be?"

Clarence laughed, glancing back at Quin. "The legitimate one, of course. Me."

Judge Jeffries pursed his lips, looking Clarence over. "I see. I wasn't quite sure which one of you is the bastard."

Quin smiled at the affronted look on his brother's face.

Edward rose to his feet. "Your Honor, we have prepared an inventory of all items that belong to Stanton Shipping."

With a nod, the judge motioned to Edward to come forward. "That was very gracious of you. May I see it?"

Edward passed the paper to the judge and returned to his seat.

Quincy held his breath, waiting for the judge's reaction. The plan could fall apart now if Judge Jeffries disagreed. The judge scanned the paper, blinked, and put on his spectacles for a closer look.

He looked over the top of his eyeglasses at Quincy and Edward with a glint in his eyes and twitch of his lips. "I see." He removed his spectacles and folded them neatly. "The court gladly gives Clarence Stanton the right to do with Stanton Shipping as he pleases."

"Thank you, Your Honor." Clarence bowed with a flourish. "Such a relief to know that justice can be served, even in this savage wilderness."

The judge cocked an eyebrow at Clarence. "Aye, so it can. Though it seems a great deal of trouble to come all this way for a rowboat."

Clarence straightened with a jerk. "A what?"

"A rowboat." Jeffries offered the paper to Clarence. "Stanton Shipping consists of one rowboat."

"The hell it does!" Clarence ripped the paper from the judge's hand and quickly looked it over. "Your Honor, this is an outrage. Everyone knows Stanton Shipping is an entire fleet of ships with warehouses in several ports."

Clarence's solicitor jumped to his feet. "Let me see that."

Clarence threw the paper at his solicitor and whirled back to the judge. "What has happened to the business?"

Jeffries shrugged. "It has obviously been sold."

"But the money, the money is *mine!*" Clarence banged his fist on the judge's desk.

"No one hits my desk but me." The judge glared at Clarence. "The court in London gave you Stanton Shipping. You have it, sir."

Clarence stamped his foot. "I have nothing! I've been robbed."

"An odd complaint, considering what you were doing." As Jeffries rose to his feet, everyone in the courtroom stood. "Now, I suggest you leave this savage wilderness to those who appreciate it. If you row real hard, you could be home by spring. Court is adjourned." The judge turned on his heel and left the room.

Grinning, Quincy glanced over his shoulder to where Virginia stood with her sister and aunt. The business was safe. He could take care of his wife in the manner she deserved.

Edward chuckled. "Jeffries will have a good laugh with us at the next Freemasons' meeting."

Obadiah Winkle gathered his papers. "Congratulations, for now, but I have a feeling this is not over."

"What have you done with it?" Clarence stormed over to Quin and his uncle. "The business is *mine*."

Gritting his teeth, Quin stepped toward his brother. "It is gone, Clarence. You lost."

"Never. Not to a bastard."

Quin grabbed Clarence by the cravat and yanked him forward.

"Stop it!" Edward pushed between them. "You two are brothers. Dammit, I've had enough."

For Edward's sake, Quin dropped his hand and stepped back.

"You listen to me, Clarence." Edward's voice shook. "We have all lost. Quincy and I worked all our lives to build a business, and it is gone. Now go home and leave us in peace."

Clarence stepped back, glowering at the floor. Edward and Obadiah Winkle passed by, headed to the exit.

Quin had turned to leave when he heard his brother's voice.

"This is not over."

He paused. "Give it up, Clarence."

"How can I? Do you think I can go back to my father empty-handed? I *have* to deliver."

Quin almost felt sorry for his brother, knowing the improbability of anyone ever pleasing his father. "He's using you."

Clarence's face reddened. "No, he's not. It will all be mine someday. No one will take it from me. Not even you."

"It is yours now. Enjoy your rowboat."

"Damn you, you've hidden the business somewhere. You wouldn't sell it all." Clarence moved closer. "I'll find it,

Quincy. And when I do, everything you own will be mine. Every ship, every sail"—his eyes shimmered as he glanced to the back of the room, where Virginia stood waiting—"every lovely bit will be mine."

Quin's blood ran cold. "Touch her and I'll kill you."

Clarence glared back with steely gray eyes. "We'll see who dies, brother."

Quin nodded once to accept the challenge. He strode toward his wife. *Damn that Clarence.* He wanted everything. Even Virginia.

He screeched to a halt with a staggering realization.

She was in double jeopardy. She possessed the body Clarence craved and the business.

"Are you all right?" Virginia asked him.

Good Lord, by signing his business to her, he had endangered her. How could he have been such a fool not to realize it?

"Quin?"

"Aye." Was it his greed, his desire to keep what was his, that had blinded him to reality? He had made his wife a target.

"What's wrong? I thought it went very well."

He looked at his wife. How could he tell her? She would hate him for this. "Aye, it went well enough."

"That look on your brother's face was priceless. Caroline had a terrible time not giggling out loud."

"Aye."

"Aunt Mary is actually speaking to Edward today. She invited us to her house to celebrate. She and Caroline have already left with your uncle."

Quin swallowed hard. Celebrate? If Clarence learned the truth, the easiest way to obtain the business would be to marry Virginia. Then, he could lock her in a hole somewhere and forget about her. No, he wouldn't do that. He would keep her in his bed, servicing him.

"Shall we go? 'Tis a lovely day. Not too cold. I thought we could walk."

"Aye." Quin offered his arm and escorted her down the street. He should warn her of the danger, but how could he? From what he could tell, she was already unhappy with the marriage. She didn't speak of it, but it seemed obvious to him.

Whenever he wasn't home, she ran back to her aunt's house and spent the day there. He was too cowardly to ask her about it, fearing she would bring up the notion of an annulment again. All he could do was show her how much he needed her each night. She responded sweetly to him in bed, but he could sense a sadness in her.

No, he couldn't admit what he had done. He would watch over her carefully to ensure her safety. And he would watch his own back, for the only way Clarence could marry her would be if she were a widow.

Clarence would have to kill him.

CHAPTER EIGHTEEN

Tuesday, January 2, 1770

"Josiah, take this to the Blockhouse Tavern." Quin handed the boy a few coins. "And here is some extra if you'd like to buy a few suckets on the way home."

"Oh, thank you, sir." Josiah pocketed the coins with a grin. "What would ye like from the tavern?"

"Nothing. You're to give the money to the Marine Society. They're meeting tonight."

Virginia looked up from her knitting. "You're not going to the meeting?"

Quin shook his head. "No, I thought I'd keep you company."

She frowned. "But you have to pay a fine if you don't go. I'll be all right if Josiah stays with me."

"Aye, master." Josiah stuck his chin in the air. "I'll take good care of me mistress."

"Take care of your errand first." Quin watched the boy leave. He didn't dare leave Virginia alone in the house with

Clarence, and Josiah was not strong enough to protect her.

She put her knitting in a basket. "I could go to Aunt Mary's and sup with them."

Quin winced inwardly. Ginny spent so much time at her aunt's, he was beginning to think she hated being in his house. He paced across the study. "I don't mind paying the fine. It goes in the Box."

"The Box?"

"Aye. The money is used to help families of captains who lose their lives at sea." *That's it.* Quin halted in midstride.

They would go to sea, sail away for a few weeks. Edward had said the house was rented 'til the fifteenth of the month. After that, the servants would be released, and Clarence would be without a home. Hopefully, his brother would return to England. Then Boston would be safe once more for Virginia and himself. Or relatively safe. There was still the rumor circulating amongst the Sons of Liberty that he had piloted the submersible. If that information reached the wrong ears, he might never be safe in Boston again.

He would check on their warehouses in different ports while Edward took care of business at home. Johnson would understand his need to leave for a few weeks. For that matter, he would tell Johnson he was ready to retire from espionage. Too many people knew about him. And while he was gone with Virginia, he would have time to convince her she had not made a mistake in marrying him.

The Forbidden Lady was en route to the Caribbean at the moment, but the new sister ship was close to completion.

Saturday, January 6, 1770

Virginia woke early and slipped out of bed to the icy dressing room, where she had hidden the packages in her trunk. Noiseless in her woolen stockings, she returned to bed and arranged the packages around her husband.

She slid between the warm sheets and inched closer to Quincy. His tanned arms lay on top of the covers, exposed to the room's chilly air. How did he stay so warm when he slept in the nude? She brushed back a lock of dark hair from his brow. With only one wig left, he had decided to let his hair grow out. She ran her fingertips along his jaw, marveling at the prickly whiskers.

A dimple appeared amongst the whiskers. "And I thought I was insatiable." He looped an arm around her shoulder and pulled her close.

"Wait. We're crushing your presents."

He blinked and looked about him. "What's all this?"

"Presents for you. 'Tis Twelfth Night."

He yawned. "'Tis morning."

"Aye, but I couldn't wait. Open your presents."

Frowning, he sat up in bed. "You didn't have to buy me anything." He opened the first one and pulled out two pairs of woolen stockings. He ran his fingers over the insteps, where she had knitted his initials into the pattern. "You made these for me."

"Aye. They should fit. I made them the same size as your others."

He opened another package. "You made this shirt?"

"Aye." She smiled at the look of astonishment on his face. "Surely, you knew I could sew and knit."

"I . . . I never thought about it. Edward and I always went to a tailor."

"Oh, well, my work may not compare to a tailor's."

"No, these are very nice. Thank you. When did you make these?"

"I've been working on them at Aunt Mary's house so it would be a surprise." She laughed at the dumbfounded look on his face. "You do look surprised."

He winced. "I am. I thought—never mind."

"Here." She handed him two more gifts. "These are from Aunt Mary and Caroline."

He stared at them in his lap.

"Is something wrong?"

He touched them as if to verify they were real. "Why would they give me presents?"

Ginny's heart ached for him. In spite of the whiskers on his chin and manly hair on his chest, he could still seem like a little lost boy. A boy who believed no one loved him. "Quin, you're a member of our family now."

She could see the movement of his throat as he swallowed hard. Aunt Mary had sewn an elegant cravat, and Caroline had embroidered two handkerchiefs with his initials.

He held them lightly as if they might take wing and fly away. "I don't deserve this."

"Quincy." She touched his cheek. "You do."

He pulled away. "No, I don't. I've endangered your life."

"What do you mean?"

"My brother, Clarence. He—"

"I know. He lusts after me, partly because I belong to you, but that's hardly your fault. You musn't blame yourself."

"Has he said anything to you, touched you?"

"No, he just leers at me." She shuddered. "I've been careful not be alone with him."

Quin slipped out of bed to build up the fire. "Is that another reason why you go to your aunt's so much?"

She hesitated. "Yes." Clarence was not the only reason she felt uncomfortable in this house. She had an odd feeling that Mrs. Millstead and Samuel were watching her. "'Tis easier to sew at Aunt Mary's. She has a full supply of needles and thread."

He glanced at her over his shoulder. "You don't?"

She shook her head. "I left most of my supplies at home in North Carolina. I didn't realize I wouldn't be going back."

Frowning, he came back to the bed. "You should have told me. When we arrive in New York, we'll buy everything you need."

"New York? Boston has everything I could need."

"I have a surprise for you, too, Ginny. We're leaving town today."

"She looks just like *The Forbidden Lady*," Virginia observed as Quin escorted her down the wharf. A biting wind blew the hood off her head and she shivered. Though she would miss her sister and aunt, she looked forward to sailing to warmer climes.

"Aye, she's exactly the same, except for the name." Quin

stopped beside the schooner where the name was painted in dark letters. "I named her after you."

"*The Wedded Lady?*"

"Aye." He shifted from one foot to another. "Do you like it?"

Virginia felt like telling him it was not her name, but he looked so hopeful, so worried. "Are you asking if I like being a wedded lady?"

His cheeks reddened. "I was wondering."

She wrapped her hands around the woolen sleeve of his coat and nestled her head against his shoulder. "I love being with you, Quincy, and I love this ship."

With a wide grin, he helped her cross the gangplank. "Let me show you the captain's cabin."

Below deck, he ushered her into their cabin and bolted the door.

"I don't remember *The Forbidden Lady* having a bolt on the door."

He shrugged. "It didn't. I wasn't married then."

She wandered about the small room. Her trunk had arrived and rested next to Quincy's at the foot of the bed. The smell of wood and varnish filled the air, mixed with the aroma of food in the basket on the table. The pinewood table, chairs, and trunk at the foot of the bed reminded her of the night aboard *The Forbidden Lady*, the night Quincy had proposed.

He removed his blue woolen coat and laid it over a chair. She started to remove her cloak, then changed her mind. The air in the cabin was very chilly.

She strode to the bed to make sure there were enough blankets. "Is there a smuggler's hole underneath the bed?"

"Aye." He approached from behind, slid his arms around

her waist, and pulled her back against him. "Hopefully we won't use it. The bed is much more comfortable."

She could feel him swelling against her. "I have a feeling I'll be trying the bed soon."

He reached around her to remove her gloves.

"My hands will be cold," she warned him.

He enveloped her hands in his own and nuzzled her neck. "I know a warm place for them."

"Don't they need you on deck so we can leave the harbor?"

"The first mate will take care of it." He took off her cloak and tossed it onto a chair.

She watched the cloak slip onto the floor in a green woolen puddle. Her heart quickened, knowing the rest of her clothes would soon join it. His fingers tickled her back as he untied her laces.

"Where do you want to go, *chérie?* New York, Philadelphia, Norfolk, Charles Town?" He tugged her gown past her hips and went to work on her petticoats.

Her gown continued to slide down her legs. The skin on her arms tingled. "I want to go everywhere."

"I'll take you. We have our entire lives to explore the world." He dropped her petticoats to the floor on top of her gown. "And explore each other." He unlaced her corset.

She breathed deeply when her corset fell off. He hunched down beside her. His fingers crept up her calves, lifting her shift in search of her garters. She felt the pressure of his fingertips against her bare thighs and her garters loosen.

She looked down.

He was pulling her garters undone with his teeth.

She laughed. "Quincy. You look like a pirate."

"I am." He grinned as he rolled her stockings down her legs. "I'm planning my attack at this moment."

"Oh? Is it going to be different this time?"

He snorted. "Saucy wench." He yanked her shift over her head, leaving her naked in front of him. "I plan to lay siege to your defenses."

"You're going to starve me?"

Smiling, he motioned to the bed. "Lie down."

She slid between the sheet and blankets. Lying flat on her back, she drew the blankets up to her chin. "Don't you plan to undress?"

"In due time. This will not do." He seized the blankets and ripped them off the bed.

"Oh, dear. I'm all aquiver with fear."

He chuckled as he sat beside her. "I'll have you quivering soon enough, madam." He touched her lips with one finger, then outlined them. He ran the finger down her throat, between her breasts and across her belly.

Her skin *did* quiver. She winced as he buried his fingers in her curls. With small circles, he rubbed against her. She closed her eyes as all sensation centered on his fingers.

"Have you ever seen a castle, *chérie?*"

She opened her eyes. "A what?"

"A castle. 'Tis built for defense. Much like you."

"I don't follow."

"Then follow the path of my fingers. Can you feel me?"

"Yes." She tilted her hips toward him.

He slipped his hand between her legs and traced her with his fingers. "This is the outer wall. 'Tis the first line of defense, thick and well-padded."

"Yes." She opened her legs wider.

"I see you are surrendering the outer wall."

"Good Lord, yes."

"Now, this—this would be the outer bailey. Very warm and protected."

She sighed and nestled her backside against the freshly washed sheets. His fingers glided easily as she responded with moisture.

"And now we approach the more sensitive areas of defense. This, madam, is where the battle will be decided."

"Blast you, Quincy, you've already won." She lifted her hips, pressing against his hand.

"Patience, *chérie*. This is the inner wall, so much more delicate than the outer one, is it not?"

"Oh, yes."

"But I know how to break through this wall. You see, there's a secret portal here. If I apply the right amount of pressure, all hope is lost, so sensitive it is to my touch."

She groaned, clutching handfuls of the sheet in her fists.

"Is that a surrender, *chérie*?"

She glared at him. "Yes!"

"Then, madam, I shall invade your keep." He inserted a finger inside her.

"Oh, please." She reached for him, wanting him inside her.

"Patience. I'm not done." He leaned down and tasted her.

She jerked to a sitting position. "Quincy, what are you doing?"

"You even taste like a mermaid."

"What?"

He pushed her back down. "You have surrendered, madam. I may do as I wish."

She gasped for air through gritted teeth as he retraced the paths his fingers had made with his tongue. The spasms struck her suddenly with such force, she lay speechless and helpless, unable to breathe. When she finally took in air, she noticed him frantically unbuttoning his breeches. He plunged inside her.

"Quincy? You're still dressed."

He clenched his teeth. "I couldn't wait."

Smiling, she wrapped her arms around him. "Is that a surrender, *chéri?*"

The Boston Burglar spread his stash of jewels on the walnut table. He sipped his brandy as he admired the shimmer of emeralds, rubies, and diamonds in the flickering candlelight.

So Quincy had run away, the baseborn coward, and taken his delectable bride with him. The fool. With the bastard gone, it would be even easier to sneak into his room and plant one of the stolen jewels amongst the fancy clothes he had left behind.

It was strange, though, that Quincy went on a journey leaving his best clothes in Boston. Also strange that he sneaked out of the house on his wedding night, dressed like a poor man. Quincy seemed to completely lose his dandified behavior when in the company of Virginia or that boy, Josiah. What was the bastard up to?

The burglar enjoyed a pinch of snuff from his silver engraved snuffbox and brushed a few bits of the powdered tobacco from his claret velvet sleeve. Too bad he would have to cease his secret profession while Quincy was out of town. He selected an emerald ring from the table. An excellent piece. A shame he would have to part with it. But it would be worth it if it incriminated Quincy as the burglar. Not only would he, the real thief, be safe from capture, but Quincy would hang. And Virginia would be his.

Friday, February 2, 1770

"Are all the servants gone?" Virginia asked.

"They should be." Quin escorted her and Josiah into their old home after a month at sea. They had arrived in Boston that morning and had returned to the house to gather the belongings they had left. The owners of the house were eager to rent it out again.

Quin opened the door to the study. "Josiah, run up to the servants' floor and make sure they've moved out."

"Aye, Uncle Quin." Josiah grinned and scampered up the stairs.

Quin turned to Virginia. "Uncle Quin?"

She smiled. "I suggested on board *The Wedded Lady* that he call me Aunt Ginny. The Uncle Quin part was his idea."

"I'm still his master. I cannot have the boy thinking he doesn't have to mind me."

She sighed. "Has it occurred to you that he might mind you because he loves you? You're his hero."

Quin hooked a finger in his neckcloth to loosen it. "I . . . we have work to do."

He pivoted on his heel and stalked into the study, straight for the secretaire. *Uncle Quin.* Of all the ridiculous names. He jerked open the desk drawers, searching for anything that was his. Everything that pertained to his life as a spy had long ago been burned. He stacked his books into a cloth sack.

Virginia handed him a few skeins of knitting wool rolled into balls. "Who actually owns this house?"

"The Higgenbottoms." Quin dropped the yarn into his bag. "'Twas their home before Mrs. Higgenbottom decided it was too small and the furnishings too plain."

"Oh, so Priscilla lived here as a child."

"Aye, I suppose." Quin spotted some movement in the hall. "Josiah, is that you?" He strode into the hall as two figures dashed for the front door.

Samuel ran out the door, and his mother shut it behind him.

"Mrs. Millstead? Why are you here?"

The cook nervously wrung her hands. "I . . . we was living upstairs to keep an eye on the place for the Higgenbottoms. We heard ye come in and thought we'd make sure ye're weren't no burglars."

Quin swung the cloth sack over his shoulder. "We're gathering our possessions. Where was Samuel going?"

"Oh, he—" She gulped and twisted her apron in her hands. "The thing is, Mr. Stanton, we ain't been paid for this last month."

"You should see my uncle about the matter, though I doubt you worked very hard with us gone."

"We were waiting on his lordship 'til he left."

"My brother left?"

"I, well, he ain't living here." Mrs. Millstead glanced over her shoulder at the front door.

Quin stepped toward her. "He's still in Boston?"

"I don't know nuthin'." Mrs. Millstead darted past him to the back of the house. The back door slammed, echoing through the cold, empty house.

Virginia approached him, frowning. "Mrs. Millstead behaved so strangely."

"Aye." Quin started up the stairs to fetch the expensive clothes he had left. He paused. Something wasn't right. "I think we should leave."

"Why?"

"I'm not sure." He yelled for Josiah to come down.

The clattering sound of horseshoes on cobblestones echoed in the street.

Quin gripped the banister. "Ginny, leave out the back. Head straight to Edward's. I'll find Josiah and meet you."

Her face paled. "I don't want to leave you."

The front door burst open as a dozen redcoats marched in, carrying muskets. Colonel Farley entered after them.

Virginia gasped and stepped back.

Quin descended the stairs at a leisurely pace. He hoped his calm demeanor appeared genuine. "Good afternoon, gentlemen. I say, dear Colonel, what a smashing surprise." He reached the ground floor and dropped his sack on the floor. "Such a delight to see you again." He swept his tricorne off his head and made a leg.

Lifting his chin, the colonel narrowed his eyes. "We've been waiting for you to return to Boston, Mr. Stanton."

Quin set his hat back on. "To what do I owe the pleasure? Are you planning to rent this house next?"

"You will remain here while my men search the house." Colonel Farley motioned to the soldiers. One soldier headed for the study, while four more bolted up the stairs.

"What a curious homecoming." Quin brushed imaginary lint off his sleeve, feigning nonchalance while he tried to figure what these men could be looking for.

Colonel Farley grabbed the cloth bag and emptied the contents on the floor. The balls of wool unrolled across the floor.

Did they know he was a spy? Quin forced a smile. "Ah, you caught me. I've been knitting naughty things."

The colonel flung the cloth bag on the floor. "You know very well what evidence we seek."

"I assure you, I have no idea what you seek." Quin ambled toward Virginia. Noting her pale face, he took her hand.

The soldier who had examined the study brushed past them. Quin felt Ginny flinch and tightened his grip.

"There's nothing in the study, sir," the soldier reported.

The colonel nodded. "We'll find it."

A yell from upstairs sounded. The four soldiers bounded down the stairs, their boots pounding on the steps.

"We found it, sir." A redcoat handed a small item to the colonel. "'Twas in his clothespress."

"An emerald ring." Colonel Farley held the piece of jewelry up to catch the light. "I believe Mrs. Ashford will be able to identify this as the one stolen from her by the Boston Burglar."

Quin blinked, caught off guard. "You cannot possibly believe that I—"

The colonel interrupted, "I know for a fact that you were present at each place a robbery occurred."

"So were many people."

Colonel Farley continued, "I know that the robberies ceased for the past month you were out of town."

Quin snorted. "That proves nothing. I'm a wealthy man. I have no reason to steal." The so-called evidence was ludicrous. He swallowed hard when he realized what was happening. He would be in jail, unable to protect Virginia.

The colonel lifted the ring with a satisfied smile. "And the final proof—this ring found in your bedchamber. You're under arrest, sir. The Boston Burglar has been found."

"No!" Virginia advanced toward the officer. "Quincy is not a thief."

Colonel Farley stared down his nose at her. "Calm yourself, madam."

"Virginia," Quin spoke quietly. "Take Josiah and go to my uncle."

She spun around and stared at him. "I'll not leave you."

Quin gritted his teeth. "May I have a word with my wife, Colonel?"

The officer nodded. "A brief one."

Quin grabbed her arm and pulled her across the hall. He leaned over to whisper in her ear. "You're in danger, Ginny. Get the hell out of here and go to my uncle."

"Me?" she whispered back. "Quin, it is you they will hang."

He squeezed her arm. "Ginny, do as I say."

Her eyes filled with tears.

"Enough," the colonel announced. "It is time, Mr. Stanton." The soldiers surrounded him and yanked his hands behind his back to tie them.

Colonel Farley eyed him with scorn. "So much for the Boston Burglar. What have you to say for yourself now?"

Quin shrugged. "Pardon me, do you have any *Grey Mouton?*"

Chapter Nineteen

Virginia stumbled back as the redcoats led her husband out the front door. She sprinted to the back door, wrenched it open, and halted.

Josiah. He was still in the house. She swiveled toward the stairs and dashed up, calling Josiah's name. No answer. He must be on the third floor amongst the servants' quarters.

"Josiah?" She flung open a door and froze.

Clarence Stanton stood across the room, one arm looped around Josiah's neck, the other holding a knife to the boy's cheek. "So kind of you to come, my dear. We've been waiting for you."

She glanced at Josiah to reassure him, but the terror in his wide blue eyes filled her heart with dread. *You're in danger.* Quin's words echoed in her head. How had he known?

Clarence stepped toward her, dragging Josiah along. "I asked the boy to call you here, but the little wretch refused to cooperate. Lucky for him, you came anyway."

"Let him go."

Clarence sneered. "As you wish." He smashed the hilt of

the knife against the boy's head, and Josiah crumbled to the floor.

"No!" She lunged forward.

Clarence seized her arm. "You're coming with me."

"No." She twisted and kicked at him.

"You'll come or I'll kill the boy."

She stilled. If she cooperated 'til Clarence was a distance from the house, Josiah would be safe. "Very well."

She allowed him to escort her down the stairs. Quin had known of this danger. How?

"This way." Clarence ushered her out the back door.

An icy gust swept a flurry of snowflakes in her face. She shivered, grateful for the chill that sharpened her senses. She recognized Quin's coachman, tied and gagged just inside the fence.

Clarence led her through the back gate. "So kind of my brother to bring his coach."

She noted the new driver of the carriage. Samuel Millstead. "You shouldn't steal the coach. It belongs to Quin and Edward."

"Actually, you're wrong." Clarence opened the carriage door and motioned with his knife for her to climb in. "I've learned some very interesting news. The coach, the ships— everything belongs to you."

That was why he wanted her? Virginia settled in the middle of the backseat, spreading out her skirts to take up the entire space. She'd never realized how valuable she was until now.

He sat across from her and closed the door. The coach sprang forward.

She pulled her woolen cloak tightly about her shoulders and mentally reviewed the facts. Clarence had discovered she owned the business. The redcoats had arrested Quin as the Boston Burglar. Samuel Millstead had run out the door shortly before the arrival of the redcoats. Now he drove the carriage. "The Millsteads are working for you?"

Clarence shrugged. "I promised them a nice reward when this is over."

She gazed out the window of the carriage. She could fling open the door and jump, but she should wait 'til they were farther away from Josiah. And the cobblestones would make for a hard landing. Better to wait for a mound of snow to make her leap. Meanwhile, she needed to decipher this puzzle.

Samuel must have alerted the redcoats that she and Quin were in the house. Clarence had been upstairs, waiting. He knew Quin would be arrested, so he must have known about the stolen ring in Quincy's clothespress. He must have planted it.

Clarence smiled at her, his eyes gleaming. "You seem very calm for someone who's been abducted."

"I've been kidnapped before."

He snorted. "That was a childish prank. This is the work of a genius."

"A genius? I thought you were a common thief."

His face grew pale. He tightened his grip on the knife. "You're too clever for your own good. Fortunately, for you, I need you alive." His lips curled into a sneer. "That is, until we're married. Then who knows? Accidents do happen."

The hair on the back of her neck prickled. "You cannot marry me. I have a husband."

He laughed. "Not as clever as you thought, are you? Why do you think I was willing to part with one of the rings? I had to incriminate Quincy. I don't need to kill the bastard if the government will do it for me."

She swallowed hard as the full extent of his plan became clear.

"I would suggest, my dear, that you keep whatever limited intelligence you have to yourself from now on. I find clever women quite unattractive." His eyes roamed over her. "But the rest of you is pleasing enough, and you will please me, madam, whenever I wish."

Her stomach cringed. "The law may not allow you to marry your brother's wife."

"If the problem arises, 'twill be easily handled. My father has only to swear in court that Quincy is not his son. He has never admitted to the bastard."

She glanced out the window. She would have to jump soon.

"Why, look." He followed her line of vision and peered out the window. "We have reached the gallows at the Neck. I wonder if this is where Quincy will hang?"

A gibbet swayed in the breeze, the decaying body of a criminal encased inside. White snow outlined the form like a hideous snowman. Her stomach churned. *No, never, not Quincy.*

"I do hope they will construct a gibbet large enough for Quincy. I would hate to see the old boy crammed into one that was too short." Clarence turned to her with an amused smile. "A good fit is so important, don't you think?"

She reached for the silken cord overhead and yanked.

It happened so suddenly, she sat and gawked, her fingers still curled around the looped cord. Taken unaware, Clarence had not made a sound. He lay, slumped awkwardly on the front seat under the heavy iron bar. His knife clattered to the floor. The open trapdoor swayed with the movement of the coach.

She couldn't afford to let Samuel Millstead know what had happened, so she would still have to jump from the moving carriage. She reached for the door and paused. When Clarence awoke, he would come after her. She needed as much time as possible.

She searched his pockets, pulled out a large handkerchief and tied it around his mouth, knotting it behind his head. A large bump on his head was swelling fast.

Recalling the hidden compartment under the backseat, she lifted the cushioned seat and looked inside. Three muskets and two knives lay inside—weapons she shouldn't leave with the enemy. She grabbed a length of rope and tied Clarence's hands behind his back. Hopefully, Samuel would keep driving for hours, oblivious to his employer's dilemma. She looked out the window. Mounds of snow lined the road.

She threw the three muskets and knives out a window, tossed out Clarence's knife, opened the door and jumped.

Snow muffled the sound of her landing, but did little to ease the shock to her body. Moaning, she lifted her head and looked around. Her body was slowly sinking into a drift of snow, the cold seeping through her clothes to settle into her bones. She rolled over onto her backside and looked at the coach in the distance. The forward movement of the coach had caused the door to shut. She had escaped without notice.

She sloshed through the knee-high snow, stepped into an unseen hole and plunged in up to her hips. Icy-hot pain shot through her ankle. She limped to the spot where the muskets and knives had landed and gathered them up. It didn't take long to realize she couldn't carry the extra weight all the way back.

Her stiffening limbs objected when she eased onto her knees by the gallows. She burrowed a hole in the snow close to the dead man and dropped in the weapons, keeping one knife for protection.

The gibbet creaked with a rusty scrape as a gust of frigid air blew past. She shivered, watching the snow-covered body sway before her eyes.

"I only hope you will not have company soon."

The metal groaned in response as the gibbet slowly rotated. The dead man's face came into view. Two hollow eye sockets stared back at her.

A wave of nausea doubled her over. She grabbed a handful of snow and pressed it to her brow. *You cannot give in.* She stood, wincing at the pain in her ankle, and hobbled down the road into Boston.

A few blocks down Orange Street, a cart stopped next to her.

"Can I offer you a ride, mistress?"

She glanced up, flexing her grip on the knife inside her woolen cloak. The young driver looked familiar. "Do I know you?"

"I work at the bookseller's on Hanover Street. I'm delivering books today. I can take you somewhere."

Of course. He had delivered Josiah's books months ago. "Yes, p-please."

He helped her onto the cart, and she gave him directions to her aunt's south-side house, the closest place of safety. When they arrived, the youth escorted her to the door.

"Thank you so much." She opened the door and glanced back. He was already driving away.

"Aunt Mary, Caroline!" She limped into the hall, dropping the knife to the floor.

Aunt Mary took one look at her and yelled to Caroline to fetch hot water. She ushered Virginia into the parlor and sat her on the settee by the fire.

"What has happened?" She added wood to the fire.

Virginia's teeth chattered as she began to shake. "They arrested Quincy. Clarence k-kidnapped me."

"My stars! You poor dear, are you all right?"

"Yes. Aunt Mary, he's the B—B-Boston Burglar."

"Clarence? How do you know?"

"He planted one of the rings he s-stole in Quin's clothes-press, so the redcoats would arrest Quincy instead of him."

Caroline entered with a large pot of hot water.

"Set it in front of her," Mary ordered. She dropped to her knees in front of Virginia to pull off her shoes. "Good Lord, lass, your ankle is swollen."

"Aye." Virginia cried out when her aunt plunged her feet into the hot water.

Mary dragged a wooden chair close to Virginia and set a plump pillow on it. "Prop your foot up, Ginny. Caroline, tell George to fetch Edward Stanton here, immediately. Quincy has been arrested."

"Good Lord!" Caroline fled from the room.

Mary sat next to Virginia and took her hand. "Tell me what happened."

Virginia settled against the cushions to retell the day's events, then jerked up straight. "Josiah! I have to go to him. He's hurt and all alone."

Mary pushed her back. "You're not going anywhere. When George returns, we'll send him."

Virginia had finished her story when a pounding on the front door startled her. "Can that be Edward, so soon?"

Caroline and Mary dashed to the front door. Virginia watched the parlor entrance, waiting for the visitor.

"Josiah!" She laughed when the boy threw himself on her lap and wrapped his arms around her.

"Aunt Ginny, I thought I lost you."

"No, sweetie. Are you all right?" She examined the blood-matted cut on the side of his head. "Caroline—"

"I know." Caroline headed for the kitchen. "More hot water."

"How did ye get away from that scurvy bugger, Aunt Ginny?"

Virginia described her escape once more while she cleaned the cut on Josiah's brow.

His bottom lip quivered. "I wanted to protect you, but I couldn't. I came here, looking for help. I untied the coach-man, and he ran to Edward Stanton's house."

Virginia blinked, fighting off tears she had no time for. "Josiah, you're the bravest little man I know."

Footsteps sounded in the hallway as George and Edward barged in unannounced.

"Tell me everything," Edward demanded.

Virginia sighed and retold the story while Josiah cuddled up close.

"George." Edward passed him a few coins. "Rent a carriage and bring it here immediately."

"Aye, sir." George sprinted from the room.

"Do you wish me to come with you?" Virginia asked.

"Yes." Edward cleared his throat. "Mary, I want you and Caroline to pack some clothes. Your servants, also. Your entire household will come with me."

"What?" Mary leapt to her feet.

"I cannot keep you safe here. You must move in with me."

Mary sputtered. "I cannot possibly live in your home. What would people think?"

Edward stepped toward her. "You don't understand the gravity of this matter. Clarence will stop at nothing to get what he wants."

"I understand Ginny must live under your protection—"

"Mary," Edward interrupted her. "If Clarence cannot get his hands on Ginny, he'll come after you or Caroline or anyone else she cares about in order to lure her into his possession. You're all in danger."

Mary gulped. "Caroline, you will inform Edward that he may bully me into living in his house, but he cannot force me to speak to him."

Caroline grinned. "My aunt says—"

Edward gritted his teeth. "I heard her."

Monday, February 5, 1770

Virginia limped into Edward's parlor. Although her ankle had improved, she tried to keep off of it as much as possible. She surveyed the spartan room with dismay. Two plain Windsor chairs flanked the hearth, the mantelpiece above adorned with a single pewter candlestick. The walls and windows remained bare of any decoration; only a plain wooden table rested alongside one wall. Edward's home on Prince Street had obviously been the domicile of two single men who valued work over comfort.

Her sister sat in one of the Windsor chairs in front of the fireplace.

"Caroline, where is Aunt Mary?"

"She—she's not in her bedchamber?" Caroline's brow furrowed as she concentrated on her knitting.

"No, I looked. Where could she be?" Virginia eased into the other wooden chair.

"Are you all right, Ginny?"

"I . . . I'm not sure." At first Virginia had believed the recent shocking events to be responsible for her bout with nausea, but she had experienced another episode this morning. After a month at sea with Quin, she suspected this was not a nervous disorder.

"What's the latest news about Quincy?" Caroline asked.

"Edward's solicitor, Mr. Winkle, has requested a meeting with the judge tomorrow. They're hoping to get the case dismissed without a trial." Virginia sighed and gazed at the fire. "Poor Quincy. Edward told me his cell is icy cold."

"Aye, so I heard. I'm making him a scarf and mittens."

"Oh, that's sweet of you, but I hope he'll be released tomorrow. I wish they would let me see him. Where *is* Aunt Mary?"

Caroline winced when she dropped a stitch. "Now look what you made me do."

Virginia frowned, suspecting her sister knew more than she was telling. "Where is she?"

"She'll be back soon. There's no need to worry."

"She *left*? Edward will be furious." Virginia clutched her middle when her stomach twinged.

"Ginny, are you ill?"

"I don't think so. I . . . I wanted to talk to Aunt Mary. I believe I'm with child."

Caroline flung her knitting to the side. "Ginny, that is marvelous news!"

"'Twill not be marvelous if the child has no father. Or if he grows up with all of Boston thinking his father's a criminal."

Caroline reached over to squeeze her hand. "Everything will be fine."

"It is not fine. Edward told us not to leave the house. Why did Aunt Mary disobey him?"

"She's determined to pay Edward back the money he gave her, and Josiah told her about these shops where you can sell your jewelry. So she took Josiah and her old wedding ring. No one will know."

"I think Edward should know about this."

"Oh, no, Ginny, you mustn't tattle on Aunt Mary. She'll be so vexed with you."

"Then she can stop talking to me, too." Virginia limped into Edward's study.

After hearing about Mary's escapade, Edward threw on his coat and charged to the door.

"That woman! She'll learn to mind me." He slammed the door shut.

Virginia winced. Caroline stood at the entrance of the parlor, shaking her head.

They returned to the parlor and were deep in a discussion about making things for the baby when a loud banging on the front door interrupted them.

"Good Lord!" Virginia jumped in her seat. "Who could that be?"

"I'll find out." Caroline dashed to the front door.

Virginia rose to her feet. "Be careful."

When her sister squealed, Virginia hobbled into the hall and stopped short. "Papa?"

Jamie Munro released Caroline from a big hug and strode toward Virginia. "Ah, lass, 'tis happy I am ye're all right." He enveloped her in his arms. "I thought I'd never find you two. I went to Mary's house, and 'twas all locked up. What is happening here?"

Virginia leaned against his strong chest, breathing in his familiar scent of pipe tobacco and wool. "'Tis a long story. Oh, Father, I'm so glad you came."

"How are Mama and Fergus?" Caroline asked.

"Yer mother and brother are fine. They send their love." Jamie pulled Caroline toward him so he had an arm looped around each daughter. "Thank God ye warned me, Caroline. I came as fast as I could. Ginny, how could ye marry the bastard who tried to purchase you?"

Virginia stepped back. "Father, he's not a bastard."

"Well, actually, he is." Caroline shrugged when Virginia glared at her.

"Doona fash yerself, lassie. I've come to take care of the matter."

Virginia frowned. "What do you mean?"

"Now, doona look all sour-faced at me, Ginny. I've come a long way, and I'll no' be thwarted." He planted his fists on his waist. "I mean to kill the bastard."

Virginia groaned.

Caroline snorted. "You'll have to wait in line."

"Have you seen a lady, about so tall, accompanied by a boy?" Edward asked the shop owner.

"Aye." The shopkeeper spit on a grubby glass case and smeared the grime around with a tattered cloth. "She would have sold me the ring, but that wretched boy told her to try elsewhere. Thought he could force me up on me offer, the little bugger."

"Thank you." Edward proceeded down the narrow lane, weaving through piles of snow-covered garbage. At least, most of the refuse was so frozen it didn't stink. He passed a millinery shop that, by the looks of the half-naked woman in the window, masked a brothel.

How could Mary do this? Her childish behavior put herself and the boy at risk. She must have suffered greatly in the past to be so touchy.

A snowball hit him on the chest. He stopped and watched a group of young boys dressed in ragged clothes run away. Out of a doorway stepped two familiar forms, Mary and Josiah.

"Mary! What are you doing? This is no place for a woman—" He forgot his anger when she ran toward him, her green eyes sparkling.

"Edward, I'm so glad you're here!"

He smiled. "You're talking to me again."

"Of course, this is important. When Josiah and I were in the shop down the street, I noticed a diamond brooch in the glass case. Then, Josiah and I tried this shop, and I saw a ruby ring."

Edward shrugged. "Do you want me to buy it?"

"No! I recognize it. 'Tis the ring that was stolen from Mrs. Higgenbottom. And I believe the diamond brooch down the street must be the one stolen from Mrs. Oldham."

Edward stared at her, then laughed. "Do you know what you've done, Mary? You've saved Quin!" He grabbed her by the shoulders and planted a kiss on her mouth.

It took a little time, but Edward convinced the two shop owners he was willing to pay a reward for the capture of the real Boston Burglar. To collect the reward, they were to come to the courthouse the next day and tell what they knew.

Edward escorted Mary and Josiah back home. She had remained silent since he had kissed her. "Are you all right, Mary?"

"Oh, I almost forgot." She fished out a handful of coins from her purse. "This is the first payment for what I owe you."

"I don't want your money." Edward mounted the steps to his front door.

"But I sold my wedding ring to do this. I'm serious, Edward."

"I'm serious, too." He opened the door with a sly smile. "I'll buy you another."

"Another what?"

"Another wedding ring."

Her mouth dropped open. A grinning Josiah slipped past her into the house.

Edward touched her shoulder. "Come in, Mary. 'Tis too cold out here."

She ambled inside with a dazed look.

He shut the door and called out. "Ginny, I have good news!"

A huge, redheaded man barreled out of his parlor. "There ye are, ye bastard!" The man raised his fists. "Prepare to defend yerself."

"Who the hell are you?" Edward asked.

Mary gasped. "Jamie! What are you doing here?"

Jamie glared at her. "Stand aside, woman. I've come to kill the man."

Mary leapt in front of Edward. "Ye'll no' hurt him!"

Edward leaned over to whisper in her ear, "As much as I love this sign of devotion, Mary, I can fight my own battles."

"Father." Virginia tugged at her father's arm. "He's not Quincy."

Jamie glowered at Edward. "He looks like him. But ye're a wee old for my daughter, don't ye think?"

"I'm Quincy's uncle, Edward Stanton."

Jamie turned to his daughter. "This is no' the bastard ye married?"

"No, I married another one." Virginia winced. "Quincy is a fine man."

"Aye? Then where is this fine man?" Jamie asked.

Virginia glanced at Edward. "Well, he . . ."

Caroline grinned. "He's in prison."

CHAPTER TWENTY

Tuesday, February 6, 1770

"Can you describe the man who sold you the ruby ring?" Obadiah Winkle asked as he crossed the courtroom.

The shopkeeper pushed a greasy strand of hair from his face and hooked it behind an ear. "Aye, I can." He glanced sidelong at the judge. "I didn't know the ring was stolen."

"Of course," Winkle agreed. "The man's description, please."

"Well, he had black hair, cut short, like he might wear them fancy wigs, and he was dressed in real fine clothes."

Colonel Farley rose to his feet. "Your Honor, this man is describing Quincy Stanton. I assure you, I arrested the right man."

"I'm inclined to agree with you, Colonel." The judge eyed Quincy with a look of disgust.

Sitting behind the defendant's table, Quincy kept his face carefully blank and his posture stiff. It was hard to appear calm and dignified when he hadn't slept or bathed in days. With his dirty, rumpled clothing and unshaven face, he knew he looked every inch a criminal.

"Mr. Stanton, will you please stand?" Winkle asked.

Quincy rose to his feet. He was too exhausted for anger, but still capable of shame. Why had Edward brought Virginia here to witness this? And if circumstances weren't bad enough, she had her father with her. The large redheaded man was scowling at him as if contemplating different methods of torture.

"Is this the man who sold you the ruby ring?" Winkle asked the shopkeeper.

"No, he ain't."

The colonel gaped, then quickly regained his wooden composure. "The witness is mistaken, Your Honor."

"No, I ain't." The shopkeeper twisted in his chair to face the judge. "The man what sold me the ring was shorter and broader. His skin was pale."

"I see." The judge frowned at Quincy. "How do you explain the ring found in your clothespress?"

Quincy cleared his throat. "Your Honor, my wife and I were out of town for the month prior to the search. Anyone could have planted the ring during that time in order to incriminate me."

"Your Honor." Edward stood up beside Quincy. "We have a second shopkeeper who will corroborate the first one's testimony."

The judge nodded his head. "Quincy Stanton, do you know who would wish to set you up in this manner?"

"Aye—"

"We have no idea," Edward interrupted. He sat and pulled Quincy into his chair.

Quin whispered to his uncle, "What are you doing?"

Edward laid a hand on Quin's shoulder. "You're like a son to me, but Clarence is still my nephew."

Quin shrugged off his uncle's hand. "I cannot believe this."

"You wish to see your own brother hang?"

"He deserves it." Quin gritted his teeth. "'Tis what he planned for me."

"I am prepared to rule," the judge announced. "In light of the new evidence, I'm dismissing the charges against Quincy Stanton. Colonel Farley, I suggest you look elsewhere for the Boston Burglar. Perhaps, if you start with an accurate description of the man, you will have better success."

Colonel Farley nodded, his face reddening. With a final glare directed at Quincy, he pivoted and marched from the courtroom. As the judge rose to his feet, everyone stood.

Quin leaned toward his uncle. "Edward, if you don't turn in Clarence, I will. He's still a threat to Virginia and our business."

"Don't worry. I have a plan." Edward motioned to their solicitor. "I need to talk to Winkle. Why don't you give your wife a hug?"

Because I don't deserve her. Quincy watched Virginia rush toward him, smiling. He groaned inwardly when he saw the slight limp in her steps. It was his fault for placing her in danger.

"Quincy!" She wrapped her arms around him.

He held her tight and breathed in the scent of lavender he

had missed as much as sleep and warmth. "Thank God you're all right."

Edward had described her escape from Clarence, thinking the news would cheer him during his stay in prison. It had, for a few moments. Then guilt and shame had crept in like the icy drafts through the thin walls to settle into his bones. He had endangered her. He had failed to protect her.

He eased away from her embrace. "I need a bath."

"Aye, ye do." Mr. Munro towered behind his daughter. "I've met polecats that smelled better."

"Father, please." Virginia frowned at him. "Quincy cannot help his condition. He's been in jail for several days."

"Humph. So I hear." The huge Scotsman narrowed his eyes.

"How do you do, sir?" Quin extended a hand and restrained from wincing when Mr. Munro tried to crush his bones.

"Congratulations." Mary Dover kissed him on the cheek.

"Thank you." Quin accepted another hug, from Caroline. "Can we go home, now? I think I could sleep for a week."

Wednesday, February 7, 1770

"I beg your pardon. I didn't realize you were here." Having just entered the study, Quin turned toward the door to leave.

"Doona fash yerself. Come in, lad." Virginia's father sat up on the pallet by the hearth and stretched. "All the bedchambers are full, so I'm sleeping in here. Would ye care for a wee dram?"

"Yes, thank you." Quincy approached the warmth of the glowing coals and sat down. After sleeping all night and most of this day, he felt better equipped for this confrontation. He had no doubt Virginia's father wanted a few words with him.

Mr. Munro poured two drinks and handed him one. With a yawn, the Scotsman settled in another chair. "Feeling better, are ye now?"

"Yes." *No.* He could hardly face his own wife.

"Ginny and yer uncle explained the situation to me, how yer father wants to steal yer business."

"Mr. Munro, I assure you, if I had realized beforehand the danger to Ginny by ceding the business to her, I would never have agreed."

"Call me Jamie. Would ye have preferred to lose yer life's work?"

"I would prefer anything other than endangering my wife."

Jamie Munro sipped his whiskey and studied Quin with narrowed eyes. "After I finish my drink, I'll be wanting to bash you around a wee bit."

Quin sighed. "I deserve that much, no doubt."

"Aye, ye do, for whining like a wee bairn. Do ye think I raised my children to be helpless fools? If ye insult their intelligence, I'll be taking it personally."

"Excuse me?"

"I raised my children to take care of themselves. My lassies are quick and clever. They doona need a man to look out for them."

Quin gulped down some whiskey. "It is my duty to protect my wife."

"Aye, and 'tis also yer duty to protect yer land, or in yer case, yer business. But ye're no' alone, lad. Ginny can fight alongside you. She has the blood of Highlanders in her veins."

Quin set his glass down with a clunk. "No offense, sir, but I do not wish to rely on Ginny's bloodlines to keep her safe. Nor do I expect her to fight like a man."

Jamie banged his glass down. "Doona ever underestimate a Highlander. She has intelligence and bravery to see her through. Just look how she handled that Clarence bastard when he kidnapped her."

"I know she saved herself." Quin jumped to his feet and paced across the room. "I should have been there. Dammit, I should have been honest with her. She had no idea Clarence would come after her."

"Why did ye no' tell her?"

Quin halted, staring at the bookcase before him. Ledgers for the last twenty years of Stanton Shipping filled the shelves—ledgers he had painstakingly learned to keep in order to please his uncle, even though as a young boy he had hated it. He had lived with the fear that Edward would reject him. Just like his father had. "I was afraid she would leave me." He heard Jamie pouring himself another drink.

"I may still have to bash you in the nose."

Quin turned to face the Scotsman who appeared to bark more than bite. "What have I done now?"

"Hasna Ginny said she loves you?"

Quin shifted uncomfortably. "Aye."

"Do ye think I raised my children to be liars?"

"No, of course not."

Jamie downed his drink and settled on his pallet in front

of the hearth. "Lad, when the woman says she loves you, ye should believe her. She'll no' be leaving you."

Quin ambled over to where the huge redheaded man stretched out on the pallet. "I expected to hear something to the effect that I'm not good enough for your daughter."

Jamie yawned. "That goes without saying, but ye'll do."

"You think so?"

"Oh, aye, I knew that when I heard ye were in trouble with the British authorities. To a Highlander, that's a positive trait." Jamie rolled onto his side. "Good night, laddie."

"**W**hy should I listen to you, Stanton? You were wrong about your brother. Quincy Stanton is not the burglar." Colonel Farley took a seat behind the desk in the Ashfords' study.

Clarence calmly sipped his Madeira. "Has it occurred to you, Colonel, that Edward Stanton may have paid for the testimonies from those shopkeepers? You saw them. Those types could easily be bought."

"Damn!" The colonel slammed his fist on the desk. "These Americans have embarrassed me for the last time."

Clarence studied his buffed fingernails. "There have been other times?"

"Aye, blast them. I had two of those damn rebels in my grasp after the destruction of *The Sentinel*, but they escaped."

"A pity." Clarence rose to his feet and sauntered over to the sideboard to refill his glass. In spite of his cool demeanor, he fully sympathized with the colonel's desire to curse and hit furniture. He had sacrificed a valuable piece of jewelry in order to trap his brother, and the blasted plan had not worked. That damned wench, Virginia, had put a knot on his head the size of an apple, and now Quincy was free. "These Americans are far too arrogant."

"I agree. My men cannot go anywhere without the Colonials flinging mud and curses at them."

Clarence returned to his chair. "How did the two rebels escape?"

"'Twas the night of your brother's wedding. We were to deliver the men to a British frigate, which we did, but then the two men disappeared."

Clarence gripped his glass tighter. "It happened on Quincy's wedding night?" He had ordered Samuel Millstead to watch his brother, and that had been the night when Samuel had seen Quincy sneak home through the back gate dressed in common clothes. Had Quincy helped the two rebels escape? "Did you ever discover who destroyed *The Sentinel?*"

"No. But since he handled that submersible so well, I believe him to be a sailor."

Or a sea captain, Clarence thought, sitting up in his chair. That was the night Quin came home late with the story he had been with Virginia when, according to the Millsteads, he had been at the harbor with Josiah. "Your men chased someone onto Quincy's ship, did they not?"

"Aye, but we found no one."

"Think, man. Have there been any other odd occurrences?"

The colonel leaned back in his chair. "Yes, an important letter disappeared off this very desk, and the next day it was in all the papers. At first I suspected one of Mrs. Ashford's servants, but none of them can read. So I can only conclude it was one of her guests."

"Do you remember which night that was?"

"Of course. 'Twas the night of the ball when that damned burglar robbed Mrs. Ashford." Colonel Farley sipped his drink. "You remember. Captain Breakwell and I searched the men. 'Twas your suggestion."

"And the missing paper was not found."

"No, nor the jewels. Whoever it was, he must have sneaked out and hidden—I say, do you think the Boston Burglar stole the paper, too?"

"An interesting notion." Clarence thought back. That was the night Quin and Virginia had dashed from the party in a great hurry. When they returned, he had stashed the jewels in Quin's carriage. And a very interesting carriage it was, with the hidden rod in the ceiling and compartment under the backseat.

Clarence nodded his head slowly. He could still be rid of his brother. The title would be his. The business, the fortune, everything. And Father would never threaten to disown him again.

Smiling, Clarence lounged back in his chair. "I think you are on to something, Colonel. My brother is much more than the Boston Burglar. I believe we can prove he's a spy."

Thursday, February 15, 1770

"I believe I'm with child." Virginia stopped when she saw the surprised look on her aunt's face. "I'm amazed Caroline didn't tell you."

"No, not a word." Mary gave her an excited hug. "This

is marvelous news! I'm so happy for you. I always wanted to have children."

"It may not be too late for you, Aunt Mary."

"Och, now, doona be silly. Certain things require a husband." Mary busied herself pouring them two mugs of hot chocolate.

Virginia smiled. "I believe there's a willing candidate here in this house."

Mary blushed. "Enough of me, lass." She handed a mug to Virginia and sat across from her in Edward's parlor. "Now, how did Quincy take the news?"

Virginia curled her fingers around the pewter mug. The heat seeped through the metal into her cold hands. "I haven't told him."

"Why not? It might cheer the man up. He seems a wee grim these days."

"I know." Virginia chewed her lip. Quincy's behavior had been much on her mind the past week. He insisted she stay home, where she could be safe, but rarely spent time with her. She had an odd feeling he was embarrassed in her presence. His lovemaking had a tinge of desperation to it that disturbed her. "I believe it is very difficult for him—the way his British family treats him. His own brother wanted him to hang."

"Aye, poor Quin," Mary agreed. "But Edward tells me he has a plan to send Clarence home to England for good. With the testimonies from those shopkeepers, he can threaten Clarence with exposure if he doesn't leave."

"I see." Virginia lifted her mug of chocolate and breathed in the comforting aroma. "We will certainly rest easier then."

"Aye." Mary nodded and sipped from her mug. "The only

problem is Edward cannot threaten Clarence 'til he finds out where the man is hiding. My stars!" Mary stared at her brother when he sauntered into the parlor. "What have you done, Jamie?"

Jamie smiled lopsidedly with a puffy cheek and cut lip. "I came looking for a wee bashing, and I found one."

Virginia frowned. "You didn't hit Quincy, did you?"

"Nay, lass. 'Twas a few of those filthy redcoats. Whatever is in this pot?" He lifted the lid and snorted. "Chocolate. The stuff is for bairns."

"Aye, so it is." Mary gave Virginia a knowing smile.

"Father, you shouldn't pick fights with the soldiers."

"Now, lass, the wee beasties were askin' for it." Jamie splashed whiskey into a glass. "They attacked a group of ropemakers for no good reason. One of the soldiers asked for work, and a ropemaker kindly offered to let him clean his privy." With a grimace, he swallowed his drink.

"You should clean that cut," Mary said.

"The whiskey will take care of it." Jamie turned his head when Quincy appeared in the doorway. "Ye missed a good fight, lad."

Quin leaned on the doorjamb. "I hear there's a brawl with the redcoats every day now."

"Aye," Jamie agreed with a smile. "This Boston is a lively place."

Virginia sighed. "Father, this is not a game. The British are armed with muskets and cannon."

"Aye, I was thinking, we should get some muskets, too." Jamie pivoted to Quin. "Are there any in the house?"

"Only one. I had more, but they were in the coach my brother stole." Quin scowled at his shoes.

"Clarence doesn't have them," Virginia announced. "I threw them out and hid them by the gallows on the Neck."

Quin raised his head and stared at her.

Jamie chuckled. "That's a good lass."

A banging on the front door drew their attention. Quin strode toward the door. Virginia set down her mug and followed her aunt and father into the hall.

Colonel Farley and a dozen redcoats marched in. Virginia felt a shiver creep down her spine. *No, not again.*

"What's the meaning of this, Colonel?" Quincy demanded. "We proved I am not the Boston Burglar. If you want him, I suggest you look for my—"

"I suggest you hold your tongue, young man." Colonel Farley unrolled a document. "You'll not pay your way out of this one. I thoroughly investigated the matter. Found a man who rows a boat on the Charles River with an interesting story. He identifies you as the pilot of the submersible used to destroy *The Sentinel*."

Quin's face visibly whitened.

Virginia rushed forward. "That's not true. He was with me that night. Remember, Aunt Mary? 'Twas the night he proposed to me."

The colonel dismissed her with a scornful look. "I would expect you to defend your husband, but 'twill not help. We have all the proof we need. Quincy Stanton, you're under arrest for high treason."

★ ★ ★

CHAPTER TWENTY-ONE

Virginia clutched her stomach as a wave of nausea swept through her. She swallowed hard, determined not to be ill in front of Quin.

His face harsh and pale, Quincy stood quietly while a soldier tied his hands behind his back.

Jamie strode toward the door. "I'll come with you, lad."

"No," Quin spoke through gritted teeth. "I'll go alone. Stay here and watch Virginia."

"We'll send Edward and Mr. Winkle." Virginia approached Quin and pressed the palms of her hands against his cold cheeks. "'Twill be all right. We'll not give up."

His jaw tightened, the muscles rippling under her hand. "Stay with your father. He can protect you." Quin pivoted and marched from the house with the soldiers.

As the door shut, it blurred before Virginia's tear-misted eyes. "Nooo." Her voice filled the silence with a soft, mournful cry. Her knees buckled, and she collapsed in a heap of woolen skirts on the hallway floor.

"Jamie, move her into the study by the fire," Mary ordered. "She can lie on your pallet."

"Aye." Jamie helped Virginia to her feet.

She felt as if she were floating and their voices were far away. This couldn't be happening. Her father set her down on his pallet and stoked the fire.

Smoke stung her tear-filled eyes. It crept into her nostrils with the memory of death.

Her stomach lurched. She grabbed a leather fire bucket from the hearth and retched 'til her stomach was empty.

"Ginny." Mary hunched down beside her, offering her a handkerchief. "Lie down. You must be strong for the sake of the baby."

"Baby?" Jamie jumped to his feet. "Are ye expecting a bairn, lass?"

Virginia splayed her hand over her belly as she rolled onto her side. "Aye, but he'll not have a father." Tears rolled across her face, dropping onto her father's pallet. "What will we do?"

"'Twill be fine, Ginny." Jamie squatted beside her and rubbed her back. "He was released before when they thought he was a burglar. 'Twill be the same way with this treason nonsense."

"'Tis not nonsense, Papa. Quin did blow up *The Sentinel*."

Jamie sat back on his heels. "He blew up a British ship? How?"

"With a submersible. And a bomb with some sort of delayed flintlock device. Quincy tried to explain it to me. He's very knowledgeable about such matters."

"So all that fancy fop business is pretense?"

Virginia nodded. "Aye. Quincy is a spy."

Jamie stood upright. "Ye have a fine man for a husband, lass. Are ye certain he's no' part Scots?"

Friday, February 16, 1770

"I have to wonder, William, why you would come to the home of an accused traitor." Virginia sat across from Captain Breakwell in the parlor.

He shifted uncomfortably in the plain wooden chair. "I have debated over the wisdom of this, but I feel I should offer my condolences."

She flinched inwardly. The man had already buried her husband. "We believe these charges will be dropped."

"May I be of some service to you through this trying time? My investment in a slave ship has given me a small fortune. I could send you away from this distress."

Her first inclination was to scream at him never to court a woman while her husband yet lived. She gripped her hands together and took a deep breath. "Actually, William, there is a matter where you may be of assistance. So far, the jailer has not allowed me to visit my husband. If you could do something?"

"Of course. It is admirable that you continue support the man—"

"My husband is innocent. I believe he is the victim of a conspiracy."

The captain frowned. "How so?"

"Quincy's brother had him arrested for burglary. I'm certain he's behind this charge of treason, also. He will not stop until he is rid of my husband."

"Why would Clarence wish his brother harm?"

She explained the situation including Clarence's attempt to kidnap her, but carefully avoided anything incriminating to her husband. "We can prove Clarence is the Boston Burglar. He'll do anything to reestablish his wealth, even if it means killing his own brother."

William fell back against the wooden frame of the chair, his mouth agape. "I had no idea. What an unscrupulous wretch! Do you plan to turn Clarence in to the authorities?"

"Edward wanted to use the proof to force Clarence to return to England, but we don't know where he's hiding."

"I know where he is. Mrs. Higgenbottom offered him a room in hopes he would court Priscilla."

Virginia winced. "Poor Priscilla."

"Yes," William agreed with a frown. "I saw her a few days ago. She's not at all happy about the matter."

"Of course not. No woman could be safe married to Clarence. He threatened to dispose of me after obtaining my wealth. Oh, dear." Virginia gripped the arms of her chair. "Priscilla is an heiress, is she not?"

William leapt to his feet. "She could be in danger."

Caroline entered with a tea tray. "I have brought refreshments."

"My apologies. I cannot stay." William sprinted out the front door.

Caroline watched his quick exit with a confused look. "What happened to him?"

"He's charging to the rescue." Virginia stood and paced about the room. "Has Edward returned from his visit with Quin?"

"No." Caroline set the tray down. "Because of the captain, I made some real tea. Would you like a cup? It might help calm you."

"How can I remain calm with Quincy in jail?"

"Mr. Winkle said this could drag on for weeks. You must think of the baby."

Virginia stopped at the window and leaned her brow against the snow-frosted glass. She shivered as the cold seeped into her. How many cold, sleepless nights must Quin endure? "You mean I should think of the baby because it will be all that remains of my husband."

"I didn't mean it like that." Caroline pulled her away from the window. "Come, sit down. We must remain hopeful."

Virginia sat and listened halfheartedly to Caroline's description of the magnificent cradle Jamie planned to build for the baby. The front door creaked as it opened and shut. She watched Edward tramp across the hall into his study without a word. Her eyes blurred with tears. There was no good news to report.

"Excuse me, Caroline." Virginia rose to her feet and ambled to the entrance of the study. Edward sat slumped over his desk, his face resting in his hands. "Did you deliver the scarf and mittens Caroline made?"

Edward lowered his hands and nodded his head. "Aye. And the blankets. They should help to keep him warm."

"Captain Breakwell stopped by. He says Clarence is staying with the Higgenbottoms."

"I see." Edward stared blankly at his desk.

"We could force Clarence to leave."

"Aye, or I could turn him in." Edward surged to his feet

and strode to the sideboard to pour a drink. "Splendid! I can see both my nephews hang. We can make it a family reunion."

She winced at the pain that shook his voice. "We mustn't give up hope."

"Ginny, this is my fault! *I* convinced Quin to spy. I talked him into it." He slammed his glass down on the sideboard, spilling the contents. "Damnation! I was so stupid, so bloody patriotic, I didn't stop to consider the danger."

He beseeched her with tear-filled eyes. "What have I done? Quin is a son to me."

Her eyes stung with hot tears. "You shouldn't blame yourself. Quincy understood the risk he was taking."

Edward paced toward the hearth and planted his fists on the mantel. He slouched forward, gazing at the fire. "There will be a hearing in a few days. The governor wants to make an example of Quincy and send him to England for trial."

He would be gone forever. Her heart constricted in her chest. The tears brimmed over to stream down her cheeks. She drew in a shaky breath. "I have to see him before he goes."

"No."

"Captain Breakwell will obtain permission from the jailer so I can see him."

Edward shook his head. "Ginny. The jailer doesn't mind if you see Quin or not. I just told you that to spare your feelings."

"What are you saying?"

Edward turned his head, regarding her sadly. "Quin doesn't want to see you."

She stumbled back a step. "No."

"He doesn't want you to see him in jail. He has his pride."

"*Pride?* 'Tis more like shame. I demand to see him, Edward. He needs me."

"It is the one request he has made."

She marched up to Edward. "I am with child. He has the right to know."

"With child?" Edward pushed away from the mantel. "Bless you, Ginny. I will take you. Quin needs to hear good news for a change."

"What news?" Jamie strolled into the study.

Virginia wiped her cheeks dry, savoring the small victory. "Edward is taking me to see Quin."

Jamie raised his eyebrows. "Och, that's good. The lad has come to his senses now?"

Her small moment withered. She slumped into a chair. "You knew he didn't want to see me?"

Jamie touched her shoulder. "Ginny, the man does love you."

She shook her head. "I'm not so sure." Why was Quincy rejecting her now?

Jamie snorted. "What is the problem with the two of you? Ye canna believe ye love each other?"

"He has never told me."

"Ye heard him, lass. When they arrested him, all he could think aboot was you and yer safety. He loves you more than himself."

She made a sound like a sob confused with a laugh. "More than himself? Papa, he doesn't love himself very much!"

Jamie crossed his arms across his broad chest. "Well, he's certain to be learning quick. Any man facing death should acquire a wee amount of self-appreciation. I'm sure, in time, he'll realize how much he loves you."

She shook her head. "He doesn't have time."

CHAPTER TWENTY-TWO

Monday, February 19, 1770

"Damn."

Quin's curse, softly spoken, did little to make Virginia feel welcome in the dismal surroundings. She peered down the empty corridor as her eyes adjusted to the dark.

Her footsteps on the stone floor echoed about her ears. The stench of full and forgotten chamber pots assailed her nostrils. A thick wall of stone rose to her left, gray and damp to the touch. To her right, a row of iron bars ran the length of the hallway, interrupted by brick walls to separate the different cells.

A sliver of a window, positioned high on the back wall of the first cell, faintly lit the room with differing shades of gray. A blast of frigid air blew in the uncovered window and rustled the loose rushes on the stone floor. The cell was empty.

With a shudder, she proceeded down the corridor. "Quin?"

"Who's that?" A gruff voice emerged from the second cell. "Come closer, darlin'. Let me see you."

"Ginny, stay close to the wall." Quin's voice came from the cell at the end of the hallway.

She veered closer to the stones just as the man in the second cell made a grab for her through the bars. With a yelp, she jumped back.

"Dammit, Ginny. This is no place for a lady." Quin stood, a grimy cheek pressed against the bars as he watched her progress. "Why did you come here?"

"I had to see you."

"Like this?" He stepped back as she hastened to him. Dark circles lined his eyes while four-day-old whiskers shaded his jaw.

"Yes. You're my husband. For better or worse."

"I've certainly provided you with the worst." His wry smile faded. "And it only took me two months."

She curled her fingers around the icy metal bars. "You provided me with the best."

His eyes glimmered with moisture. "Thank you. It was the happiest two months of my life." He turned his back and roamed toward the back of the cell.

She pressed against the bars. "Quincy." How could she reach him? He was retreating into this jail of cold rock, distancing himself from her to dull the pain.

He stopped at the back wall. Splaying his hands against the glistening stone, he leaned forward and rested his forehead. Snowflakes drifted through the small window above him and landed on his head and shoulders.

"Come away from there, Quin. 'Tis too damp and cold."

"What could happen? I could freeze to death. Or catch a fatal illness. Both preferable to what awaits me."

She gripped the bars tighter. "We brought blankets to keep you warm."

He sighed and ambled over to the wooden bench that served as his cot. "Thank you." He sat on the blankets, rested his elbows on his knees and leaned forward to study his hands. Slowly, he eased a silver ring down a finger of his left hand.

"Caroline knitted the scarf and mittens for you. We're all very worried about you."

He remained silent, sliding the ring up and down his finger.

"Is there anything else we can bring you?"

"There are a few things you can do for me."

She pressed her face against the cold, clammy bars. "Anything."

"Sell the business and leave Boston. Go home with your father. With the money you'll make, you can live comfortably—"

"Stop it! Stop talking like you're dead."

He snapped his gaze toward her. "I *am* dead. It was wonderful, Ginny, but it is over. The sooner you realize that, the sooner you can get on with your life."

"No! I love you, Quincy."

He leapt to his feet. "How can you? I failed you as a husband. At least I provided you with enough funds—"

"Stop!" She reached an arm between the bars, stretching toward him. Tears filled her eyes. "I only wanted you. Please, don't give up hope."

"I have hope—hope that you'll put this behind you and find joy in your life. I want you to be happy, Ginny."

The tears rolled down her cheeks. "I don't want happiness if you're not with me."

He paced about the small cell, kicking the rushes with his shoes. Small clouds of dust and debris floated around his feet. He stopped and stared aimlessly at the wall in front of him. "There's a part of me that cringes at the thought of you finding happiness with another man. But I know that is selfish. I *do* want you to be happy. I love you."

She covered her mouth to stifle the sobs that threatened to break loose. Now she heard the words she had longed for? Now, when she was going to lose him?

He grimaced. "Dammit, I'm causing you more pain. Go now, Ginny, and leave Boston. I would not have you endure the shame of being the widow of a criminal."

She wiped her cheeks. "I could never be ashamed of you."

He wandered to the back wall. "Thank God we have no children."

She froze. "What?"

"I grew up with shame. It is not something I would wish on a child. Take Josiah and go home with your father."

She staggered back. The news of their child would give him no comfort. Her back collided with the stone wall. Cold shivers shot down her spine.

"Good-bye, Ginny," he whispered.

"No! I'm not leaving town. I'll see you again." She raced down the gloomy corridor and wrenched open the door to the jailer's office.

She remained silent on the walk home with Edward.

He guided her across the street of churned-up mud and snow to his house. "Did you tell Quin about the baby?"

She moistened her chapped lips. Cold air stung her swollen, tear-filled eyes. "No."

Edward sighed. "I shouldn't have taken you." He held her arm as they ascended the icy steps.

"He wants me to leave Boston." She stepped into the hall. "He wants me to sell the business and leave, like this was all a bad dream."

Edward closed the door behind them. "From Quin's standpoint, it must look entirely hopeless, but I'll not give up."

She removed her cloak and shook off the snow. "Neither will I."

Caroline peeked out of the parlor. "There you are. We have guests."

Virginia wandered into the parlor. Priscilla Higgenbottom dashed toward her and embraced her. Captain Breakwell paced about the room.

"I'll bring refreshments." Caroline headed to the kitchen.

Edward hovered at the parlor door, frowning at the redcoat officer.

Captain Breakwell bowed. "Excuse our intrusion into your home, sir, but I didn't know where else I could take Miss Higgenbottom."

Virginia noted Priscilla's red, swollen cheek. "What happened?"

Priscilla grasped Virginia's hands. "It was terrible! I don't know what I would have done if William hadn't been there." She glanced at the captain with adoring eyes. "He saved me."

"Saved you from what?" Edward asked.

"Clarence." Priscilla collapsed into a wooden chair. "He attacked me."

"Good Lord." Virginia sat across from her. "What happened?"

"William calls on me every afternoon while Mama is resting in her room." Priscilla blushed and gave the captain an apologetic look. "Mama doesn't quite approve of him."

"I rented a carriage to take Priscilla for a ride in the country," William explained. "She went upstairs for her cloak."

"I found Clarence in my bedchamber, digging through my jewelry," Priscilla said.

Virginia winced. Clarence must be short of funds again.

Priscilla continued, "I ran toward the stairs, but he caught up with me. He told me he had bought me a gift and was putting it in my room for a surprise. I knew he was lying for William had told us the truth about him."

"You know he's the burglar?" Virginia asked.

"Yes, but Mama refuses to believe it. She still thinks your husband—" Priscilla winced. "I'm sorry."

"That's all right. Continue, please," Virginia urged.

"When I told Clarence I would tell the authorities, he slapped me. I ran down the stairs, but he followed me. Then William dashed out of the parlor and punched Clarence again and again." Priscilla beamed at the captain. "He was so brave."

"Where is Clarence now?" Edward asked.

"I left him knocked out at the Higgenbottoms'," William said. "I was more concerned with Priscilla's safety at the time, so I brought her here in the coach. I didn't think you would mind."

"No, not at all. If you will excuse me." Edward bowed and left the room.

Virginia followed him out. "Edward, what will you do?"

"I'll convince Clarence to go home, but if he ever sets foot in America again, wreaking havoc with my family, I vow I'll kill him myself."

"Wait. He may be dangerous. Take my father with you."

Edward shook his head. "Jamie should stay here to protect you."

Virginia watched Edward leave, then headed back to the parlor. She stopped short in the entryway. Captain Breakwell and Priscilla were locked in a passionate embrace, totally unaware of her presence. She eased back and tiptoed to the kitchen.

Caroline glanced up as she placed cups and saucers on a tray. "'Tis almost ready."

Virginia sat at the kitchen table. "I believe they would prefer to be left alone for a while."

Caroline raised her eyebrows. "Priscilla and William?"

Virginia nodded. "At least some good has come from all this."

Tuesday, February 20, 1770

Edward saw the dismay on her face as they neared the coffeehouse on Union Street. "What's wrong, Virginia?"

She stalled at the entrance. "Quin took me here once."

Edward examined her face—the red swollen eyes edged with dark circles, the raw nose, and chapped lips. He opened the door. "I'm sorry. This is where Johnson asked us to meet him."

With a sigh, she entered. "I don't understand how Quincy's secretary can help us."

Edward led her to a table in a corner. He positioned a chair close to Virginia and sat. "Johnson is not a secretary, but an employer."

"I don't understand."

Edward leaned closer. "Johnson recruited Quin to work for him."

"You mean—"

"Aye." Edward nodded. "Johnson is the man in charge for the Boston area."

"Oh, I never knew."

"You weren't supposed to." Edward greeted the waitress who approached them.

"Good evenin'. Me name's Sukey. What can I get for you?"

"Hot chocolate and coffee," Edward ordered.

Sukey inspected Virginia. "I remember you, miss. This is a different man ye have now. Did ye give up on the other one?"

Virginia shook her head. "No, I have not."

Sukey narrowed her eyes. "Good." She strode toward the kitchen.

Virginia removed a crumpled handkerchief from her purse and dabbed at her nose. "Any news about Clarence?"

"No." Edward had hurried to the Higgenbottoms' house the day before, hoping to catch his nephew. "Clarence took off with Quin's carriage. No one knows where he is. He must be lying low, waiting for Quin to be deported."

"What do you think he'll do next?"

Edward shrugged. He feared Clarence hadn't given up his hopes of acquiring Stanton Shipping through Virginia, but he didn't want to cause her more worry at this time. He was saved from answering her when Mr. Johnson entered the coffeehouse.

The short man, dressed in brown wool, sat across from them at the table. "Good evening, Edward. Mrs. Stanton." He nodded his head to each of them.

Edward leaned forward. "Is there anything you can tell us?"

"Nothing new. They want Quin to stand trial in England."

Edward shook his head. "We cannot allow that. We should rescue Quin when the British move him to the transport ship."

Johnson studied his clasped hands on the table. "Quin and I rescued the other two men that way. The British will be prepared for something like that. Such a plan cannot work twice."

Edward searched his mind for other ideas. "We have to do something."

Johnson spread his hands on the table's surface. "It is already done."

"Then you have a plan?" Virginia asked.

"All I can say is Quincy has the means to escape the execution."

"What do you mean?" Edward asked. "He has no weapons."

Johnson drummed his fingers on the wooden surface. "There is nothing I can do without endangering more of my men."

"Then don't use them. Ginny's father and I will do whatever is necessary." Edward heard Virginia gasp and turned to her. "What's wrong?"

She grabbed Edward's left hand. "You have no ring. I

thought Quin's ring was from the Freemasons, but then you would wear one, too."

"What are you talking about?"

She pointed at Johnson's left hand. "He has a ring just like Quincy's."

Johnson raised his eyebrows. "You're an observant woman, Mrs. Stanton." He flicked open the top of the ring to reveal a fine white powder. "All my men wear one of these, myself included, just in case." He snapped the lid into place.

Virginia muffled a sob with her handkerchief.

Edward stared aghast at the ring. "I don't believe it."

Johnson clasped his hands together. "Quin accepted the ring."

Edward leapt to his feet. "That is your solution? *Poison?*"

Johnson looked about. "Calm yourself, Edward."

Edward sat, gripping the edge of the table. "I will not accept this. Neither will Quin."

Johnson shrugged. "He agreed to wear it."

"Damnation." Edward hit his fist on the table. "That was before he was married and expecting a child."

Johnson glanced at Virginia. "A child?"

She nodded her head and wiped her eyes with the crumpled handkerchief.

They remained silent as Sukey approached with a tray. She placed the coffee and chocolate in front of Edward and Virginia. With a glare at Johnson, she clunked a mug of coffee in front of him. "Ye didn't place an order, so I brought you whatever I felt like." She arched an eyebrow at him. "Sometimes I like to play God and make decisions affecting other people's lives." She marched off in a huff.

Johnson watched her departing figure, his expression grim.

Edward wrapped an arm around Virginia's shoulders. "We will not accept this."

Johnson stood, reached in his brown wool coat and tossed a few coins on the table. "Quincy knows what to do." He swiveled on his heel and strode out the door.

Thursday, February 22, 1770

Four paces from the bench to the jail bars. Quincy heaved himself to his feet and walked the four steps. If a man could die of boredom, he'd already be a lifeless corpse. He turned and faced the back wall. Ten paces from the bars to the window. He shuffled to the back wall and stood under the open window.

The window was both friend and enemy. On nights like this, he could look out at the stars and pretend he was at sea with his old stellar friends watching over him. But the comfort came at a high price. He could only tolerate the frigid air for a short while.

He ambled back to the bench and sat. He had tried bribing the guards with his silver shoe buckles or ring. They refused to let him go, but offered to take the silver in exchange for allowing him more comforts. He had asked for a candle, thinking he could use his small stash of gunpowder to escape, but that request had been refused. Johnson had ordered his other spies to stay away rather than risk exposure.

Quin sighed and leaned back against the cold, gritty wall. What to think about next? Anything but Ginny and the pain he had caused her. The cell seemed a bit smaller each day, a bit darker each night. Once again the bastard was shut away in a cold, dark room. But now he was no longer a child. He had too much to live for.

Now he was loved.

Somehow, he needed to escape before they deported him. Here he had friends and family who would help him. Once in Britain, his chances would be limited. He flipped open his ring. He could barely see the poison in the dark.

He snapped the ring shut. Better to die attempting an escape.

Sunday, February 25, 1770

"Is she asleep?" Edward poured himself another mug of coffee.

"Aye." Jamie tucked a blanket around his daughter where she lay on his pallet in the study. "Puir lass. She's exhausted, trying to stay awake every night."

Edward nodded. He felt the same way. How could he sleep, fearing that Quincy might decide in the cold of night to take the poison? Every morning he rushed to the jail to see if Quincy still lived. He beseeched his nephew to give him the ring, but Quin refused.

The hearing had taken place on Friday. The judge had marched in and announced that Quin would leave on the eighth of March to stand trial in England. The judge refused to listen to any petitions from Winkle. In a matter of minutes, Quin was doomed to die a traitor's death.

Edward leaned back in his chair at the desk. "I'm grateful you have remained in Boston. If Quin thought Ginny was leaving with you, I'm afraid he would take the poison immediately."

Jamie paced about the room. "Aye, we'll stay. I tell you, this town is growing more angry each day. The funeral for the wee lad is tomorrow."

"Aye." Edward knew the Seider family, who would be burying twelve-year-old Christopher the next day. A gang of youths had attacked a customs employee who had retreated to his house and fired a musket at the boys. Young Christopher had died.

Edward sipped his coffee. "As tragic as it is, I think the atmosphere of violence may work to our favor."

Jamie stopped in front of him. "Ye mean the redcoats are too occupied with the brawls in the streets."

Edward nodded. "They may not be watching the jail so carefully."

"I was thinking the same thing." Jamie leaned over the desk. "We have ten days before the lad goes to England."

"I know the layout of the jail. I've been there every day."

"We should do it at night. The guards will be different and no' recognize us."

"I agree." Edward grabbed his penknife to sharpen a quill. "If I present Johnson with a workable plan, he might agree to it. Some of Quincy's friends have volunteered to help."

"How about a week from tomorrow?"

"That would be Monday, the fifth of March." Edward reached for a blank sheet of paper. "Pull up a chair, Jamie. We have plans to make."

"I want to be in on it." From the pallet, Virginia heaved herself to her feet.

Jamie frowned at her. "I thought ye were sleeping."

"Just resting a bit. I want to help."

Edward exchanged a doubtful look with her father. "This could be dangerous."

"Aye," Jamie agreed. "Ye should thinking of the bairn, lass. Ye'll be risking more than yer own neck."

"I am thinking of the baby. He needs a father." Virginia sat at the desk, a stubborn look etched on her tired features. "I intend to rescue my husband."

CHAPTER TWENTY-THREE

Monday, March 5, 1770

Jamie stopped the coach a block south of the jail.

Edward stepped out and helped Virginia, Mary, and Caroline dismount to the deserted street. "Everyone knows what to do?"

Caroline nodded. "I'm the lookout. I'll be two blocks down from you and scream as loud as I can if any redcoats come." She wrapped a knitted scarf around her neck. "I'll be on my way. Good luck." She dashed down the street.

Mary pulled the hood of her blue woolen cloak over her head. "You have yet to explain how I am to assist you, Edward."

"We'll distract the guard outside the jail."

Mary frowned. "Yes, but how?"

"Don't worry. You'll see." Edward looked at Jamie, still in the driver's seat. "Have you heard from the boys?"

"Aye." Jamie clucked at the restless horses. "George and Josiah have found two dozen lads who will help them torment the sentry in front of the customs house on King Street. They should be moving into place now."

"Good." Edward nodded. "Quin's friends and the other Sons of Liberty are meeting with Johnson at the Bunch of Grapes Tavern. They'll be converging on King Street soon. The redcoats will be too busy there to interfere with our plans here."

Jamie winked at Virginia. "Ye make me proud, lass. I'll be waiting for you." He flicked the reins, and the coach rolled away.

Edward gave Virginia one last warning. "Wait 'til you see the coast is clear. Good luck."

She nodded, her face pale in the moonlight. Her knuckles whitened as she tightened her grip on a bottle of rum. With a swish of woolen skirts and green woolen cape, she turned and ran to the side street to the west of the jail.

Edward grasped Mary's hand and led her to the side street to the east of the jailhouse. At this time of night, two soldiers guarded the jail, one posted outside the door and one inside the office. Once he and Mary distracted the guard outside, Virginia would deal with the guard inside. Jamie would pick up the boys at King Street and wait for the rest of them to arrive. The coach, borrowed from Johnson, had a hidden compartment under the backseat. Quin would hide there while Jamie drove overland to Concord.

As Edward advanced onto the empty street in front of the jail, he spotted the guard standing outside. He stopped where the guard could see him and faced Mary. "Did I tell you the good news? My factor in London has located George Peeper's little sister. He's putting her on the next ship here."

Mary smiled. "Edward, that's marvelous! George will be so happy. How can I thank you?"

Edward glanced quickly at the guard. The young soldier was watching them. "Well, Mary, you could come to my bed."

Her mouth dropped open. With a huff, she flushed bright red. "Edward Stanton, I thought you were a decent man."

He shook his head. "You'll have to do better than that. Slap me."

"What?"

"Slap me." He seized her by the shoulders and ground his mouth against hers.

She wrestled free and slapped him hard.

He grimaced, rubbing his stinging cheek. "Not bad. Can you scream at me now?"

"Have you lost your senses?"

"A little louder, sweetheart." He fell to his knees and shouted, "I cannot bear it any longer! You must marry me."

She stepped back. "What has come over you?"

"Oh, cruel woman! Why do you torture me this way?"

"Come on, lady." The young soldier wandered toward them a few steps. "Give the poor man what he needs."

With a huff, Mary pivoted toward the soldier. "I will thank you to mind your own business."

Edward cried out, "For twelve long years she has tortured me!"

The soldier grimaced as he approached. "Twelve years? Give it up, man. There are other women in the sea and more willing than this cold fish."

Mary gasped. "How dare you!"

Edward clutched the hem of her skirt. In the distance, he

spotted Virginia slipping inside the jail. "I can never give her up. I love her."

Mary paled. She stepped back, jerking her skirt from his hands. She glanced at the soldier and back to Edward. "Ye're just saying that because—ye doona mean it."

"I do. I have loved you for twelve years. I named *The Forbidden Lady* after you. I did business with your husband for your sake. I have always tried to take care of you. I love you so much."

Mary's eyes shimmered with tears. "Oh, Edward. I never knew."

"Marry me, please."

"Come on, lady," the young soldier said. "Have a heart."

Mary laughed as the tears streamed down her face. "All right. I will marry you."

Edward whooped as he sprang to his feet. He kissed Mary gently on the mouth.

"Congratulations." The fresh-faced young soldier grinned.

"Thank you." Edward smiled at him, then punched him in the jaw.

The soldier crumpled onto the street.

Mary gasped. "Did ye have to do that?"

"Yes." Edward seized the redcoat under the arms and dragged him to the side street.

Mary followed him. "Did you mean what you said, Edward? You weren't acting merely to distract this poor boy?"

"I meant every word." Edward pulled a length of rope from his coat and tied the soldier's hands and feet.

Loud voices shouted in the distance. Edward straightened to listen. "That sounds like more than a few dozen boys."

Church bells rang out. They echoed over Boston, alerting the citizens of impending danger. People poured into the streets. They shouted, waving their arms and shaking their fists. Edward dragged the unconscious soldier out of the way of trampling feet. Mary jumped to the side to keep from being swept down the street with the sea of people surging toward the customs house.

Shouts of "Town born! Turn out!" mingled with feigned Indian war cries. Torches, held high, cast strange lurching shadows and stunk of burning pitch. Those who were empty-handed ripped planks off fences and crates, promising pain to any redcoat in their path.

Mary yelled, straining to be heard over the roar. "Is this part of the plan?"

Edward shook his head. "No."

"I thought the bells meant there was a fire."

"Not this time. These people are armed with sticks and bats, not fire buckets. This is a mob!"

Mary watched the people pouring past them, her eyes wide with alarm. "It will keep the redcoats busy, won't it?"

"Yes, but these people are headed for King Street where Jamie is waiting. He'll never be able to drive the coach through this crowd. Stay here and help Virginia. I'll find Jamie."

Edward lunged into the middle of the street. A wave of human bodies, electrified with excitement, accelerated toward King Street, shoving him along in its wake. There he spied a line of redcoats in front of the customs house, their muskets leveled at the crowd.

"No!" he shouted.

Musket fire rang out, followed by screams. Smoke filled the air and hovered over the street like a menacing cloud.

The crowd panicked and reversed its direction, turning on itself. More musket fire exploded. Screams fractured the air, shrill and terrified. Pushing bodies entangled and trampled each other, desperate to escape. Edward scrambled to a recessed doorway as arms and legs struck and kicked at him.

He pressed against the wooden door. The smell of gunpowder and horror-inspired sweat hung thick in the air. Screams of panic gave way to sobs of despair. What on earth had happened? Johnson had planned a mere distraction, not a full-fledged riot with gunfire.

As the smoke cleared and the crowd thinned, he peered out of the doorway. Several bodies lay in the street. Kneeling beside them, mourners cradled the dead, their cries rending the night, forever branding the fifth of March as a day of massacre.

Edward stumbled from the doorway. Americans shot down in the street by British redcoats. Was this the beginning of war?

He approached each of the dead, fearing to find Josiah or George. He spotted their overturned carriage in the distance and sprinted toward it. "Jamie?"

No one answered.

Edward peered inside the carriage. Empty. A wheel, suspended in the air, slowly turned. The horses were gone.

"Damn." The mob had destroyed their means of escape. He headed back in the direction of the jail, searching for his missing comrades as he ran.

"Visitors are not allowed at night, miss." The young jailer rose from his chair.

Virginia advanced slowly. "But I came to visit with *you*."

The young man smiled as he inspected her. "How did you get past the guard outside?"

"I told him I was yer grandmother."

He laughed. "You don't look like an old woman to me."

Her gaze traveled the length of his body. "And ye don't look like no little boy." She sidled up to the iron brazier and lifted her skirts with one hand to warm her calves. "Ye won't make me leave, will ye? 'Tis awful cold out there."

His head tilted as he examined her new, improved skirt length. "Don't you have a place to go?"

She shook her head, wide-eyed and helpless. "No, me mistress threw me out. I have no money, no bed, only a wee bottle of rum to keep me warm." She slipped the bottle from her cloak.

"I could help you with the rum."

She lifted her skirts a little higher. "Could ye help me find a warm bed? I'll make it worth yer while."

He stuck a finger in his neckcloth to loosen it. "Aye." He looked nervously at the front door. "We'll have to be quick."

"Good. That's how I like it—hard and quick."

His eyes lit up. "Me, too."

What a pig. She gulped when he ripped off his coat and flung it to the floor. "Wait! I need a bed. I won't do it on this cold stone floor."

"Oh." He stopped to consider. "There are cots in the prison cells."

She shivered. "Ooh, sounds excitin'."

"Aye." With a grin, he reached for the key ring hanging from a peg on the wall. He inserted a key into the lock on the heavy wooden door that led to the prison cells.

Stepping behind him, Virginia raised the bottle of rum and focused on the back of his head.

He spun around suddenly.

She inspected the upside-down bottle in her hand. "Oh, look, me bottle's half-empty."

The look on his face indicated he suspected her mind was in a similar state. "I was going to say it is quite cold in there."

She shrugged. "Ye know how to keep a lady warm, don't ye?" She cursed inwardly at the missed opportunity. She had hoped to have the man unconscious before he opened the door, for fear that Quin might see her and call her by name.

The door creaked on its hinges, opening to the dark, cold corridor. The smell of dirty chamber pots assaulted her nose. She clung to the shadows. Perhaps Quin would be asleep.

The jailer picked up a lit candlestick, along with the key ring, and stepped into the corridor. "This way. We'll use the second cell. The prisoner was released this morning, so the bench has a pallet of fresh straw."

"Oh, me lucky day." She heard the sound of steps shuffling through loose rushes. Quin was awake. She raised her voice so he would hear. "We ain't been introduced. Me name's Polly."

The jailer bowed his head. "My pleasure."

She grinned as she pushed back her hood. "Aye, it will be."

"No!" Quin's shout came from the darkness. "No!"

She jumped back, as if startled. "Here now, I thought we'd be alone. There ain't no murderers in here, is there?"

The soldier lifted his candlestick to illuminate the corridor. "There's only the one down there. Don't worry about him. He'll be dead soon enough."

"Dammit, you'll not do this!" Quin rattled the barred gate to his cell. "I forbid it."

"Bossy, ain't he?" She proceeded down the corridor. "Hush now, a girl's got to earn a livin'."

"Bloody hell, you won't! Dammit."

She glared at her raucous husband as he attempted to rip the gate from the hinges. This was the man Edward had described as uncommunicative and listless? "Some people have no manners."

The soldier shrugged. "He's usually very quiet." He turned his back to her to insert a key in the gate to the second cell.

She lifted the bottle and focused on his head.

"No!" Quin yelled. "She's dangerous!"

The soldier whipped around, finding her once more with an upside-down bottle grasped in her hand.

"Oh, look how the moonlight shines on the glass." She peered at the soldier innocently while inwardly raging over another failed attempt.

"She's dangerous," Quin repeated the warning. "She has a disease."

She gasped. "I do not."

"She does." Quin squeezed his face against the bars. "I slept with her, and I've been a lunatic ever since."

"Aye, ye are." She gritted her teeth. "Why are ye interfering in my business?" She gave the young soldier a pointed look. "Are we going to do this or not?"

The guard frowned. "Are you poxed?"

"No! The lunatic is jealous. Are ye ready now?"

"Aye, I have to unlock this gate." He turned around.

She lifted the rum bottle.

"I'll pay you for her," Quin yelled.

The soldier swiveled around, noting with a frown the upside-down bottle in her hand.

"Oh, I forgot to take the cork out." She lowered the bottle with a look of confusion.

Quin stuck his arm through the bars. "I have a silver ring. It is yours if I can have the girl first."

She narrowed her eyes at him. Why was he messing up her plan? "I ain't sleepin' with no criminal. He'll probably murder me when he's done."

Quin glared back. "Don't tempt me, wench."

"Here, now." The jailer cleared his throat. "I cannot accept payment for the girl if she's not willing. I *am* a gentleman."

Virginia tightened her grip on the bottle's neck, looking forward to bashing the gentleman.

"Come here." Quin gestured through the bars. "I'll show you my ring. 'Tis quite valuable."

The soldier advanced slowly, the key ring in one hand, the candlestick in the other.

She swung hard and smashed him on the back of the head. Rum spewed forth, splattering on the floor. Shattered glass flew in all directions. She jumped back, raising her hands to protect her face. The soldier dropped the key ring and candlestick, stumbled to the side against a cell, banged his head on an iron bar, and toppled to the floor.

With a flash, the flame ignited a puddle of rum, engulfing the key ring with fire. She gasped and froze in her steps. Hungry flames sought out more liquor, streaming out in all directions. Loose rushes caught fire, and the flames swept into an empty prison cell.

She backed away. *No, anything but fire.* She covered her face to shield her mouth and nose from the rising smoke. A loud, clanging roar assailed her ears, humming through her shocked mind without registering. She couldn't think. She couldn't hear. The fire completely blocked the corridor with Quin on the other side, so far away, lost forever behind a wall of flames.

"No!" she cried out and covered her eyes. *No.* She could not give up. She had come to rescue him. The clamor in her ears divided into discernible sounds.

The church bells were ringing. Loud voices shouted in anger outside on the streets. And Quincy, he was yelling at her. He needed her.

"Ginny!"

She opened her eyes. Flames licked at the white breeches of the soldier. She seized him by the boots and dragged him away from the blaze. She rolled him on the stone floor to keep him from burning.

She ran at the fire and flung her cloak at it 'til the corridor was clear. The fire still raged inside the empty cell—the floor of rushes ablaze along with the cot. Breathing heavily, she stared at the fire. The walls of stone and brick should keep the fire from spreading. She lifted her gaze and groaned.

The roof was made of wood. The entire jail would burn.

"Ginny, we need the keys."

She turned to her husband.

He smiled through the bars. "Find the keys, Ginny. Let's get out of here."

She searched the floor to locate the keys. "Why did you try to stop me from hitting the guard?"

"He was holding a candlestick. I thought you would catch him on fire with that rum. I was hoping to get him close enough to knock him out."

"Oh." She found the keys and jerked her hand back as the heated iron burned her fingers. With her singed cape, she lifted the key ring and scurried to Quin's cell. "Which key is it?"

He pressed against the bars, overlooking the lock. "I don't know. Try them all."

She inserted one, using the cape to insulate her fingers from the heated iron. She turned the key. The metal twisted in her hand.

He jiggled the gate. "It didn't work."

She yanked at the key. "Oh, no, it won't come out."

"Let me try." He reached his hands through the bars to grasp the key. Heated from the fire, it bent in his hands. "Damn."

"No! I was so close." She covered her face. "Oh, God, don't let this happen." Her worst terror had returned. Once again she had failed to save a loved one.

Her husband remained locked away, soon to be lost in the flames.

CHAPTER TWENTY-FOUR

"Ginny, listen."

She lowered her hands. "I'm so sorry. Dear God, I have failed you."

Quin stretched his arms through the bars and cradled her face with his grimy hands. "Listen to me. You have not failed. I've never seen you so strong and brave."

Tears streamed down her face. "I did it for you. I love you so much."

"I know." His heart filled, erasing years of loneliness and despair.

"I wanted to save you."

"Ginny, you have saved me. Now if you'll help me, together, we can get me out of here. I have a plan." He bent over to remove his silver shoe buckles.

"What are you going to do?"

"Blow my way out. Drag that redcoat back into the office, will you?" He grabbed one of the mittens Caroline had knitted and emptied the gunpowder from one buckle into the thumb. He squeezed it into the lock. After filling the other mitten with gunpowder from the second buckle, he wedged it also into a strategic place by the lock.

Virginia returned. "What do I do now?"

"Find some liquor, rum, whatever. And remind me later to thank Caroline for her presents." He grabbed the knitted scarf and tied the fringed end by the lock. Then he carried his bench to the back of the room and turned it over on its side. This would be his barricade against the blast.

"I found this canteen. 'Tis full of rum." Virginia slipped the wooden canteen through the bars.

"Good. Now I need a source of fire so I can light this." As she dashed off once again, he opened the canteen and doused the mittens and scarf with rum. He spilled a trail of liquor leading to his barricade.

She returned with a lit candle.

"Good. Now return to the office and wait behind the door." He watched her hurrying down the corridor, then darted to his barricade against the back wall. The sound of musket fire echoed outside his cell. What the hell was happening out there? The entire population of Boston seemed to be in the streets, screaming.

He dropped the lit candle into the trail of rum. Instantly the flames raced toward the scarf. He ducked behind the bench.

The explosion deafened his ears. Thick smoke filled his cell. He stayed low as he dashed to the gate.

It was wide open.

"Ginny!" He sprinted down the corridor.

She opened the heavy door.

He seized her in his arms, laughing and hugging her close. "We did it!"

She wrapped her arms around his neck. "Oh, Quin, I thought I'd never hold you again."

"My brave Ginny." He kissed her and brushed the tears from her face, leaving smears on her cheeks with his dirty fingers. "Let's go."

He hefted the unconscious guard over his shoulder and hurried from the jail. Immediately he and Ginny were bombarded by a screaming, pushing mob. Ginny held fast to his arm as the crowd swept them west.

"We're going the wrong way," Virginia yelled over the noise. "We're to meet my father on King Street."

"I don't think we can." Quin pulled her into a deserted side alley and lowered the guard onto the ground. "What is happening here?"

"I don't know. George and Josiah were planning to torment a sentry with some other lads, and your friends were supposed to distract the redcoats."

"They did a hell of a job. I've never seen such a riot. At least we'll not be noticed."

"I see you, old boy." Clarence stepped from the shadows, dragging Mary with him.

"Aunt Mary!" Virginia lunged forward.

Quin swept out an arm to hold Ginny back.

Clarence yanked Mary against him, pointing a knife at her neck. "Did you really think I'd leave town without your money?"

Quin tamped down on the growing fury inside him. "Let her go."

Clarence motioned with his head toward Virginia. "Give me your wife, and I'll let this one go."

"No. Virginia's still married to me, and in spite of your efforts, I'm very much alive and intend to remain so."

Clarence's face hardened. "You'll be a hunted man, Quincy, forever on the run. 'Twill be a miserable existence for your wife. Give her to me, and she'll live a life of luxury in London."

"I'd clobber you on the head again the first chance I get," Virginia warned.

Clarence sneered at her. "Don't worry, my dear. You've lost all your appeal to me. I only want to deliver you to my father so he can control the business through you."

"You'll not have my wife nor my business," Quin stated.

Clarence gritted his teeth and tightened his grip around Mary. "I'll kill this one! 'Twill be your fault."

Virginia stepped forward. "I'll come with you."

"No!" Quin yanked her back. "Fine, Clarence. You win. Take my bloody ships and leave these women alone."

Clarence squinted at him. "Are you serious?"

"Yes, the women are worth more than a few ships."

"Damn, you're a fool." Clarence smiled slightly. "I'll need it in writing."

Quin nodded. "Agreed."

Clarence loosened his grip on Mary, who pulled away and ran to Virginia.

Quin advanced toward his brother, balling his fists.

Clarence jumped back. "I expect you to honor the agreement."

"Haven't you heard? I'm a bastard."

"Damn you!" Clarence pointed the knife at him, his face reddening with rage. "How many times must I turn you in? Why couldn't you just *die*?"

"I have as much right to live as you."

"No! The title will be *mine!*" Clarence threw the knife.

Quin leapt to the side as a flash of metal flew past him. Anger exploded inside him, muffling the sound of Ginny's scream and the clatter of the knife landing on cobblestones.

He grabbed his brother and threw him against the wall. Clarence hit hard and sank toward the ground.

Quin jerked him up and pinned him to the wall. "Why are you so determined to see me dead?"

Clarence grimaced with pain. "You fool. You still haven't figured it out, have you?"

"Figured out what? I know you're a greedy little bastard who wants my money. But why the obsession with killing me? I'm not a threat to you."

Clarence spoke through clenched teeth. "Father will disown me if I don't deliver the business to him. I'll lose the title, everything I ever wanted."

"How can he disown you? You're legitimate."

"No, dammit. You are. Father kept his marriage to your mother a secret so he could marry my mother and get all of her money. If I don't deliver, Father will claim you as his heir."

Quin stared at his brother, stunned. All these years he'd believed himself a bastard. With a shout of rage, he gripped both hands around Clarence's neck.

"No!" Virginia yelled. "Quin, you cannot kill your own brother."

Quin paused with his hands around Clarence's neck. The look of terror on his brother's face sickened him. He loosened his grip. "Go. The title is yours. I want nothing from you or your father. Edward is my father. *This* is my country."

"Hold still!" A voice shouted behind him.

Quin released his brother and turned.

Captain Breakwell marched into the alley, his brace of silver-handled pistols cocked and aimed at Clarence and Quin.

Clarence greeted the officer with a nervous laugh. "Thank God you've come, Captain. I caught the traitor, trying to escape."

Quin slowly eased back.

Captain Breakwell motioned with a pistol. "Stay next to your brother."

"William, please." Virginia stepped forward. "Don't do this."

"They're both criminals—a traitor and a thief." The captain studied his prisoners.

Clarence cleared his throat. "But being a traitor is so much more serious. If you turn Quincy in, you'll be a hero. They'll probably promote you."

William narrowed his eyes. "Possibly."

"Don't listen to him," Virginia pleaded. "Please, it would kill me to lose my husband."

William nodded. "I understand how you feel. I would hate to lose Priscilla."

Clarence snorted. "You cannot possibly control the two of us. You'll have to let one of us go."

"I believe you're right." William pursed his lips. "So shall I be a hero for King George and turn in Quincy, or turn you in, Clarence, and be a hero for Priscilla? An interesting choice."

Clarence shrugged. "I merely helped myself to a few baubles, but my brother is guilty of treason. You should let the worthiest man go free."

"I agree." William bowed his head to Quincy. "I suggest you get as far from Boston as possible. And take good care of Virginia."

Quin nodded. "I will. Thank you."

"*What?*" Clarence shouted. "This is an outrage."

Quin didn't wait to see what happened to his brother. Grabbing his wife and Mary Dover, he hurried away. At the end of the alley, they turned west, away from King Street, on a roundabout route toward Edward's house. The crowds had thinned, but tension still ran high as shouts of murder echoed in the cold night.

A cart rolled up beside them. "Let me give you a lift," a youth called out.

Quincy stopped. The boy looked familiar. "Do I know you?"

The boy grinned. "Aye, I once helped you out when some sailors were after you."

"You're the boy from the print shop. Which direction are you going?"

The youth looked around and leaned toward Quin. "I'll take you to where your family is gathering. I promise."

Quin helped the ladies into the back of the cart, then jumped in beside them. The boy drove the cart, serpentining through the lanes and alleys 'til he arrived at the back gate of a plain house with brown riven siding.

"This way." He led Quin and the women into the house through the back door.

In the parlor, Quin found Jamie with the two boys, George and Josiah. Virginia ran to hug her father.

"Uncle Quin!" Josiah leapt at him.

Quin gave Josiah a big hug. He noticed another boy in the corner. "I know you. You're the boy who sold chestnuts by Mary Dover's house."

The boy grinned. "I was doing me job."

Jamie ambled over to Quin and offered his hand. "Good to see you free, laddie."

"Thank you." Quin shook his hand. "Do you know whose house this is?"

"No. The mob overturned the carriage, so we were making our way to the jail on foot. Then the lad in the corner said to come with him, that he knew where ye would be. He seemed to know a great deal, and Josiah and George recognized him, so we came."

The youth from the print shop joined the boy in the corner, and Quin noted the similarities between the two. "Are you boys related?"

His question went unanswered for Edward and Caroline arrived, accompanied by another youth.

"Mary, you're safe!" Edward grinned at her, then his face lit up when he saw Quin. He grabbed him and hugged him tight. "Thank God you're free."

Quin patted him on the back. "I thank God I had you for a father."

Edward's eyes filled with tears. He turned to Mary and enveloped her in his arms.

Caroline took a turn hugging each person and laughing.

Quin leaned close to Virginia. "Does the boy who came with Edward and Caroline look familiar to you?"

"Yes." She nodded. "He's the boy who delivered the books

you ordered, and he gave me a ride to my aunt's house when I escaped from Clarence."

Quin noted the boy's brown hair and brown eyes, just like the other two in the corner. "There's something odd going on here."

"Welcome. I see you have all arrived." A feminine voice sounded at the parlor door.

Quin blinked. "What the hell?"

Virginia gasped. "Sukey? What are you doing here?"

She smiled as she entered. "I live here. I'm so delighted to see you safely together once again. I told Father I'd never forgive him if you two were separated."

Quin frowned. "Your father?"

"Aye," Sukey replied. "Come along, boys. 'Tis time for you to be in bed."

The three boys grumbled and shuffled from the room.

"Thank you for helping us," Virginia called after them.

"Who are you?" Quin shouted.

"They're my children," Johnson answered from the hallway. "Good night, boys. You did well." The short man, dressed as usual in brown, paused by the parlor door. "You said it once yourself, Quincy. A child can go about unnoticed. My children are spread all over town, learning different occupations and hearing bits of information they pass on to me."

"Wait a minute." Quin held up a hand. "The boy selling chestnuts—he was stationed outside Ginny's house before I even asked her to stop spying."

Johnson shrugged. "I suspected she was the woman you were protecting. I knew how you felt about her, even if *you* did not."

Quin frowned at his know-it-all employer.

Virginia grinned. "How many children do you have, Mr. Johnson?"

"Nineteen, at last count."

Quin snorted. "Johnson, you randy old goat."

His mouth twitched. "I shall miss you, Quincy. No one makes me laugh like you."

Quin exchanged a doubtful look with his wife.

Sukey chuckled. "For my father, that was a laugh. I hope you didn't take offense at my behavior in the coffeehouse. I was merely teasing two fellow spies."

"Enough with the pleasantries." Johnson walked to the center of the room. "Edward, you will return to your house. Whether or not Mary Dover continues to live with you, will be for you to decide."

Edward looped an arm around Mary and pulled her close. "Mary has agreed to be my wife. George, you'll be staying with us. And I have good news. Your sister will be arriving soon."

Congratulations and hugs circled the room.

Johnson cleared his throat. "How quaint. Now back to business. Mr. Munro, you will borrow another coach and leave with your family. An acquaintance of mine owns a tavern along the Boston Post Road. He'll be expecting you. If the redcoats stop you, you will say tonight's horrid events frightened your girls so much, they wanted to go home to North Carolina."

"What did happen tonight?" Quin demanded.

"Death," Edward answered. "I saw it. The bloody redcoats shot Americans down in the street."

Johnson shrugged. "It was supposed to be a mere demonstration, but there is a faction that is pushing for war. They may have succeeded."

"What happens to me?" Josiah's eyes widened with fear.

Jamie winked at him. "Ye'll come with us, lad."

"Me, too." Quin rubbed his whiskered jaw.

"No, you won't," Johnson replied. "If the redcoats search for you, they'll look for your wife first. 'Tis best for you to separate."

Quin frowned. "Then how do I get out of Boston? They'll search the ships in the harbor."

"Not all of them. There's a ship of indentured servants due to set sail tomorrow. 'Tis the perfect place for you to hide. They'll never look for you amongst a group of criminals."

Quin shook his head. "I don't like it. The captain would know I was a false passenger. He could turn me in."

"We'll sneak you on board," Johnson explained. "As many people as they cart around like animals, they won't question your presence. No one would volunteer to be shackled as a prisoner and sold like livestock."

"Wait a minute. You're saying I'll be sold?"

"Aye, Wednesday, in Newport," Johnson continued. "Your wife should be there to make the purchase. I'll loan her enough money to buy you. Edward can reimburse me."

Quin scoffed. "And if she doesn't make it in time?"

Johnson's mouth twitched. "You'll have to trust her."

Virginia and her family arrived in Newport late Tuesday. Jamie took rooms for them in a tavern near the harbor so they could see each ship as it came into port.

The first to arrive was the fast-moving schooner, the newly finished sister ship to *The Forbidden Lady* and *The Wedded Lady*. Edward had sent the new ship ahead so Quin could take possession.

The British frigate docked Wednesday afternoon, and Virginia prepared to board the ship for the auction. With her money in her purse, she left her father on the wharf, insisting that Quin would not want her family to see him in chains.

The ship's deck bustled with activity as shoppers examined the human cargo and haggled over prices. Virginia winced when she spotted Quincy, already surrounded by females appraising his form. Even filthy, unshaven, and in chains he collected admirers. She scurried over before any of the women could make an offer for him.

Suddenly, they shrieked and ran away, bumping into each other in their haste. One plump, older woman remained. She circled behind Quincy to study his backside.

Quin scowled at her over his shoulder. "I told you, I killed my last owner."

"I don't believe you," the portly woman answered. "They would have hanged you then."

"Good afternoon." Virginia smiled at her husband.

He whipped his head around at the sound of her voice. "Thank God. Get me off this ship now."

She tried to recall the words he had once said to her. "I say, you're a fetching sight for someone who has traveled on this godforsaken ship for weeks—"

"Very amusing," he interrupted her. "Now buy me, and be quick about it."

"You'll not buy him." The plump woman waddled around

to the front of Quin. "I saw him first, and I'll pay handsomely for him."

He gritted his teeth. "Madam, you bear a remarkable resemblance to a walrus I once sliced to pieces just for the pleasure of it."

The woman huffed and stalked away.

Virginia wrinkled her nose. "You cut up a walrus?"

"No. I wanted rid of the walrus woman."

"Tsk, tsk, such impertinence is sure to lower your price."

He snorted. "I'll be glad to go cheap, since the money used to buy me will be my own."

She smiled. "I say, dear fellow, what *is* your price?"

He narrowed his eyes. "You're enjoying this." He lifted his chained hands. "Just wait 'til I get my hands free."

"Oh, are you threatening me? I'll leave you chained up."

"No threat, little mermaid, just excellent service. Before the night is through, you'll know just how valuable I am, every delicious inch of you." His gray eyes glimmered as they roamed up and down her body. "Satisfaction guaranteed."

She drew in a deep breath as her skin tingled with anticipation. "I'll be right back." She returned shortly, minus a great deal of cash, with ownership papers in hand.

"Excuse me," she called to the bosun. "I've bought this one here. Can you undo his chains?"

She watched the chains being removed from Quin's ankles and calmly fanned herself with the ownership papers. Her eyes met his, and she smiled. "He's awfully big. Is it possible for me to keep those chains?"

"No, ma'am. The chains stay on board." The bosun

dragged the shackles away from Quin's feet with a loud scrape against the wooden deck.

She feigned a look of helplessness. "At least let me keep the handcuffs. He's so big and fierce. I'm a wee frightened to be alone with him."

The bosun scratched his chin. "Ye should have thought of that before laying out yer money." He turned his back to her as he unlocked the handcuffs.

Over the sailor's head, Quin winked at her.

"There. He's all yers." The bosun gathered up the armload of chains and walked off.

Quin lunged toward her and snatched the papers from her hand. "I'll take those." He nabbed her by the elbow to escort her off the frigate.

"Wait a minute." She grabbed for the papers in vain. "I need those papers. They prove that I own you."

"Did my ship arrive?"

"Aye, last night."

"Good." He helped her cross the gangplank. "The first thing I'm doing after I board my ship is burn these damned papers."

"You will not. I paid a great deal of money for those."

"Aye, my money. Under the circumstances, I would say I own myself."

"You forget, Quin, you gave all your wealth to me."

He cocked an eyebrow at her and strode down the wharf. She spotted her father in the distance with Caroline and Josiah and waved at them.

She raced to keep up with Quin. "Must you walk so fast?"

"Sorry." He slowed his pace to match hers. "I was enjoying having my feet free from those damned chains. The second thing I'm doing is having a bath."

"I'll not argue with that." She wrinkled her nose.

His cheeks reddened under the grime and whiskers. "Can you purchase some food for me while I bathe? The bloody British only fed us enough to keep the fleas alive." He scratched at his chest.

She grimaced at the sight of the clothes he had worn for three weeks. "We'll burn those clothes. Edward said he would make sure all our clothing was on board your ship."

"I won't need clothes 'til tomorrow."

She gave him a suspicious look.

He grinned.

She shook her head. "I knew I should have kept the handcuffs."

"I'll tie you up if you want, saucy wife, but I would prefer to feel your bare arms and legs wrapped around me."

She snorted. "I meant the handcuffs for you, you silly man."

"Oh. Well, you needn't restrain me, Ginny. You can have me whenever you like." His eyes gleamed. "I'm insatiable, remember?"

She smiled. "Aye, you never let me forget."

He stopped in front of his new ship and eyed her proudly. "Our new home." He took her hand in his. "We can drop your father and sister at the port of their choice. Then we can sail to the Bahamas with Josiah and start a new life together."

She examined the pristine ship before her. "She doesn't have a name."

"Aye, we'll have to name her before we leave."

"Will she be another *Lady?*" She thought of suggesting *The Expectant Lady* but decided to wait 'til Quin was well fed and rested to tell him the news of her pregnancy.

"I haven't decided which name to use. I wanted to name her after you. I thought perhaps *The Treasured Lady* or *The Cherished Lady*."

She smiled. "Those sound nice."

He reached out to touch her face. "Then I thought *The Beloved Lady* would be best, for I do love you, Ginny, with all my heart."

She rested her cheek against his palm. "That one will do."

Keep reading for a sneak peek of

Wild About You

by Kerrelyn Sparks
Coming December 2012
from Avon Books

Chapter One

In the dim light of a cloud-shrouded moon, Shanna Draganesti cast a forlorn look at the flower beds she'd once tended with care. They'd become choked with weeds since her death.

To be honest, gardening had ranked low on her list of priorities for the past three months. She'd had bigger things to fret about, such as adjusting to a steady diet of blood when six years ago she would have fainted at the sight of it, and dealing with an increased amount of psychic power that made it too easy to hear people's thoughts whether she wanted to or not.

Practically overnight, she'd been expected to master all the vampire skills. Levitation? Downright scary to look down and see nothing beneath her feet. With no way to ground herself, she kept tipping over. *Mental note: never wear a skirt to levitation practice.*

And what about teleportation? She was terrified she'd materialize halfway into a tree or a rock. And why the heck couldn't she materialize ten pounds lighter? Her scientific genius of a husband couldn't answer that one. Roman had laughed, under the impression that she was kidding.

Then there were the fangs. They tended to pop out at inopportune times. Thankfully she couldn't see her scary new canine teeth in a mirror. Unfortunately she couldn't see herself, either. She'd nearly dropped her three-year-old daughter on the floor the first time she'd seen Sofia floating in a mirror, held by an invisible mother.

And that was the most difficult part of being a vampire. She was no longer the same mother she'd been before. Every scraped knee or bruised feeling her children experienced in daylight hours would be soothed away by someone else. Because during the day, she was dead.

She'd never fully appreciated what the other Vamps went through each day at sunrise. Death-sleep was easy enough, since you just lay there like a lump, but getting there was the pits. She had to die. Over and over, as the sun broke over the horizon, she experienced a burst of pain and a terrifying moment of panic. Roman assured her it would get easier in time when she learned to relax, but how could she remain calm when she was dying? What if she never woke again? What if she never saw her children or her husband again?

There was no comforting light in the distance, reaching out to her with the promise of a happy afterlife. There was only a black hole of nothingness. According to Roman, that was the way it was for vampires. As a former medieval monk, he had interpreted the darkness as one more indication that he was cursed and his soul forever lost.

He now believed differently. When he'd fallen in love with her, he'd accepted that as a blessing from above and a sign that he wasn't entirely abandoned. And then dear Father Andrew, may he rest in peace, had convinced the rest of the Vamps that they had not been rejected by their Creator. There was a purpose to everything under heaven, Father Andrew claimed, and that included the good Vamps. They were the only ones with the necessary skills for defeating bad vampires and shifters. The good Vamps protected the innocent, so they served an important purpose in the modern world.

Mental note: remind yourself every night that you're one of the good guys. It should make that glass of synthetic blood easier to swallow.

"Come on, Mom!" Constantine ran ahead of her and charged up the steps to the front porch.

Not to be outdone by her older brother, Sofia clambered up the steps, too.

"I don't have to wait for Mom to unlock the door," Tino boasted. "I could teleport inside."

Sofia scowled at him, then turned to Shanna. "Mom, he's bragging again."

She gave Tino a pointed look. How many times had she warned him to be mindful of his little sister's feelings? So far, Sofia had not displayed the ability to teleport, and she was growing increasingly sensitive about it.

"There, now." Shanna's mother, Darlene, gave Sofia a hug. "Everyone has their own special gifts."

Sofia nodded, smiling sweetly at her grandmother. "I can hear things that Tino can't."

"Mom, she's bragging again," Tino said in a high-pitched voice to mimic his little sister.

With a snort, Shanna carried her children's empty suitcases up the steps to the front door. In spite of the recent upheaval in her personal life, her kids continued to behave normally. Like the weeds, they seemed capable of thriving in any environment.

"Nice porch." Darlene looked around. "It needs to be swept, though. And you'll need to get the yard tidied up before you post a For Sale sign."

"I know." Shanna set the small suitcases down so she could unlock the door. This was the first time her mother was seeing their home in White Plains, New York. And maybe the last.

Since Shanna's transformation, they'd all lived at Dragon Nest Academy, the school she'd started for special children, mostly shifters or hybrids like Tino and Sofia. Roman had claimed she'd sleep easier, knowing their children were well supervised during the day.

He was secretly worried that she wasn't happy, that she wasn't adjusting. And deep inside, he was afraid that she blamed him for transforming her and separating her from her children. He never said it, but she could read it in his thoughts. And sense it whenever they made love. There was a desperation in his kisses and an extra tenderness to his touch, as if he hoped to eradicate her fears and heal her sadness with the sheer force of his passion.

She blinked away tears as she opened the front door. Poor

Roman. She should reassure him that she was fine, even if it was a lie.

She wheeled the two suitcases into the foyer that was already well lit. The porch light and a few lights in the house switched on each evening thanks to an automatic timer so the house would appear inhabited. "Come on in."

"Oh my, Shanna!" Darlene looked around, her eyes sparkling. "What a lovely home."

Shanna smiled sadly. "Thank you." She'd procrastinated for three months before accepting the inevitable. They had to move. No matter how much she loved this house, it no longer worked, not with her and Roman both dead all day.

Thank goodness her mother was back in her life. Only recently had Darlene broken free from the cruel mind control imposed on her by her husband, Sean Whelan. She spent all of her time now with her children and grandchildren, trying to make up for lost time.

"Come on, Grandma!" Sofia clambered up the stairs. "I want to show you my room."

"Don't forget her suitcase." Shanna handed the pink-and-green Tinkerbell suitcase to her mother. "She can bring whatever toys she can fit in there."

"I want my Pretty Ponies!" Sofia shouted, halfway up the stairs.

"And there's another suitcase in her closet," Shanna said. "She needs more clothes."

"No problem." Darlene started up the stairs. "I'll take care of it."

Shanna handed her son his orange Knicks-decorated suitcase. "Here you go."

Constantine regarded her quietly before responding. "Do we really have to move?"

She nodded. "It's for the best. There are more people at the school who can watch over you during the day."

"I don't need a babysitter."

Shanna sighed. Sofia was delighted with the move, since the school now boasted a stable of horses for equestrian classes. But Tino wasn't so easily swayed. "You'll have other kids there to play with, like Coco and Bethany."

He wrinkled his nose. "They're girls. They just want to do silly stuff."

She tousled the blond curls on his head. "Girls are silly now?"

"Yeah. They just want to dress up and pretend they're movie stars. I want to play basketball or backgammon or Battleship."

"Where did you learn those?" She knew her son played basketball with his dad, but she'd never seen him play board games.

"Howard taught me."

"Oh. That was sweet of him." Howard Barr had been the family's daytime bodyguard for several years now. As a bear shifter, he made a fierce protector, but he had such a gentle nature that Shanna had always considered him more of a honey bear than a grizzly.

"Howard loves games," Tino continued. "People always think he's slow 'cause he's so big and eats so many donuts, but he's really fast."

"I'm sure he is."

"He's smart, too." Tino narrowed his eyes, concentrating.

"He says winning is a combination of skill, timing, and . . . stragedy."

"Strategy?"

"Yeah. Howard's real good at stragedy. When is he coming back? He's been gone forever!"

She thought back, recalling that he'd gone to Alaska at the end of May, and it was now the end of June. "It's been about a month."

"Yeah! That's almost forever!"

She supposed it was for a five-year-old. "I'll call your uncle Angus and ask him, but for now, I need you to pack whatever stuff you want to take back to school."

"Okay." Instead of heading for the stairs, he positioned himself underneath the second-floor landing.

"Tino, wait—" She was too late. He'd already experienced lift-off and was quickly levitating beyond her reach. "Be careful."

He peered down at her with the frustrated half smile he always gave her when he thought she was being overly protective. "Come on, Mom. It's not like I can fall." He reached the second-floor balcony and tossed his empty suitcase onto the landing.

She gritted her teeth as he swung a leg over the balustrade and straddled the flimsy railing. He could certainly fall now if he lost his balance or the balustrade collapsed. She tensed, prepared to levitate and catch him, but he landed neatly on his feet on the second floor.

She exhaled the breath she'd been holding. "Are you all right?"

"I'm fine. Don't worry so much." He rolled his suitcase toward his bedroom.

Don't worry so much? She was a mom. How could she not worry?

His words echoed in her mind as she wandered into the family room. She *was* worried. She was afraid he'd try something really dangerous. Like teleport into a moving car. Or levitate to the top of a cell phone tower.

She'd heard him ask Angus MacKay how high a Vamp could levitate. And he was always begging Angus and the other guys at MacKay Security and Investigation to talk about the dangerous adventures they'd managed to survive over the centuries.

In the family room, she rested her handbag on the back of an easy chair to retrieve her cell phone. She'd ask Angus about Howard and remind him that the guys needed to be careful what they said around an impressionable five-year-old boy.

Her gaze drifted to the space between the sofa and coffee table where Tino had taken his first baby steps. Why was he in such a hurry to grow up? If he attempted something dangerous during the day, she wouldn't be there to stop him. How could she live with herself if something happened to her children while she was unable to protect them?

The solution was obvious. Howard needed to come back. He could guard her children better than anyone. Tino wouldn't dare disobey when a Kodiak were-bear told him no.

With a twinge of shame, she realized she'd been too fixated lately on her own problems. She should have realized something serious was happening with Howard. It wasn't like him to be gone for so long. In the six years that she'd known him, he'd only taken a day or two off each month so he could go to his cabin in the Adirondacks and shift. Was he having some sort of personal problem? Was he ill again?

She recalled the way he had looked when she'd first met him—a balding, middle-aged man with a broken nose. He'd had a ready smile and a cheerful sense of humor, so she had never guessed that he was ill.

Roman had explained that right after high school, Howard's were-bear clan had banned him from Alaska. He'd spent four years at the University of Alabama on a football scholarship, and then three more years as a linebacker for the Chicago Bears. Separated from his kind, he had no safe place to shift.

In fact, the first time he shifted in Tuscaloosa, news of a grizzly on the loose had quickly spread, and he'd spent a terrifying night dodging bullets and shotgun shells. After that, he was reluctant to risk shifting. He was even forced to play football on nights when his body had desperately needed to shift. It had taken an enormous amount of control and strength to suppress his inner nature, but he'd managed it, knowing he would lose his career and endanger his species if the truth was revealed.

Refusing to shift had caused a chemical imbalance in his system whereby he was slowly poisoning himself. He aged. His hair fell out. The injuries he incurred on the football field wouldn't heal.

It was a chance occurrence that had saved Howard's life. Gregori had dragged Roman and Laszlo to a play-off game at the old Giants stadium, where they'd sensed an ailing shifter on the field. Even in pain, Howard had managed to sack the opposing quarterback three times. Impressed, they sought him out and convinced him he would die if he continued on his current path.

Relieved to find a job where he no longer had to hide his true identity, Howard began working for Angus at MacKay Security and Investigations. He built a cabin in the Adirondacks where he could shift, and slowly, his bones mended, his hair grew back, and he regained the younger, more virile appearance that shifters normally enjoyed for centuries. But he never returned to Alaska where he had been banned. Until now.

Shanna wondered what had changed. She leaned against the back of the easy chair as she scrolled through the list of contacts on her cell phone to call Angus.

"Did you call yet?"

She nearly dropped her phone. Her son had suddenly materialized by the coffee table. "Tino, you startled me. I thought you were upstairs packing."

"I was." He climbed onto the easy chair, kneeling so he was facing her. "Did you call Uncle Angus? Is Howard coming back? Will he live with us at the school?"

"I suppose he will."

"Then why don't we pack some of his stuff?" Tino asked. "We could get a room ready for him."

Shanna glanced toward the hallway that led to Howard's rooms. Since she and Roman shared a large, windowless suite in the basement, they had let Howard use the master bedroom and office on the ground floor. As a were-bear, Howard was very territorial, so they had allowed him to treat that part of the house as his private domain. She'd seen his office a few times, but she'd never ventured into his bedroom.

She shook her head. "He wouldn't like us rummaging around in his room. Besides, he's been on vacation for over a month. He must have plenty of clothes with him."

"But he won't have his games." Tino bounced on the seat cushion. "We can't play without his games."

Shanna bit her lip. Howard might not mind her going into his room to fetch a few games.

"And he'll want his secret DVDs."

She turned toward Tino. "His what?"

"His DVDs. He has a box of them hidden under his bed. He watches them when he's not working."

"They don't sound very secret if you know where they are."

Tino shrugged. "I just call them secret 'cause he won't let me watch them. He said they're for older people."

Adult only? Shanna swallowed hard. Was there a side to Howard no one knew about? No, she couldn't believe it. Sweet Howard, who always had a smile on his face and a donut in hand? Surely he wasn't . . . "Did he say anything else about these DVDs?"

Tino tilted his head, considering. "There's a girl and two guys. The guys are called Big Al and The Hammer—"

"Okay." Shanna tried to keep any alarm from showing on her face. Good Lord, she'd trusted her children with Howard. Forget privacy issues. As a responsible parent, she had to investigate. "I . . . think I could look in his room for a few board games."

"Cool! Can I come with you?"

"No!" Shanna softened her voice to continue. "Why don't you be a sweetie and help Grandma bring your sister's suitcases down?"

Tino frowned. "All right. But remember to get the chess set, too. Howard promised he would teach me."

"I will." She waited for her son to teleport upstairs, then hurried down the hallway.

She glanced inside the office Howard used as his security headquarters. One wall was covered with monitors. A few screens normally showed the outside perimeter of the house in White Plains, while others were linked to surveillance cameras in Roman's townhouse on the Upper East Side. The monitors were all dark now, since no one was living at either place.

Her gaze wandered across the room. A file cabinet topped with a few trophies and awards Howard had earned during his football career, a plain wooden chair, a pair of hand weights on the floor. Fifty pounds each? Good Lord. Howard would be formidable if ever crossed. It was a good thing he was so sweet-natured. Or was he? How well did she really know him? She eyed the handcuffs on his desk.

Howard loves games. Tino's words slipped back into her mind with a new and disturbing meaning. No, this was easily explainable. Howard was their security guard. He needed silver handcuffs to prevent bad vampires from teleporting away. But what about the adult-only DVDs under his bed?

The door to his bedroom was locked, but that didn't present a problem with her new vampire strength. *Mental note: repair the splintered doorframe and broken doorknob before the house goes on sale.*

She flipped on the light as she entered the bedroom, then stopped with a small jolt of surprise. This was how Howard had furnished his room? She'd visited his hunting cabin on several occasions when Connor had hidden the Draganesti family there in dangerous times. The cabin was exactly what you would expect from an Alaskan were-bear. Lots of wood, leather, Indian blankets in shades of earth and sky, and a few animal heads mounted on the walls.

There was nothing rustic about this bedroom. Sleek, sophisticated, and modern, it didn't seem to match Howard. Was there a secret side to him that no one knew about?

The king-sized bed was covered with a black-and-white striped comforter and bright red pillows. The bedside tables were chrome and glass. Across from the bed, a shiny black dresser was topped with a wide-screen TV. A black leather recliner rested in the corner next to a glass and chrome bookcase. She spotted the games Tino wanted on the bottom shelf.

But what about the secret DVDs? As she approached the bed, the unusual headboard drew her attention. Tin ceiling tiles?

She ran her fingers over the embossed tin. How interesting. The tiles were mounted on a piece of plywood to make a headboard. Had Howard made this himself? Apparently, there was a lot about Howard that she didn't know. With an uneasy feeling, she dropped to her knees and peered underneath the bed.

There it was. A black alligator-skin box. She pulled it out, then took a deep breath and opened it.

Homemade DVDs. She rummaged through the stack, reading the labels Howard had written and attached to the plastic cases. *Elsa in London. Elsa in Amsterdam. Elsa in Berlin.* This Elsa certainly got around. *Elsa in Pittsburgh. Elsa in Cincinnati.* Was this like *Debbie Does Dallas?*

Shanna inserted the first disc in the DVD player on Howard's television, then lowered the volume in case she happened across a scene with loud moaning.

A collage of stately old homes rolled across the screen, then the title of the show appeared. *International Home Wreckers*. A map of the U.K. and the Union Jack flashed by, followed by the photo of a well-dressed man. Alastair Whitfield aka Big Al. The outline of Germany and its flag, followed by another photo. Oskar Mannheim aka The Hammer. And finally, the map and flag of Sweden, followed by the photo of a beautiful blond woman, dressed in cut-off jeans, a plaid shirt tied beneath her breasts, a pair of work boots, and a utility belt resting on her hips. Elsa Bjornberg aka Amazon Ellie. A commercial began for the network, HGRS. Home and Garden Renovation Station.

"Oh my gosh," Shanna breathed. "I love this channel." She glanced back at the tin-tiled headboard. Howard was into home décor?

As the show began, the two male stars were gutting a Victorian townhouse in London that had fallen into disrepair. Alastair, dressed in an expensive designer suit, was selecting new wallpaper for the parlor. Oskar, wearing jeans and a T-shirt, was ripping up a hideous orange shag carpet to expose a wooden floor underneath.

"It's extremely important to preserve a site's proper heritage," Alastair explained in a crisp British accent. "But at the same time, we must be sensitive to the needs of the family who will be calling this home. They have their hearts set on a more modern, open concept, so we have agreed to take down part of the wall separating this parlor from the room behind it. Fortunately, we have the perfect person for busting down a wall. Elsa!"

Shanna sucked in a breath as Elsa Bjornberg strode into the room. Good Lord, she had to be over six feet tall. Either that or her costars were a little short. She wore a pair of white overalls splotched with paint and a short-sleeved T-shirt, also white, that contrasted nicely with her golden, tanned skin. Her long blond hair was pulled back into a ponytail, and the upper part of her face was covered with an enormous pair of safety goggles. In her gloved hands she carried a large sledge-hammer.

She wasted no time, just hauled off and slammed her hammer right through the wall.

Shanna watched, amazed. No wonder they called her Amazon Ellie. She was a big woman. Big bones, big muscles, and a big smile she flashed at the camera as the last of the wall crumbled to dust.

Returning to the black box, Shanna inspected the contents more thoroughly. A TV guide listed the show as coming on in the afternoon. That explained why she'd never seen it. But why was Howard being so secretive about his interest in house renovation?

Underneath the DVDs she discovered a magazine article with an interview of Oskar, Elsa, and Alastair. And underneath that she spotted a stack of photos that looked like they'd been printed off the Internet. Every one of them showed Elsa. Elsa in her cut-off jeans, which highlighted her long, tanned legs. Elsa in an evening gown showing off her generous curves. A close-up of Elsa's face and her pretty green eyes.

"Oh my gosh," Shanna whispered. This was why Howard was watching the show. He had a crush on Amazon Ellie.

She glanced up at the television just in time to see Elsa rip a bathroom sink off a wall. "Wow."

Her heart pounding, Shanna rose to her feet. Howard had found the perfect woman for a were-bear!

She turned off the television, and with trembling hands, she returned the DVD to the black alligator-skin box. The perfect woman for Howard! She had to make sure he met her. But he was watching the show in secret. At this rate, he'd never meet his dream girl. He needed some help.

Her heart lurched. The old gate house! Just the other night, she and Roman had discussed the possibility of making the old house their new home. Only a few miles from the school, it was part of the estate, so they already owned it. Unfortunately, it was in sad shape. A money pit, her mother called it.

But that made it the perfect project for the International Home Wreckers! It was exactly the sort of historic gem that they specialized in renovating.

She shoved the box back under the bed and jumped to her feet. Did she dare do this? Play matchmaker to a were-bear? Her heart raced, and for the first time in three months, she realized she was grinning.

She grabbed the games off Howard's bookcase and rushed back to the family room. In a few seconds, she had Angus's number ringing on her cell phone.

"Hi, Angus. Can you bring Howard back right away?"

"Is there something wrong, lass?" he asked.

"I'm worried about my children's safety during the day,

especially Tino. I'm afraid he'll try something dangerous, and Howard is the only one who can keep him safe for me. I need him back."

There was a moment of silence before Angus replied. "His vacation time ran out over a week ago. There was a mission I wanted to send him on, but he refused to go."

"What?" Her nerves tensed. "He's not quitting, is he?"

"He dinna say he was, but the bugger stopped answering my calls. I sent Dougal and Phil to hunt him down."

Shanna winced. "He's not in any danger, is he?"

"We doona know," Angus said. "That's why we're looking for him. I would have sent more lads, but we have three missions going on right now. We're short on manpower."

"I see." She took a deep breath. Finding a babysitter for her children probably seemed trivial compared to the other issues Angus had to deal with. But that didn't make her worry any less. "If you find Howard, can you tell him that we need him? Tino is asking for him."

"Aye, we'll tell him."

"Thank you." Shanna dropped her cell phone back into her handbag.

It wasn't like Howard to take more vacation days than he was allotted. Or to ignore phone calls from his boss. Angus had sounded annoyed that he'd been forced to track him down.

What on earth was Howard up to?

Chapter Two

Howard peered over the edge of the cliff. Even in the dim light of a cloud-covered moon, his sharp eyesight could make out the jagged rocks where Carly had been discovered all those years ago, her body broken, her long brown hair matted with blood. His first love, the girl he'd hoped to marry. Murdered on the night of their senior prom.

His gaze drifted to the small collection of lights that marked the nearby town of Port Mishenka on the eastern coast of the Alaska Peninsula. Twenty years had passed since he'd last been here, but not much had changed. The most noticeable lights were still those that illuminated the high school football field. He'd been a hero there at one time, but none of the residents would welcome him back now. Not when they believed him guilty of Carly's murder. Her family still claimed he had thrown her off the cliff along with a few guys.

It was impossible to deny all the charges. He had tossed three guys off the cliff. Werewolves. He'd believed them all dead until two months ago. Now he knew the truth. The worst of the three had survived.

He didn't blame Carly's family for turning against him. They were heartbroken over her death. He'd felt the same way for years. Heartbroken and guilty, for there was a kernel of truth to the family's claim. Their daughter had died because of him. She'd become an unwitting pawn in Rhett Bleddyn's game of revenge.

He had found little solace in believing he'd killed Rhett. The bastard had found the perfect way to torture him by making him feel responsible for Carly's death.

But now the truth was out. Rhett Bleddyn was still alive.

And the game was back on. Unfortunately Rhett had the hometown advantage. Recently acknowledged as the Pack Master of all of Alaska, he had hundreds of werewolves on his team. Howard could only call on a few were-bears from their dwindling island community. What he lacked in manpower, he had to make up for with superior timing and strategy.

Speaking of timing, it was about time for the two men climbing up the mountainside to finally reach him. The scent of werewolf wafted toward him, and Howard instinctively squeezed his fist around the carved wooden hiking stick he'd borrowed from his grandfather. The staff was thick enough to use as a weapon and about six foot four inches long, ending right at his eye level.

He relaxed his grip. This werewolf was one of the few Lycans he called friend. Werewolves always assumed they had the most advanced sense of smell, but that was one area where a were-bear had them beat. He could distinguish Phil's scent over two miles away. Not that Phil normally smelled differently from other werewolves. It was the influence of his wife, Vanda, that made him unique. She had him using some kind of fancy shampoo and conditioner.

Phil had obviously caught Howard's scent and was tracking him down. What the werewolf might not realize was that Howard wanted to be found tonight. It was all part of the strategy.

Phil's companion was a little harder to figure out. The lack of any strong scent indicated a vampire. The smell of damp sheep suggested a kilt-wearing Scotsman who'd been caught in a light rain. But which Scottish vampire? Was Angus so pissed that he'd come in person?

They were moving quietly up the mountain path, as if they could sneak up on a were-bear. The thought made Howard smile. There was no mistaking the soft swish of a kilt or the grinding of Phil's boots.

Not Angus, he decided. Phil was taking the lead, and he wouldn't do that if the boss was with him. Ian or Robby? Or maybe it was Connor, resuming his work after a long honeymoon.

Howard's smile faded. All of the guys were getting married, having children. That sort of domestic bliss was unlikely to happen for him. There were a few female were-bears on the island, but they were either taken or related to him.

His gaze drifted back to the rocks where Carly had died twenty years ago. She had trusted him completely, even after he'd confessed to her that he was a were-bear. Since her, he hadn't met another mortal female he had felt he could trust with his secret.

There had been a time when the pain and guilt of Carly's death had nearly crippled him. All through college and his football career he'd allowed himself to suffer as a way to punish himself. But as the years went by, his burden of guilt slowly changed. Instead of feeling guilty for wanting to forget, he now felt guilty that he could barely recall her face. How cruel life was that she had paid the price for Rhett Bleddyn's rage.

Death was too good for Rhett. Howard wanted to watch the sick bastard squirm. He'd have to go about it secretly and stealthily in order to keep his people safe, but with the proper strategy, he felt confident about pulling it off. And if he avenged Carly, then maybe he could finally lay his guilt to rest. He'd been banished for long enough.

A cool breeze swept up from Mishenka Bay, and he closed his eyes to focus fully on the scent—a glorious mixture of salty sea and lush forest. *Home.* He took a deep breath to let the comforting fragrance seep into his soul, and a new face formed in his mind. Elsa. Beautiful Elsa. She was invading his thoughts more and more each day. Unfortunately that only proved that no matter how clever a strategist he tried to be, he was still a fool.

Elsa Bjornberg was a celebrity, a breathtaking, gut-wrenching beauty, who traveled the world for her successful career. Why would she want to meet some guy from an obscure island in Mishenka Bay, Alaska? Especially a guy who was oversized and turned into a real bear on occasion. The cold reality was that they would never meet. He'd known months ago that his obsession with her was ridiculous. Pathetic. Juvenile. It was embarrassing, so he kept it secret.

And yet, whenever he saw her on television, he felt drawn

to her. Not just mildly attracted but somehow irrevocably attached to her. It didn't make sense, but knowing that didn't make the strange feeling go away.

The soft scuffle of a footstep behind him made him stiffen. Holy crap, he'd allowed himself to get distracted. He masked his reaction by swinging the staff up and across his shoulders, gripping each end with his hands.

With his back to them, he listened carefully as he gazed up at the moon, a dull silver disc shrouded in clouds. It would be full tomorrow night. If everything went according to plan, he'd score a touchdown. "Hello, Phil."

There was a moment of silence, then a whoosh of air as Phil Jones exhaled. "How did you know it was me? Alaska is overrun with werewolves."

"They don't use that fancy, girly shampoo." Howard smiled when he heard a low growl in response.

A slight mechanical click emanated from the vampire behind him. Could it be Dougal Kincaid? The Vamp had lost his right hand in combat a few years ago, and Roman had recently fitted him with a mechanical one.

"Dougal?" Howard turned, widening his smile when he saw he'd been correct. "It's good to see you again. You arrived last night?"

The Scotsman tilted his head, studying him. "Someone told you?"

"No. It rained last night, and your kilt smells like wet sheep."

Dougal's mouth curled with amusement. "Ye're in trouble with Angus, ye ken."

"Not enough trouble, if he only sent two of you."

"Believe me, he's pissed," Phil grumbled, then shoved his long, shaggy hair back over his shoulders. "It's cheaper to use the same shampoo that my wife buys."

"I understand." Howard gave him a sympathetic smile. "I won't mention it again since you're so . . . sensitive about it."

Phil's eyes narrowed.

Dougal chuckled. "We have orders to take you back to Romatech immediately."

Howard nodded, still smiling. "Good luck with that."

Phil snorted. "What the hell are you up to, Howard?"

"I thought you'd never ask. I need more players on my team."

"Team?" Dougal asked. "Ye're playing a game?"

"Yes. It's called Payback. It'll be easier to score if I have a few more hands." Howard slanted a wry look at the Vamp's fake right hand. "No offense."

"None taken." Dougal wiggled the fingers on his mechanical hand. "Ye'd be surprised what I can do."

"Tell it to the ladies." Howard motioned to Phil. "Are you in?"

"If you're getting back at Rhett Bleddyn, then yeah, I'm in. Angus can wait."

Dougal scoffed. "Now there are two of you no' following orders. Angus will be royally pissed."

"Maybe not," Phil argued. "He knows what an asshole Rhett is. The guy tried to force my sister into marriage. He was going to kill off my entire family and steal all our land and followers. He's a power-hungry, ruthless bastard."

Dougal nodded, then turned to Howard. "I can see why Phil wants revenge, but what do ye have against him?"

Howard remained silent, then swung his staff off his shoulders and planted one end in the gravelly dirt next to his feet. "I have my reasons. Are you in?"

Dougal's hand produced a series of clicks as he curled the fingers into a fist, then stretched them back out. "What is the purpose of yer game? Are ye wanting to kill Bleddyn?"

"Do I look like a murderer?" Howard frowned when the two guys exchanged glances. "Okay. You've seen me kill, but only in battle."

"You're ferocious," Phil muttered. "You rip heads off with a single swipe."

"So I'm efficient," Howard grumbled, then smiled. "No one has ever complained about my efficiency before."

Phil snorted. "We're just relieved you're on our side."

Howard's mouth twitched. "Are you sure about that?"

Phil stiffened. "You big lummox, why don't you—"

"Enough." Dougal lifted a hand, then shot an annoyed look at Howard. "I need to know more before I decide. Do ye plan to lure Rhett into battle?"

"No." Howard pointed his staff toward a few lights twinkling far out in Mishenka Bay. "You see that group of islands out there? They're called the Bear Claw Islands 'cause there's a big round one and four narrow ones extending north."

Dougal moved closer to the cliff edge. "That's where ye grew up?"

"Yes. On the big round one called The Paw."

"We saw on your bio that you went to high school down there." Phil motioned at the town below and snickered. "A were-bear playing football for the Port Mishenka Marmots? That had to be embarrassing."

Howard arched a brow at him. "I kicked ass on that field. Would you care for a demonstration?"

"Enough, you two." Dougal gestured to the Bear Claw Islands. "Does yer family still live there?"

"Yes. That group of islands and Kodiak Island to the north are where most were-bears live. We're down to about a hundred now."

"Shit." Phil frowned at the islands. "You're in danger of extinction."

Howard sighed. "There was a time, a few hundred years ago, when were-bears flourished and covered the mainland. There were over a thousand of us. But then settlers began moving in, searching for gold, and werewolves moved in, wanting the land. The Alpha wolves tended to bite any guy who found gold, so he would become their minion."

"And then they would have his gold," Phil muttered.

Howard nodded. "The werewolves quickly amassed land and wealth. If someone had something they wanted, they simply bit him to bring him in line."

"The were-bears dinna bite people?" Dougal asked.

"Not usually. It's not in our nature to live in packs. Especially the male bears. We're loners. Unfortunately, that always worked against us. We were spread out thin, each male bear taking a huge territory, and it made us vulnerable. A single were-bear might be able to defeat a small group of wolves, but they started attacking us in packs of thirty and forty."

Dougal muttered a curse. "Ye wouldna stand a chance."

"No. Eventually, in order to keep the cubs safe, most of the were-bears moved to these islands. To make a living, many of the men turned to fishing, but whenever a storm capsized a boat, we would lose five or six of them. With our numbers depleted, a loss like that was devastating."

Phil winced. "The werewolves know which islands your people are living on?"

"Yes. Rhett has over five hundred followers, so we can't afford to draw him into battle." Howard gritted his teeth. "I just want to play with him, make him wish he was dead."

"What did he do to you?" Dougal asked.

Howard stabbed at the ground with his staff. No way was he going to discuss lost love with two guys. "He deserves far worse than what I have planned. Are you in the game?"

Dougal gave him an apologetic look. "I may no' be much help to you. I'm lucky if I'm able to stay awake for more than a few hours at night. The blasted sun here is always up."

Howard smiled. "You could use that as an excuse for not reporting in. Then maybe Angus would send more men."

Dougal tilted his head, his eyes narrowed. "Is that why ye stopped returning his calls? So he would be forced to send us?"

Phil scoffed. "You jerk, you had us worried about you. Why didn't you just ask for help?"

"If I asked, Angus could refuse." Howard leaned on his staff. "Any chance of getting more guys here?"

Dougal gave him an irritated look. "Angus will have smoke coming out his ears."

"Then he should come and help," Howard suggested.

"He's busy coordinating three other missions right now," Phil grumbled. "A lot has happened since you left for vacation."

Howard frowned. After the skirmish with Rhett in Montana, everything had seemed to calm down. "What's going on?"

"We're still trying to find Russell," Phil began. "J.L. and Rajiv went to China to hunt for him."

"That's good." Howard had often wondered how Russell was doing. The former Marine and newly turned vampire had gone AWOL in China after their last mission there. As Russell's sire, Angus probably felt some responsibility for him. Everyone assumed Russell was hunting for Master Han, the evil vampire who had left him in a vampire coma for forty years.

"There was an outbreak of murderous Malcontents in Albania," Phil continued. "Angus sent some guys there to help Zoltan track them down."

"I see." Howard knew that as Coven Master of Eastern Europe, Zoltan was charged with the task of protecting mortals in his jurisdiction. It wasn't a job he could always do alone, so he often requested help from Angus.

"And then we got an urgent request from President Tucker," Phil muttered. "And when the government asks for our help, we have to comply."

Howard nodded. Now that the president knew about vampires and shifters, he and the CIA were likely to make many such requests in the future. "What is it this time?"

"Seven American tourists taken hostage by a drug cartel in Mexico," Phil explained. "The president asked us to locate them and teleport them out. The only safe way to do it is to have a vampire for each hostage. So that's seven more Vamps. Carlos went with them as their day guard and translator."

"Now ye ken why Angus wasna pleased with yer antics,"

Dougal said. "He's short on manpower. He had to call me away from my station in Texas."

"I understand." Howard had hoped for a bigger team, but he could manage with only two more. "If you both join us, then we'll have a team of six. The three of us. A journalist and good friend, Harry Yutu, in Anchorage. And two young were-bears from the island, my twin cousins, Jimmy and Jesse."

"What's the plan?" Phil asked.

"We call it Operation Three Little Pigs," Howard replied. "We're attacking three of Rhett's houses. Our first target was one of his fishing cabins. We removed everything from inside, stashed it in our trucks, then huffed and puffed and knocked the walls down. It wasn't too hard, since it was just a shack."

"That was yer house of straw?" Dougal asked.

Howard nodded. "Some hungry cubs on The Paw are enjoying the food, and an old woman got a new wood-burning stove she was needing. My grandfather is very happy with his new rod and reel."

Phil crossed his arms. "You probably left your scent behind. Rhett will know it was you."

"My cousins left behind some deer and squirrel carcasses. The place will be a magnet for hungry animals. There'll be a lot of scents there by the time Rhett discovers it." Howard took a deep breath, then continued, "Last week, we tackled the house of sticks, Rhett's vacation home on the coast of the Kenai Peninsula. We emptied it so we could give all the stuff to some needy were-bears, then took a few axes to the stilts and watched the house slide down the bluff and break apart on the rocks. Most of it floated out to sea."

"I like it." Phil grinned. "And the house of bricks?"

"It's log and stone, actually. One of Rhett's main residences." Howard glanced up at the sky. "We'll hit tomorrow night when the moon is full, and Rhett and his minions are away from the house on their monthly hunt."

"He'll leave behind a few guards," Phil warned.

"That's why I wanted more men. If they discover us invading his home, there could be trouble. I was hoping to get a few Vamps on our team so we could use your mind control or at least teleport away if we need to. We could really use your help." Howard extended a hand, palm down. "What do you say? Are you in?"

Phil gave them a wolfish grin. "Yeah, I'm in." He slapped a hand on top of Howard's.

Dougal snorted, then rested his mechanical hand on top of theirs. "Aye, I'm in as well."

ABOUT THE AUTHOR

Former tap dancer and high-school French teacher, *New York Times* bestselling author KERRELYN SPARKS has always searched for creative ways to express herself. A prolific reader since childhood, she discovered that writing her own stories provided the ideal way to combine her love of comedy, language, and history. And what a relief that the voices in her head have led to a paycheck instead of a padded room! A native Texan, Kerrelyn lives with her husband and children in the Greater Houston area.

Kerrelyn loves to hear from readers and you can visit her at www.kerrelynsparks.com.

Give in to your impulses . . .
Read on for a sneak peek at three brand-new
e-book original tales of romance
from Avon Books.
Available now wherever e-books are sold.

MATING SEASON
A CABIN FEVER NOVELLA
By Alice Gaines

NINE LIVES OF AN
URBAN PANTHER
By Amanda Arista

LAST VAMP STANDING
By Kristin Miller

An Excerpt from

MATING SEASON
A Cabin Fever Novella
by Alice Gaines

Gayle and Nolan have been professional rivals for years. But now, stuck together out in the wild, these two scientists will discover that there's a fine line between feuding and foreplay. The competition *really* heats up when their research on animal mating habits moves from theory to practice . . .

AN AVON RED NOVELLA

CHAPTER ONE

The four-wheel drive monstrosity came over the crest of the hill with a growl of gears and headed down the path toward the cabin, bringing Gayle Richards's worst nightmare with it. Professor Nolan Hersch didn't drive any old SUV to research sites, like normal people did. No, he had to command something hypermacho, a vehicle one might pilot out into the bush to harass lions.

The trees had stopped dripping after the recent early fall rain, but the ground remained damp, and the ferns drooped with moisture. The redwood duff, which in summer had consisted of a fine powder that coated everything that touched the ground, now made an equally fine mud. Hersch's vehicle followed the path her own tires had made until he pulled up in front of the cabin and turned off the engine.

Dressed in khakis and with his sandy hair attractively tousled, he resembled a big game hunter more than what he was—an evolutionary biologist with an ego almost as big as his reputation. She instinctively took a step backward as he climbed out. She would have wrapped her arms around her ribs, too, but he'd recognize that as a defensive gesture, so she let them hang by her sides.

He gave her his usual killer smile—perfect teeth and all—and extended his hand. "Professor Richards."

She gave him her own hand and shook firmly. Business-like. Assertive. "Welcome, Professor Hersch."

Somehow, despite Northern California's notorious fog, his arms were tanned and covered with bleached golden hairs that set off the silver band of his heavy watch. His wrist made hers appear tiny as his hand engulfed hers. Appealing and intimidating all at once. When she'd satisfied the bounds of collegiality—and stopped staring at his skin—she pulled back.

"Good of you to have me," he said. "I enjoyed your last paper."

Oh he had, had he? Despite the fact that it blew a hole the size of his SUV through his own last journal article? Courtesy would suggest she compliment his work in return. She didn't.

He put his hands on his hips and glanced up at the cabin, which gave her a view of his Adam's apple and the gap of his shirt where he'd opened the top two buttons to reveal more tanned skin.

"Good-looking facility," he said.

"Room for four," she answered. "Where are the others, by the way?"

"There's a road washed out back a few miles. I barely made it through," he said. "Dave and Susan should make it here in a couple of days."

"Days?" she repeated. She'd arranged for four researchers

on this trip. She'd written that specifically into the grant proposal. She might need this man's collaboration on her research to win herself more visibility in her field and therefore more advancement at her university, but she sure as hell hadn't arranged a vacation for the two of them. Especially not one that involved watching large animals having sex.

Elk might not be closely related to humans, but the males had penises and they did the deed doggie style, with a lot of grunting and snorting. So no, she hadn't planned on watching animal porn alone with Nolan Hersch.

"Something wrong?" he asked.

"There's a lot of work," she said. "There's supposed to be four of us."

"It's only a few days," he said. "The mating season will last longer than that."

"I know how long mating season is," she said. "I just didn't think . . . you and I . . ."

Oh, brother. That wasn't a sentence she could finish anytime soon, if ever. She wouldn't tell him about where her mind wandered during his presentations at conferences. She wouldn't mention her delusions that every time he mentioned receptive females his gaze lingered on her. She wouldn't share the fact that every time he turned to a chalkboard she rememorized the curve of his ass.

Just because she didn't bring any of those things up didn't prevent him from watching her whenever she became uncomfortable in his presence. Like right now. There was that pleasant expression—the half smile—that did little to hide the fact that he was assessing her with as much care as he used in studying his research subjects.

She lifted her chin and smiled right back. "I guess we have enough supplies."

He gestured with his head toward his SUV. "I have more than enough for myself. We can share."

"No need. I'm well stocked. Come on inside." She turned and climbed the stairs to the cabin. Because he still had to unload his things, it would take him a while to follow, and she could catch a breath before having to allow Nolan Hersch into her space. She'd spent the last two days alternating between steeling herself for his arrival and telling herself it was no big deal.

The others were supposed to come with him. His two graduate students would have acted like a buffer, always underfoot, always between them. She wouldn't have had to imagine him alone in the next bedroom because he'd have a roommate, as would she. And when he spouted some bit of sexist bullshit from his research, she'd have support from at least one other woman. Alone, she'd end up wanting to tear him apart one way or another in an hour. Two, tops.

She went to the kitchen area of the cabin, poured herself a glass of water from the tap, and turned to lean against the counter to drink it. After a minute or two, Hersch entered with more than enough stuff for a season in the field. He needed several trips to haul it all in. Among the boxes and cases stood one of those canvas carriers wine stores sold. The necks of six bottles stuck out the top.

"A treat," he explained. "You and I can share a bottle before the others get here."

"I don't think—"

"Say, that's a fine genealogy you've done." He walked to the wall where she'd unrolled butcher paper so that she could create a visual display of the relationships among the animals they'd be observing.

He lifted a hand to trace one particular family's line. "You have three generations here."

"I've been studying these guys for years."

"So why did you invite me?" he asked.

An innocent question. A logical one. She could lie and tell him that she'd come around to his way of understanding animal sexual behavior. Or she could give him the truth . . . that he was top in the field and papers they did together had an easy shot of getting into the best and most-read journals. She wouldn't add that spending time with him in the forest was supposed to be chaperoned by the others.

"I thought it was time we collaborated," she said.

"Instead of yelling at each other at conferences?" His eyes took on the gleam of challenge she'd seen in them so many times. The blue of his irises always seemed to darken, as they did now.

"I don't yell."

He made a noise that was half humph and half snort. Maybe more than half snort.

"All right, I raise my voice," she said. "But your theory ignores the female in the mating equation."

He crossed his arms over his chest. "I promise you, I've never ignored the female."

Cute. Double entendre. His typical ploy to make his presentations "sexy." "But you do. You make it sound as if the cows stand around, grazing, while the bulls do all the work. Fighting with each other. Then she has no choice and the winner climbs on and slam-bam-thank-you-ma'am."

He laughed. "I don't think I ever put it quite like that."

"That's what you mean."

"You think I believe that?" he said. "That females have no sex drive at all?"

She glared at him, using every bit of willpower not to grind her teeth. "We're talking about animals here."

"I am. What are you talking about?"

"The way you look at things," she said. "You're completely androcentric."

One of his sandy brows quirked upward. "You think I'm fixated on the male point of view and incapable of understanding the female?"

"Something like that." Damn it all, it hadn't even taken an hour for him to get under her skin. Not even half an hour.

"And I imagine you're going to show me how females look at things," he said.

"Animals."

"Animals," he said. "Should be interesting."

An Excerpt from

NINE LIVES OF AN URBAN PANTHER

by Amanda Arista

Violet Jordan, B movie writer-turned-shapeshifter (and a few other things), is back! She and Chaz are engaged, her pack is finally coming together, and her latest script is a hit. Sounds like the perfect time for the fur to start flying!

CHAPTER ONE

Dear Diary,

Eight months ago, I was attacked in the back alley of my townhouse and rescued by an über-hot guy named Chaz. He told me that there was a prophesy about me and that I might turn into a werepanther. He was right on both counts. Then Spencer, the guy who bit me, tried to convince me to join the dark side. It didn't work. So he poisoned me and left me for dead. My best friend, Jessa, an undercover fairy princess, saved the day but bonded us together as the dynamic duo for opening and closing the Veil.

Six months ago, in an epic battle for the world, Spencer jumped through the Veil into the Neveranth, and I ended up killing his father. As he lay dying, he gave me the Haverty Legacy and the hellfire that comes with it.

I thought life was going to get better. After four assassination attempts, I finally changed my mind. When the Haverty pack needed a new leader and I was the one holding the Legacy, I quickly found that having loyal followers really helped when the elemental Carlisle started *killing his way through all competition for leader of the Dallas Pride. When push came to claw, Carlisle got thrown into mirror jail, and I got crowned as the Prima.*

Yep, I think that's about it. All I have to do is keep sane, even with the prophetic dreams I keep having, run a pack, keep my "real" job, and have some sort of personal life with my shiny fiancé.

Being a queen was exhausting. This was the first of four meetings for the day, the first of three appointments with new pack members, and my second latté with an extra espresso shot.

As I waited at my favorite coffee shop for my caffeine and my ten o'clock appointment, I stretched my neck and slipped off my pointed heels. Cute but deadly. Now that I was a Prima, looking like a leader was starting to get tiring as well. The life of jeans and tee shirts was behind me. I had to look more responsible now, and my feet were paying the price.

The cool wooden floor soothed the pain burning up my legs and let me relax for just one moment. This place was my second home, and I'd single-handedly brought it back from extinction with a string of new customers by making it the unofficial hotspot for the new Dallas Pride.

Secret club's got to have a clubhouse, right?

I looked down at my watch, my dreaded new accessory, and played with the charm at my neck. My ten o'clock was late. It had been hell to pin him down for a meeting. He was the last of the new members of my little family that I had to meet with before our first full moon together. I actually had to call his office to get an appointment. Neither of us was very happy about that.

My frustrated thoughts were quickly redirected by the feel of coarse fur brushing up my spine. I turned around to see a tall man enter the coffee shop and pause. His dark suit and briefcase were a stark contrast to the bohemian feel of the café.

He looked around the shabby chic décor, and when his cool blue eyes landed on me, I knew him, even though I'd never seen his human form before. This was my ten o'clock: Peter Delmont, lawyer/wolf.

He wore his power like he wore his sharply tailored suit and slick blonde hair: on the outside, letting everyone know he didn't mess around. As he crossed the small space in long, purposeful strides, I was frozen in his gaze. The look. The suit. It was damn effective, and for a split second, I almost thought I didn't have the claws for this one.

He stopped just short of stepping on me, and I had to look up at him. Something that, with my 5'11" frame, I rarely needed to do. He didn't bother with putting up borders to contain his power, and his scent overwhelmed me. Under the cologne I was sure he wore because it made the women in his office swoon, his power, his wolf, smelled distinctively of leather and sandalwood.

"Miss Jordan?" His voice was low and deep as his eyebrow rose with his question.

My spine reacted to his power, going stiff and straight. "Mister Delmont."

"May we sit?" His eyes flicked to the open table in the back.

"I was just thinking the same thing."

He strode over to the table, and I looked back to the counter for my drink.

The young girl behind the counter had my coffee in her hands, her mouth wide as she stared over at Delmont. Good. So it wasn't just me.

I waved my hand in front of her face so she would relinquish my coffee. The girl jumped and spilt a bit of the coffee, sloshing the white porcelain counter.

With a sigh, I took the mug and headed back to the table. Usually, I would have said something about the waste of good caffeine, but I was going to need my strength for the conversation ahead. I had a feeling my usual new member spiel about safety in numbers and checking-in and full moon responsibilities wasn't going to work with this one. I sealed my borders, keeping my power close to my vest, and knew the macchiato would get me through this.

This man had his suit, and I had my twelve ounces of hot coffee.

Delmont had turned my usual table into his personal office, his briefcase already popped open. "I'm sorry this meeting is so delayed."

An apology? Now that was unexpected. I sat slowly on the chair across from him and waited for him to stop shuffling papers. "No problem. I've had a few things to organize."

He closed the briefcase, opening up the space between us. In the right light, he was handsome—slender and broad shouldered. But I knew underneath this forced perfection was an animal, a silver-mantled wolf, easily the size of my panther. His energy had been primal when we'd bonded six weeks before, when he had pledged his power to me and that pledge connected our magical souls. Even now, as we sat civilly across the table from one another, Peter Delmont was different. Where the others' connections were silvery threads that I gently nudged this way and that, his was a rough-hewn twine that bound him to me as his Prima.

Now, more than with any of the other fourteen, I was wondering why me. He was powerful, in this incarnation and in his animal form. He had been a high-ranking member of the Haverty Pride before I'd come in and destroyed it all. Yet when push came to claw in the battle between my few and the darker Wanderers, he had chosen me as his master.

That was the story I wanted to hear. The story I was slowly coaxing out of all the Wanderers who had given me a piece of themselves, chosen me as their leader.

Delmont looked down at the papers in his hand. "I was Haverty's lawyer and the executor of his will." His voice was quick and succinct, with so very little affect that I would have believed his act, if it hadn't been for the twisting of the twine between us, something undulating under the coifed façade that pulled at me.

"Must have been an honor, with you being so young."

All he gave me was a curt nod as he slid the stack of papers across the table toward me. "Reade Haverty directed that the next leader of the pack should get all of his properties and assets."

A sudden void of white formed in the space between my ears, and the words bounced around in there as if it were a wind tunnel. "What?"

Delmont licked his lips. "Of course, he meant it to be his

son, Spencer, but, well, we know that didn't quite work out, what with you throwing him into the Neveranth and all. So, it seems, as the new leader of a majority—by one—of the pack, you are now the beneficiary."

"I didn't throw Spencer into the Neveranth. He jumped," I corrected. I looked down at the stack of papers. "I always got the impression Haverty was loaded."

"A full list of assets is included." He folded his long fingers in his lap. "Including houses, foreign accounts, and domestic holdings, it would come out to around 1.3 billion if you were to sell everything. Which I don't recommend in this market."

I gulped and set my coffee down on the table. No need to waste the coffee by spilling it all over my new dress, though I thought this meant that I could buy a million more cups of coffee if I needed, and a million new dresses for that matter.

"Why?"

His steely blue eyes finally rose to meet mine. "With the crown comes the kingdom."

His words settled around me like an ice-cold blanket, and my skin prickled. It had taken me over three months to assume the title of Prima. I wasn't ready for a kingdom.

"I never asked for this."

The smooth monotone of his voice didn't help. "No, you didn't."

I licked my lips and cursed Haverty. Yet another burden he'd left me with. Like the Legacy, the collected family power he'd forced upon me as he lay dying, this fortune was just another trap to tempt me in the direction everyone else in my line had gone, straight into the darkness.

"I know this is a lot to take in, Miss Jordan, but I will need a decision on the next step fairly soon. The property has been in limbo far too long."

"Of course." It had been in limbo for five months, since last December, when I'd killed Reade Haverty and his cowardly son had jumped into a parallel dimension. Don't imagine they have paperwork for that sort of thing.

A million storylines ran through my head about wealth, including a few scenes of Scrooge McDuck swimming through his money piles and all the horror movies I'd written with insane benefactors and large mansions and late-night feasts. But wasn't that one of the special little bonuses of being Violet Jordan, knowing the darkness so I could avoid it?

I wrapped my hands back around the hot coffee. "I'll need a little more time to think about it, Mister Delmont."

"Very well. Call my office for an appointment."

He moved to leave the table, as if this meeting was over.

I chuckled and wrapped my fist around the charm on my necklace. It usually kept me hidden from other Wanderers, specifically the baddies out for blood. But covered like this, it let me push my power out and flow over Delmont.

He froze six inches from the seat as if I'd pushed the pause button on his movements. His eyes darted to me as he felt the power again and smelled the burned magnolia fragrance of his Prima.

"Not so fast, Stretch. I booked you for an hour."

He gulped, and his tanned face went pale. It was the first crack I'd seen in his façade since he'd come in. He returned to his seat and smoothed out his jacket.

I released the pendant and leaned back in my chair. Like this, the world was a little duller, but I'd gotten used to it. It was better than jumping at every shadow in the window, convinced the undefined *they* had found me again.

"I do appreciate the business portion of our meeting." I tried to ignore the packet of potential just sitting between us and get down to the real meat and bones of this confrontation. "But I coordinated this to learn about you."

Delmont licked his lips and was seemingly speechless. He finally mustered, "What do you want to know?"

I figured we'd start simple. "Did Haverty place you in your law firm, or did he get to you afterward?"

He adjusted in his seat again. "You really don't play around, do you?"

"No," I answered quickly. "But I'm also not testing your alliance. We both know what you did. I just want a little more as to why."

Delmont's eyes dropped to the stack of papers. "Haverty treated me very well. And yes, he did help me get a place at the firm. In return, he asked only that I waive my retainer fees."

I frowned. "That seems tame for him."

"I was a little fish in his very big pond."

I nodded. "And what do you think about the pond now?"

He looked down at his briefcase and measured his words, seeming to roll them around in his mouth before he spoke. "I've been told you appreciate honesty."

"Above almost all else."

Delmont cleared his throat. "Dallas isn't better, just different. There are still holes that need to be filled, and if they aren't, I predict there will be chaos."

I was glad for the charm around my neck that helped keep my power reined in, because it also helped me hide when my emotions made my power jump, as now. His comment had just made my whole being tense in fear. What could he know that I didn't know?

I took a sip of my drink to buy some time for my answer. The coffee soothed my frazzled nerves. The sheer power of him was making me fray by the second. "Chaos is a strong word, Mister Delmont."

His blue eyes were brave enough to look straight into mine. "It is an accurate word, Miss Jordan. You may have secured the affections of the shapeshifters in Dallas, but what of the witches and the vampires and the elementals, some of whom are still nursing their wounds from six weeks ago?"

"They can't all be treading on the dark side. I watched them fight against Carlisle's men. They helped us defeat him."

"That just means they didn't want him to rule things."

I ran my fingers through my hair in frustration. It was a habit I'd picked up from no less than three men in my life. "None of them have made a move to try to challenge me."

He began to pinch the flesh of his pinkie finger as his hands lay in his lap. "They might not see a need to. The shifters have their own way of doing things, other breeds have theirs. I wouldn't be surprised if the elementals were naming their Akasha as we speak."

I would have let the sentiment go as a concern, but the fidgeting of his hands got me. Little things, like the fall of a shoulder and the pinch of a pinkie, had greater meaning to a person who had spent most of her adult life watching from the outside than a string of words put into a sentence. "You're not telling me everything."

His eyes darted down to his hands, and he spread them wide on his thighs. He knew I'd caught his tell.

I was right. He was keeping things from me. Dangerous things about the others in the city. I could force him to tell me, literally pull the information from him, but then where would I be? Connected to an embittered pack member? Not the best way to start out this whole leader thing.

"The other breeds have not made a move. Dallas has been quiet. I'd rather focus my efforts on my pack, making them feel safe, protected. I don't know what you knew of Haverty's methods, but given the stories I've heard in the past month, these people need healing, and I won't use them as pawns in another war."

"For now," he said.

I straightened, looking into the deep blue eyes I knew to be almost silver when he shifted. "Excuse me?"

"To protect them, you will need to use them, their strengths and their weaknesses."

"And how are you so sure about that?"

Delmont took in an unnervingly calm breath. His long fingers traced the edge of his briefcase. "This is not my first pack. Been in one or another my whole life, Miss Jordan. It will happen."

I licked my suddenly very dry lips. "If you knew this, then why choose me? Why bind yourself at all?"

Delmont opened his mouth. A sliver of cold wavered around him and pushed against my own radiating power. He shut his mouth just as a cold, stony look covered his face, and he hid behind his borders for the first time in our conversation, creating a void before me. He was nothing like the confident man who had strode through the place, power out all willy-nilly.

I knew in an instant there was a story here, a painful memory he shut away with his steel trap border. Those bound to me were like books, and stories like that are best served willingly. Just like the information that I would need to get from him about the others in the city. Mother always said you catch more flies with honey.

I took in a breath and exhaled, again formulating the right words to use. "Unfortunately, I will need to use your legal skills. And if you happen to see a little of that chaos, I might want a heads-up."

Delmont nodded. "Yes, ma'am."

I grimaced at the title but went on with the same speech that I had given all of my new wards. "I want you to feel safe. I want you to live your life. But I do expect you to be at the next full moon."

"I'll have my secretary put it on my calendar."

I smiled. I doubted he could resist the full moon. It was just a line to make him feel more important, probably said out of habit more than necessity. "I'll get her the information."

He moved again to stand, and I nodded. He rose, buttoned his suit coat, and picked up his briefcase. He turned to me and paused.

I expected him to simply say goodbye, but as of late, I wasn't about to assume anything about anyone. Nearly cost me my life last time.

He spoke slowly—and with a little hope, if I was reading his tone correctly. "This was an interesting conversation, Miss Jordan. I'd like to do this again."

I was in a state of shock for a moment. "Well, I do have some papers to sign for you."

"Thank you." He nodded and walked across the coffee shop, leaving a small bit of sandalwood in his wake.

As his exit from the shop sent the bells on the door into fits, my entire body relaxed. I was exhausted. The others had been easy. Mothers, students, hermits. No one had set me on edge like Delmont, testing me like he did. And no one else had as much of the information I desperately needed to maintain this peace.

An Excerpt from

LAST VAMP STANDING
by Kristin Miller

Kristin Miller's Vampires of Crimson Bay are back and facing their most dangerous fight yet. Dante, not quite a vampire, not quite a shifter, stumbles onto a secret vampire hideout—and its sexy protector, Ariana—just in time for war to break out. True love is put to the test as Dante and Ariana fight to save their lives . . . and their love.

PROLOGUE

Dante threw up his hand to guard against another one of *her* attacks. "You finished yet?"

She thwacked him again, right across the shoulder. And again, upside the back of the head, for good measure. She couldn't have thought she was actually hurting him. "I wasn't ready to leave, dammit, take me back!"

"That's not happening." He shooed her with an annoyed wave of his hand, glad the shakes and chills had finally subsided. "Now just calm down, would you?"

After glaring at him for a few moments, she planted her hands on her hips like a pissed-off little teapot. At least she wasn't hitting him. He supposed it was progress. To think, not twenty minutes ago, at the elder black market, Dante had wanted her hands all over him. Ask and ye shall receive, right?

Stifling a laugh, Dante sat forward on his haunches, rubbed his aching head, and tried to slow her words down. *Take me back.* "Why on earth would you want to go back there?"

"Why on earth would you think I needed your rescuing?"

She mocked him, a stubborn yet downright adorable pout pushing out her heart-shaped lips.

The elder black market wasn't exactly the slime-slathered gutters of San Francisco, but it was a far cry from the Hilton. She'd been captured. Bound. Restricted from using her mawares. That bastard Juan Carlos was beating her around. She'd been *sold*, for Christ's sake!

He'd saved her.

Only as Dante looked around from his position squatting in a mound of wet, muddy earth, spotted an unfamiliar forest and a woman who looked like she'd rather kill him than thank him for removing her from that place, Dante realized he looked more like the one who needed saving.

To hell with that.

Mustering all his strength, Dante tested his legs by shooting one out from beneath him, kneeling on it, then following suit with the other. He crouched in the mud, listening to the elder take sharp, quick breaths over him. When he finally got to his feet, he regained his balance by grasping a thick Douglas fir tree on his right. Teleporting always wiped him physically, but this time his head felt painfully muddled. Like he would've chopped off his left leg for an adrenaline drip.

Dante looked around. They were in some sort of tiny clearing, surrounded by fir trees with a hollowed-out mud pit in the middle. From where they stood, the forest went uphill in every direction until the land crested just out of sight, no doubt leading to hundreds of other tree rings and mud pits. Thick trunks popped up like daisies through moss-clotted earth. No city sounds buzzed on the cool midnight air. Was that salt he picked up on the breeze? Ocean? They were far from San Francisco, Dante figured out that much right away. But the ocean? How far had he traveled? Pain seared through his temples. Disorientation must've been fucking with his head.

Although teleporting wasn't an exact science, he'd have liked to think that over his fifty years on this earth he'd learned a thing or two about it. But he'd never, not once, teleported to a place he hadn't been before. And for the life of him, he couldn't remember his head ever hurting so damn much.

"Hel-lo?" she asked, leaning into his line of sight to catch his eye. Her long braid swung to and fro like one of those freaky pendulums in psychologists' offices. His mundane parents had insisted on taking him to dozens of those places throughout his childhood to figure out why he wasn't "normal" like the rest of the kids. *Why doesn't he sleep? Why doesn't he ever eat?* That had been before he'd realized being abnormal wasn't always a bad thing.

"I asked you a question," she said, louder, with more fire behind it. "What the hell kind of right do you have to scoop me up like some knight in shining armor? Did you hear me ask for your help?"

No. He hadn't. He couldn't remember hearing much before this moment, actually. Although anger was pitching her tone octaves too high, causing his ears to ring, it was still the most beautifully ringing orchestra he'd ever heard. Like wind chimes blowing in a soft southern breeze. "I thought I was doing you a favor." He heeled his boot against a tree and scraped off a clod of mud, thinking about how off-target her questions were. She should've been asking *how* he'd teleported. Not *why*. But he sure as hell wasn't about to pony up any information she could use against him.

"Some favor," she said, swiping smatters of dirt off her robe. It was so dirty that the burgundy had turned gunpowder brown. "Next time you might want to ask the damsel if she's in distress before you stick your nose where it doesn't belong."

With a swish of her braid, Miss Priss hiked up the heavy swells of her robe, spun around, and high-stepped over a fallen log to the outskirts of the circle. As she made her way out of the small ring of fir trees in a very straight and determined line westward, Dante realized he had no idea where the hell he was. Or how to get back. Yet she didn't seem to have any confusion about which way to go to get out of the thicket. She trudged uphill, in and around scattered rows of trees, with purpose.

Damn it. He was gonna be in trouble deeper than the mud sucking at his boots if he didn't bring this elder back to help him decipher the scrolls. *Don't let her get away.*

He scrubbed his hands over his head. "Son of a bitch."

"Excuse me?" She whipped around, her robe flaring out in a perfect circle before wrapping around her legs. "What'd you just call me?"

"Shit." Dante closed his eyes tight and lifted his face to the heavens. "I wasn't talking to you."

It wasn't like he expected solace, at least not from the Big Guy Upstairs. But he would've appreciated a break every now and again. He would recover from the physical energy-suck. His brain would even shift into high gear at some point and stop grinding like a beat-up Pinto. But why did it seem like everything was a fucking battle—waged uphill, staring into the sun—against more powerful enemies using superior weapons?

He didn't know what he'd expected when he jumped her out of the black market. Maybe some gratitude and a rewarding kiss? Certainly not this . . .

She trudged a few steps back down the hill. "A real man, if he had something to say, wouldn't wait until a woman turned her back before letting his balls drop."

Oh, Miss Priss has a mouth. Small pulses of adrenaline tingled across Dante's chest, settling in his lap. It was like the initial rush of a fight. Like an erotic kiss, drawing his mouth open in rebuttal.

Dante took a step closer, holding her mahogany eyes in his sights. "A real man, who'd saved you from certain death, wouldn't expect a thank-you in return. He'd rescue your beautiful ass and ride off into the sunset to be virtuous for the sake of virtue." He advanced, stepping over the same fallen log she had. Shock widened her eyes as he closed the distance between them. She retreated, her back pressing against the wide span of a fir. "A real man wouldn't try to take advantage of the situation at hand." She was still as stone, her chin high. Her expression like a marble statue's, regal and poised. Her skin glowed, luminescent in the soft streams of moonlight peeking between overhead branches. Dante stepped closer still, an odd twinge in his belly humming in anticipation. "But I'm not a real man. I'm not virtuous. And not only would I appreciate a goddamn thank-you for getting you out of that mess, but something tells me you know where we are. Now you're gonna share that with me, or we can keep going round and round all night."

She shook her head, rubbing it against the bark behind her. Standing over her five-foot-nothin' frame, Dante noticed how small and fragile she looked, despite the roughness of her mouth. She had a button nose. Heart-shaped lips that turned up at the edges, even without the trace of a smile. Cute, pointed chin. Looking down upon her, nothing but a breath between them, Dante could hear the flutter of her heartbeat as it pattered like a bird in the canopy above their heads.

"You know where we are." He was certain of it. "You've been here before."

"No. You're wrong."

"And you're a horrible liar."

"You have no idea what you've done." Her breath caught as he pressed against her. The cool glimmer in her eyes simmered down.

"Why not tell me so I can get the hell out of here and away from you." Oh, how things had changed. To think . . . he'd actually felt something for this elder at the black market. Now, looking into the hard glare in her eyes, Dante realized the feeling he'd had must've been pure pity. She wasn't strong. She wasn't a woman to be respected. She was just a spoiled brat with mud on her robe and a chip on her shoulder. "The least you could do is point me in the right direction."

"Go to hell." She slipped around the tree and took off up the hill at a sprint.

Dante sighed, chewed on his lip and his options. Even if his energy were restored full-force, could he risk teleporting somewhere else—to somewhere he knew? What if he'd jumped to a different dimension completely? Where would he be then? He might never find his way back. And he needed to find a way to contact Ruan. He pulled his cell out of his pocket and tossed it into the mud pit he'd just stepped out of. Another jump, another dead phone. This shit was getting expensive. AT&T was going to own his ass.

Just when Dante thought he was going to have to follow the elder and come up with some sort of pathetic excuse for an apology, she stopped right at the top of the nearest ridge, spun around, and faced him. Wind ruffled wisps of hair around her face and fanned her robe so that it clung to her body. She was tinier than he'd thought. Curvier at the hips, too. He wondered what else she was hiding beneath the weight of that cloak.

"You can't follow me, though I can see you're more stubborn than a mule, and will probably try it anyway," she said, raising her voice so that it carried down to him. "It's forbidden to pass here, punishable by death."

"I hardly think—"

"If I tell you the way back to the city, will you promise never to think of this place, or me, ever again?"

Dante couldn't explain it, but two seconds before, all he'd wanted was to find a way back to San Francisco and ReVamp. To get out of this forest and back to civilization. Now, the thought of leaving this elder behind, not knowing anything about her, letting her vanish into the night felt . . . wrong.

"You're not coming back to the city?" It was the only thing he could find to say, though he hated the concern lacing his voice.

She shook her head and clasped her tiny hands together in front of her. "I don't belong there. Never did." She looked content in this place. At peace. As if she'd run over the logs in this forest a thousand times.

How had her loathing of him dissipated so quickly? She'd easily lashed out at him with her tongue, been rude without regard. But now, her eyes were softer. Her words feather light. Even the air around her seemed surreal. As if she were standing behind a veil of water, the waves rolling up and down her body. Was her maware some sort of protective shield? Was that why her demeanor had changed—because she was now protected?

Dante moved up the hill and watched her go rigid again.

"No," she snapped, throwing up her hands. She glanced over her shoulder, as if with one step backward, she'd tumble off the ridge, right into oblivion. "Don't come any closer."

The air around her wavered and rippled, as if his movements had caused a disturbance in her aura. But he had to know what was going on. Had to understand the switch from pissed-off beauty queen back to the concerned angel he'd first laid eyes on.

"*Please*," she whispered, just like she had in the black market, in a way that made Dante's blood still. It had the same soothing effect on him, even now. "I wasn't supposed to bring you here. Please don't come any closer."

"Where's *here*?" He stilled.

"It's the Black Moon."

Puzzled, Dante looked up, peeking between umbrellas of fir. The moon was full, far from blending with the black vastness of space. "What are you so afraid of?"

She pointed through the trees. "Head due east." Warm currents in her voice wrapped around him, tugging him into compliance. "When you come to a series of warm springs, turn and head north. Within half a mile, you'll come to a meadow with two large boulders leaning against one another in the middle." She whispered now, leaning forward out of the shadows. "Touch them with the palms of your hands and think about where you want to go." She turned.

"Wait," Dante said, keeping his voice low, though he didn't have a goddamn clue why. "At least tell me your name. It's not like I'm ever going to see you again anyway." The words stung, although he knew they were the truth.

The slight curve of her mouth lifted into a coy smile that flipped Dante's stomach. "Ariana." She glanced over her shoulder. When their eyes met again, the smile was gone. "My name's Ariana. Seekers are coming. Go."

The air between them rippled with such intensity that Dante thought he was dreaming, although he'd never actually had a dream to measure it against. His mind couldn't seem to grasp what he was seeing. He could make out Ariana through the fog of air circling her—her mahogany braid tied with a pale blue ribbon, draping down the front of her cloak, her face downturned—but she was fading. Wavering. Shifting as the air shifted.

Dante reached out, his fingers sinking into the cool air as if it'd transformed into some kind of portal. Then, with a rush of winter wind that howled through the trees, she was gone. The air stilled behind her.

Just when he was about to shadow her footsteps and stand where she'd stood at the top of the ridge, two words echoed through the forest. They reverberated against the earth, the starless sky, off the tall and stoic trees. They came from everywhere, yet nowhere at all.

Thank you.

Dante stopped in his tracks, full of the feeling the words were for him. Feeling somehow vindicated, he smiled and slowly turned down the hill, in no hurry to get back to the monotonous life he dreaded living.

He took a single step in the direction Ariana had pointed, and the branches above him rustled with movement. He glanced up. Falling from the sky, right into the open palm of his hand, was a baby blue satin ribbon.

The one Ariana had tied around her braid.

A smoldering inside him—a knowing—told Dante he'd meet Ariana again. Someday he'd find his way back here, wherever *here* was, and get the explanation owed to him. As he wrapped the ribbon around his wrist and looped it into a knot, he wondered how she'd made an impression on him so quickly. And why she made him feel like there was more life to be lived in one curl of her lips and one melody of her voice than in thousands of days and nights on this earth.

Next month, don't miss these exciting new
e-book love stories only from Avon Books!

THREE SCHEMES AND A SCANDAL
by Maya Rodale

Charlotte Brandon is a schemer. But when her latest plot creates a rather compromising position for James Beauchamp, the rakish man who once broke her heart, chaos ensues. Tired of Charlotte's conniving, James has had enough; now it's time for a scheme of his own. Will James manage to outwit Charlotte—and win her heart—with a proposal to end all proposals?

SKIES OF STEEL
The Ether Chronicles
by Zoë Archer

The Ether Worlds are becoming treacherous, and Daphne Carlisle must journey into perilous territory to free her parents from a warlord's clutches. Her only hope is Mikhail Denisov, a rogue Man O' War as seductive as he is untrustworthy. Mikhail thinks he has the mission and Daphne figured out, but he's about to learn that in the Ether Chronicles, appearances can be deceptive.

FURTHER CONFESSIONS OF A SLIGHTLY NEUROTIC HITWOMAN
by JB Lynn

Maggie Lee's back—and life's more complicated than ever. After all, being an amateur hitwoman with maid of honor duties and a niece in a coma isn't easy. But when the one job Maggie can't take is the only way to keep Katie in her custody, will Maggie be able to make it out alive?

HOT AND HAUNTED
by Saranna DeWylde, Lauren Hawkeye, and Megan Hart

AN AVON RED ANTHOLOGY

Halloween is the only time of year when the doors between worlds open to ghosts, werewolves, zombies—and unknown pleasures. Let yourself be dragged in for some tasty tricks and treats as popular erotica authors Saranna DeWylde, Lauren Hawkeye, and Megan Hart serve up three tales of chilling, thrilling passion.

BLOOD BY MOONLIGHT
by Jocelynn Drake, Terri Garey, and Caris Roane

Just in time for the scariest season of all, three beloved paranormal authors come together to tell tales of romance . . . in the heart of evil. Join fan favorites Jocelynn Drake, Terri Garey, and Caris Roane for some seriously spooky love stories.

MIDNIGHT IN YOUR ARMS
by Morgan Kelly

When medium Laura Dearborn mysteriously inherited an old mansion, she never expected to find a link to her own cryptic past. Through her psychic abilities, Laura discovers the mansion's previous owner, Alaric, and the story of their love—half a century in the making. Kept apart by time, will they lose their newfound romance to the ages, or will they find a way to defeat death itself?